CHRIS CARTER

HUNTING EVIL

SIMON &
SCHUSTER

London · New York · Sydney · Toronto · New Delhi

A CBS COMPANY

First published in Great Britain by Simon & Schuster UK Ltd, 2019
A CBS COMPANY

Copyright © Chris Carter, 2019

The right of Chris Carter to be identified as author
of this work has been asserted in accordance with the
Copyright, Designs and Patents Act, 1988.

3 5 7 9 10 8 6 4 2

Simon & Schuster UK Ltd
1st Floor
222 Gray's Inn Road
London WC1X 8HB

Simon & Schuster Australia, Sydney
Simon & Schuster India, New Delhi

www.simonandschuster.co.uk
www.simonandschuster.com.au
www.simonandschuster.co.in

A CIP catalogue record for this book
is available from the British Library

Hardback ISBN: 978-1-4711-7952-5
Trade Paperback ISBN: 978-1-4711-7953-2
eBook ISBN: 978-1-4711-7954-9
Audio ISBN: 978-1-4711-7956-3

Typeset in Sabon by M Rules
Printed and bound by CPI Group (UK) Ltd, Croydon, CR0 4YY

MIX
Paper from
responsible sources
FSC® C020471
FSC
www.fsc.org

Author's Note

Hunting Evil is the tenth novel in the Hunter thriller series. It's also the first ever sequel I've written. It follows on from *An Evil Mind*, the sixth novel in the series, where this story really begins. Though all other books in this series can be read individually, as the storyline in one novel does not depend on a previous book, *Hunting Evil* is different. I would recommend that you also read *An Evil Mind* at some point to fully understand the history between Hunter and Lucien.

*

In all of my novels I have always tried my hardest to use factual locations not only in and around the city of Los Angeles, but also wherever else the story might take Hunter and Garcia. For that reason, I feel the need to apologize. To better suit the plot in *Hunting Evil*, I have taken the liberty of creating a few fictitious establishments and localities inside the United States of America.

I also feel that I owe everyone an apology for altering a scene in *Hunting Evil*. At the end of my previous novel – *Gallery of the Dead* – I give readers a quick preview of what's to come in the next book. *Gallery of the Dead* ends with what is essentially the first chapter in *Hunting Evil*. After revising that chapter, once I started writing *Hunting Evil*, I decided to add a little more impact and tension to that initial scene. Therefore, the opening chapter in this novel differs slightly from the final chapter in *Gallery of the Dead*, including a character name change. Please forgive me for that.

This novel is dedicated to all the readers from all around the world for the most incredible support over so many years.

From the bottom of my heart, I thank you all

One

That morning, due to a broken-down truck partially blocking one of the slip roads on US Route 58, it took Jordan Weaver exactly twenty-eight minutes and thirty-one seconds to drive the almost nine miles between his house and his work place; about twelve minutes longer than usual. Parking and the walk from his car to the staff entry door cost him another one minute and twenty-two seconds. Security check, clocking in, dumping his bag in his locker and a quick trip to the bathroom added another eight minutes and forty-nine seconds to his time. Grabbing a quick cup of coffee at the staff cafeteria and the final walk down the long, L-shaped, west-wing corridor that led to his station – one minute and twenty-seven seconds, which meant that in total it took Jordan Weaver, an infirmary control-room guard at Lee high-security federal prison in Virginia, exactly forty minutes and nine seconds to go from his front door to the worst day of his life.

As he rounded the hallway corner and his eyes settled on the squared control station just ahead of him, Weaver felt his throat constrict and his heart pick up speed inside his chest. The station, which was encased in large bulletproof-glass windows, was never, ever left unattended, but from where he was standing Weaver could see no one inside the control room, which was worrying fact number one. Worrying fact number two was that the room's assault-proof door had been left wide open, an absolute no-no according to the rulebook, but what really sent a shiver of fear down Weaver's spine, making him drop his cup of coffee and pray to God that this was just a horrible dream, were the blood splatters and smears that he could see running down the inside of the windows.

'No, no, no . . .'

Weaver's voice got louder as he went from walking to the fastest sprint he'd ever done. With each step, the large ball of keys that hung from his belt bounced loudly against his right hip. He reached the control-room door in four seconds flat and nightmare became reality.

On the floor, inside the bulletproof enclosure, the bodies of Guards Vargas and Bates lay in one massive pool of blood, both of their heads twisted back awkwardly, revealing the extent of the injuries to their throats – thick, crude lacerations that ran the width of their entire necks, slicing through the internal jugular vein, the common carotid artery and even the thyroid cartilage.

'Fuck!'

Across the room from the two guards was Nurse Frank Wilson – a 24-year-old Asian American who had recently graduated from Old Dominion University in Norfolk. His body was draped out of shape over a swivel chair. His throat had been slashed so ferociously, it was a miracle he hadn't been decapitated, but unlike Vargas and Bates, Wilson's eyes were still wide open and full of terror. Oddly, given the angle in which his head had fallen, Wilson seemed to be staring straight back at Weaver, as if even after death he was still begging for help. All three bodies had been stripped of all their clothes, with the exception of their underwear. The guards' weapons were also missing.

'Jesus H. Christ! What the hell happened here?'

Confused and shaken, Weaver had to step over Vargas's body to reach the main control console and the alarm button. As he slammed his right palm against it, the entire complex was instantly enveloped by the deafening screams of sirens.

The facility's west-wing infirmary housed eight individual medical cells and according to the daily manifest, only one prisoner had stayed overnight – the prisoner in medical cell number one. Weaver's eyes immediately moved to the blood-splattered monitors just above the central console, more specifically to the one on the far left – cell one.

The cell was empty, its door wide open.

'Shit! Shit! Shit!'

Weaver felt his legs weaken under him. He'd been an infirmary guard at Lee federal prison for nine long years and in that time, not a single prisoner had ever escaped.

'Shit!' Weaver yelled at the top of his voice. 'How the hell did this happen?'

His gaze rounded the control room one more time. Weaver had never seen that much blood before and despite the perils of being a maximum-security prison guard, he'd never lost a colleague to the job.

'Shiiiiiiiiit!'

Suddenly Weaver paused, his brain at last registering something that it had somehow missed until then.

A blinking faint white light that was coming from inside a semi-open drawer.

'What the hell?'

Once again, Weaver had to step over Vargas's body to get to where he needed to go. As his right foot touched the ground, the thick film of blood that lay between his sole and the linoleum floor caused his foot to slip. Instinctively, Weaver's hands shot forward, desperately searching for something to hold on to. His left hand found nothing, but his right one managed to grab hold of the semi-open drawer, where the blinking light was coming from,. As he tried to steady himself, his foot slipped again. As a consequence, his grip tightened on the drawer, fully pulling it open.

Even through the loud shriek of sirens, Weaver heard the odd 'click' that came as the drawer was pulled open.

It was the last sound he ever heard before his entire head exploded into a mess of blood, bone and gray matter.

Two

The National Center for Analysis of Violent Crimes (NCAVC) was a specialist FBI department conceived in 1981, but only officially established in June 1984. Its main mission was to provide assistance in investigations of unusual or repetitive violent crimes to law-enforcement agencies not only inside US territory, but also across the globe.

The head of the NCAVC, Adrian Kennedy, coordinated most of the division's investigations either from the department's headquarters, located at the FBI training academy near the town of Quantico in Virginia, or from his spacious office on the top floor of the famous J. Edgar Hoover Building in northwest Washington DC. That morning though, as luck would have it, when his cellphone rang inside his breast pocket, Kennedy was in neither of his offices. He had flown to Los Angeles to conclude a joint serial-murder investigation between the FBI and the Los Angeles Police Department.

'Special Agent Larry Williams' funeral will be in two days' time,' Kennedy said, addressing Detectives Robert Hunter and Carlos Garcia of the LAPD. His naturally hoarse voice, made worse from decades of smoking, sounded fatigued. 'It will be held in Washington DC. I just thought you'd like to know, in case you guys can make it.'

'We'll make arrangements and we'll be there,' Hunter said in return. He too sounded tired, the heavy bags under his eyes giving away how little sleep he'd had in the past few days.

Garcia nodded his agreement. 'We'll definitely be there. Special Agent Williams was a great agent.'

'One of my best,' Kennedy confirmed, his voice coated by sadness. 'He was also a good friend.'

'It was an honor to work with him,' Hunter added.

Kennedy paused, his stare distant and unfocused, as if he was reflecting on something. It was right then that he felt his work cellphone vibrate inside his pocket. He lifted his left index finger, asking both detectives to give him a minute, before bringing the phone to his ear.

'Adrian Kennedy,' the NCAVC director said into the mouthpiece. The next few moments were spent listening. Within the first couple of seconds, Kennedy's facial expression morphed into a confused one. Two seconds later, it went from confused to disbelief. Two seconds after that, from disbelief to shock.

'What do you mean, *he's gone*?'

Those words prompted Hunter and Garcia to look back at Kennedy expectantly.

'When did this happen?' A sliver of trepidation managed to find its way into Kennedy's voice.

'What's going on?' Garcia asked, frowning at the director.

Kennedy signaled both detectives to wait.

'How the hell is that even possible?' Kennedy's shoulders came up in a shrug, the trepidation in his voice quickly turning into anger. 'Because correct me if I'm wrong here, but wasn't he supposed to be in a *high-security* facility?'

. . .

'So how does an inmate, who is being held in a high-security federal prison, manage to waltz out of a heavily guarded building, through the outer perimeter gates and straight into freedom without being stopped? What kind of amateurish, circus security do we have running down there?'

. . .

'I'm sorry, he was transferred where?' Kennedy's livid stare met Hunter's worried one for just a split second.

. . .

'Still, security should've been—' Kennedy paused mid-sentence. 'He killed how many guards?'

As Kennedy heard the answer, his hand shot up to his forehead and he began massaging his temples with his thumb and forefinger.

'A booby-trap in the control room?' Kennedy's eyes widened. 'How can he have set a booby-trap in the control room? Using what?'

. . .

'How in God's name did he get hold of a . . . ?' Kennedy paused again, finally realizing that, at this point, the 'hows' made absolutely no difference anymore. 'OK. I want a nationwide APB to go out immediately,' the NCAVC director ordered. 'And I mean *immediately*, am I clear? Every law enforcement office and station in the country, no matter how small. I want everyone mobilized on this . . . everyone. Also, I want you to inform the Department of Justice that this will be a joint fugitive hunt between the United States Marshals Service and the Federal Bureau of Investigation, you understand? They're not going after him by themselves.' Kennedy took in an angry lung of air. 'And I want the name of the prison warden. Someone is paying for this incompetence. You can bet on— There's more? What else can there be?'

He listened for another ten to fifteen seconds.

'Wait, wait,' he interrupted the caller. 'You're going to have to repeat that. Take a breath, calm the hell down and repeat what you just told me, but this time do it slowly.'

Kennedy glimpsed at Hunter and his facial expression morphed again, this time into a pained one. 'Are you sure of that?' he asked the caller. 'All right.' His voice sounded half defeated. 'I need you to send me an image confirmation of that; and I need you to do that right now, do you hear me?'

. . .

'Yes, right now.'

Kennedy disconnected from the call and, so as not to throw his cellphone against the wall, he took another deep breath and held it in his lungs for as long as he could.

'What's going on, Adrian?' Hunter asked, his voice full of concern.

No reply.

'Adrian,' Hunter asked again. 'What the hell is going on?'

The look in Kennedy's eyes as he finally looked back at Hunter was vacant and lacking in comprehension, but Hunter also noticed something else in the NCAVC director's stare. Something he couldn't quite identify yet.

'He's gone, Robert,' Kennedy replied at last. 'He's escaped. Walked out of a federal high-security facility as if no one was even there. Killed three guards and two infirmary nurses in the process.'

'Who escaped?' Garcia asked, confusion covering his face like a mask. 'It can't be the killer we just caught.' He shook his head at Hunter. 'He hasn't been sentenced yet, which means he was never at a high-security prison, though I'm sure he will be.'

'No, it's not the killer you just caught,' Kennedy confirmed.

'So who are we talking about here?' Garcia insisted.

Once again, Kennedy's gaze moved to Hunter. The look that the LAPD detective had failed to identify just seconds earlier was still floating in Kennedy's eyes. This time Hunter read it like an open book. It was an apologetic look – an 'I'm sorry' of sorts.

Hunter felt an empty pit start to form inside his stomach because he didn't have to ask. He already knew the name Kennedy was about to throw at him.

Garcia, on the other hand, still had no idea of whom the NCAVC director was talking about, but he clearly saw the silent exchange between Kennedy and his partner.

'Who escaped?' he pushed yet again.

'Lucien,' Kennedy finally revealed.

Hunter closed his eyes and breathed in pain.

'Lucien?' Garcia asked, his eyes playing ping-pong between Hunter and Kennedy. 'Who's Lucien?'

Hunter reopened his eyes but said nothing in return. It was Director Kennedy who clarified.

'Lucien Folter.'

As he said the name out loud, his entire demeanor changed into one leaden with anguish.

Garcia had never seen his partner look the way he did right at that moment. If he didn't know better, he could've sworn that Hunter looked almost scared.

'Who the hell is Lucien Folter?'

Three

Detective Robert Hunter grew up as an only child to working-class parents in Compton, an underprivileged neighborhood of South Los Angeles. His mother lost her battle with cancer when he was only seven years old. His father never remarried and had to take on two jobs just to cope with the demands of raising a child on his own – a child whose brain seemed to work at a different pace to everyone else's – a much faster pace.

From a very early age it was obvious to everyone that Hunter was different. School never really offered him a challenge, on the contrary, it bored and frustrated the young Robert Hunter to such an extent that after finishing all his sixth-grade work in less than two months, he sped through seventh-, eighth- and even ninth-grade books just for something to do. Not surprisingly, that feat grabbed the attention of the school principal who, after consulting Hunter's father, got in contact with the Mirman School for the Gifted in Mulholland Drive, North West Los Angeles. After a battery of tests, both academic and psychological, Hunter was offered a place at Mirman as an eighth-grader. He was only twelve years old.

By the age of fourteen, Hunter had glided through Mirman's English, History, Biology, Mathematics and Chemistry curriculum. Four years of high school were condensed into two and at fifteen he'd graduated with honors. With recommendations from all of his teachers, Hunter was accepted as a 'special circumstances' student at Stanford University, the top psychology university in America at the time.

In spite of being an attractive young man, the combination of being too thin, too young and having a strange dress sense made Hunter unpopular with girls and an easy target for bullies. He didn't have the body or the aptitude for sports and preferred to spend his free time in the library, where he chewed up books on a plethora of subjects with incredible speed. It was then that he became fascinated with the world of criminology and the thought process of individuals dubbed 'evil'.

Maintaining a 4.0 Grade Point Average – the highest possible – during his university years had been a walk in the park, but he soon grew tired of the bullying, the beatings and of being called 'tooth-pick boy'. Following the advice of a friend, he decided to join a weights gym and started taking martial arts classes. Despite the physical exhaustion that came with the workouts, Hunter stuck to it with the enthusiasm of a professional bodybuilder. Within a year the effects of such heavy training were clearly visible. His body had bulked up impressively. 'Tooth-pick boy' became 'fit boy' and it took him a little less than two years to receive his black belt in karate. The bullying stopped and all of a sudden girls began paying attention to him.

By the age of nineteen, Hunter had already obtained a degree in Psychology – *summa cum laude* – and at twenty-three years of age he received his Ph.D. in Criminal Behavior Analysis and Biopsychology. Thanks to one of his professors, Hunter's thesis paper, titled 'An Advanced Psychological Study in Criminal Conduct', became, and remains, mandatory reading at the FBI Academy in Quantico, Virginia.

But only two weeks after receiving his Ph.D., Hunter's entire world was turned upside down for the second time.

For the past three and a half years, his father had been working as a security guard for a branch of the Bank of America in Avalon Boulevard. During a robbery gone wrong, Hunter's father took a bullet to the chest. The operation to try to save his life took several hours, at the end of which Hunter's father slid into a coma. There was nothing more anyone could do but wait.

And wait Hunter did, sitting by his father's side, watching him slip away little by little each day, until he finally passed away twelve weeks later. Those twelve weeks transformed Hunter. He could think of nothing else but revenge and when the police told him that they had no suspect, Hunter knew they'd never catch his father's killer. He felt utterly powerless and the feeling filled him with rage. It was after the burial that he made the decision that studying the minds of criminals wasn't enough. It would never be enough. He would have to go after them himself.

After joining the police force, Hunter moved through its ranks at lightning speed, becoming the youngest ever officer to make detective for the LAPD. As a detective, he was immediately assigned to the Homicide Special Section (HSS) – a dedicated branch within the LAPD's Robbery–Homicide Division that dealt solely with serial and high-profile homicide cases requiring extensive investigative time and expertise. But when it came to homicides, the city of Los Angeles was like no other city on earth. For some reason, it seemed to attract, or even breed, its own very particular type of psychopath, which triggered the Mayor of Los Angeles and the LAPD to create an elite entity within the HSS. All homicides involving overwhelming sadism and brutality were tagged by the LAPD as Ultra Violent Crimes. Hunter was the head of the LAPD's Ultra Violent Crimes Unit and as such, he had seen more brutal homicide crime scenes than anyone else in the entire LAPD ... ever. Nothing ever really fazed, scared or shocked him anymore. And that was what had surprised Garcia so much.

'Who the hell is Lucien Folter?' he asked again, his gaze still traveling between Hunter and Director Kennedy.

Eye contact was not reciprocated.

'Robert,' Garcia called. This time he sounded like an annoyed parent reprimanding a disobedient child. 'Who the hell is Lucien Folter?'

'To put it in simple terms ...'

Though Hunter had finally locked eyes with his partner, the reply came from Director Kennedy, his voice sounding even more ominous than it did just a moment ago.

'Lucien Folter is ...'

Garcia turned to face him.

'... evil in human form.'

Four

By the time Director Kennedy received the phone call informing him of the prison break, Lucien Folter had already crossed
the border between Virginia and Tennessee and was now fast
approaching the city of Knoxville. His target destination, at
least for the time being, was a small wooden shack by a remote
wetland in southern Louisiana, but Lucien knew that the worst
thing he could do right at that moment was to keep on running.
He knew that by then the alarm at Lee high-security penitentiary would've been raised, the FBI and the State Attorney
General's office would've been informed and US Marshals
had probably already been mobilized. His face wouldn't have
made the early morning news – not enough time to get that
particular ball rolling – but urgent 'breaking-news' bulletins,
reporting his escape would be hitting the airwaves in a hurry
and by lunchtime his mugshot would be splattered all over
the country. Before continuing on his way, Lucien needed to
change his appearance – drastically – and for that he needed
a few supplies, which in a city as large as Knoxville wouldn't
be that hard to come by, but first things first. Before getting
to Knoxville, Lucien needed to ditch the silver Chevrolet
Colorado he'd been driving.

The pickup truck belonged to prison guard Manuel Vargas. After murdering everyone inside the infirmary control room, Lucien had taken their clothes, their weapons, their wallets and their car keys. With the alarm raised, it wouldn't take long for them to realize that Lucien had taken one of the guards' vehicles. By now, Lucien was certain that an APB on the Chevrolet Colorado had already been put out. Every cop in the country would be on the lookout for that car. He needed to get rid of it and he needed to do it pronto.

Suddenly, as Lucien considered his options, Lady Luck smiled at him. A rest area was coming up on his right and from about two hundred yards out he could see that there was only one other car parked there – a jet-black Audi A6, one of the newer models.

'Well, hello there,' Lucien said to himself as he straightened up, slowed down and veered off into the rest area. As he approached the parked vehicle, he saw a woman in the driver's seat talking on her cellphone. There was no one sitting next to her. There were no kids in the backseat.

'Perfect.'

Lucien parked four spaces away and quickly scanned the surrounding area for a short while – he could see no one in the bushes, in case the woman's passenger, if there was one, had needed an emergency bathroom break. He smiled at himself and allowed his attention to return to the Audi driver. The woman, who had her window shut all the way, looked to be around forty years old. From where he was sitting, her profile just missed beauty – her chin was a bit too pointy, her nose a bit too round. Her black hair was cut short and neat and she wore a thin brown leather jacket.

So as not to look suspicious, Lucien got out of the car and

pretended to check his driver-side tires. For the next twenty seconds, Lucien studied the woman from afar. Her cellphone hand was blocking the view to her mouth, which kept him from reading her lips, but the expression on her face, her eyebrow movements and the way in which she gesticulated every now and then, suggested that she was having an argument with someone.

Lucien rounded the truck to check the tires on the other side, all the while keeping an eye out for any other vehicles slowing down to enter the rest area. None did. When he looked back at the Audi, he saw that the woman was now off the phone, her body slumped forward, her eyes shut, her head low, buried against the steering wheel. It was obvious that the argument she was having on the phone hadn't ended too well.

That was his chance.

Lucien dusted his hands against each other, checked his reflection on one of the truck windows and tentatively approached her car.

At six-foot-one, he bent over just enough for the woman to be able to see his face.

'Excuse me, ma'am.'

Lucien was a master impersonator. At the drop of a hat he could put on any voice, any accent, any intonation he saw fit. As he spoke, his voice sounded velvety and deep, possessing an almost hypnotic effect. His accent carried an impeccable Tennessee drawl.

The woman kept her eyes closed and her hands and head against her steering wheel. Lucien noticed the empty space on her wedding finger. A light dented and discolored skin band marked exactly where her ring used to sit.

The woman didn't reply.

'Ma'am?' Lucien called again, this time using his right index knuckle to knock on her window.

The knock, even though gentle, startled the woman. Her shoulders bounced up, her breath caught in her throat and her body jerked back awkwardly. Her head twisted left in a fright and her teary blue eyes locked with Lucien's dark brown ones.

'Is everything all right, ma'am?' he asked. The concern in his voice was mimicked by the look in his eyes.

'What?' the now confused woman asked without rolling down her window. She seemed annoyed at the stranger disturbing her.

'I'm very sorry,' Lucien said in a charming but apologetic tone. 'I don't mean to pry, but I saw you with your head against the steering wheel and now I can see that you've been crying. I was just wondering if everything is all right. Are you feeling OK? Do you need a drink of water or something?'

In silence and for the next several seconds, the woman studied the stranger standing at her car window. There was no doubt that he was an attractive man – tall and muscular with high cheekbones, full lips and a strong, squared jaw. His eyes seemed kind, possessing a penetrating quality that she immediately associated with knowledge and experience. His dark brown hair was long enough to cover his ears and his beard was thick, but well kept.

The woman's eyes left Lucien's face and refocused on his clothes. He wore a dark blue, military-style uniform. There was some sort of large emblem sewed onto the right sleeve shoulder, but she couldn't quite make out what it said. Just above his shirt pocket there was another sewed-on patch. This one said, 'M. Vargas'. A thick, black leather belt rounded his waist.

'Are you a cop?' A mist of confusion and hesitation still clouded the woman's eyes.

Lucien saw that that was his chance to get her to roll down her window. He pointed to his ear and gave her a slight shake of the head, as if the combination of the closed window and the noise coming from the highway was blocking the sound of her voice.

'I'm sorry, what was that?' he said.

It worked, at least partially, because the woman lowered her window just shy of halfway before repeating her question.

Lucien smiled back shyly. 'No, not exactly, ma'am.' He then twisted his body just enough for her to be able to read the official patch stitched onto his right shoulder. 'I'm a United States federal prison guard. I work at Lee Penitentiary. Just ended my shift, actually.' He didn't give her a chance to comment. 'Why? Are you in need of some police assistance, ma'am? Is that why you pulled into this resting area? I could radio them from my truck, if you want. It will get them here much faster than a phone call.'

Lucien injected just enough concern into his tone of voice and facial expression to ease most of the woman's doubts.

'No,' she replied. 'I don't need the police, thank you.' Her voice deepened into sadness. 'I pulled in here because I got a phone call.' She shrugged. 'A bad one. No way I could drive, talk and . . . cry at the same time.'

Lucien gave the woman a new, subdued smile, mainly as a reward for her keeping her sense of humor through something that was obviously hurting her.

'I'm really sorry to hear that, ma'am. Is there anything I can do to help? Would you like some water? Maybe a candy bar? Sugar can be good for you at times. I've got some back in my truck.' He threw his thumb over his right shoulder.

The woman lowered her window all the way and studied Lucien one more time. That was when he knew that he had sufficiently weakened her defenses to be able to push past them. He could see that she didn't see him as an imminent threat anymore. Why would she? He was handsome, polite and well spoken. He had shown concern for her well-being. He worked for the United States Federal Government as a penitentiary guard and he had just offered to radio the police for her if she so wished.

The woman's eyebrows arched. 'Right now, what I need would be something a lot stronger than water.'

A new smile from Lucien. 'I hear you. Unfortunately, all I can offer you right now is water . . .' He paused and scratched his chin. 'Or a cigarette.'

Lucien didn't smoke, not anymore, but he had seen a couple of cigarette packets inside the glove compartment of the pickup truck.

'I quit two years ago,' the woman said, as her head tilted to one side. At the same time, a thoughtful look came over her. 'But do you know what?' she continued. 'Fuck it. I quit just to please that cheating, good-for-nothing piece of shit.' She shrugged. 'Well, he can go fuck himself.' Her gaze returned to Lucien. 'Yeah, I'd love a cigarette.'

'Sure. Give me just a sec.'

Lucien turned on the balls of his feet and walked the short distance between the Audi and the Colorado. As he reached into the glove compartment, he heard the Audi door open and close behind him. He stopped the smile before it reached his lips. When he turned around, she was leaning against the driver's door, looking out in the distance, away from the highway. As Lucien moved to her, he unwrapped the cigarette packet, tapped one out and offered it to the woman.

'Thank you,' she replied, placing the cigarette between her lips.

Lucien took one for himself before lighting both of them. Hers first, of course.

As the woman took her first long and melancholic drag, her eyes closed and her head tilted back almost sensually. The expression on her face relaxed into one that was clearly full of pleasure, a pleasure that she had unwillingly given up.

'Oh my God!' she said, staring at the cigarette between her fingers. 'This feels soooo good.'

Lucien also took a drag of his cigarette, but said nothing in return. Instead, and without giving it away, his eyes studied her a little bit more attentively.

The woman was about five-foot-six and voluptuous. Her hands had been professionally manicured. Her clothes and shoes had clearly come from designer stores, and on her right wrist she sported a $3,000 Omega Constellation watch.

Lucien peeked at the highway. Still no cars seemed to be slowing down to enter the resting area, but Lucien knew full well that toying with Lady Luck was a very risky game, one that he had no intention of playing.

'Yeah, I know,' he said, walking around to the front of the Audi. 'I've given up a bunch of times, but I always end up going back to it. We're all going to die anyway, right? Might as well have some enjoyment.'

'I'll smoke to that,' the woman said, having another drag as she joined Lucien.

That was exactly what he wanted. Now he had her Audi offering cover between them and the highway.

She leaned against the hood of her car.

'I'm Alicia, by the way,' she said, extending her hand. 'Alicia Campbell.'

'A pleasure to meet you, Alicia Campbell,' Lucien replied as he took her hand into his. 'My name is Lucien. Lucien Folter.'

Alicia frowned at the man standing in front of her.

'Lucien Folter?' she asked skeptically, while nodding at the nametag stitched onto his shirt. 'So who is M. Vargas?'

Lucien closed his eyes for just an instant, as if searching for something inside of him. When he reopened them, something about his entire persona had changed. When he spoke again, his voice was as serene as a religious scholar's, but the Tennessee accent he'd been using had completely vanished. His eyes refocused on hers and what she saw in them filled her with fear.

'Oh, him?' Lucien replied. 'Don't worry about him. He won't be needing this uniform anymore. Not ever.' He winked at Alicia as his grip tightened against her hand with so much strength, she was unable to free herself. 'Just like you won't be needing your car anymore, Alicia ... not ever.'

Five

'Lucien Folter is . . . evil in human form.'

Those seven words from Director Kennedy seemed to thicken the air inside Hunter and Garcia's office.

Garcia consulted his partner with an intrigued look, but Hunter's thoughts appeared to be somewhere else entirely.

'*Evil in human form?*' Garcia asked Kennedy. His tone carried a hint of sarcasm. 'No offense, I know that you folks back at the FBI's NCAVC deal with some very heavy hitters, but this is the LAPD Ultra Violent Crimes Unit. The "clue" would be in the words "Ultra Violent". "Evil in human form" could be used to describe every single murderer we've ever chased.'

'No offense,' Kennedy replied in an identical tone to Garcia's. 'Ultra violent or not, believe me when I tell you that you've never chased anyone quite like Lucien Folter. No one has . . . except Robert.'

Immediately, Garcia's attention reverted back to Hunter. They'd been partners at the LAPD's UVC Unit for the past ten years.

'What does he mean, Robert? When have you chased this guy before?'

Hunter finally seemed to disengage from the trance-like

state he'd been in for the past few seconds, but instead of issuing Garcia a reply, he addressed Kennedy.

'Which prison was he at, Adrian?' His voice was calm, his demeanor unaltered. 'You said that he killed three guards and two infirmary nurses as he escaped. Where was he being held?'

Kennedy hesitated.

Hunter's eyebrows lifted.

'At Lee federal high-security penitentiary in Virginia,' Kennedy replied.

'*High-security* penitentiary?' The look Hunter gave Kennedy was full of doubt. 'What was he doing in a *high-security* penitentiary?'

No answer came.

'Lucien should've been at a supermax,' Hunter continued. 'And in complete isolation. How did he end up in a high-security facility?'

Kennedy breathed in as he uncomfortably shifted his weight from foot to foot.

'Adrian,' Hunter pushed. 'How come Lucien was being held at a high-security penitentiary and not at a supermax?'

Kennedy looked up to meet Hunter's stare. 'Because we wanted him as close to Quantico and the NCAVC as we could, Robert. The closest Federal supermax to us is in Colorado.'

Hunter didn't have to ask. He knew exactly why Kennedy would have wanted Lucien Folter to be close to Quantico.

'And he *was* in isolation,' Kennedy reassured Hunter. 'Always has been, since the day we caught him. Even when he needed to be transferred to the infirmary.' Kennedy shook his head, clearly angry. 'I just can't understand how he managed to escape. Fine, it wasn't a supermax, but it was still a federal high-security facility. You don't just break out of one of those,

Robert. He must've had help from someone, or someone made the biggest and certainly the last mistake of his career. I will find out exactly how Lucien managed to break out and I will personally make sure that whoever is responsible for this pays. Lucien should've been—'

'What difference does it make how he managed to get out, Adrian?' Hunter cut in, leaning against the edge of his desk. 'He's out. He's gone . . . and as a fugitive, he's now the responsibility of the Justice Department and the US Marshals Office, but as an inmate of a high-security facility, I'm sure that Lucien was exposed to the same few guards day after day, am I right? The guard who brought him food, the guard who brought him a book, the guard who accompanied him to the infirmary, or whatever.'

'Yes, so?' Kennedy didn't seem to follow Hunter's line of thought.

Hunter's eyes widened. He was clearly surprised by Kennedy's naivety.

'So we're not talking about just another serial killer here, are we, Adrian? We're talking about Lucien Folter, probably the most psychologically apt murderer on the planet. Would you like to have a wild guess on which other psychology field he excelled at?' Hunter didn't wait for a reply. 'Hypnotism.'

Kennedy breathed out a visibly painful breath.

'You give someone like Lucien the chance to see the same guard every day,' Hunter carried on. 'The chance to talk to the same guard every day and you might as well hand him the keys to his cell and a loaded weapon.'

'He was only transferred to the high-security facility about a week ago,' Kennedy tried to counter.

Hunter looked back at the NCAVC director as if he was

looking at a complete stranger. 'Are you suffering from dementia, or are you just trying to cover your ass, Adrian?'

Kennedy's jaw tightened. Very few people would have the nerve to talk to him in that tone.

'How long does it take an expert to place an unaware subject under hypnotic control, Adrian?' Hunter asked. 'You've seen it happen before, haven't you?'

Kennedy looked away, knowing that Hunter was right.

'But I also heard you say something about a booby-trap,' Garcia cut in. 'What was that about? What sort of trap?'

'I'm not one hundred percent sure,' Kennedy replied, turning to face Garcia. 'What I was told over the phone was that after Lucien escaped his cell and killed four people, he apparently set up a booby-trap inside the infirmary control room, which killed one other guard as he arrived for his shift this morning, almost half an hour after Lucien had escaped. This was the guard who finally raised the alarm.'

'What sort of trap?' Garcia asked again. 'What did he use?'

Kennedy's eyes moved to the window just past Hunter. 'If I open that window, can I smoke in here?'

'Nope,' Hunter replied.

Kennedy ran his tongue over his lips impatiently. 'It looks like Lucien used a sawn-off twelve-gauge shotgun,' he said, finally answering Garcia's question. 'A flashlight and a piece of nylon string – something like a fishing line or something similar.'

'A fishing line?' Garcia queried.

'Don't ask,' Kennedy said. 'What I was told was that the nylon string was somehow attached to the back of a drawer at one end and to the shotgun at the other. When the drawer was pulled open, the shotgun, which was hidden behind some boxes, fired, blowing the guard's head off.'

'Jesus!' Garcia exclaimed.

'Still,' Hunter took over again, 'none of this really matters now, Adrian. Nothing can be done about it. All we can do is allow the Justice Department and the US Marshals Office to do their job. Like I've said, it's their responsibility now.'

'You're right,' Kennedy replied. 'Lucien is now the responsibility of the Justice Department and the US Marshals Office, but they're not going after him by themselves.'

Hunter stayed quiet.

'I'll talk to the US Attorney General myself. Nathan and I go back a long way. This manhunt *will* be a joint effort between the Justice Department and the FBI, but I'll also set up a parallel special task force.' His right index finger pointed to Hunter. 'And *you* will be heading it, Robert.'

'Woah!' Both of Hunter's hands shot up in a 'back-up' gesture. 'Wait a second there. What do you mean – I'll be heading a special task force? I'm not an FBI agent, Adrian. I'm an LAPD detective. And despite the fact that we're talking about Lucien Folter here, he's not my responsibility. Not anymore.'

Garcia frowned at his partner.

'Like I've said,' Hunter continued. 'He's a fugitive and the task of bringing him in falls to the US Marshals Office. If you want to run a joint operation with the Justice Department, that's between you and them. If you want to run a parallel special task force, that's your prerogative, but none of that involves the LAPD.'

'Are you telling me that you don't care if Lucien is behind bars or not?' Kennedy countered.

'That's not what I've said,' Hunter came back. 'If it was up to me, I would've locked him down in a dungeon and thrown away the keys.'

The frown in Garcia's face turned to wide-eyed surprise.

'And that was where he was supposed to be,' Hunter continued. 'But you decided to place him in a high-security facility closer to Quantico just so you could study him further, right? Pick at his brain? You couldn't just let it go, could you, Adrian? What we've found . . . all his notebooks, his research . . . they weren't enough for the NCAVC, the BAU, or for you.'

'Study him?' Garcia had to jump in. 'Notebooks? Research? Who the hell is this guy, Jack the Ripper?'

'Jack the Ripper is a well-behaved kindergarten kid when put next to Lucien Folter,' Kennedy replied before turning to face Hunter once again. 'Yes, I wanted to study him further, Robert. You of all people should understand the reasons why. His knowledge of how a serial killer's mind works is unprecedented and unparalleled, but all that is now beside the point. Like you've said: he's out and right now the only thing that matters is bringing him in.'

'Agreed,' Hunter said. 'And again – that responsibility belongs with the Justice Department and the US Marshals Office, not the LAPD. I'm not part of this.'

'Unfortunately,' Kennedy said, 'yes, you are, old friend.'

'Says who?' Hunter countered.

Kennedy looked troubled by what he was about to say.

'Says Lucien himself.'

Hunter paused and studied Kennedy's facial expression. He looked like a card player who'd been holding on to a top trump card for the entire game, waiting for the optimal time to play it.

'And what's that supposed to mean?' Hunter asked. 'What haven't you told me yet, Adrian?'

Kennedy straightened up. 'They found a note inside Lucien's cell, Robert,' he replied. 'It was addressed to you.'

Six

Lucien had never been to the city of Knoxville before, and as he drove around its streets looking for a parking garage, he couldn't help but marvel at the sheer beauty of the place. On the banks of the Tennessee River and nestled in a breathtaking valley just west of the Great Smoky Mountains, the city had indeed a sort of irresistible and disarming charm to it, where nineteenth-century buildings sat effortlessly among modern-architecture ones and history seemed to ooze out of every street corner. Ten minutes driving around the city center was all Lucien needed to convince himself that he would have to come back to Knoxville and explore it a little better as soon as he could afford the time.

Lucien drove past three valet-parking garages before he came across a self-parking one on the corner of State Street.

'Here we go,' he said out loud as he veered the Audi A6 into the building's entrance. After grabbing a ticket from the machine by the barrier, Lucien drove around the floors slowly, his eyes scanning not only for a parking spot, but also for CCTV cameras.

The first floor had no spaces left. On the second floor, Lucien came across a couple of spots, but they were in a direct line with a security camera. It was at the very end of the third floor that Lucien found the perfect spot – by the wall and no CCTV cameras in sight. He quickly reversed into it.

'OK, let's see what else you've got for me, Mrs. Campbell,' he said to himself as he switched off the engine and reached for Alicia Campbell's handbag that was resting on the passenger's seat. The first thing he found was a Bottega Veneta leather wallet.

'Wow, very fancy,' he said with a chuckle as he unzipped the wallet open. 'And we have ... one hundred and twenty-seven dollars in cash. Not bad at all.' He put the money in his pocket before going back to the wallet. 'Five credit cards, a driver's license, a few coins, a bunch of calling cards: "Alicia Campbell",' he read from one of the cards. '"Independent mortgage adviser". Huh, that I would've never guessed.' The last pocket inside the wallet contained a photograph. Lucien studied it for a second. 'Oh, is this the guy who broke your heart?' he asked as if Alicia was sitting right next to him. 'Maybe I'll pay him a visit sometime soon and teach him a lesson, how about that?'

Lucien took out Alicia's driver's license and randomly chose one of the credit cards before placing them in his pocket. That done, he put the wallet to one side and returned to the handbag. Ruffling through the rest of its contents, he found a small makeup bag, which he also kept – makeup could always come in handy – a keychain, containing house keys or something similar, two pens, a bunch of useless receipts and two boxes of prescription drugs. He checked their labels – Xanax XR (3mg tablets) and Valium (10mg tablets).

Lucien's eyes widened in surprise. He was very familiar with both drugs. Xanax was the best-selling alprazolam in the country. Alprazolam was a benzodiazepine that affected chemicals in the brain that might've been unbalanced in people who suffered from anxiety. It was used in the treatment of anxiety, panic disorders and chronic depression. Valium was the best-selling diazepam in the country, which also belonged to the benzodiazepine group. Though it was also used in the treatment of anxiety, Valium was an anticonvulsant, which meant that it was widely used in the treatment of alcohol withdrawal symptoms, muscle spasms and in the prevention of seizures. Both drugs had also gained cult status all over the world as recreational drugs. To put it simply – since benzodiazepines affected chemicals in the brain, half a tablet of either Xanax or Valium would get most people high. A full tablet would put most people to sleep. Lucien could benefit from both effects. He smiled at his good fortune.

There was nothing else inside the handbag.

Lucien placed the bag back on the passenger's seat and opened the glove compartment. Inside it he found the vehicle's manuals, a plastic box containing the wheel-bolt key and Alicia's cellphone. He pressed the button to wake it up and was met by a picture of a forest, the cellphone clock and a message saying, 'use fingerprint or swipe screen to unlock'.

He swiped the screen and was immediately asked for a password.

'Fingerprint it is,' Lucien told himself, pressing the button to release the trunk lid.

He leaned forward on his seat and checked the garage's parking floor. No movement anywhere.

Lucien had left just enough space for a person to fit between the rear of the Audi and the garage wall. He rounded the vehicle, checked the parking floor one more time and pulled open the trunk lid. In there, the body of Alicia Campbell lay – her neck broken, her face still showing the terrifying fear that had petrified her in place as Lucien grabbed her face with both hands, stared straight into her horrified eyes and, in one violent move, twisted her head to one side one hundred and eighty degrees, fracturing the cervical vertebrae near her skull and severing her spinal cord at the same point. With that, three things had happened to Alicia. One – since the spinal cord is the pathway between the brain and the body, her brain was separated from her body below the level of the injury, instantly paralyzing her, including her respiratory muscles. Two – consequently, she stopped breathing. Three – her body lost the ability to control her heart.

Now, one thing that Lucien knew very well was that – unlike what was portrayed in Hollywood films and kung fu movies – death from a broken neck and a severed spinal cord did not come instantly. The victim would suffer in agonizing pain anywhere up to three and a half minutes, depending on resilience and body strength. Alicia Campbell lived for another one minute and twenty-two seconds before she suffocated from respiratory failure.

Lucien had considered disposing of her body at the resting area by the highway, but quickly decided that it was too risky. The bushes around the area weren't thick enough to properly hide a body during daylight. It would've been easily discovered by whoever pulled into that resting area next. Lucien could also have left her inside the Chevrolet Colorado he'd been driving, but by now every law enforcement agency in the country would be looking for that pickup truck. If it hadn't been spotted yet, it would be in the next hour or so, maybe sooner, Lucien was very certain of that. If they found the truck, they would find her body. If they found her body, identification would come quickly and the search would jump from the Colorado to the Audi A6, which meant that Lucien would have to find another way of getting around pretty sharpish, and right then he could do without that sort of hassle. He still had to get to Louisiana, and he liked how comfortable and powerful the Audi was.

After weighing his options, Lucien had decided that his best move would be to put Alicia's body in the trunk of her car and keep it there until he had left Knoxville. He did not intend to stick around the city for longer than an hour . . . two, max, just enough time for him to be able to buy some supplies and change his appearance. He was sure that he would find an ideal place to get rid of her body soon after he left town, but right now he needed to unlock that cellphone.

Lucien reached for Alicia's right hand, singled out her thumb and placed it against the fingerprint reader. A second later, the cellphone screen unlocked.

First Lucien called up the 'settings' screen on the phone. He knew that he wouldn't be able to change the 'lock screen and security settings' to keep the screen permanently unlocked without entering a password, so he did the next best thing – he changed the 'lock automatically' time from five seconds to half an hour. Now, as long as Lucien touched the phone screen within every thirty minutes, the phone wouldn't lock on him and he wouldn't need to use Alicia's fingerprint again.

Next, Lucien called up the cellphone's map application and searched for 'Costume shops in downtown Knoxville'. He got three results. The closest one was less than half a mile away from where he was.

'How about that?'

Lucien wasn't only a master impersonator, he was also

a wizard when it came to disguise. Armed with the right makeup and just a few simple props, easily obtainable in most costume shops, he was able to drastically change his appearance and make himself completely unrecognizable in a matter of minutes.

He used the screen map to check the directions to the store. Walking would be just as simple as driving, and since Lucien also needed to pick up a few random items that he wouldn't find in the costume shop, he decided to make his way there on foot. He locked the car and set off towards the address shown on the cellphone screen.

Seven

Hunter kept his focus on Kennedy, expecting him to develop on what he had just told him, but the NCAVC director offered nothing more.

'What are you talking about, Adrian?' Hunter asked, his voice still composed. 'What note?'

'I know I have no need to explain protocol to anyone here,' Kennedy replied. 'You all know that once an inmate escapes, the first place that gets scrutinized to hell is that inmate's prison cell, right? Marshals will be looking for plans of the escape, notes, drawings, letters exchanged with someone on the outside ... any sort of clue that can point them in some sort of direction.'

Hunter's reply was a single nod of the head.

'Well,' Kennedy continued, 'Lucien's cell has already been turned inside out and upside down, they found absolutely nothing.'

'They wouldn't have.' Hunter shrugged. 'Lucien would've kept whatever plan he came up with locked in his head, no matter how complex it might've been.'

'Maybe,' Kennedy accepted it. 'But Lucien didn't escape from his cell.'

'Yes, I know,' Hunter said. 'You told us that he killed two nurses as he broke out, which obviously means that he escaped from the infirmary.'

'That's right,' Kennedy agreed. 'He was transferred to Lee Penitentiary's infirmary yesterday afternoon – apparently due to a violent stomach bug. He wouldn't stop vomiting.'

'Yeah, right.' The comment came from Garcia.

'Anyway,' Kennedy carried on, 'inside his infirmary cell they did find a short note. From what I heard, Lucien left it on his pillow.'

'On his pillow?' Garcia asked.

'That's correct,' Kennedy confirmed.

'And that note was addressed to me?' Hunter asked.

Kennedy gazed back at Hunter, but the nod he gave him wasn't that convincing.

'Well, yes,' he replied. 'But in a charade kind of way.'

Hunter questioned with a look.

At that exact moment, Kennedy felt his cellphone vibrate inside his pocket, but this time it vibrated only twice and in quick succession, indicating that he had received a text message.

'Just give me a minute, will you?' he said, as he checked his cellphone screen. 'Yeah.' Kennedy nodded after a couple of seconds. 'The note is addressed to you, all right. No question about it.' He extended his right arm, offering Hunter his cellphone. 'Here, have a look.'

For an instant, Hunter debated what to do, as though if he declined to look at the phone, the whole nightmare would simply go away. Garcia, on the other hand, lost no time at all, stepping forward like a hungry kid who had just been offered a candy bar.

Hunter allowed his partner to read whatever was displayed

on Kennedy's cellphone screen before finally walking across his office to where they were.

'I'm confused,' Garcia said, his eye narrowing first at Kennedy then at Hunter.

Kennedy aimed his phone at Hunter, who paused about a foot away and tucked his hands into his trouser pockets, his eyes at last settling on the small screen. It showed a rectangular piece of white paper, resting on a crispy white pillowcase. The words on it seemed to have been written in blood. Hunter read them slowly.

'You should've taken me out inside that plane when I gave you the chance, old friend. That chance is well and truly gone. Now it's my turn. Get ready, Grasshopper, because we're going to play a game.'

'Am I wrong?' Kennedy asked. 'About this note being meant for you?'

Hunter shook his head. 'No, you're not wrong.' This time his voice sounded labored.

'I am *made* of questions right now,' Garcia said, confusion all over his face like a second skin.

'And I'm sure Robert will answer them all for you as soon as I'm gone,' Kennedy said as he quickly checked his watch. 'Which will be very soon.' He addressed Hunter again. 'You know Lucien a lot better than I do, Robert, but I've been dealing with psychopaths my entire career and to me, this . . .' He nodded at his cellphone. '. . . doesn't sound like an invitation . . . and if it is, it's not the type one can simply choose to decline. Lucien won't let you do that.'

Hunter said nothing because he knew Kennedy was right. That note wasn't an invitation, it was an ultimatum wrapped around a challenge.

Kennedy checked the time once again. 'I have to get back to DC. I'm sure things are already boiling just about everywhere over there, but I'll be in touch by the afternoon.'

'I'm not heading an FBI manhunt task force, Adrian.' Hunter was resolute.

Kennedy paused by the door and looked back at both detectives. Before he exited the office, all he did was give them both an ever so subtle acknowledgement nod. What he never told either Hunter or Garcia was that, in his mind, it didn't matter if Hunter wanted to go after Lucien or not, because the one thing Kennedy was very sure of was that Lucien would be coming after Hunter.

Eight

As soon as the door closed behind Kennedy, Garcia faced Hunter.

'You and I,' he said, his index finger bouncing between the two of them. 'We've got to talk.'

Hunter accepted it with a head gesture before taking a seat behind his desk.

Garcia stood.

'All right,' he said. 'I'm all ears here. Who the hell is Lucien Folter?' He lifted his right hand. 'And please, don't give me that "evil in human form" crap.'

Hunter sat back on his chair, rested his elbows on its armrests and laced his fingers in front of his chin. He knew that he had no easy way out of this. 'I'm guessing that you'd like the long version.'

'I've got all day,' Garcia replied.

Hunter took a moment, as if he needed to choose the right words to describe who Lucien really was. He began his explanation with a shrug.

'Lucien Folter is one of the most intelligent people I've ever met. He's self-disciplined, determined, focused, resourceful, very skilled, an absolute master when it comes to psychological manipulation and deception, and to top it all off, Adrian wasn't lying – Lucien really is pure evil.'

Garcia still looked unimpressed. 'You've ever *met*?' he asked. 'When was that?'

Hunter hesitated for a split second. 'When I was sixteen years old.'

The unimpressed look on Garcia's face fast turned into complete surprise. 'What? Sixteen?'

Hunter nodded. 'On my first day at Stanford University. We were both assigned to the same dorm. Lucien was my roommate.'

Garcia's jaw almost hit the floor. 'I think I better sit down for this.' He leaned against his desk.

'Just like myself,' Hunter continued, 'Lucien was also a psychology major.'

From the vacant look in Hunter's eyes, Garcia could tell that his memory had taken him back to his college days. Garcia waited.

'We hit it off straight away,' Hunter said. 'Which was something I wasn't expecting.'

'What do you mean?'

Another shrugged. 'He was friendly.'

Garcia frowned. 'And that surprised you?'

'In part, yes.'

'Why?'

'As I've said,' Hunter explained, 'I was sixteen when I started college, which meant that I was at least a couple of years younger than everyone around me. As a kid, I had never been the physically active type. I wasn't into sports, or exercising, or anything like that. I was skinny and awkward, and I dressed very differently from most Stanford students at the time.'

'Different how?'

'We were very poor,' Hunter replied, without sounding apologetic. 'Most of my clothes had come from second-hand shops. A lot of it didn't really fit me well, but it was all we could afford.' He smiled. 'I used to wear torn jeans when torn jeans weren't a fashion statement. Lumberjack shirts before grunge rock made them popular.' His eyebrows lifted at Garcia. 'So, I was younger than most, comically skinny, geeky and wearing mainly ill-fitting and torn clothes.' Hunter gave his partner an extra second to grasp the mental image. 'Are you starting to get the picture now? I was a bully magnet, Carlos.'

From Hunter's look and physique alone, Garcia would've never guessed that he had been a scrawny kid. He looked more like he had been the captain of the wrestling team or the university boxing champion.

'At the time,' Hunter carried on. 'Lucien was nineteen, he loved sports and he worked out at least five times a week. He was the perfect picture of a jock-type who would have a field day with someone who looked like me.' Hunter chuckled as he recalled. 'I remember entering my dorm room for the first time all those years ago, carrying a box of books and a bag with all my clothes. Lucien was on the floor, doing push-ups.'

'That's so sad,' Garcia commented.

'As soon as I saw him,' Hunter said, 'I readied myself for what I was certain was coming my way.' He shook his head. 'But it never happened. Lucien didn't say anything about how skinny I was, or how scruffy my clothes were, or even about how nerdy I looked. No sarcastic comment of any kind. No digs, no jokes ... nothing. He actually helped me with my things.'

'I never knew that you were bullied when you were a kid,' Garcia said.

'Hard to escape it when you looked the way I did,' Hunter replied. 'I was so used to it that I actually thought that Lucien was just saving it all for later, you know? Being nice at first ... gaining my trust, but in time I would get it all – the pranks, the jokes, the physical abuse, the humiliation ... you name it.'

'And it didn't happen.'

Another shake of the head. 'None of it. In fact, Lucien came to my rescue on a couple of occasions, when other students tried to gang up on me. He was the one who got me into martial arts and gave me tips on how to exercise, eat well and bulk up. All in all, during my college years, Lucien was my best friend.'

Garcia looked like he'd missed something. 'I'm a little confused, Robert. I keep on hearing that this Lucien character is evil personified, but the person you're describing sounds like a pretty decent guy.'

'That's just one of his tricks, Carlos,' Hunter said, sitting back on his chair. 'Deception. And Lucien is the best there is at it.' He paused, measuring his next words. 'There's no confirmed number, and I'm not sure that there ever will be, but the presumption is that he has murdered over one hundred people.'

Now Garcia looked impressed. 'What?' He knew that Hunter would never joke about such a thing. 'But that would've made him one of the most prolific serial killers in US history.'

'Yes, it would,' Hunter agreed.

'So how come I've never heard of him?'

'No one had. No one knew who he was or what he was doing until we caught him, just a few years ago.'

'We?' Confusion had recolored Garcia's face. 'We who?'

'I was helping the FBI and the NCAVC.'

'When was that?'

Hunter breathed out. 'About three and a half years ago.'

'Three and a half years ago?' Garcia's confused look intensified. 'We've been partners for ten and I don't remember that at all.'

Hunter said nothing.

'When, three and a half years ago? Where was I?'

'On vacation.'

'On vaca—' Garcia paused, frowning at thin air, as the memory exploded inside his head. Three and a half years ago, after concluding a serial murder investigation that had almost cost him his life together with his wife's, Anna, Hunter and Garcia were ordered by their captain to take some time off – two weeks, to be exact. Garcia took Anna to New Orleans, while Hunter was supposed to have gone to Hawaii. The memory that had just popped up inside Garcia's head took him back to the morning he and Hunter met again, after Garcia and his wife had come back from Louisiana. It had been inside that same office. Garcia remembered their conversation almost word for word.

'You don't look so tanned for someone who's just been to Hawaii,' he had said, before frowning at his partner. 'You did take your vacation, right?'

'Sort of,' had been Hunter's reply.

'And what does that mean?'

'I did take my break. I just didn't go to Hawaii in the end.'

Garcia had found that a little strange, as he knew how much Hunter had always wanted to visit Hawaii, but never really had the chance to.

'So where did you go?'

'Nowhere special, just visiting a friend back east.'

Garcia had never pushed for a more informative answer, but now it all made sense. 'Visiting a friend' – Adrian Kennedy – 'back east' – Quantico, Virginia.

'So that was your "sort of" vacation?' Garcia asked, incredulous. 'You went to Quantico to help the FBI?'

'I wasn't given too much of a choice, Carlos,' Hunter explained. 'I was all packed and ready to go when I got a call from our captain.'

'You got a call from Captain Blake?'

'That's correct,' Hunter confirmed. 'She asked me to come by the office. Said that something really important had come up and it couldn't wait. I got here and Adrian Kennedy was in her office. He had flown all the way over here because the FBI had, by chance, arrested someone in Wyoming who could possibly be connected to a double homicide.'

'By chance?'

Hunter nodded. 'Consequence of a freak accident.'

'This is getting better by the second,' Garcia said, taking a seat behind his desk. 'OK, let's hear this one from the beginning.'

Nine

For the next hour or so, Garcia listened in almost complete silence as Hunter proceeded to tell him most of what had happened during those fateful two weeks, three and a half years ago, but not exactly everything. The personal details ... the revelations that changed Hunter's life forever were kept locked away somewhere inside his mind. Somewhere cold, dark and overflowing with sorrow and hatred. Nevertheless, Hunter's facial expression gave nothing away.

'So what you're telling me,' Garcia said when Hunter was finally done recounting the facts, 'is that this Lucien character went on a lifelong killing spree because he wanted to write a ...' He paused and searched the air around him for a word. '... "murder manual" of sorts?'

'It was much more than that, Carlos,' Hunter rectified. 'Lucien documented everything he possibly could: victims' names and addresses, what specifically triggered his desire to kill them, his planning, every detail of every different MO he experimented with, his signatures, his emotions ... everything. His notebooks read like a self-psychological evaluation of the kind of insanity and turmoil that goes through the mind of a killer, before, during, and after the murder act. So no, he wasn't writing a manual. He was writing an encyclopedia.'

'How many notebooks did you say you found again?'

'Fifty-three,' Hunter replied. 'Every one about three hundred pages long.'

Garcia shook his head at the thought. 'That's just absolutely nuts.'

'For most people, yes,' Hunter agreed. 'But for Adrian Kennedy, getting hold of those notebooks was a must.'

Garcia pinched his bottom lip as he pondered on that for an instant.

'Though it sounds like madness,' he said, 'as the head of the FBI NCAVC and the BAU, I can understand why he would want them.'

'Yes,' Hunter said. 'I'm not debating that at all. It's just that—'

'Wait a second,' Garcia said, pausing and narrowing his eyes at Hunter.

'Something wrong?' Hunter asked.

'These notebooks you're talking about,' Garcia replied. 'That was how you found him after he escaped for the first time, isn't that right?'

'That's correct,' Hunter agreed. 'We crosschecked the false names Lucien had been using against the names of his male victims and—'

'Yeah, sure,' Garcia interrupted him with a wave of the hand. 'I got the name crosschecking thing. I know that was how you finally caught him in the end, but you also told me that before you figured out that he'd been taking over the identity of some of his victims, you scrutinized his notebooks for safe-house locations, didn't you?'

Hunter looked back at his partner thoughtfully. He knew where Garcia was heading with his question because he had thought about it as well.

Hunter had just told him that Lucien had documented everything he possibly could in his 'murder encyclopedia', including the locations of obscure places he either bought or took over. Places no one knew about – safe houses. Those safe houses, which were distributed all over the land, had been used mainly as torture chambers, so Lucien could experiment with his victims, but they could very easily serve as hide-out shelters for when he felt threatened, and that was what Garcia was talking about.

Upon escaping, the first order of play for any fugitive, no matter who he or she was, was to find a place where they could hide – a safe shelter where they could lie low, at least for a while. Knowing that, as soon as Hunter realized that Lucien had noted down the locations of every safe house he'd ever used, Hunter got Kennedy to quickly assemble a team of ten speed-readers. That team, which Hunter was part of, spent several hours going through Lucien's notebooks, searching for every location mentioned in the text. As they reached the last page of Lucien's fifty-third notebook, they had identified a total of fifteen shelters, spread around fifteen different states. Within the space of a couple of hours, FBI SWAT teams had stormed into all of them.

'I know that you've said that the FBI SWAT operation was unsuccessful,' Garcia said, following through with his line of thought. 'Lucien wasn't found in any of those fifteen locations, but let me ask you this – does Lucien know that the FBI stormed his hideout locations? Does he know that those addresses have been compromised?'

'Probably not,' Hunter replied. 'At least not per se.'

'And what does that mean exactly?'

'I don't think that Lucien was ever told that the FBI's first plan of action had been to check his safe houses.'

Garcia made a face at Hunter, as if his point had just become obvious.

'But,' Hunter carried on, 'Lucien knows that the FBI has seized all fifty-three volumes of his makeshift encyclopedia. He knows that Adrian and the NCAVC have by now completely picked it apart – every page, every word.' Hunter paused before accepting Garcia's suggestion. 'Yes, you're right. Right now, what Lucien needs the most is a place to hide, somewhere where he considers safe.' He gave Garcia a subtle headshake. 'No location, no address, no name mentioned in any of those pages is safe anymore, Carlos, because the FBI has them, and Lucien knows that fully well. He's not heading to any of those fifteen addresses. He's much smarter than that. He probably has one, maybe even more, ghost places. Somewhere only he knows about. Somewhere he never mentioned to anyone, or wrote down anywhere.'

'You don't know that for sure, Robert,' Garcia countered. 'Lucien has been locked up in almost complete isolation for the past three and a half years. From what I gathered, in that time, he's had no contact with the outside world.' He paused by Hunter's desk. 'It doesn't matter how intelligent he is. Right now he's got every law enforcement agency in the country looking for him, including the FBI and the US Marshals Office. Yes, I'm sure you're right and Lucien is completely aware that every location, every address, every name he mentioned in his notebooks has been compromised, but right now, he's a desperate man, running on borrowed time, and you and I know that desperate people will usually resort to desperate measures, no matter how risky they might seem.'

Hunter couldn't fault Garcia's logic, except for one little detail – Lucien didn't do desperate. He didn't panic . . . ever.

Despite all that, he had to agree that staking out those locations once again could be worth a shot.

'So my next question to you is . . .' Garcia said. 'Those safe houses: do they still exist, or did the FBI shut them down for good?'

Hunter shrugged. 'I don't know, but it doesn't really matter, does it?'

Garcia quickly saw Hunter's point.

'No, it doesn't . . . because Lucien has no way of knowing that either.'

Hunter nodded as he reached for the phone on his desk.

Ten

Lucien had been correct in his assumption – by mid-morning, urgent 'breaking-news' bulletins reporting his escape were all over the airwaves, and by one o'clock, his mugshot had made the lunchtime headlines of just about every major TV network in the country. The photo shown was almost four years old and in truth, Lucien hadn't changed much. He didn't even seem to have aged, but that didn't make an ounce of difference. Within forty minutes of him parking his newly acquired Audi A6 on the third floor of the 24-hour garage on State Street, Lucien already looked like a different person.

Across the road from the garage, Lucien found a grocery store, from which he purchased a pair of scissors, shaving cream, a disposable razor, a small mirror, three large bottles of water, several candy bars, two bags of beef jerky, a roll of paper towels, a baseball cap and a pair of sunglasses. A couple of shops down the road, Lucien came across a small clothes store. In there he bought a pair of blue jeans and a long-sleeved dark shirt that said 'Straight out of Knoxville' across his chest. Less than twenty yards past the clothes store was a large McDonald's.

'That will do just fine.'

Lucien really only needed to use the bathroom, but as he entered the fast-food restaurant, he noticed a sign on the door that read: 'Our restrooms are for our customers only.'

He wasn't one to pay much attention to signs or follow rules, but he saw no reason to risk calling any unwanted attention to himself, plus he could really do with some food.

Wearing the baseball cap and the sunglasses, he observed the four young cashiers from a distance, picking his target in less than a minute – a ginger-haired, acne-ridden teenager, who looked like he hated his job, his parents, and possibly his whole existence, all of it with a vengeance. The kid barely looked up from his cash register as he took orders from customers.

Lucien waited until the kid was free before approaching him and ordering a cheeseburger, some fries and a small chocolate milkshake. Just like with the previous customers, the kid kept eye contact to a bare minimum as he rang in Lucien's order.

Tray in hand, Lucien took the last table at the far corner of the restaurant, well away from the window, making sure that he sat facing the wall, with his back towards everyone.

Lucien had never really been a McDonald's fan, but it had been way over four years since he'd had a cheeseburger with fries, and he couldn't even remember the last time he had sipped a chocolate milkshake – McDonald's or not, junk food or not, right then, it all tasted like food from the gods.

He finished his meal in just under five minutes, picked up his shopping bag and returned to the ginger-haired kid.

'Could I please use the restroom?' he asked, his voice timid, his tone soft.

'Sure, man,' the kid replied with a shrug. 'Knock yourself out. I'll buzz you in.' His head jerked slightly to the right.

As Lucien got to the bathroom door, the kid pressed a

button hidden behind the counter and the door unlocked with a muffled hiss.

Once inside the large, white-tiled restroom, Lucien lost no time, quickly locking himself inside one of the four available cubicles that ran against the east wall. In there, he closed the toilet lid and placed his shopping bag on it.

Over the last few months, Lucien had allowed his hair to grow to just past his ears, a look that he was quite fond of, but it was now time to get rid of all of it.

From the shopping bag, he first retrieved the pair of scissors and the mirror he had just purchased and began trimming his hair to as short as he possibly could, being careful to collect it all into the shopping bag. That done, he took out the shaving cream, the disposable razor, one of the bottles of water, and the roll of paper towels. He then proceeded to carefully shave off what little hair was left on his head.

Lucien's beard had also grown to a thick, annoying and quite itchy stubble, something that he disliked immensely, but it served a purpose. Without a doubt, Lucien's most recognizable facial feature was a one-inch-long diagonal scar on his left cheek – a memento presented to him over twelve years ago, when one of his victims got lucky with an arm swing. Lucien saw it late, but still he managed to twist his body enough to evade the full power of the blow. What he didn't see, or count on, was the chunky rock ring she had on her finger. The punch missed Lucien completely, but her ring managed to graze him hard across the left cheek – cue in the scar-covering beard.

Lucien knew that the picture the FBI would be circulating on the Internet and sending to all the newspapers and TV networks across the country would be his mugshot, taken around three and a half years ago – no beard. He also knew how the human brain worked.

When tested, the average person was only able to accurately recall a very small percentage of a visual memory that the subject had seen only once. The reason for that was because when presented with a visual image for the first time, the human eye tended to concentrate mainly on features that the brain considered to be out of the ordinary. In the case of a human face it could be a variety of things, like for example, something that the subject's brain perceived as beautiful – striking eyes, perfectly shaped lips, a beauty spot, and so on – or something that the subject's brain considered odd – a crooked nose, a scar, strangely shaped eyebrows, etc. Once Lucien's mugshot hit the media, the feature that most people would automatically remember would be the scar on his left cheek. Lucien knew that, and that was why he needed the costume shop. With a tiny amount of latex, or even just the right makeup, Lucien could easily make his scar disappear, but he had no idea what he would be able to find at the shop, and though he was dying to shave his itchy beard off, for now, it was a necessary annoyance.

'This will do,' Lucien whispered, as he checked his freshly shaved head in the small mirror. He wasn't looking for perfection. All he really needed was to avoid detection for the next twenty minutes or so, just until he made it to the shop and then back to the car.

With the head shaving done, Lucien swapped his military-style uniform for the shirt and trousers he had bought in the clothes shop. After placing everything back into the shopping bag, he exited the cubicle and checked his full profile against the large bathroom mirror. The result brought a smile to Lucien's lips.

Phase one of his transformation was certainly complete.

Eleven

Adrian Kennedy had just boarded his private FBI Hawker jet when he received the call from Hunter. Kennedy had been so consumed by anger since he'd heard the news of Lucien's escape that he had completely forgotten about Lucien's safe houses. He had forgotten that three and a half years ago he had been the one who had green-lighted what he had called Operation EvilMind, where fifteen FBI SWAT teams had simultaneously stormed into a list of locations scattered around the country. Locations which had been extracted from Lucien Folter's 'murder encyclopedia' itself.

'It's a very long shot, Adrian,' Hunter explained. 'Lucien knows that every one of his notebooks has been analyzed, every name checked out, every location verified. Trying to run back to any one of those fifteen safe houses is the kind of risk that someone like Lucien doesn't usually take.'

'Understood,' Kennedy replied. 'But I think that this is a long shot that's worth taking, don't you?'

'Perhaps,' Hunter accepted it.

'I'll get on it straight away,' Kennedy said.

'Keep me posted.'

'Of course.'

As Hunter disconnected from the call, Garcia walked over to the coffee machine on the corner and poured himself a cup from a freshly brewed pot.

'As a Detective,' he said. 'I've seen a lot of crazy shit throughout my years with the force, but there's something that I just don't get about this whole Lucien Folter thing.'

'And what's that?' Hunter asked.

'Lucien used a piece of nylon string and a sawn-off shotgun to set a trap inside the infirmary control room, right?' The question came with a shake of the head that was quickly followed by a shrug. 'Why?'

Hunter shrugged back. 'Because he's Lucien.'

Garcia sipped his coffee. 'Oh, OK, that's that bit totally explained now. Thank you.'

Hunter stood up and approached the window. Outside, the sky above LA was a marble of blue and white, with clouds paling the late morning sun just enough to keep the temperature out on the streets in the 'pleasant' bracket.

'Lucien is the kind of person who wouldn't miss an opportunity to demonstrate his resolve, Carlos.' Hunter finally began elaborating on his answer. 'Any other inmate, anywhere in the country, if given the chance to escape, would simply take it and run, right? The faster they got the hell away from those walls the better.' He crossed his arms in front of his chest. 'Not Lucien. I don't know exactly what happened in that infirmary control room, but I can guess.'

'Well, I can't,' Garcia said. 'So let's hear your take on it. What do you think happened in there?'

Hunter leaned against the wall to the right of the window. 'If an opportunity to escape presented itself to Lucien out of the blue, he would've jumped at it, no questions about that, but I don't think that that was the case.'

'You think it was all planned?' Garcia had another sip of his coffee.

'I have no doubts it was.' Hunter nodded. 'All of it, with the exception of the trap he set up – that was the opportunity that presented itself.'

Garcia looked intrigued and unsure at the same time.

'From the second Lucien was taken into custody, he would've already been trying to come up with a escape plan. That's what he does. That's how his brain works. And he never gives up. All he really needed was for his opponent – the FBI, the state, the government, whoever – to let their guard down for just an instant.'

'And that happened when he got transferred to the high-security penitentiary in Virginia,' Garcia said, picking up on Hunter's line of thought.

'Exactly,' Hunter agreed. His attention returned to the window and the world outside it. 'And his plan worked out perfectly – Lucien managed to reach the infirmary control room without raising any alarms. Once there, he killed everyone because – why let them live?'

Garcia finished his coffee and placed the empty cup on his desk. 'How about the trap?'

'What I think happened was ... Lucien's plan probably worked out better than what even he had anticipated. Somehow he managed to avoid every little glitch that could've interfered with his getaway and got to the control room a lot faster than he'd expected.'

'Fine,' Garcia accepted it. 'So he's ahead of his own schedule. Great! Still, why not just get a move on? Why set a trap to kill one more guard who posed him no threat whatsoever? The guard wasn't even there. According to what Director Kennedy told us, he arrived around half an hour after Lucien had escaped.'

'Because like I've said,' Hunter replied, 'Lucien is the kind of person who wouldn't miss an opportunity to demonstrate his resolve.' He halted Garcia with a hand gesture. 'Picture this, Carlos – Lucien gets to the control room way ahead of schedule. He either knew beforehand what time the next shift was coming in, or found out as soon as he got there; anyway, he now knows that he doesn't really have to rush. Anyone else would've used that extra time to gain an even bigger head start on everyone, but Lucien isn't like anyone else. Instead of getting a move on, he looks around the control room and finds a sawn-off shotgun, together with some nylon string.' Hunter snapped his thumb against his forefinger. 'Right there and then a new idea comes to him and he takes his time not only to devise a trap, but also to set it all up, running the risk of another armed guard, a nurse, or whoever, walking in on him at any time. Can you see what Lucien is doing here? He's not setting up a trap just to add another victim to his body count. He couldn't care less if he killed one more person or not.'

'He's showing off,' Garcia said, catching up with his partner's reasoning. 'Giving everyone the finger, as it were.'

Hunter nodded. 'That too, but most of all, he's showing everyone how calm, calculating, narcissistic and in control he can be, even under the utmost pressure.'

Garcia scratched the underside of his chin. 'Qualities that will make a serial killer infinitely more dangerous.'

Hunter agreed.

'Now I understand how come Director Kennedy knew that the cryptic note Lucien left behind was meant for you,' Garcia said, before quoting: '"You should've taken me out inside that plane when I gave you the chance, old friend." He was talking about when you captured him.'

Hunter nodded. 'And just to make absolutely sure I knew that the note was meant for me, Lucien ended it with a very personal reference.'

'You mean, "Grasshopper"?' That was about to be Garcia's next question. He'd been wondering about that since he'd read the note.

'Back then,' Hunter explained, 'we were both very much into this TV show called *Kung Fu*. It was a rerun from the 70s, but it was still a great show.'

'I don't know it,' Garcia said with a headshake. 'What about it?'

'In every episode,' Hunter continued, 'there would be at least a couple of flashback scenes, where an old and blind Shaolin kung fu master would explain his teachings to his young apprentice. The master always called the apprentice "Grasshopper". As a joke, every now and then, when Lucien wanted to belittle me, he would call me "Grasshopper". It mostly happened during martial arts classes. He would put on a pretty good Chinese accent and say something like, "You need to be patient, Grasshopper".'

Garcia thought about that for a second.

'So by calling you Grasshopper once again,' he said, 'he's trying to psychologically take you back to your college days, when he was the master and you were the apprentice ... so to speak.'

Hunter agreed with a nod.

'And what do you think he means when he wrote: "We're going to play a game"? What kind of game?'

Hunter locked eyes with his partner. The conviction with which he spoke his next few words brought an uncomfortable chill to Garcia's spine.

'I don't know for sure, but I can tell you this – what Lucien calls "a game", everyone else calls "the seven rings of hell".'

Twelve

Unlike Los Angeles, the sky over Knoxville was completely clear of clouds, which allowed the late April sun to bathe the city in warmth, its rays reflecting from car tops and building windows like laser beams.

Once Lucien was back on the street, it took him just a few minutes to reach the costume shop he'd been looking for, and it pleasantly surprised him. The place was huge, a lot bigger than he had expected, with a varied stock that catered just as much for adults as it did for children.

Despite its size and the mesmerizing number of items on its shelves, Lucien spent less than ten minutes inside the store, in which time he picked up a sixteen-ounce bottle of liquid latex, two different makeup kits, two wigs, four sets of colored contact lenses and one tube of natural makeup cream, the tone of which matched his skin.

'Are you having a party?' the middle-aged African American lady behind the counter asked, as she rang the last item through her till. The happy lilt in her voice was one hundred percent legit.

'No, not really,' Lucien replied in a perfect southern Tennessee accent. 'I just ... want to hide from people.'

The cashier let out an animated laugh that seemed to come from deep within her belly. Her glasses slid down to the tip of her nose and she used her index finger to push them back up again. 'I know exactly what you mean. That's me most days.'

Lucien gave the lady a sympathetic smile as he handed her the money. 'Keep the change.'

'Oh, thank you very much.' Her smile gained a whole new dimension. 'You now have a good day hiding away, you hear? Don't let them catch you.'

'I don't intend to,' Lucien replied, winking at the cashier before finally exiting the store.

Less than eight minutes later, Lucien was passing the same McDonald's he'd been in not so long ago. He considered going back into the restrooms, shaving off his annoying beard and using some of the liquid latex he had just bought, together with some of the makeup, to cover his scar and maybe even enhance his cheekbones just a little. That would certainly move him way past the 'recognizable' borderline, but that would also cost him valuable time, and apart from getting rid of his itchy beard, he saw no real reason to change his appearance any more that what he'd already done.

Listening to his better judgment, Lucien skipped going back into McDonald's.

For the duration of his trip to Louisiana, interaction with people would be kept to a bare minimum, if any at all. Lucien would take bathroom breaks only when absolutely necessary, and rather than using restrooms in gas stations, he would use a bush by the side of the road or a rest area. Gas station would be used exclusively for refueling.

For obvious reasons, during the first several hours following a prison break, highway gas stations tended to be on high alert, especially the ones in and around the state where the break had occurred. True, given his head start, Lucien could've gone in any direction following his escape, but if they hadn't already, it was just a matter of time before US Marshals found the pickup truck he had left behind at the rest area by Maynardville Highway, revealing that he had traveled southwest and into Tennessee. Though US Marshals wouldn't necessarily know which vehicle Lucien was now driving, they would still instruct state police and the Tennessee sheriff's office to set up roadblocks at strategic points.

Knowing that, Lucien would do his best to avoid highways for the rest of the trip. His plan was to circle around Cherokee National Forest and drive back into Virginia before moving south into North Carolina, then South Carolina, Georgia, Alabama, Mississippi and finally Louisiana. The theory behind his plan was that since Lucien had just come from Virginia, traveling southwest into Tennessee, most of the roadblocks, if not all of them, would be placed in that same general direction. No one would really expect him to drive back into Virginia after he'd just escaped from there.

The maneuver, according to Lucien's calculations, would add anything from ten to sixteen extra hours to his journey, not ideal by any means, but in Lucien's world, 'cautious' would win over 'ideal' any day. In total, including the long way around, Lucien had estimated that if he averaged between 45 and 50mph, he'd be driving for a maximum of thirty-two hours before he reached his remote wooden shack in southern Louisiana. He had more than enough water to last him the trip. If hunger became a problem, he had the candy bars and the beef jerky he had bought in the grocery store back in Knoxville.

Lucien had also noticed that one of the computer dashboard

displays in the Audi indicated how far the vehicle should go on the amount of gas in its tank. It was a big car, with a big tank; when full, it would cover around six hundred miles before it needed refueling. With about half a tank still left in the Audi, Lucien would only need to make about two gas stops, three at a push, before he reached his final destination.

Once he got back to the Audi, Lucien placed both of his shopping bags on the passenger seat, jumped back behind the wheel and fired up its engine. As he began moving the car out of its parking spot, Lucien checked the satnav map on the dashboard just to make sure which way to turn once he'd left the garage. His attention diverted from driving for only a split second, enough to cause him to fail to notice the silver BMW that had just turned the corner and was moving toward him at speed. The BMW honked loudly while swerving hard left, barely missing another parked car. Lucien immediately slammed on the brakes, bringing the Audi to an instant halt. The contents of both shopping bags on his passenger seat shot forward and onto the floor.

'Sonofabitch!' Lucien said to himself. 'That was a close call.'

'You motherfucker!' Lucien heard the driver of the BMW yell from inside his car.

He had pulled into an empty parking space, a few yards ahead of the Audi. Lucien saw the BMW driver's door open and a tall and very muscular figure emerge.

'You motherfucker!' the man yelled again, this time pointing an angry finger at Lucien, while making his way toward him.

Lucien unclipped his seatbelt and quickly jumped out of his car.

'Are you fucking blind, you bald-headed lump of fuck?'

Lucien barely had time to close his door before 'muscleman' got to him.

'Who the fuck taught you to drive,' the man said, his finger about an inch from Lucien's face, 'Stevie Wonder?'

The man looked to be in his early forties, with a military haircut and a curved nose that had been broken at least a couple of times, a clear giveaway that he was no stranger to fighting. He wore a white T-shirt that was visibly a size too small, making his already large biceps, triceps and pecs stretch out the thin fabric to just a hair from ripping, enhancing his bloated physique even more.

Lucien took a step back and kept his composure. There was no need to get into an argument.

'I'm terribly sorry, sir,' he said in a shy and apologetic voice. 'It was my fault. I wasn't looking and I didn't see you coming.'

'How can you not have seen me coming?' the man asked, his anger still at top notch. 'Look at the size of my car. Are you blind as well as stupid?'

Lucien breathed in the man's rage. 'Once again, I'm very sorry. I should've been more attentive.' He gave the man a timid smile. 'Thankfully we've escaped a collision and no harm has come to either of us.'

'No harm?' The man's voice was still a few decibels louder than normal. 'You made me spill my coffee all over my fucking trousers, you imbecile. Look at this.' He pointed to a wet patch over his left thigh no bigger than two inches.

Lucien looked at it and bit his tongue so as not to make a sarcastic comment.

'I'm very sorry for that too, sir.'

This was taking too long already.

So he could end the silly argument and be on his way, Lucien was about to offer to pay for the man's laundry, but the man beat him to the punch.

'Sorry will not cut it, buddy,' he said, looking Lucien straight in the eye, his demeanor becoming even more aggressive. 'This is gonna have to go to a dry-cleaners and guess who's gonna pay for it.' He poked Lucien's chest with his index finger. 'That's right, fuckface . . . you. You are paying for my dry-cleaners.'

Lucien's eyes filled with fire.

The chest poking was a mistake.

A very bad mistake.

Thirteen

Lucien held the man's stare for a short while. He'd met plenty of people like him before. The world was full of them, actually – bullies who, due to their muscle size, enjoyed intimidating others just for the fun of it. They were the ones who, even if they could, even if they had the ability to, had no interest in arguing a point using reason and conversation because they took pleasure in terrorizing others. It fed their egos. It gave them a sense of belonging. It made them feel superior, but the reality was that in almost one hundred percent of the cases, the bullying, the terrorizing, the intimidation was just something those people did to make up for some sort of inadequacy in their lives. More often than not, that inadequacy could be traced back to a point in their childhood.

It was obvious that the BMW driver didn't really need or care for the dry-cleaners money. His trousers probably wouldn't even be taken to a dry-cleaners. He demanded it because bullies like him would never miss an opportunity to intimidate others.

Yes, Lucien had met plenty of people like him before – in school, in college, on the streets, at work, at home . . . and he had hated them all.

'Give me your wallet,' the musclebound man ordered.

Lucien frowned at the man while taking another step backwards.

'Your wallet, asshole.' The man turned the palm of his right hand up and motioned his fingers. 'Give it to me. Now'

Lucien hesitated.

'You better give me your goddamn wallet right now, or this is gonna end up very bad for you.'

Lucien glanced left. There were no cars coming their way. No one else other than the two of them on that third floor.

'I don't have a wallet,' he replied.

The man fixed Lucien with a dead cold stare. 'You drive an Audi A6 and you don't have a wallet?' He smiled sarcastically while nodding. 'OK ... OK.' He pretended to look away for an instant before his right hand shot toward Lucien, grabbing him by the shirt at chest height. 'Look here, you shiny-head cock-sucker.' The man brought Lucien's face to about two inches from his. 'If you don't give me your fucking wallet, I will fuck you up right here, right now. Do you know what I'm saying?'

If poking Lucien on his chest had been a bad mistake, grab-bing him by his shirt had been a fatal one, but Lucien didn't get angry. He was actually enjoying the 'macho' display. He was confident that those theatrics would work on most people – having a mammoth of a man grab you by the shirt and threaten to beat you up in an isolated spot inside a parking garage probably had a way of making a lot of people wet themselves.

Lucien's composure stayed solid, but he injected just the right amount of trepidation into his voice to convince the man that he was scared.

'Sir, I really don't have a wallet, but I do have some money on me.'

'Attaboy!' The man smiled. 'See? Now we're getting some-where.' He let go of Lucien's shirt. 'Let's have it. All of it.'

Lucien, acting as if he were almost too frightened, used his right hand to reach into his right trouser pocket.

'Sorry,' he said, his lips trying to stretch into a smile, but failing. 'Wrong pocket.' He then used his left hand and reached into his left pocket before bringing out all the money he had taken from Alicia Campbell's purse. 'One hundred and twenty-seven dollars is all I've got.'

'That should cover it,' the man said, reaching for the money, but before he could take it, Lucien closed his hand and took one more step back, placing him behind the Audi and com-pletely out of eyeshot from any vehicle or anyone that could've surprised them.

'Wait,' he said.

The man's dead cold stare was back, this time with an extra pinch of anger. 'Have you lost your goddamn mind? You better give me that money or I'll crush your bald head like a rotten egg.'

'Let me show you something first,' Lucien said, opening his arms as wide as he could, as if he was about to hug the man or be crucified.

The man paused, his forehead creasing with confusion. 'What the hell are you doing?'

'Hear me out, OK?' Lucien looked right, indicating his stretched-out right arm. The palm of his hand faced the man. 'As you can see, I've got nothing in my right hand.' He wiggled his fingers to emphasize his point before looking left to indicate his left arm. 'In my left hand, I've got one hundred and twenty-seven dollars.'

'Yeah, my one hundred and twenty-seven dollars,' the man came back.

'Fine,' Lucien agreed. 'Your one hundred and twenty-seven dollars, but this is what I propose.' He looked left once again, dragging the man's attention back to his left hand. 'I will give you those one hundred and twenty-seven dollars, plus the keys to this car . . .' His head jerked slightly to one side, indicating the Audi. 'All you have to do is pick the correct hand.'

'What?'

With his arms still wide apart, Lucien slowly crumpled the money in his left hand into a messy ball. He then closed his fingers over it. His right hand, nonetheless, stayed where it was – palm facing the man, fingers stretched out.

'So, my question to you is – where's the money?' Lucien asked. 'Left or right hand?'

The man looked back at Lucien as if he were insane.

'What? Are you mental or just plain stupid?'

'Pick a hand,' Lucien said again. 'Where's the money? You pick the correct hand, the money and the car are yours.'

The man looked at Lucien's empty right hand then at his left one – fingers closed into a fist over the money ball he had just crumpled.

'I guess you are both – mental *and* stupid, aren't you?' the man said, his tone a lot less angry than moments ago. 'I can see that your right hand is empty. You didn't even close your fingers.'

'Pick a hand.'

'And you didn't even hide your hands behind your back, or anything. There's nowhere else where that money can be . . . unless you dropped it.'

The man looked down at the floor – nothing.

To help him out, Lucien stretched out two fingers in his left hand, showing the man that the crumpled money ball was still safely in his palm. 'No, I didn't drop them.' He then closed his fingers back into a fist. 'Pick a hand,' Lucien insisted.

'You're nuts.'

Lucien's eyes quickly darted in the direction of the entrance to the garage's third floor – still no cars . . . no one coming.

'Where's the money?' he asked one last time. 'Left or right hand? Get it right and you'll get the car too.' Lucien's empty right palm was still facing the man.

'Your loss, freakshow,' the man said with a smirk on his lips before looking at Lucien's left hand. 'Left hand . . . I pick your left hand.'

Lucien closed his eyes, as if he had to look at something that was hidden behind his eyelids. A moment later he reopened them, together with his left hand, to once again show the man where the money was.

'Ha, there it is, see?' the man said. 'You really are one stupid sonofabitch.'

'Do you know what the first rule of a magic trick is?' Lucien asked, still keeping his arms wide open.

'What?' The man frowned at Lucien, as if he'd heard wrong. 'Magic trick what?'

'Misdirection,' Lucien explained, adding to the man's confusion. 'The performer makes his audience look one way, while the trick is actually happening somewhere else. Like here for example. Since all of your attention was on the money I was holding in my left hand, you completely disregarded my right one.'

The man began turning his head to his left to look at Lucien's right hand, but it was all too late. Lucien's right fist was already moving toward the man's head. Firmly clenched between two of his fingers, with its pointy end sticking out, was the key to the Audi. The man had barely been able to move his head when Lucien's fist struck him over the left temple with supreme precision. Lucien heard an odd screeching sound, similar to that of someone stepping over broken glass with heavy shoes.

That sound had been a consequence of the key rupturing skin and fracturing the man's skull.

Lucien's left hand had also moved. It had let go of the money and it too had moved toward the man's head, but not to strike it. Its objective was to grab the back of his neck, keeping his head from jerking back from the punch.

'Easy there, big fellow,' Lucien said, as he angled the man's head slightly toward him, so their stares met. The man's eyes, now overflowing with terror, shot wide open. The pain that had exploded inside his head, caused his legs to lose most of their strength and his whole body to go just a shade away from limp, but Lucien held him up by grabbing hold of his nape. 'It's almost done now,' Lucien whispered, still staring straight into the man's eyes.

In an effort to speak, the man's lips parted, but his weak vocal cords were unable to produce much more than a primal, unintelligible grunt.

'You see? This is the problem,' Lucien began, keeping the man's attention on him. 'The world is practically overflowing with assholes just like your bad self. You guys are like ants – you're everywhere – in schools, on the streets, at work ... you're always pushing people around, doing your best to make others feel inferior just to try and fill your own egos with the delusion that you are the big fish. But that cup never really gets full, does it?'

The man tried to say something again, but again his vocal cords failed him.

'Oh, you won't be able to speak,' Lucien continued. 'The trick here is that my punch hit you over your left temple ... inch-perfect, I might add, but then again, I've been doing this for some time. Anyway, the important thing here is that located directly behind the left and right temples is the thinnest part of the human skull. It's so because it's actually a junction of bones. It's where four of the skull bones come to meet and that's how come I was able to pierce it so easily using just a regular key, which is now embedded in your cranium.'

With that particular section of the garage's third floor having no CCTV camera, Lucien had some freedom of movement. He quickly let go of the man's nape and using his left arm, hooked the man under his right arm so he could carry him the short distance between the Audi and the BMW.

Lucien checked the floor entrance once again – still no movement.

The man was big and heavy, but Lucien didn't have much difficulty dragging him from one vehicle to the other. As he got to the BMW, he reached into the man's pocket and retrieved his car keys. A simple button-press released the trunk lid.

'But the most interesting fact about the human temple,' Lucien decided to resume his explanation, 'is that running just behind it is a large artery called the middle meningeal artery. This artery supplies blood to the outer covering of the brain.'

The man's eyelids fluttered as he threatened to slip into unconsciousness.

'No, no, no,' Lucien said, letting go of some of the pressure that he was applying to the key. 'Stay with me just for a while longer, will you?' He accepted his mistake. 'Sorry, I was probably boring you with all this medical explanation. You didn't need to know any of that. But here's what you do need to know. If the temple is hit hard enough, one of the four bones that junction at that point can fracture inward and lacerate that artery. If that happens then blood will collect and build up around the brain, compressing it with a lot more pressure than the brain can handle. If not treated promptly, brain tissue will bulge from that pressure causing unimaginable pain and consequently ... death, of course.'

Though the man couldn't speak, Lucien knew that he could still hear and understand him.

'Now, my friend, you will not be treated promptly. In fact, you will not be treated at all.' He paused for effect. 'And what I'm about to do right now will guarantee that the middle meningeal artery in your head is severed.' He winked at the man. 'This is going to hurt ... a lot.'

In one firm movement, Lucien twisted the key embedded in the man's skull. The friction between metal and bone produced a soul-chilling sound, reminiscent of someone crushing a mouthful of dry cereal with a single bite. That sent a new colorful firework of pain traveling into the man's brain, which made him convulse as if he was being electrocuted.

Lucien used his left hand to momentarily gag the man, as he knew that with that new burst of pain, the man's vocal cords would, even if ever so briefly, find a new rush of strength.

The scream came, but it died just as fast, muffled in Lucien's palm.

With that, the man's body went full limp, but he was still semi-conscious.

Lucien let go of his mouth and pushed him into the trunk of his own car. As Lucien extracted the key from the man's skull, he gave it one final twist to free it from bone and skin. Inside the trunk, blood began spurting out of the wound to the man's head. Lucien lost no time, immediately slamming the trunk lid shut.

There would be quite a significant amount of blood pouring out of the man's head before he succumbed to his injury and allowed death to take him, but the blood wouldn't seep through the car's trunk. Depending on who the man was and where he was heading before the whole incident happened, it could be hours, even days before he was found. But even if he were found in the next ten minutes or so, it would make no difference to Lucien.

Seconds later, like a man without a care in the world, Lucien was back on the road.

Next stop – Louisiana.

Fourteen

It rained during Special Agent Larry Williams' funeral. Not a heavy downpour, but a steady, uncompromising rain that began in the early hours of the morning and didn't let go until late in the evening.

Hunter and Garcia had taken an early flight from LAX to Dulles International airport in Washington DC. They weren't staying the night, so upon landing they took a cab straight from the airport to Oak Hill Cemetery, a 22-acre garden cemetery located in the Georgetown neighborhood of DC.

At the ceremony, Director Kennedy was standing next to the priest, his face almost frozen in a mask of grief as they slowly lowered the cherry-colored coffin into a grave that had been dug into the earth like a painful wound that only time would be able to heal. As the coffin came to a stop at the bottom of the six-foot hole, two attendants, holding shovels and wearing bright yellow raincoats, started to cover it with earth.

The crowd, most of it FBI agents who had at one time or another worked with Special Agent Williams, slowly began to disperse. Hunter and Garcia, on the other hand, stayed until the last shovelful.

Kennedy stayed as well, his head low, his eyes hidden behind standard-issue FBI sunglasses.

As the grave was finally filled with soil, the priest said a few final words, crossed himself and shook Kennedy's hand before he too walked away. With it all done, Kennedy walked over to Hunter and Garcia.

'Thanks for coming,' he said, shaking both detectives' hands.

'It was a nice service,' Garcia said.

Kennedy looked back at the grave. 'Simple. That's how Larry would've wanted it anyway.' He faced both detectives. 'Where are you staying?'

'We're not,' Hunter replied, consulting his watch. 'We're catching a flight back to LA in just a little over two hours.'

'Really?' Kennedy frowned. 'When did you get here?'

'About an hour and a half ago,' Garcia replied.

Kennedy's gaze jumped between both LAPD detectives. 'That's nuts. It's a five-hour flight from here to LA.'

'Tell me about it,' Garcia said. 'Given the three hours time difference, I've been up since three this morning, but there's nothing we can do, we need to be back at LAPD headquarters first thing tomorrow morning.'

Kennedy nodded. 'OK, in that case, let me give you guys a ride to the airport. We can talk on the way.'

Though it had been less than forty-eight hours since they last saw each other, Kennedy seemed to have aged at least a couple of years.

'Which airport are you flying from?' Kennedy asked as the three of them took the backseat inside the large black SUV that was parked just around the corner, by a white mausoleum.

'Dulles,' Hunter replied.

Kennedy instructed the driver before taking off his glasses

and loosening his tie. He used a paper tissue to dry his face. Hunter and Garcia did the same.

'We've got nothing,' he said, his tone half-defeated, half-exhausted.

Both detectives knew Kennedy was talking about the 'second coming' of Operation EvilMind.

Just a few hours after leaving LA and landing in DC, after he received the call from Hunter, Kennedy had his FBI SWAT teams assembled and ready to strike. Their orders had been simple – stealthily approach Lucien's hideout locations, use fiber optics to gain eyes into the properties and strike only if certain that Lucien was in there, otherwise the teams were to retreat and a surveillance operation would begin in the hope that Lucien could still turn up.

'It's been over forty-eight hours since Lucien escaped,' Kennedy said. 'If he was heading to any of the safe houses that we have knowledge of, he should've been there by now.'

'I said it was a long shot,' Hunter said.

'I'm going to keep the surveillance teams in place for another forty-eight hours, after that it becomes pointless.'

Hunter and Garcia agreed.

'And by the way,' Kennedy added, addressing Hunter. 'You were right on the money.'

'About what?' Hunter asked.

'About how Lucien managed to escape,' Kennedy clarified. 'He hypnotized an infirmary guard. I watched the CCTV recordings. That night, as one of the guards is doing his final late-night rounds, Lucien is seen uttering something to him – a command of some sort – and just like that.' Kennedy snapped his fingers. 'The guard becomes almost catatonic. Another command and the guard unlocks his cell. The guard then enters the cell and Lucien moves him to the toilet corner – CCTV camera blind spot. Now here's the thing; that particular guard was about the same height and build as Lucien. Lucien kills him, takes his clothes and walks back to the control room. At the security door, he never looks up at the camera, but one of the two idiots inside the room still buzzes him through. From then on is pure carnage. There was no CCTV camera inside the control room, so the exact sequence of events that followed is unknown, but as we well know, he kills everyone inside that room and sets up a trap to kill another guard, or nurse, or who- ever turns up first, and he did all that in less than five minutes.'

'He obviously didn't escape on foot, did he?' Garcia asked.

'No,' Kennedy replied. 'He took a truck, a Chevrolet Colorado. It belonged to one of the guards he killed in the control room.'

'Have you found the truck yet?' Hunter asked.

'We did. It was left on a rest area on Maynardville Highway in Tennessee. He obviously swapped cars, but we have no way of knowing to which one. Now, Maynardville Highway leads to US 441, where Lucien could've changed directions and gone north, toward Kentucky, but we're looking at the possibility of him having carried on moving south and into the city of Knoxville.'

Hunter's question came with a simple look.

'Yesterday morning,' Kennedy explained, 'a male body was found inside the trunk of a BMW. The car was parked on the third floor of a garage building in downtown Knoxville. The victim, a Mr. Ross Baxter, forty-three years old from Knoxville itself, had a wound to his left temple.' He shrugged. 'Some not-so-sharp but also not exactly blunt instrument. Not very long either, probably just about three inches, but long enough to break through Mr. Baxter's skull and rupture the middle meningeal artery. Death came from a combination of bleeding-out and swelling of the brain due to excessive blood pressure inside the skull. Though the body was only found yesterday, time of death was placed somewhere between eighteen and twenty-four hours earlier, which would match Lucien's time-frame for reaching Knoxville. The reason why it's hard to be sure if this was Lucien's doing or not is because, apparently, Mr. Baxter was well known for his bullying. According to what Knoxville PD detectives have found out, it seems that he'd been a bully for as long as most people can remember. The list of people who disliked Mr. Baxter reads like the yellow pages. His murder could've been payback from someone who'd been pushed around one too many times.'

'Has the car been checked for prints?' Garcia asked.

'Yes. Lucien's prints weren't found anywhere.'

'No CCTV cameras inside the garage?'

'A few, but as our luck would have it, Mr. Baxter's BMW was parked on a blind spot. We've got no footage of what happened. What we do have is footage recorded by the cameras at the entrance and exit to the garage. The FBI and the US Marshals Office are checking the whereabouts of every vehicle recorded entering and leaving the garage on the day Mr. Baxter was murdered.'

'Any luck?' Hunter asked.

'We don't know yet,' Kennedy replied. 'They have identified and located every vehicle, with the exception of two.' He reached inside his breast pocket for his notepad. 'A red Ford Mustang, Nashville license plate, and a jet-black Audi A6, Charleston license plate.'

'Charleston?' Garcia queried.

'West Virginia,' Kennedy confirmed before proceeding. 'The Mustang is registered to a Mr. Frank O'Brien, thirty-three years old from Little Rock in Arkansas. He's a musician who's been living in Nashville for the past seven years. What we've managed to find out is that Mr. O'Brien has a tendency to drop off the grid every now and then – tours, gigs, recordings, that kind of thing.'

'Does he live alone?' Garcia asked.

'He does indeed,' Kennedy confirmed. 'His neighbors haven't seen him for at least a couple of days and no one we've talked to has any idea of where he could be. He's not answering his cellphone either.'

'How about the other car?' Hunter asked.

'The Audi is registered to Alicia Campbell, forty-one years old from Charleston. She's an independent mortgage adviser. Her husband, Warren Campbell, is an attorney at law. On the morning Lucien escaped, Mr. Campbell and his wife had a bad argument. She took off in the car and hasn't been seen since. She's also not answering her phone. APBs have been issued on both cars all over the country, but neither have been sighted yet.' Kennedy returned his notepad to his pocket. 'The problem is that it's been two days since Mr. Baxter's death. Two days since either vehicle was seen. Even if Mr. Baxter's murder was Lucien's doing and he was indeed driving either the Mustang or the Audi, chances are that he would've dumped the car by now. Probably swapped for another vehicle.'

'How about physical sightings of Lucien?' Garcia asked. 'His mugshot has been splattered just about everywhere now.'

Kennedy let out a deflated breath. 'Yes, we've received way over one hundred calls so far. According to them, Lucien's been seen all over the country – West Virginia, Kentucky, Tennessee,

North and South Carolina, Ohio, Indiana, Alabama, New York . . . you name it. Believe it or not, we've even received a call from someone who thinks he saw Lucien in a local supermarket in Alaska.'

Hunter wasn't at all surprised. Every time the photo of a fugitive made the national news, hundreds of bogus sightings were reported, not usually out of malice, but because people truly believed that they had spotted the person on the photo. The fact that most people believed that there would probably be some sort of reward for the information also contributed to the high number of calls logged by the authorities.

'The truth is,' Kennedy continued, 'Lucien's been on the run for over forty-eight hours and we don't have a clue where he might be. There's no one who we can talk to. For the past three and a half years he's been locked up and completely incommunicado. He's never had a visitor. He's never received or sent out any correspondence. He's never even made a phone call. No attorney either. He waived his right to one. The only people he talked to after being arrested were BAU psychologists and a handful of prison guards, most of whom he's just murdered.'

Hunter's cellphone vibrated inside his jacket pocket. He reached for it and checked the display screen – 'unknown number'.

'Give me a second,' he said to Kennedy as he accepted the call. 'Detective Hunter, Ultra Violent Crimes Unit.'

'*Hello, Grasshopper.*'

Hunter's heart stopped beating.

'*Long time no talk, old friend.*'

Fifteen

After leaving Knoxville, Lucien drove for about an hour before he reached a long and dense cluster of trees alongside Dixie Highway, just south of the banks of the French Broad River.

'Yep, this is what I'm talking about,' Lucien said, as he slowed down, looking for a turn, a path, a trail . . . any sort of track that would take him deeper into those trees.

After searching for a couple of minutes, he finally spotted a small dirt road that veered off Dixie Highway and disappeared into the forest. Without an ounce of hesitation, Lucien took the turn and followed it until he could drive no further. There, he parked the Audi, opened its trunk, threw Alicia Campbell's body over his shoulder and carried her on foot, due north, for an extra ten minutes, until he reached a very distinctive group of trees. The area seemed unspoiled. He looked around, but saw no signs of anyone ever being there – no litter, no camping marks, no bonfire residues, no cigarette butts . . . nothing. What he did find were wolf tracks.

'This is where we say goodbye for good, Alicia,' Lucien said, placing her body on the ground by one of the trees. 'It was a pleasure meeting you.'

From his pocket, he retrieved the pair of scissors he had bought back in Knoxville, kneeled down next to Alicia's body and, in one precise and powerful move, slit her throat from left to right.

Blood didn't exactly gush out of the cut, as her heart-pumping activity had seized over two hours ago, but some did surface from her wound, trickling down her pale white skin and dripping onto the leaves and the ground under her body. That was all Lucien wanted. Soon, the scent of her flesh and blood would be picked up by wolves and whichever other animals roamed those woods. By the morning, there wouldn't be enough left of her body to fill a cereal bowl.

'Dinner is served, boys. Come and get it,' Lucien said out loud. Before making his way back to the car, he placed Alicia's handbag on a tree branch, high off the ground so the wolves wouldn't drag it away.

Save a couple of obligatory fuel stops and bathroom breaks, Lucien drove nonstop for the rest of the day and all through the night. His plan to drive back into Virginia before moving south again, this time through North Carolina instead of Tennessee, worked better than he had expected. Once the pickup truck he'd abandoned at that rest area had been found, the US Marshals in charge of re-apprehending Lucien had immediately ordered roadblocks to be set up at tactical points scattered around southern Tennessee, including the borders with Georgia, Alabama, Mississippi and Arkansas. By driving north back into Virginia, then south again via North Carolina, Lucien managed to circumvent the entire US Marshals' operation, avoiding every single one of their roadblocks.

Almost twenty-nine hours after leaving Alicia Campbell's body to the mercy of the wolves, Lucien reached the remote wetland in southern Louisiana by which his wooden shack stood. He did make two final pit stops in a nearby town just before getting there. First, a hardware store, where Lucien purchased a small list of items he had put together during his trip. Second, the local grocery store. He could really do with a home-cooked meal.

By the time he finally got to his property, Lucien felt exhausted, but he still had work to do before he would at last allow himself to rest.

First on the agenda was to get rid of the Audi.

Besides being in a remote enough location, Lucien's shack was hidden away behind so much vegetation that he didn't really have to worry about anyone spotting the car from a distance, unless they were specifically looking for his property, which was an almost impossibility.

Lucien had bought the small hut from a Mr. Joe Topanga, over eight years ago. The hut had originally belonged to Joe's father, a troubled and lonely man, who in the early 1980s, and for his own reasons, had decided to live as far away from modern society as he possibly could. Mr. Topanga senior had built the entire house from scratch, making it his home ever since, until he passed away nine years ago. With his death, the house fell to Joe, who hated everything about the place – the location, the surrounding area, the smell of the wood planks, the frog noises that came at night, all of it ... but most of all he hated the memories and how sick to the stomach the shack made him feel every time he went near it.

Lucien had met Joe Topanga in a bar in New Orleans eight months after Joe's father had passed away. They spent the night drinking together and when Joe told him about his father's property, how remote it was and how much he disliked the place, Lucien jumped at the opportunity.

*

'How much do you want for it?' Lucien asked.

'Seriously, man,' Joe replied, 'you don't want to buy that place. It's like a goddamn serial-killer hideout. Something out of a horror movie – "The Cabin in the Swamp".' He laughed. 'It's so hidden away that even with instructions, people would struggle to find it.'

'It sounds perfect,' Lucien said.

'Perfect if you want to hide from the world.'

Lucien finished his drink. 'Maybe someday that's exactly what I'll do.'

They had talked for the rest of the night, and Lucien had used the opportunity to get to know Joe a little better. Just like his father, Joe was also a loner – no wife, no kids, no girlfriend, no brothers or sisters, and just a handful of friends. His mother had passed away ten years before his father, and Lucien had gathered that that had been the trigger that had caused Mr. Topanga senior to become a hermit. That night, right there at the bar, Lucien bought the place for one thousand dollars cash. He threw in another five hundred just so Joe would drive him there to show him exactly where it was. Conveniently, two days later, Joe Topanga overdosed on heroin, a substance that he had never, ever used before.

The shack was absolutely perfect for what Lucien had in mind and he decided that it would become his fail-safe place. A place that he would never talk or write about, not even in his 'murder encyclopedia'. A place that no one else would ever know existed.

Over the years, Lucien had made several trips back to Louisiana, readying his property for an eventuality just like this one – for when he needed to disappear for good. But before doing so, Lucien had a score to settle.

At the back of his wooden hut, Lucien had buried a couple of suitcases. Inside them he had kept several driver's licenses, a small number of passports, plenty of cash, a multitude of high-quality disguise props, and a small but very diverse arsenal. In one of the suitcases, he had also stored a very prized possession, something he had acquired years ago, something he had never actually used before, but now the time seemed to be fast approaching.

Despite knowing that no one would be able to find him there, keeping the Audi was still a risk, and risks, no matter how small, were something that Lucien always did without whenever possible. In a place surrounded by swamps – some of them deep enough to submerge an entire articulated truck – making a car disappear was kids' play. Within half an hour of getting to his shack, Lucien had driven the Audi to one of those deeper marshlands, put the car in gear, dumped a heavy rock over its gas pedal and watched it slowly vanish into the murky waters.

On foot, over rough and wet terrain, it would take Lucien around four hours to get from his hut to the nearest town, but that didn't worry him. He had enough supplies to last him a week, though he had no intention of spending more than one, maybe two nights hidden away in southern Louisiana.

Finally alone and isolated, Lucien at last allowed himself to rest.

Sixteen

Since Lucien was talking to Hunter and not a stranger, he saw no reason to disguise his voice.

'*I'll admit that I'm really disappointed, Grasshopper, maybe even a little hurt by the fact that you never came to visit me while I was inside.*'

Hunter's pained stare moved first to Garcia then to Kennedy. Neither had to ask to know who the caller was.

'You have got to be kidding me.' Garcia mouthed the words, his entire face lighting up with disbelief.

Hunter placed his cellphone on the seat between him and Garcia, signaled everyone to be quiet and switched the call to speakerphone. Next, he called up a phone-call recording application and pressed 'record'.

'*You do know that I'm not inside anymore, don't you, Grasshopper?*'

There wasn't an ounce of trepidation in Lucien's tone of voice. In fact, he sounded rested, as if he'd been on holiday for the past two nights.

Hunter said nothing in return.

'*But of course you do,*' Lucien continued. '*I bet that you were the first person that that lump of excrement, Adrian Kennedy, contacted after he heard the news.'*

Kennedy was way too experienced to even flinch at such a comment. His attention stayed on Hunter's cellphone screen, as if he was looking straight into Lucien's eyes.

'I also trust that you've seen the note I've left you, haven't you?'

Still nothing from Hunter.

'Oh, c'mon, Robert, are you really going to give me the silent treatment. You're not sixteen anymore, old buddy.'

'You didn't have to kill them all, Lucien.' Hunter finally broke his silence.

'Well, hello there, old friend. It's good to hear your voice again. So how have you been?'

'You didn't have to kill them all.'

'I'm assuming you are talking about the guards in that shithole that I was put in. Of course I didn't "have" to, Grasshopper, but that's what I do, remember? I'm a ... how should I put it?' There was a short pause, while Lucien searched for the right words. *'"Investigator of murderous acts and the psychological effects they might have on the human brain". I'm a scholar, if you will. One could even say that I'm an ever-evolving method-researcher.'* A dismissive chuckle. *'I like that, actually – I'm a method-researcher – but I'm going to be honest with you here, Grasshopper, it felt reaaaaally good to kill again. I didn't expect to miss it that much. I had never taken that long in between acts before, did you know that?'*

Hunter didn't find it amusing that Lucien used the word 'acts' instead of 'murders'.

'Three and a half years, Grasshopper,' Lucien continued. *'Three and a half years locked in a cage. Three and a half years*

enduring interviews by the most brainless of psychologists, if you could even call them that. Who do they hire at the NCAVC and the BAU, anyway? It was like every day was amateur day.'

All of a sudden, Lucien's voice became overtly serious.

'*Three and a half very long years inside a fucking box and I can tell you this – you think about one thing and one thing only while you're inside. Do you know what that is?*'

No reply.

'*Time,*' Lucien said. '*You think about it every second, every minute, every hour, every day. The clock becomes as vital to you as your own heart. You can feel them beating and ticking side by side.*' There was a long and heavy pause. When Lucien spoke again, he pronounced every word slowly and in a steady monotone. '*The last three and a half years of my life have all been about time, Robert. Time to think. Time to be honest with myself. Time to plan. Time to visualize the future. Time to elaborate. Time to wait ... and then ... they transferred me to a "high-security" penitentiary.*' A sarcastic laugh. '*What did they expect? That I would spend more time inside?*'

Hunter's gaze crawled over to Kennedy.

Kennedy didn't match it, keeping his eyes low.

A pinch of amusement crept into Lucien's voice. '*But since you've mentioned what happened inside that control room, how impressive was that little trap I set up, huh? Damn, that "was" ingenious. And the idea popped into my head just like that. As soon as I saw that nylon string reel on the shelf, I knew that I had to leave them one last surprise before I left.*'

After booby-trapping the drawer inside the infirmary control room, Lucien had no real way of knowing if the trap had actually worked or not, he had no way of knowing if he had claimed another victim or not, but knowing the outcome was irrelevant. What Lucien was doing right there was boasting about his quick thinking. Hunter knew that and he wasn't about to indulge him.

'Good trap,' Hunter said, his voice controlled, his breathing steady. 'Too bad it didn't work.'

Hunter's reply caused Lucien to pause in hesitation. He certainly wasn't expecting it.

Hunter read the hesitant pause and quickly tagged his reply with an explanation. 'They found the trap before anybody else got hurt.'

What came through the tiny speaker on Hunter's phone was a contrived laugh.

'*No they didn't,*' Lucien said. '*That trap was perfectly placed. Perfectly hidden. No one could've found it without opening that drawer – and as soon as anyone did ... game over. You're losing your touch, Robert. You used to be very good at hiding the truth. You're getting old, my friend.*'

'Sure,' Hunter came back, spotting the perfect opportunity to attack Lucien's ego, but not by trying to prove a point. That wouldn't work with someone like Lucien. Hunter's trick was to leave him wondering. 'By all means, Lucien, carry on believing that everything you do is infallible ... that we can all lose our touch, except you ... that three and a half years of total inactivity and isolation wouldn't affect you in any way ... that you could've never have made such a simple mistake like the piece of nylon string that you forgo—' Hunter deliberately left the sentence unfinished. 'You know what? It doesn't matter.'

This time it was Lucien who stayed quiet.

Hunter knew that Lucien was right then rushing through his memories, searching for a mistake he could've made inside that control room.

'Yes,' Hunter accepted it. 'Time can certainly do all those things you've mentioned, but it also has its own imperceptible way of rusting things up.'

A long and tense silence.

'*I'm glad that you think I'm rusty, Grasshopper.*' Lucien finally came back to Hunter. '*Because I will be delighted to be able to prove you wrong. And here is a taster. Are you ready? Knoxville, Tennessee – there's a garage building on State Street.*'

Hunter looked at Kennedy, who nodded, confirming that that was where they had found Ross Baxter's body inside the trunk of the silver BMW.

'Yes,' Hunter said. 'We suspected that that was you.'

'*So you've found the BMW, I see.*'

Hunter replied with an affirmative silence.

'*The curious thing here is that his death could've been avoided,*' Lucien explained. '*If he hadn't been such an asshole, but boy was he a dick? Anyway, with that one, I'm sure I did a lot of people a favor. Now, taster number two.*'

Hunter, Garcia and Kennedy exchanged concerned looks.

Lucien proceeded to give Hunter the exact coordinates of where he had left Alicia Campbell's body.

'*You might not find much of her. There were wolves in those woods, you know? But for identification purposes, I did leave her handbag hanging from a tree. What can I say? Sometimes I'm nice like that. Anyway, I've got to run, Grasshopper. I've got to go back to my work . . . to my research. You know what I'm talking about, don't you?*' Lucien gave Hunter no time to reply. '*But of course you do, after all, you and the FBI took it from me, remember? All of my life's work. All of my research. But don't worry, old friend, I'm not angry. Not in the least.*'

At the end of the day, that was the intention of the whole study. What good would a research be if the results weren't shared and appreciated by others? The problem is ... I wasn't done, Grasshopper. There were still a few avenues I hadn't explored ... methods I hadn't tried ... situations I hadn't put myself through ... emotions I hadn't experienced. And I can't wait to resume it all. Like I've said – three and a half years is a long time, and boy, did I miss it.'

The pause that followed was long and uncomfortable.

'Keep your phone close, Robert, because I'll be in contact a lot sooner than you think.' Lucien laughed again, this time a short amused laugh. *'Let the games begin, Grasshopper, let the games begin.'*

The line went dead.

Seventeen

'I guess you can tell your boys and the US Marshals Office to stop searching for the Audi and the Mustang,' Garcia murmured to Kennedy, as soon as Hunter disconnected from the call.

'We'll find out for sure soon enough,' Kennedy replied, retrieving his cellphone from his pocket and quickly pressing a number on his speed-dial. Once the call was answered at the other end, Kennedy passed on the coordinates that Lucien had given them over the phone and the details of what should be found at that particular location. He then instructed the agent to contact the sheriff's office in Tennessee and tell them to send a patrol car to that site ASAP.

'I also need a full trace location on the last call made to the following cellphone . . .' Kennedy nodded at Hunter, who slowly dictated his number. 'I need this by yesterday, do you understand me? Call me back as soon as you have anything.'

'Do you know what really bothers me about this?' Garcia said, as soon as Kennedy had ended the call. 'The fact that since his escape, which was only two days ago, he's killed, what, seven people?' He looked at Kennedy. 'Three guards, two infirmary nurses and now two civilians?'

'If the body in the wood confirms,' Kennedy agreed. 'Yes, the count stands at seven.'

'And according to what he just said over the phone,' Garcia continued. 'The "games", as he put it, haven't even begun yet. Seven victims and that's a "taster"?'

Right at that moment, Kennedy's phone rang in his hand. He answered it before the second ring.

'What have you got for me?'

Kennedy listened for a total of three seconds before his naturally rosy cheeks went ghostly white.

'Are you sure about this?' he asked the FBI agent at the other end, already knowing that there was no way he could've made a mistake. His gaze settled on Hunter. 'Thank you,' he said, before putting the phone down.

Hunter waited in silence.

Garcia wasn't as patient.

'What happened?' he asked.

The SUV slowed down as it hit some traffic on Dulles Toll Road.

'We've traced the last call made to your cell, Robert,' Kennedy replied. 'Lucien was using a prepaid cellphone, but we've got the location. Would you like to have a guess where he was calling from?'

Hunter took a deep breath and leaned back against the car seat. 'Los Angeles?'

Kennedy frowned at him. 'How did you know?'

'I didn't,' Hunter replied. 'At least not for sure, but I know Lucien and if he wants to "play a game" with you, he won't wait until you go to him. He'll come to you.'

'Hold on a second,' Garcia said, lifting his hands. 'This psycho drove all the way from Virginia to Los Angeles in a stolen car, straight after escaping from a high-security facility, and he wasn't spotted anywhere, by no one?'

'No,' Kennedy replied. 'He didn't drive . . . he took a plane.'

'Sorry . . .' Garcia's jaw dropped open. 'He did what?'

'The location where the call originated from,' Kennedy explained. 'It was traced to LAX. He called you from the airport in Los Angeles, Robert.'

Eighteen

Lucien disconnected from the call he'd made to Hunter, swung his rucksack over his right shoulder and exited the terminal building at LAX airport. As he stepped outside, he dropped the prepaid cellphone he had just purchased into the closest trashcan.

Lucien knew that as soon as Hunter answered his phone, they'd begin tracking the call, and Lucien would've wanted it no other way. His only regret was that he wouldn't be there to see Hunter's face once he found out that the call had come from LAX.

Outside, Lucien paused by a group of four friends who were busy trying to fit a ridiculous amount of luggage into the trunk of a rental Toyota Avensis. Lucien quickly identified their accent as Texan – the drawliest of the Southern drawls.

The bright blue sky above their heads was completely unspoiled and within seconds of standing there, Lucien could feel beads of sweat starting to form on his forehead. The digital display on the billboard clock not that far from where he was standing read sixteen degrees Celsius, which would fall into the expected temperature for a typical LA spring early afternoon, but the lack of clouds, coupled with no wind at all, made it feel as if Lucien had landed right in the middle of the Los Angeles summer.

Despite the heat, Lucien closed his eyes and allowed the sun to beat down on his face for a few seconds. Freedom was without a doubt a thing of beauty.

The four Texans gave up on stuffing the car trunk with their luggage, finally accepting that they would have to place some of it on the backseat. The argument was now about who would share that backseat with the suitcases.

Lucien was just wondering if he should take a cab or a bus to town, when he saw two police officers walk out of the same terminal exit he had done just moments earlier. For someone like Lucien, that was too good an opportunity to miss, so he took off his sunglasses, adjusted his rucksack on his shoulder, ran a hand through his longish blond wig, and approached the two policemen.

'Excuse me, officers,' he said, pausing right in front of them. His accent was now identical to the luggage-struggling four-some. 'Could you tell me how long it would take me to get from here to downtown LA? I've never been here before,' he lied.

'If you've never been here before, then I think a better question would be – how much do you want to spend?' the younger of the two officers replied. He had a long, jagged scar across his chin that hadn't healed too well. Lucien could tell it had come from a glass-bottle wound. 'A cab will cost you anywhere between . . .' The officer looked at his partner for confirmation. 'Eighty and one hundred and fifty dollars, depending where you're being dropped off.'

The second officer nodded. 'Yeah, that sounds about right.'

'And it can take you anywhere from forty minutes upwards,' the young officer continued. 'That'll be subject to traffic and in this city, there's no telling.'

'Or you can take a Flyway bus to Union Station and jump

in a cab from there,' the second officer said, taking over. He looked to be at least fifteen years older than his partner, with a thick moustache that was perfectly groomed. 'The Flyway bus will cost you seven bucks, but it will easily take you way over an hour just to get to the station.'

'One option is faster,' the younger officer said. 'The other is cheaper. The choice is yours.'

Lucien's dark brown eyes, which were now blue thanks to his contact lenses, slowly moved from one policeman to the other, as if he was waiting for one of them to recognize him.

Neither did.

'Thank you,' Lucien finally replied with a smile. 'I think I'll probably go for the cab option then, as money isn't really a problem.'

The younger officer angled his head at Lucien. 'You might not want to advertise that kind of information around, sir. Not in a city like LA and definitely not inside an LA cab.'

Lucien nodded a little apologetically. 'Thank you again, officers. Very much appreciated.'

'The nearest taxi rank is that way, sir,' the senior officer said, pointing to the opposite direction Lucien had taken.

'Sorry, dumb me.' Lucien replied, putting his sunglasses back on and spinning around on his feet.

How's that for losing my touch after three and a half years, Robert? he thought, as he walked past the two officers. *I hope you're ready, old friend, because here I am . . . and I'm coming for you with a bag full of surprises.*

Nineteen

'Lucien took a *plane* into LAX?' Garcia asked Kennedy, his eyes narrowing at the NCAVC Director. 'How the hell wasn't he spotted?'

The SUV finally cleared traffic and began making good headway toward Dulles airport.

'When Lucien was arrested last time,' the reply came from Hunter instead of Kennedy, 'a collection of ID cards, driver's licenses, even passports were found inside one of his safe houses. All of them authentic . . . all of them belonging to male victims, who he had carefully chosen according to their height, body frame, skin complexion, age and similarity in appearance, though the appearance wasn't that important.'

'How's that possible?'

'That's the thing about Lucien,' Hunter explained. 'He's a genius when it comes to changing his appearance. He's an expert with makeup and liquid latex, which means that if he has access to the right materials, he can pretty much make himself look whichever way he wants. Matching a photograph in a passport or a driver's license wouldn't be that hard for someone with his skills.'

'Lucien was always planning ahead,' Kennedy jumped in.

'According to what we found out through his notebooks, he never kept the same identity for more than twelve months ... never stayed in the same place for longer than that either. He was always moving around, always assuming a brand-new identity, and the more he did it, the better he got at it, to the point that he could stop you on the street, have a conversation with you and you would've never known it was him. So ... to answer your question, Detective Garcia, clearing a boarding desk on a domestic flight, where a bored airline clerk barely looks at the photo on your ID, would've been a stroll in the park for Lucien.'

As they neared Dulles airport, a 747 on the approach to landing flew directly above their SUV, making all the windows rattle.

'I can't delay this any longer, Robert,' Kennedy announced, as he again reached for his cellphone. 'I'll have to inform the Attorney General and the US Marshals office that we've figured out that the note that was found inside Lucien's infirmary cell was addressed to you. I'll also have to tell them about the phone call you've just received. If Lucien is now in LA, the entire manhunt operation will have to relocate.'

Hunter said nothing in return because there was nothing to be said.

Once again, Kennedy quickly connected to one of his speed-dial numbers. This time, the person who picked up the call at the other end was Peter Holbrook, the special agent in charge of the FBI team that had been working together with the US Marshals Office. The conversation was concise and to the point. Kennedy told him about the new victim in Tennessee, Alicia Campbell, and that they had positive information that Lucien was now in Los Angeles.

Once Kennedy ended the call, Garcia let out a questioning chuckle.

'The two of you speak of this Lucien character as if you both admire him. He's not a rock star, he's a psychopath, and from what I've heard so far, quite a delusional one at it. Fine, he's clever, he's good with makeup, he knows psychology and he knows how to hypnotize people, so what? Except for the makeup expertise, which I'm not sure we need, we can do everything he can.' He paused and thought better of what he'd just said. 'Well, you can.' He nodded at Hunter. 'I don't know how to hypnotize people. Anyway.' Garcia's tone became serious again. 'There's no way this guy can win, Robert. He's a lone player on what seems like a vendetta mission against you. The problem is – he's not facing a lone opponent in this "game" he wants to play.' He used his fingers to draw quotation marks in the air. 'He's going up against the FBI, the US Marshals Office and now the LAPD. Call me crazy, but I'll take those odds against him any day.'

'I like where your head's at,' Kennedy said, an approving look across his face.

'And the way I see it,' Garcia proceeded, 'Lucien just made his first big mistake.'

'What mistake is that?' Kennedy asked. The approving look turned to thoughtful.

'He's now in Los Angeles,' Hunter replied. Though he knew exactly what Garcia was talking about, he didn't quite share his partner's excitement.

'Exactly,' Garcia agreed. 'He's now in Los Angeles and that's our turf, our house. We know the streets, we know the neighborhoods and we've got contacts everywhere. Clever or not, this Lucien guy just jumped into a frying pan . . . our frying pan.'

'I can't really disagree with your partner's logic here, Robert,' Kennedy said.

'Yes, sure,' Hunter said. 'We know the streets of LA. We know the neighborhoods and we've got contacts, but there's something you're forgetting, Adrian.'

'And what's that?' Kennedy asked.

'You've had Lucien in custody for three and a half years,' Hunter replied. 'You've been studying him for three and a half years. I'm sure that you know him a little better now. Carlos is right – Lucien *is* a loner, but he's so by choice. He will never depend on anyone. He will never trust anyone.'

'I don't follow,' Kennedy said.

'What I'm getting at is that Lucien will not roam the streets of LA looking for partners, or weapons, or drugs, or anything. Whatever he needs, he'll find a way to get it himself. Whatever he's planning, he will not depend on another soul to execute it. He will not act suspiciously and he will not give anything away.'

'Fine,' Kennedy agreed. 'But I still think Detective Garcia has a point. We could have an advantage here that Lucien might have overlooked.'

'You still don't get it, do you, Adrian?' Hunter asked, shaking his head at the NCAVC director.

Kennedy seemed oblivious to what Hunter was referring to. 'What don't I get, Robert?'

'Even if we were arresting Lucien right this second,' Hunter clarified, 'seven innocent people have already lost their lives because of your ego trip. Seven people in two days, Adrian.' Despite being angry, Hunter's voice was still composed. 'You know what Lucien is capable of . . . and he's now on the loose, walking around in a city like Los Angeles.' Hunter paused to allow his words to sink in for just a second. 'We don't have a clue what he's got planned and no one can predict how many more innocent people will perish, how many more lives will be destroyed before we get to him . . . *if* we get to him. That's what you've done, Adrian. What you don't get is that this "game" that Lucien wants to play . . . no matter what happens from now on . . . we've already lost.'

Twenty

After almost an hour walking the streets of Lynwood, a majorly Hispanic neighborhood that sat between Compton and South Gate in the southern portion of the Los Angeles Basin, Lucien finally came across exactly what he was looking for – a hotel that rented their rooms by the hour, day, week, month, year . . . any sort of arrangement could be reached – no questions asked, no ID needed – as long as it was all paid for in cash and in advance. The derelict building, with a faded blue façade and dirty windows, was sandwiched between a dry-cleaners and a shoe repair shop at the bottom of a nondescript road, where potholes were starting to look like plunge pools.

As he stepped inside the small and badly lit entry lobby, Lucien immediately picked up the distinct smell of sweet perfume, combined with cheap booze and old tobacco. The patterned carpet that greeted whoever walked through the front door was dull, ripped at one end and dotted with cigarette-burn marks. Puerto Rican reggaeton played out of a portable radio sitting behind the empty reception desk.

Lucien rang the bell and waited.

Nothing.

He rang it again.

This time he heard a noise coming from behind the door at the back of the reception area, but still no one appeared.

Lucien rang it one more time, keeping his finger on the buzzer until he got a reply.

'*Calmate puto*. I'm coming already,' an angry and heavily accented male voice called from behind the door. 'Enough with the bell, *ese*.'

Lucien finally let go of the buzzer.

A couple of seconds later, a short and overweight man, wearing elasticated trousers, brown loafers and a checked long-sleeve shirt that was buttoned up to his collar, came out of the door. His hair had been clipped to a number-one cut.

'*Que quieres, ese?*' the man asked, at last getting to the front counter.

Lucien regarded him in silence. The man's breath smelled of refried beans and onions. His eyes were bloodshot and a small blob of some sort of brown sauce hung from the right corner of his mouth.

'What do you want, *ese?*' the man asked again, matching Lucien's analytical stare.

'You missed some,' Lucien said, first touching the right corner of his own lips before pointing to the man's.

'What?' The man frowned at Lucien, clearly annoyed at having been disturbed.

'You've got some sauce on your lips.' Lucien said. He maintained the Texan accent he had picked up at the airport.

The man used his right hand to wipe his mouth clean then licked the sauce from his finger.

Lucien waited patiently.

'OK, so what do you want, *cabron?*'

Seeing that he was standing in a hotel lobby, Lucien looked back at the man, waiting to see if he would realize how silly his question sounded. He didn't.

'A room,' Lucien finally replied.

'*Cuánto tiempo?*' the man asked, looking down at the register book. 'How many hours?'

'Let's start with four days,' Lucien said. 'How about that?'

The man looked back at Lucien with an odd expression on his face, before angling his head to look past him, in the direction of the entry door. There was no one else there.

'*Cuatro días?*' The man's tone of voice was skeptical, to say the least. 'You want a room for four days? *Estás seguro?*'

Lucien realized that though the hotel advertised their rooms by the hour, day, week or month, it was really the sort of establishment that people would bring working girls to, have their fun, then leave a couple of hours later. No one really stayed the night, never mind four whole days, but that had been precisely why Lucien had chosen that specific hotel.

'That's right,' he replied. 'Let's start with four days. If I need to stay longer, I'll let you know at least a day in advance. Sounds fair?'

The man carried on eyeing Lucien for a moment longer. '*Pagando en chavos, ese?* You paying cash?' He rubbed his thumb against his index finger.

'Of course.'

'Then yeah, *ese*, it sounds fair,' the man agreed, giving Lucien a stained-teeth smile. 'A room for four days will cost you . . . one hundred and eighty dollars.'

Lucien saw no point in haggling. Instead, he reached inside his pocket, took out the exact count and handed it to the man.

'Plus thirty bucks deposit,' the man added, his eyes alight

with greed. 'In case you break something in the room, *ese*, you know? You'll get it back when you leave. *Te prometo.*'

With ice-cold eyes, Lucien held the man's stare long enough to make him feel positively uncomfortable.

'Of course,' Lucien finally agreed, handing the man the extra thirty dollars.

The man counted the cash before putting it in his shirt pocket.

'I like you, *ese*,' he said, writing something down in the register book. 'And because I like you, I'll give you a room on the top floor. All the rooms here are the same,' he explained. 'But a room on the top floor means that you won't have anyone directly above you, *comprendes*?' He used his index finger to point at the ceiling. 'You'll probably still hear some banging noises coming from the room next door or the one under you. That will be the *chacha*.' He gave Lucien a 'you know what I'm talking about' smile. 'You might also hear some slapping noises, some screams, some name-calling . . .' The man shook his head. '*No te preocupes por nada* . . . nothing to worry about, *comprendes? Eso es normal aquí.*'

Lucien simply nodded in silence.

The man put the opened register book on the counter and turned it so it faced his new guest. '*Firme aquí, por favor.*' The man smiled. 'Use any name you like.'

Lucien took the pen and quickly scribbled something onto the line the man had indicated.

The man laughed as he picked up the book and read what Lucien had written down. 'Your name is "Ese Puto"?'

'Why not?' Lucien said. 'That's what you called me, right? Why change it?'

The man smiled. '*Si, Por qué no?* Ese Puto it is.' He handed

Lucien a key. The keyring read 215. 'As I've said, top floor. Turn left when you come out of the lift.'

'I'll take the stairs,' Lucien said.

'Still,' the man replied. 'Turn left when you get to the top floor. It will be the last room on your right.'

As Lucien reached for the keys, the man leaned over the reception counter and whispered at him. 'If you're looking for a party, *ese* . . . any time . . . all you have to do is come see me, *tranquilo*? I can get you anything you need, ese . . . *anything*.' The stained smile was back on the man's lips. '*Chicas, yayo, cachimba, todo lo que quieras, comprendes?* Whatever you need, I'm your man.'

Lucien had to take a step back to avoid the full weight of the man's onion breath.

'Actually, there maybe is something you could help me with,' Lucien said.

Greed returned to the man's eyes.

'Do you know anyone who could help me find out which home address is registered a specific cellphone number?'

The man regarded Lucien anxiously while scratching his large belly. Dodgy requests were something that he was no stranger to. 'I know a couple of people,' he replied. 'But it's gonna cost you, *ese*.'

Lucien stood still, his piercing eyes once again making the man feel a little uneasy. 'How much?'

The man thought about it for a couple of seconds. 'One hundred dollars.'

'You'll get the money when I get the address.'

The man smiled. 'Of course. Do you have the number?'

Lucien wrote Hunter's cellphone number down on a piece of paper and handed it to the man.

'*Dame una hora* … give me one hour and I'll have an address for you.'

Lucien thanked him with a simple head gesture before calmly taking the stairs up to the second floor.

Twenty-One

Despite the three-hour difference between Los Angeles and Washington DC, it was past 11:00 p.m. by the time Hunter finally got back to his small one-bedroom apartment in Huntington Park, southeastern Los Angeles. After pouring himself a dose of Port Askaig, Sherry Cask, fifteen–year-old, he switched off the lights and sat in silence in his living room, staring out the window at the never-dying city lights far in the distance.

He tried to organize some of the thoughts in his head, but since the news of Lucien's escape, Hunter's mind had been a grotesque mess of images, memories and emotions, starting from three and a half years ago and angrily dragging him all the way back to his college days. The more he tried to think clearly, the murkier his thoughts became.

Hunter had another sip of his Scotch, closed his eyes and allowed the dark golden liquid to completely envelop his taste buds, and envelop them it did – sweet and smoky with notes of citrus and just a hint of violet. Hunter couldn't remember when he had acquired that particular bottle, or who had recommended it to him, but it was indeed a very nice dram.

Single malts were Hunter's biggest passion and though he

would never consider himself an expert, the small collection he had obtained over the years was no doubt diverse and very accomplished, probably able to satisfy the palate of most connoisseurs.

The sound of a not so distant ambulance siren pulled Hunter away from his moment of pleasure. As he reopened his eyes, he saw a blonde woman, who seemed to be in her mid-forties, close the curtains on an apartment window across the road from him. A moment later, her lights were switched off.

Hunter checked his watch: 11:48 p.m. For most, a very reasonable time to go to bed, but Hunter wasn't like most people, especially when it came to sleeping.

In the USA, it was estimated that one in five people suffered from insomnia. In most cases, the condition was brought on by a combination of work, financial and family related stress, but then again, Hunter's case wasn't like most cases.

Insomnia had grabbed hold of him for the first time just after his mother lost her battle with glioblastoma multiforme – the most aggressive type of primary brain cancer known to medicine. Hunter was only seven years old at the time. Back then, he would sit alone in his room at night, desperately missing her, trying to understand what had happened, trying to keep his tears from drowning him. Sadness became the daily companion he'd never asked for, and with sadness came the shattering nightmares, so powerful and vivid that out of an instinct of pure self-preservation, his brain did everything it could to keep him awake for as long as possible. Sleep became a luxury and a torment in equal measure and to keep his mind occupied during those endless sleepless nights Hunter took to books, reading ferociously night after night, as if they gave him some sort of magic power. Books became his sanctuary, his safe place ... his shield against a sadness he couldn't control or understand.

As the years went by, Hunter learned how to live with insomnia instead of fighting it. On a good night, he would probably be able to find four, maybe even five hours of consecutive sleep, but as he watched another light across the road from him being switched off ... another curtain being drawn shut, Hunter already knew that tonight wouldn't be one of the 'good nights'.

Just as he had another sip of his whisky, Hunter's cellphone vibrated on the coffee table that centered his living room, startling him. His heart skipped a beat as his eyes immediately shot toward the phone display screen, fully expecting to once again see the words 'unknown number' written across it, but he was wrong. Instead, the name on his screen read: 'Tracy'.

Without even realizing, Hunter breathed out in relief while allowing a timid smile to grace his lips.

Hunter had met criminal psychology professor, Tracy Adams, a few months back in one of the many libraries inside the UCLA campus in Westwood. The attraction on both sides had been undeniable and immediate, but despite liking her a lot more than what he would like to admit, for his own reasons and to Tracy's frustration, Hunter had never really allowed romance to properly blossom.

'Hey,' Hunter answered the call, returning his attention to the city lights outside his window. 'I would've thought you'd be asleep by now.'

'Really?' Tracy replied, her tone a tad amused. 'When have you known me to go to sleep any time before one in the morning?'

As coincidence had it, Tracy also suffered from insomnia, albeit not as severely as Hunter.

'True,' Hunter accepted. 'So how was your day?'

'Pretty normal,' Tracy replied. 'Though two students had to excuse themselves today and rush out of class and into the bathroom. Some of the images that accompanied one of my lessons this afternoon were too much for them.'

'Really?' Hunter asked. 'Who were you talking about?'

'Ed Gein.'

Hunter laughed. 'Let me guess – the images were of the human skin suits.'

Edward Theodore Gein was an American serial killer whose victim count was pretty low when compared to some of the most notorious murderers in American history – officially he was only found guilty of two murders. What set him aside from most other serial killers was the violence and the level of his insanity. Ed Gein was severely delusional. He used to dig up bodies of women who reminded him of his mother, cut up patches of their skin and then use it to make suits and masks for himself, which he would wear around the house. He also used some of their body parts to create belts, lamps, bowls, ashtrays and various other household items. Ed Gein was the true inspiration behind some of the most horrifying Hollywood serial killers ever created, including Norman Bates (*Psycho*), Jame Gumb (Buffalo Bill in *Silence of the Lambs*), and Leatherface (*Texas Chainsaw Massacre*).

Tracy chuckled. 'Yep, you got it,' she said. 'The skin suits. It gets them every time. Anyway, how was the flight . . . or flights, I should say.'

'Long and tiring.'

'I can imagine. It's been some time since I last went to DC, but there and back in the same day is a tough call. I'm surprised you're not crashed out after twelve hours of flying.'

'Yeah ... unfortunately it looks like sleep won't come that easily tonight ... if at all.'

Tracy picked up a hint of worry in Hunter's voice, but she knew better than to ask. Instead, she threw him a very different question.

'Would you maybe like some company? I was correcting some papers earlier in the evening and I still feel wide awake, plus I have no classes tomorrow morning.'

The invitation was certainly tempting.

'Isn't it quite a long way for you to come over at this time of night?' Hunter asked.

Tracy lived in West Hollywood, which was around sixteen miles away from Huntington Park.

'It would be,' Tracy agreed. 'But can you do me a favor? Can you have a look out your window?'

'What?' Hunter frowned. 'I *am* looking out my window.'

'I know,' Tracy replied. 'But look down, by the lamppost to your left.'

Hunter did.

Tracy, who was wearing a long black coat, waved at him, her phone still held against her right ear.

Completely surprised, Hunter waved back. 'Why didn't you just come up and knock?'

'I didn't want to intrude.' She smiled up at him. 'Does that mean that you *would* like some company?'

'Yes,' Hunter gave in, returning the smile. 'I'd love some company.'

*

As they disconnected from their call and Tracy made her way into Hunter's apartment block, neither of them noticed the tall figure hiding behind a tree several yards away.

Lucien had been standing there for a while. He saw Hunter arriving not that long ago. He saw the lights go on inside an apartment on the third floor before they were switched off again. He saw Hunter's shadow step up to that window and stare out into the distance, as if contemplating the inevitable and then ... surprise. Lucien saw the stunning redhead approach from the other side. He saw her look up at the apartment block, as if she was searching for something. From that distance it was hard to be certain, but as Lucien tried to follow her stare, he could swear that she was looking at the same window as he was.

'Well,' he whispered to himself. 'This looks interesting. So who might you be, you pretty little thing?'

He then saw the redhead reach into her handbag, take out her phone and dial a number, her eyes still looking up at the building before her. Again, from that distance there was no way Lucien could make out any of the conversation, or even read her lips, but he felt every hair in his body stand on end as he saw Hunter standing by his window with his cellphone glued to his right ear. A few seconds after that he saw the redhead smile then wave.

Lucien looked up.

Hunter waved back.

Jackpot.

'Well, hello there, beautiful,' Lucien whispered again, excitement intoxicating his body like poison injected straight into his bloodstream. His eyes followed the redheaded woman as she returned her phone to her handbag and walked over to Hunter's apartment building.

Lucien smiled at his good fortune.

'It is so . . . so nice to make your acquaintance, my beautiful red rose . . . whoever you are.'

Twenty-Two

Garcia was already at his desk when Hunter opened the door to their UVC Unit office, which was located at the far end of the Robbery Homicide Division's floor, inside the famous Police Administration Building in downtown LA. The room was nothing more than a claustrophobic 22-square-meter concrete box with a single window, two desks, three old-fashioned filing cabinets, a printer, a coffee machine and a large white magnetic board pushed up against the south wall, but it was still a complete separate enclosure to the rest of the RHD floor, which, if nothing else, kept snooping eyes and the never-ending buzzing of voices locked out.

As Hunter closed the door behind him, Garcia took one look at his partner and chuckled.

'Well,' he said, 'I guess that asking you if you had a good night's sleep is quite pointless, isn't it?'

'I did get about three hours,' Hunter said.

Garcia accepted it with a sideways nod. He knew that in Hunter's case, three hours of sleep was actually good going.

Hunter took off his jacket and fired up his computer, but before he had a chance to sit down, the door to their office was pushed open once again, this time by the captain of the Robbery Homicide Division, Barbara Blake.

Captain Blake had taken over the division's leadership a few years back, after being handpicked for the job by one of the force's most decorated captains, as he finally stepped down from a position he had occupied for over fifteen years. The decision to appoint a woman to such a high-profile job did anger a long list of contenders, all of them male. But angering people was something that Barbara Blake had grown very accustomed to throughout her career in the police force.

Despite being greeted by a fair amount of hostility as she took over the RHD's captaincy, she quickly gained a reputation for being a hard-to-the-core, no-bullshit captain. Barbara Blake wasn't one to be easily intimidated. She also took no crap from anyone, including her superiors in the police department, and she had absolutely no qualms about upsetting government officials, high-powered politicians, or even the media, if it meant sticking to what she believed was the right thing to do.

Within just a few months of taking over the RHD job, the initial antagonism began to dissipate and slowly but surely, Captain Blake gained the respect and trust of every single detective under her command.

As Captain Blake held the door to Hunter and Garcia's office open, both detectives realized that she wasn't alone. Standing directly behind her were two tall individuals.

'Captain,' Hunter said in greeting, offering her a single head-nod.

Garcia followed suit, but frowned as soon as he noticed the two visitors behind her.

'Robert, Carlos,' Captain Blake said, returning the head gesture. Her long jet-black hair was gracefully pulled back into a braided ponytail. She wore a silky pearl blouse, tucked into a well-designed navy-blue pencil skirt and black shoes. The look across her face spoke for itself: *We were expecting this, weren't we?*

Captain Blake waited for the two guests to step into the office before closing the door behind them.

'This is US Marshal Tyler West,' she addressed her detectives, as she indicated the six-foot-two, African American gentleman standing to her right.

West was in his early forties with a military haircut that framed a bland and squared face. His nose was clearly no stranger to being punched and the look in his dark eyes was focused, secure and almost menacing. His perfectly fitted pinstripe suit looked like it had just come from the dry-cleaners that same morning.

'And this is Special Agent Peter Holbrook with the FBI.' the captain continued, now turning to her left, where a willowy man stood. He was elegantly dressed in a black suit, with moderately tanned skin and a full head of dark brown hair that was combed straight back – Dracula style.

They all shook hands and West was the first to speak.

'I'm sure you've been brought up to speed on what this is all about, right?' he asked Hunter. His voice was smooth, but quite deep. 'I'm the US Marshal in charge of Lucien Folter's manhunt operation and Special Agent Holbrook here is leading the FBI team that's tagging along with us.'

From the corner of his eyes, Hunter noticed the look on Holbrook's face harden and he knew exactly why. 'Tagging along' didn't quite rhyme with 'joint operation'.

'I understand that you received a call from our fugitive yesterday, early afternoon,' West continued. 'Is that correct?'

'Yes, that's right,' Hunter replied.

'And may I ask why you didn't immediately contact us?' West's voice got deeper still and the look in his eyes crossed the line from focused to menacing.

Hunter didn't mind West's tone of voice nor the look in his eyes. None of it fazed him.

Captain Blake, on the other hand, who knew nothing of the phone call, did not look too pleased. Her eyes first widened at the news before quickly homing in on West.

'There was no need for me to call you,' Hunter calmly replied, finally taking a seat behind his desk.

'There was no need?' West's eyebrows almost hit the ceiling.

'The NCAVC director,' Hunter explained, 'Adrian Kennedy, was sitting next to me when I received the call, which I placed on speakerphone. He heard the entire conversation. Once Lucien disconnected, the first thing Director Kennedy did was call Special Agent Holbrook with every detail.' He nodded at the agent who was now standing in front of Garcia's desk. 'Adrian told us that Holbrook was leading the FBI team in the *joint* investigation between the US Marshals Office and the Bureau.'

This time Hunter noticed the look on Holbrook's face soften and his lips twitch as he held back a smile. It looked like Hunter had just made a friend.

'So,' Hunter continued. 'I already knew that the "manhunt operation task force" had received the information about the call, including where it had originated from, seconds after the call had ended.' He shrugged. 'Me placing an identical call to you would have been a little pointless, don't you think?'

'Hold on,' Captain Blake intervened. 'He called you yesterday?'

'Right after Special Agent Williams' funeral,' Garcia replied.

Captain Blake's intrigued look went nowhere. 'And I just heard you saying something about the location where the call had originated from,' she said. 'So the call was traced?'

Garcia looked at Hunter, who nodded.

'Lucien made the call from LAX,' he replied.

'He's here?' Captain Blake's voice was eighty percent surprise, twenty percent outrage. Her gaze moved first to the two newcomers, then to her detectives.

'Why do you think we have the two lead agents running this manhunt operation standing in our office, Captain?' Garcia asked. 'It's not just because of a phone call.'

Captain Blake pinned West and Holbrook down with a look that could've cut glass. 'You never mentioned the fact that Lucien Folter was in Los Angeles when the two of you stormed into my office.'

It was West's turn to shrug. 'We thought you knew. How are we to know that your detectives don't communicate with their captain?'

This time Captain Blake really didn't like West's tone of voice, not to mention his implication.

'Oh, we communicate fine,' she replied, her voice taking a special tone of its own – one that Hunter and Garcia knew only too well. 'What we don't do too well is—'

Garcia got comfortable and stiffened a smile. He had front-row seats for the show that was about to take place, but Hunter knew that a confrontation between Captain Blake and a senior US Marshal wasn't really the best way to start the day.

'You can listen to the call, if you like,' Hunter quickly cut in, interrupting his captain.

All eyes moved to him.

'It's been recorded?' West asked.

Hunter reached for his cellphone and placed it on his desk. Everyone except Garcia gathered around.

'Can you connect it to your computer speakers?' West asked.

Hunter nodded and did just that before calling the application he had used to record the call.

For the next four and a half minutes, Hunter and Garcia's office went absolutely still. Captain Blake, US Marshal West and Special Agent Holbrook listened to every word Lucien had said with the utmost attention. No one interrupted. It was only when the recording came to an end that West came to life.

'So,' he said, addressing Hunter, his voice, once again, hostile. 'If I understood this correctly, and I'm pretty sure I did, you knew that the cryptic note that was found inside Folter's infirmary cell was meant for you, and you simply decided not to forward that information to us?'

'We thought you knew,' Captain Blake cut in.

West looked back at her sideways.

Garcia smiled. 'That's my captain.'

'We did indeed assume you knew,' Hunter intervened again.

'And why would you assume that?' West asked.

'Because Director Kennedy knew,' Hunter came back.

West's concerned gaze navigated to Holbrook, who was looking a little lost.

'I wasn't aware that Director Kennedy knew who the note was meant for,' he said, his tone defensive. 'I was never told.'

West didn't seem to buy Holbrook's reply.

'What difference does it make if you knew that the note was meant for me or not?' Hunter took over again, bringing West's attention back to him. 'That knowledge doesn't get you any closer to arresting Lucien. Today or yesterday.' He lifted his hand to stop West before he had a chance to retort. 'Clearly there was some sort of misjudgment in communication from our part and from the FBI, but none of it was done on purpose, US Marshal West. Believe me when I tell you that we all want Lucien back behind bars as fast as possible. No one is playing games here.'

'Well, he is,' West came back. 'And I'm glad that you have said that *we* all want Lucien back behind bars, because the game that he wants to play clearly involves you, Detective Hunter. So, whether you like it or not, you're now part of this manhunt operation.'

West placed both hands on Hunter's desk and leaned forward until he was just a few inches from the detective.

'And we really need to talk. And I mean . . . right now.'

Twenty-Three

For the second time in the same week, Hunter had to run through the story connecting him to Lucien, this time so that Captain Blake, US Marshal Tyler West and FBI Special Agent Peter Holbrook could understand why Lucien seemed to be so obsessed with involving Hunter in some sort of 'catch me if you can' game.

Just like Garcia, West, Holbrook and Captain Blake were utterly shocked by what Hunter had told them, all three of them finding it hard to believe that someone, anyone, no matter how delusional they were, had spent their entire adult life torturing and killing people as part of some crazy, self-indulgent experiment – just so he could document his own insanity.

'This has got to be the most mind-boggling, crazy-ass story I've ever heard,' West said when Hunter was finally done.

Neither Captain Blake nor Holbrook seemed to disagree with his assessment.

To Garcia, it all sounded even more unbelievable the second time around.

'We have a team armed with state-of-the-art face-recognition software analyzing all of LAX CCTV footage from around the time Lucien placed the call to you,' Holbrook said. 'If we manage to identify him and what sort of disguise he was wearing, then there's a chance that a bus driver, a cab driver, someone would remember him . . . maybe even remember dropping him somewhere.'

'In a city like LA,' Garcia cut in, 'that's a hell of a long shot.'

'We know that,' Holbrook accepted it. 'But right now, long shots are all we've got.'

Hunter kept a steady face, but the thought swimming around in his mind was: *Lucien never left anything to chance.*

Lucien had spent almost five minutes on the phone to Hunter, more than enough time for the call to be traced. Lucien knew that. In fact, Hunter had no doubt that Lucien *wanted* the call to be traced. He wanted Hunter to know that he was in Los Angeles. It was all part of the 'cat and mouse' game Lucien wanted to play. It not only added to the overall tension of entire situation, but it also served as a testimony to how confident he was.

If Lucien knew that the call would be traced to LAX, then of course he expected the FBI and the US Marshal's Office to sieve through all of the airport's CCTV footage. The problem was, that same state-of-the-art face-recognition software had been operating in most USA international airports for years now, including LAX. Airports are among the first to be put under alert in case of a prison break. They are among the first to receive a photo and full description of the fugitive, a photo that without a doubt would be immediately fed into this 'state-of-the-art face-recognition software'. Still, yesterday Lucien waltzed out of LAX without a single red flag being raised.

State-of-the-art or not, the only way the program would pick up Lucien out of a crowd was if Lucien wanted it to, and if he ever did, there would be a reason behind it.

'Can I ask you something, Detective Hunter?' West asked,

and immediately followed it through, without waiting for
Hunter's reply. 'What do you think are the chances of this
Lucien character, your old college pal, coming for you? Because
from what you told us and from that phone conversation
we've just heard, one thing is very clear to me – he blames you
for his arrest, for stopping him, for putting an end to his . . .
"research", if one can even call it that. He's obviously angry,
and in his own words – he spent the last three and a half years
counting time and plotting revenge. To top it all off, he's here,
in your city – so really, what do you think are the chances of
him coming for you, Detective?'

Hunter, who had already considered that possibility, held
West's determined stare for a moment.

'The chance is very real,' he finally admitted. 'But if he
comes after me, he won't do it straight away.'

'I don't follow,' West countered. 'Why not?'

'Because first Lucien will do exactly what he said he would,'
Hunter replied. 'He'll turn this into a game. A game with no
rules on his side, but plenty on ours. A game where he'll control
everything. A game that has already cost seven innocent lives,
and the scary thing is – I don't think he has started playing it
yet. Those seven lives were just a warm-up.'

West uncomfortably scratched the tip of his skewed nose.

'I wish he would come for me straight away,' Hunter added.

West looked back at him with doubt in his eyes.

'I'm not saying that because I want to sound tough, Marshal
West,' Hunter clarified. 'I'm saying it because if Lucien was
coming after me now, then there would be a chance that this
would end here. No more innocent lives would be lost. Either
I would kill him, or he would kill me, or both. But he won't do
that . . . and do you know why?'

'Because he's a coward?' West shot back.

'Because to Lucien that would be no fun,' Hunter corrected the US Marshal. 'You've all heard the phone call recording, right? Lucien wants to go back to his "project", to his "research", because like he'd said, he wasn't finished with it yet. So why not make it fun and pair all of that with a "catch me if you can" game?'

'A game where he's completely outnumbered,' West suggested. 'A game he knows he can't win.'

'That's the problem,' Hunter said. 'If you want to look at this as a win or lose situation, then he's already won . . . seven times. Every life he claims is a victory to him and a defeat to us. A defeat we can never win back.'

A disconcerting silence spread itself across Hunter and Garcia's office like a suffocating blanket.

West was the first to break it.

'Well,' he said, 'on the off chance that you're wrong and your old pal decides to pay you a direct visit straight away, I think that we should assign a twenty-four-hour surveillance team to you.' His gaze moved to Captain Blake.

'He's got a point, Robert.' Her words were followed by a firm nod. 'It doesn't take an expert to figure out that this Lucien character is a cocky sonofabitch, and he clearly has got a beef with you. He's also unpredictable, and if there's a sliver of a chance that he might come looking for you . . .' She didn't need to finish her sentence. 'I'll give SIS a call straight after this meeting.'

The LAPD Special Investigation Section was an elite tactical surveillance squad that had been in operation for over forty years, despite the never-ending efforts from various human rights and political factions to shut it down. The reason was that their kill-rate was higher than any other unit in the department, including SWAT and the Gangs and Narcotics Division.

SIS teams were mainly used to stealthily watch apex predators – individuals suspected of highly violent crimes who would not stop until caught in the act. SIS officers were expert marksmen and essentially masters in surveillance. Their main tactics were to wait and observe until they witnessed a suspect committing a new crime before moving in to make the arrest. Because they usually waited until they caught the suspect red-handed, lethal force was often used, and that was why they were such a controversial tactical LAPD squad.

'We'll also need to bug your phone, Detective,' West added. 'In his call to you, Lucien said that he would be in touch again a lot sooner than you thought. When he does, we'll need to know pronto.'

Hunter knew that no matter what he said, the US Marshals Office would bug his phone anyway. Chances were that they had already done it.

'No SIS,' Hunter said.

Captain Blake frowned at him. 'Why not?'

'Two reasons – first, if Lucien comes for me, he won't do it at my place. He's not going to sneak up behind me and shoot me in the back of the head either. Too easy and not spectacular enough for him. If he comes for me, he will go for something more dramatic. And second – I understand that the LAPD SIS are the best of the best when it comes to surveillance and stealth, but everything Lucien does, he does it like a chess player. What I mean by that is that he always plans several moves ahead, that's how he works. He would've anticipated the chances of a surveillance team being put on me. If he's coming after me, he will look out for that team and, no matter how good they are at stealth operations, there's a chance that Lucien will spot them. If he does, he won't be scared, he won't run away, and he won't just give up either. He will try to take them out first.'

Garcia looked alarmed. 'This Lucien guy is capable of taking out an SIS team?'

'He's capable of much more,' Hunter replied.

'How about a tracker?' Holbrook this time. 'Something small you could hide in your belt, your wallet, your watch, whatever . . . something with a distress button that you could easily activate if you were in trouble.'

'Adrian Kennedy tried something similar when we had Lucien in custody for the first time,' Hunter explained. 'When Special Agent Courtney Taylor and I followed Lucien to one of his hideouts. Adrian gave us a shirt button that doubled as a listening device. I warned Adrian about it. I told him Lucien would spot it and he did. Lucien isn't that easy to fool.'

'I'm sure that between the tech units of the LAPD, the FBI and the US Marshals Office we can come up with a "Lucien-proof" tracking device, Detective Hunter,' West said, taking over again. 'But we can do that a little later. Right now, I need you to think. Is there anyone else in or around LA who you think Lucien might try to contact?' He paused and shrugged. 'Or murder? Maybe someone from your Stanford days?'

Hunter had also already run through that possibility in his mind.

'I can't think of anyone,' he replied. 'The only other person who used to hang out with us back then was Susan Richards, and like I told you, she was the first person he murdered all those years ago.'

'Is there anyone else from back then who *you* keep in contact with?' West insisted. 'Maybe even one of your old professors?'

'No,' Hunter replied. 'No one.'

West stood up straight and ran a hand across the back of his neck a couple of times, massaging it. 'No offense, Detective Hunter, but it seems to me that you are snapping these answers out without any due thought.'

Hunter understood the US Marshal's frustration. 'I'm not,' he said, his tone unoffended. 'The reason why right now I don't need to think about my answers is because I've already done that. I've been through that same line of questioning in my head over and over again. I've been going through it for the past three days. There really is no one I can think of.'

West gave up trying to read Hunter's demeanor after a few seconds. Though he read people for a living, he just couldn't get a beat on the LAPD detective.

'Still,' this time it was Special Agent Holbrook who took over, 'we have a team preparing a list of names as we speak. All of them people who attended Stanford University at the same time you and Lucien were students there. All of them psychology graduates. We would be grateful if you could have a look at the list once we have it, Detective Hunter, and see if any names jump out at you. Maybe a name could refresh your memory about something ... an incident, a conversation ... anything, really. Maybe someone else who Lucien might've had a grudge against. The list will include their respective Stanford yearbook photographs to help you remember them.'

'Of course,' Hunter agreed. 'Just send me the list once you have it and I'll look it over.'

Twenty-Four

In total it took Lucien four days to finalize his plan – half a day to acquire all the items he needed, which was done from four different stores so as not to raise any suspicions; two and a half days roaming around town to find the perfect location; and an extra full day to put everything together.

Lucien would much rather have had his own workshop, preferably somewhere away from the city, where he'd be able to work quietly and calmly for as long as he deemed necessary, but to find such a place would take time, time Lucien wasn't prepared to spare. Besides, he couldn't wait to get started, so instead of a workshop, Lucien had to make do with his dingy hotel room. It certainly wasn't the ideal environment, but the environment didn't affect the final product.

The first thing Lucien had done after arriving at his hotel four days ago had been to place a call to a small courier company back in Louisiana. He had left a package with them, something he had retrieved from one of the two suitcases he'd dug up from his backyard. The package had come with specific instructions. All the company needed to finally ship it was a legitimate delivery address, which had been the reason for Lucien's call.

The package had finally arrived at Lucien's hotel yesterday afternoon.

Lucien had worked throughout the night, taking short breaks every two hours or so, and though the job was laborious and quite complex, he had managed to have it all done by breakfast time. As he finally put down his tools, Lucien got up from his seat and stretched his arms high above his six-foot-one frame. His body felt stiff from working in the same position for hours on end, but it was nothing a hot shower and some rest wouldn't be able to fix.

'Yep,' he said to himself, inspecting his work. 'Not as perfect as I would've liked, but this will do.'

The item was indeed crude. It did lack a little in finesse, but the aesthetics of the final product didn't really matter. What mattered was that it worked.

Lucien slept for six hours before having a long hot shower to relax his aching muscles. After that, he spent around two hours before the mirror perfecting a brand-new character. A character that was totally different from the one he had stuck to for the past week. This time Lucien went for a more sophisticated look.

His wig was black, with short, elegantly trimmed hair, parted to one side. With the help of the liquid latex, Lucien gave himself a squared chin with a dimple, an elongated nose with a cute round tip, and some prominent cheekbones. His scar was once again completely hidden under latex and makeup. He also gave himself a whole new forehead, practically free of wrinkles, showing thinner, more defined eyebrows. The eyes were now dark brown, which were Lucien's natural color, but still he used contact lenses to hide his real irises. He also decided to go with a pair of clear-lens glasses. It gave him a somewhat studious look. His new teeth were gleaming white sitting in fleshy gums, giving him a car-salesman smile.

To match his new look, Lucien decided to go with an Angelino accent, born and raised in the City of Angels, but his tone and demeanor were a lot more elegant than masculine, a persona that Lucien believed would better suit the location he had chosen.

He wore black trousers and a dark blue shirt under a brown blazer jacket, which he had purchased the day before from a second-hand shop all the way across town.

Standing in front of the large mirror in the bathroom, Lucien regarded his new creation: Joseph – a name he borrowed from the sales clerk who had sold him the blazer. Joseph's posture had to be that of a man who was very proud of the way he looked – straight back with squared shoulders. The look in his eyes was confident without being arrogant. His voice was a lot softer than Lucien's, but not submissive. It was the voice of someone who had experienced a certain level of success in life, but still had plenty of room for more.

It took less than fifteen minutes of practice for Joseph to fully take over. When he was done, there was nothing left of Lucien in the man in the mirror.

Back in the room, Joseph packaged the item Lucien had created into a brand-new rucksack and checked his watch: 5:19 p.m. Outside his window, the sky was almost fully clear, with just a few fluffy white clouds scattered far in the distance.

A beautiful day for a walk, Joseph thought.

There was only one more thing he needed to do before the real 'show' began, and that was to call Hunter again, something he would do from one of the five prepaid cellphones he had purchased earlier in the week.

Joseph opened the bedroom window to let in some fresh air, something that the room was in much need of, before reaching for the rucksack.

He paused before the mirror one last time, giving himself a final nod of approval.

'It's show time.'

Twenty-Five

It had been three and a half days since Hunter and Garcia first met US Marshal Tyler West and FBI Special Agent Peter Holbrook back in their office. Despite all their efforts, Lucien's manhunt task force was still to obtain any significant leads. The CCTV camera footage obtained from LAX had yielded no results, nor had the list of names, dating back to his time at Stanford University, that Hunter had been given. He had gone through every name and every photo on that list, but he couldn't remember anything that would in any way link Lucien to any of them, or to anyone else for that matter.

Just like Hunter, Lucien was an only child, whose parents were also deceased. He did have two living relatives – an uncle in Rhode Island, and an aunt in Wisconsin. US Marshals had already talked to both of them, but it was a known fact that Lucien hadn't had any contact with either of them in over twenty-five years. Nevertheless, the US Marshals Office had placed a shadow on both relatives and bugged their phone lines.

With such little progress in almost four days, frustration was quickly settling in.

West and Holbrook were now beginning to question if Lucien was still in Los Angeles or not. Contrary to what they

were expecting, Lucien hadn't made a new move yet, neither
had he contacted Hunter as he'd said he would. The task force
had spent the last twenty-four hours practically sitting on their
asses and staring at walls.

It was just past six in the afternoon when Hunter and
Garcia came out of a meeting with Captain Blake. They had
just got back to their office when Hunter's cellphone rang on
top of his desk.

Sixth sense, cop intuition, premonition, whatever people
wanted to call it, Hunter didn't really believe in it, but as
soon as he heard his cellphone ring, even before checking
the display screen, he knew that the call was from Lucien.
He knew it because all of a sudden he felt his heart freeze in
place. Hunter's gaze moved first to Garcia then to his phone –
'unknown number'.

Garcia, who had just begun preparing a brand-new pot of
coffee, saw the look in his partner's eyes and followed it toward
Hunter's phone.

'Shit!' he whispered, putting down the cup he was holding
and immediately approaching his partner's desk.

Hunter waited for the phone to ring one more time before
answering it. As he did, he straightaway placed the call onto
speakerphone.

'*Hello, Grasshopper.*' Once again, Lucien used no pretend
accent, no variation to his tone and no device to modify his
voice. '*Have you missed me?*'

'With every bullet so far,' Hunter replied in a conservative
tone, as he began recording the call.

'*I would've called sooner, but there were a few things I
needed to sort out first. You know ... I wanted to get reac-
quainted with LA. Plus, all of my work, all of my research,*

was documented in the notebooks you took from me. It's been three and a half years, Robert. My mind was a bit murky about where I had left off, and since I couldn't consult my own notes to remind me, I needed to figure out where to pick up from again.'

Hunter stayed quiet, but he could read between the lines. What Lucien really meant was – he had spent the time choosing his target.

'Anyway,' Lucien continued. *'I've decided that I'm going to make this fun for both of us, and what that means is …* I'm going to give you a really good chance to get to me, Grasshopper.'

'Why don't you come over then?' Hunter said. 'You know where the Police Administration Building is, don't you? We can have a real good chat.'

Lucien laughed. *'Unfortunately that wouldn't quite work for me, old friend, but thanks for the invite anyway. But how about a little game of wits? You've always been a sucker for those, Grasshopper, and I bet that you've got even better at them now after all these years, haven't you?'*

Hunter looked at Garcia, who shrugged, while at the same time arching his eyebrows.

'So here's how this is going to go – I'm about to send a question your way, Grasshopper. Figuring out the answer to that question will earn you the right to hear a very nice little riddle that I have prepared. Figuring out the answer to that riddle will give you a chance to save someone from dying. How does that sound?'

'And if I don't figure out the answer to the first question?' Hunter asked, to Garcia's nod of approval. He was thinking exactly the same.

'Oooh, *that's a pessimistic way of thinking right off the bat, isn't it, Grasshopper? What happened, old friend? Have you lost your confidence?'*

'I just want to understand the rules, Lucien,' Hunter came back.

'*Fair enough,*' Lucien replied. '*If you don't figure out the answer to the question, then you don't earn the right to hear my nice little riddle, which is the part that will allow you to save a life.*' There was a short pause. '*Shall I spit out the rest for you as well, or do you get the gist of it now, Grasshopper?*'

Garcia pressed his lips together and narrowed his eyes in a pained face.

'*Anyway,*' Lucien carried on. '*Time is certainly of the essence now, my friend, so here's the question – ready?*'

'As ready as I'll ever be.'

There was another short pause, as if Lucien needed to get into character first. When he spoke again, there was no excitement in his voice, no wavering, no hesitation.

'*I've been conducting my research for many years, during which I've delved into innumerous exercises, seeking a better understanding of the psychopathic mind. I've learned much, much more than I first expected I would, but there have been a few darker avenues, a few tabooed paths, which I haven't yet ventured into. I think that the time for that has come.*'

Another pause, this time a little longer than the previous one.

'*What I want from you, Grasshopper, is one of these avenues.*'

Garcia looked at Hunter with a ghostly white face as he mouthed the words, 'What the hell?'

'*You have my research, Grasshopper,*' Lucien continued. '*I'm sure you've read through all of it, so what is missing from it? Which dark path have I not explored yet? In truth there is more than one, but I only need one correct answer. Get it right and you'll get to hear my riddle. You have sixty minutes. I'll call you again in exactly sixty minutes.'*

Hunter and Garcia were expecting Lucien to end the call right then, but Lucien surprised everyone.

'I'm also going to throw you a bone, Grasshopper. Not that I think you need it, because I know what you're capable of. The bone is going to the pack of dogs that I'm sure are listening in on this call – the US Marshals, the FBI and whoever else. So here's your bone – a clue that could lead you to the correct answer can be found on page one hundred and thirty-three of one of my notebooks. The notebooks that you now have. Seek and ye shall find. Sixty minutes, Grasshopper. Tick-tock, tick-tock, tick-tock.'

The line went dead.

Twenty-Six

The FBI Training Academy was located on a Marine Corps base forty miles south of Washington DC, in Virginia. The conglomerate of interconnected buildings that formed its nerve center looked nothing like a government training facility. In fact, it resembled some sort of overgrown corporation somewhere in Silicon Valley. Marines armed with high-powered rifles stood at every intersection and guarded every building inside the 547-acre complex. Recruits wearing dark blue sweat suits with FBI in large golden letters across their backs could be seen everywhere, like students on a college campus.

Director Kennedy's office was located on the top floor of the second highest building inside that complex. It was spacious without being too imposing. There was an old-fashioned mahogany desk, two dark brown Chesterfield armchairs, a furry rug that looked comfortable enough to sleep on, and a huge bookcase with at least one hundred leather-bound volumes. The walls were mostly adorned with framed diplomas, awards, and photographs of Kennedy posing next to politicians and government officials.

From his office window, Kennedy was absent-mindedly

watching the streets below when his cellphone rang on his desktop. The display screen told him who was calling.

'Robert?' he said, bringing the phone to his right ear.

'*Adrian ...*' Hunter lost no time with small talk. '*Lucien's notebooks, where are they?*'

The question caught Kennedy by surprise. 'What?'

'*Lucien's research,*' Hunter clarified. '*The notebooks we retrieved from his hideout in New Hampshire ... where are they? Where do you keep them?*'

It took about two seconds for Hunter's question to register with Kennedy. 'Umm ... they're here,' he finally replied. 'We keep them at the NCAVC's private library. Why?'

'*Are you at Quantico?*' Hunter asked.

'I am, and once again, why?'

Hunter quickly explained about Lucien's phone call.

'Page one hundred and thirty-three?' Kennedy's tone of voice did not hide his confusion.

'*That was what he said,*' Hunter replied.

'OK, but from which volume?' Kennedy asked. 'We've got ...'

'*Fifty-three of them,*' Hunter said. '*I know.*'

'Exactly, so which of the notebooks am I supposed to be looking at?'

'*Lucien didn't say.*'

'Of course not,' Kennedy accepted it. 'Why would he make this easy for us?'

'*You're going to have to get as many people as you can to help you on this, Adrian. We've got ... fifty-seven minutes.*'

'Fine, but what the hell am I supposed to be looking for on page one-thirty-three, Robert?'

'*That's the "save a life" question – we don't know.*'

'Well, that helps.'

'*What Lucien said was that there were things missing from his research. Avenues he hadn't yet explored. He also said that there is more than one, but for the purpose of this little game, he only needs one. We get that right, we get the riddle.*'

'Yes, Robert, you've told me all of that,' Kennedy replied, his husky voice getting a little tougher. 'Telling me again doesn't clarify it. We still don't know what we're supposed to be looking for.'

'*Maybe we can help,*' Hunter suggested.

'How?'

'*Maybe you could photograph a couple of pages from different volumes and send them to me via email or text and ...*'

'No can do, Robert.' Kennedy interrupted Hunter. 'That would cost us way too much time.'

'*How so?*'

'Security protocol,' Kennedy explained. 'No mobile devices are allowed into the NCAVC's private library. Not even mine. We all have to surrender them at the entrance before being allowed inside. Checking anything out of the library would require my signature of approval together with Michael Aldridge's, who's the NCAVC's Executive Assistant Director. We would never ...'

'*OK, I've got the point,*' Hunter paused Kennedy.

'We are going to have to do this from this side and it would help if we knew what we were looking for.'

'*Lucien's entire "research" was based on murdering people, right?*' Hunter began pondering about it. '*With each murder he would modify something – level of violence, MO, level of torture, something – and he did it because he was trying to experience what sort of psychological effects that would have in the mind of a psychopath. With that in mind, I think that we need to look for something related to the murdering act. What hasn't Lucien tried? What kind of MO, or torture, or whatever, hasn't he tried yet?'*

'There are fifty-three volumes to his mad encyclopedia, Robert,' Kennedy came back. 'You haven't read them all, but I have. He's been through everything – strangulation, blunt trauma, throat severing, decapitation, dismembering, exsanguination, impaling, crucifixion, removal of fatal organ while still alive, poisoning, starvation, dehydration, even trephination. The list is almost endless, Robert. He's tortured victims in every possible way. He's raped some. He's eaten their flesh . . . you name it, he's done it. If you come up with something you've never heard of, Lucien has probably tried it.'

'*Well, not according to him,*' Hunter replied. '*So get some people to look through page one hundred and thirty-three on every single one of those notebooks. Flag anything that could be related to murder – an MO, a signature, a type of victim, a location, a bizarre torture method . . . anything.*'

'The problem here, Robert,' Kennedy said, 'is that since we don't really know what sort of thing we're looking for, we could end up with fifty-three different possibilities – probably more, actually.'

'*I know that,*' Hunter replied. '*And that's why even though we now have fifty-four minutes before Lucien calls again, I would like to have that list in forty-four. That will give me ten minutes to go through it and see if I can make any sense of it.*'

'OK,' Kennedy agreed, not wanting to waste any more time. 'I'm on it. I'll call you in forty-four minutes.'

Twenty-Seven

Hunter was still on the phone to Director Kennedy when Garcia took a call that had come through to their office.

'Detective Garcia, Ultra Violent Crimes Unit,' he said into the mouthpiece.

'Detective, this is US Marshal Tyler West.' His voice was rushed and full of worry. 'We heard the call Lucien made to Detective Hunter. His notebooks, where are they?'

Garcia had forgotten that they had bugged Hunter's cellphone.

'Robert is on the phone to Director Kennedy as we speak,' he replied. 'And that's exactly what he's finding out.'

'Great,' West replied. 'We're on our way.'

Lucien's manhunt task force had set up their operations office in the US Marshals' California Central District headquarters, which was located inside the Edward Roybal Federal Building on East Temple Street. The LAPD Police Administration Building was located on West 1st Street – a mere block and a half away. It took West and Holbrook two minutes to cover that distance on foot. It took them another minute to clear security at the PAB entrance and then get up to the Robbery Homicide Division floor. By the time they stormed into Hunter and Garcia's office, they were both dripping sweat.

'The notebooks,' West asked, catching his breath. 'Where are they?'

Hunter had just disconnected from his call to Kennedy.

'Adrian Kennedy has them at the NCAVC private library,' he replied, 'inside the FBI Training Academy.'

'We need to have a look at them,' West said.

'Well,' Garcia countered, sitting back on his chair. 'Seeing that we are in LA and the NCAVC private library is in Quantico, Virginia, unless you have some sort of teleporting machine, I'd say that right now that's a pretty impossible task.'

Hunter intervened before West was able to reply to Garcia's comment.

'Director Kennedy is assembling a team to go through the notebooks as we speak,' he said. 'He understands the severity of the situation and he'll be calling me back with a list of what they find out in . . .' He checked his watch. 'Forty-two minutes.'

'Forty-two?' Holbrook consulted his watch.

'That's ten minutes before deadline,' Hunter explained. 'That will give us a chance to go over the list and decide what to do.'

'Does Director Kennedy and his team know what to look for?' West queried.

'No one really does,' Hunter replied. 'But the idea is to try to flag anything that could be related to the act of murdering someone – like an MO, a signature, a type of victim, a location . . . something that Lucien hasn't tried yet.'

'And how will they know if they come across something that he hasn't tried yet?' West asked.

'They won't,' Hunter said. 'That's why they'll make a list

of everything they find on page one hundred and thirty-three. We'll be the ones who will have to decide what to tell Lucien when he calls back.'

'On that subject,' Holbrook cut in, 'the call was traced to the area around the intersection of Flower Street and Wilshire Boulevard.'

'That's just about a mile from here,' Garcia said.

'Yes, we know,' West confirmed. 'We checked the map. Vehicles were dispatched to the location as soon as we had it confirmed.' He consulted his watch. 'They should be there by now.'

'That was a waste of time and resources,' Hunter said.

'And why is that, Detective Hunter?' West asked, his tone challenging.

'Because we have no idea what Lucien looks like at the moment,' Hunter replied. 'Even if he was still there waiting for your guys to turn up, they could bump into him and they still wouldn't recognize him.'

'And since you looked at the map,' Garcia added. 'You should've noticed that the intersection of South Flower Street and Wilshire Boulevard is less than half a block away from the 7th Street Metro Center Station, the second busiest metro station in the whole of LA. Other than Union Station, it's the only station in Los Angeles that services three different subway lines. If he were walking while on the phone to Robert, Lucien would've made it to the station before he even ended the call, not to mention that from that Wilshire Boulevard intersection he also had a pretty vast selection of buses he could catch.'

'So what were we supposed to do?' West asked. He was getting visibly annoyed. 'Nothing?'

'Unfortunately,' Hunter answered, approaching the coffee

machine, 'right now, all we can do is sit and wait for Adrian to call us back with whatever list he and his team comes up with. Like I said before, this is Lucien's game. He makes the rules that we have to abide by and everything he does is planned.' He poured himself a cup. 'It's no coincidence that he was so close to a Metro station and different bus routes when he made the call. Coffee?' He offered the room.

'I'm all right, thank you,' Holbrook replied.

West simply shook his head.

'I'm good,' Garcia said.

Hunter poured himself a large cup before continuing. 'There's also a reason why Lucien decided to split this game into two parts.'

'And what would that reason be?' West asked.

'To achieve exactly this,' Hunter said, nodding back at West. 'Frustration. He knew that his notebooks wouldn't be here in LA – why would they be? They were seized by the FBI not the LAPD.' He returned to his desk. 'By splitting his "riddle", or whatever you want to call it, into two parts, he was making sure that for the next hour there would be absolutely nothing we could do here in LA, except sit around and wait. By giving us only sixty minutes to come up with an answer, he knew that all we could do was pass on the challenge to whoever was closest to his notebooks, but none of us would be able to look at them for ourselves. So now we're not only sitting on our hands, but we are actually depending on others to figure out the answer to Lucien's question. How's that for frustration levels?'

West ran a hand over his mouth, as if stroking an imaginary beard.

Hunter sipped his coffee. 'If Lucien wants to play a game,' he said, 'it will be above all a psychological one.' He looked at

West. 'This frustration you're feeling right now, the inability to do anything, Lucien wanted it that way. And the worst of it all is ... this is only the beginning. It will get worse. It will get a lot worse.'

Twenty-Eight

West threw his hands up in the air, puffed his cheeks and breathed out slowly. Hunter was right. He had never felt this frustrated in his entire career as a US Marshal.

'Well,' he said, facing Hunter. 'I haven't seen any of Lucien's notebooks, but you have, right?'

Hunter nodded.

West's gaze moved to Garcia, who shook his head.

'I'm as new to this as you are,' he said.

West knew that Holbrook had also never seen any of the notebooks. 'All right,' he addressed Hunter again. 'It looks like you're the only one here with knowledge of the contents of this "murder encyclopedia", Detective Hunter. So what do you think Lucien was referring to when he mentioned avenues he hadn't yet explored. Things still missing from his research? What hasn't he tried yet?'

Hunter put down his cup of coffee.

'I haven't read all of his notebooks,' he said.

'Still,' West insisted, 'you're the only one out of all of us who has even seen them, so let me ask you again, Detective Hunter, what do you think he means? What might he be planning?'

'In truth,' Hunter replied, 'and considering that we're

talking about Lucien, it could be just about anything. Like I told Adrian – he could be referring to an MO he hasn't yet tried, or a type of victim he hasn't yet murdered—'

'Type of victim he hasn't yet murdered?' Holbrook interrupted, giving Hunter a shrug and a slight headshake. 'Such as?'

Hunter pinched the bridge of his nose, as if what he was about to say would trigger the most unbearable of headaches.

'Lucien's victim count is easily in the hundreds,' he began. 'And with every single one of his murders, he tried something different because he wasn't killing them to satisfy some uncontrollable urge, like most psychopaths.'

'Yes, we know,' West cut in. 'He was experimenting.'

'That's right,' Hunter agreed. 'And the purpose of those experiments was to generate an emotion inside of him. He wanted to experience the pleasure, the pain, the ecstasy … whatever it was that other psychopathic killers experienced when committing those murders.'

'If there was ever an out-of-the-fucking-park, lunatic idea in this messed-up world,' West said, 'that was it, right there.'

Hunter simply disregarded the comment.

'But as we all know,' he continued, 'there are two major types of aggressive psychopaths: violence-centered, which are the ones to whom the victims are secondary, and victim-centered, where the victim itself is the most important part of the equation. With the first type, what drives the perpetrators, what makes them tick is the violence itself, the torture that they put their victims through. They don't care if the victim is old, young, male, female, blonde, brunette, black, white, fat, thin … it doesn't matter, just as long as they suffer … just as long as they can hurt them.' Hunter paused for breath. 'Victim-centered predators, on the other hand, fantasize about a *specific* type of victim. Everyone the predator chooses has to match that specific profile, which usually boils down to physical type. With victim-centered psychopaths, the whole fantasy revolves around the way the victim looks. It's the victim's physical attributes that excites and turns them on. Most of the time because it reminds them of someone else. In those cases, there's always some sort of strong emotional connection, and nine out of ten times their fantasies will involve some sort of sexual act. The victim being sexually assaulted either before, during, or after the murder act is almost a certainty.'

'And since all that Lucien's been doing for God knows how long is experimenting,' Garcia suggest. 'He probably fits both profiles – victim-and violence-centered.'

'He does. Yes.' Hunter agreed.

'And do you think that there's any victim-type he hasn't gone for yet?' West asked.

Hunter ran a hand through his hair. 'I think that until now he has managed to stay away from murdering kids, infants, elderly people, people with disabilities and pregnant women.'

Hunter's words brought a deafening silence into his office.

'I don't think that Lucien has ventured outside of the realm of homicide either,' Hunter added.

'What do you mean?' This time the question came from Garcia.

'Lucien has always stuck to trying to psychologically identify the feelings experienced mainly by serial murderers,' Hunter replied. 'Most of them people who suffered from a compulsion they couldn't shake – an urge that eventually overwhelmed them, forcing them to reoffend. It had always been a "one-on-one" affair. Maybe stepping out of that zone was what Lucien meant by avenues he hadn't yet explored.'

'Wait a second,' Garcia said, lifting a hand. 'Are you talking about . . .'

Hunter nodded. 'Mass murder. Lucien has never ventured into mass murder.'

'Mass murder?' West questioned, wide-eyed. 'I doubt that this Lucien character would be that dumb.' He shrugged. 'Or maybe he would.'

Hunter knew why West seemed so doubtful – statistically, in the USA, ninety-five percent of mass murderers perished during or directly after their ordeal. Many of them by their own hands. The remaining five percent were usually apprehended.

According to the FBI, by definition, a 'mass murder' is when four or more people are murdered in one single event, without a 'cooling-off period' between the murders, unlike a serial murder, where a 'cooling-off period' always separates the murders. A mass murder also typically occurs in a single – usually public – location, like a school, a shopping center, a bank, a music concert, or similar. If Lucien was really considering experimenting with mass murder, chances were it would be his last ever act.

Hunter was trying to consider every scenario – that was why he mentioned mass murder – but he found it hard to believe that that was what Lucien had in mind. The only way he could see Lucien moving into that field was if he had come up with a way of inverting those odds.

Garcia got to his feet and grabbed his jacket.

'Where are you going?' West asked.

'Out for a walk,' Garcia replied. 'We're making no progress here. All we're doing is increasing our frustration by speculating. Like Robert said – this is probably exactly what Lucien wanted to begin with. We don't have the notebooks, which means that we can't look for ourselves. All we can do is wait for Director Kennedy to call us back with whatever he finds. If all I can do is wait, I might as well do it outside.' He pointed to the window. 'It's a nice day. I'm going to go grab a coffee in a café or something.' He looked at Hunter. 'How long before Kennedy calls back?'

Hunter checked his watch. 'Thirty-five minutes.'

'Enough time for a coffee and a donut,' Garcia said before closing the door behind him.

Hunter thought about following his partner when his cellphone rang on his desk. It was Adrian Kennedy.

'*Robert*,' Kennedy said as soon as Hunter answered his phone. '*We've already got a problem.*'

Twenty-Nine

The NCAVC's private library occupied half of the first-level basement floor, directly underneath the building where Kennedy's office was located. As soon as he disconnected from his call to Hunter, Kennedy rushed out of his office, his cellphone back against his right ear.

'Daryl,' he said in a hurried voice once Special Agent Daryl Jensen answered the call.

Jensen had been with the NCAVC for nine years. He held a degree in law and a Ph.D. in psychology and he had been one of the few who, in the past three years, had been given access to Lucien's encyclopedia. He had also interviewed Lucien five times since his incarceration.

'How many agents and or cadets can you gather up in the next five minutes?' Kennedy asked. The urgency in his voice was almost palpable.

'Depends what for, sir?' Jensen replied. 'Internal or external task?'

'Internal and extremely pressing. I need you and the agents to meet me at the NCAVC private library in five minutes, preferably sooner. Time is absolutely crucial here.'

'For an internal task I can probably get as many as you'd like, sir. What is it for exactly?'

'I'll explain when you get to the library,' Kennedy replied, and quickly tried to calculate a number on the fly. There were fifty-three volumes to Lucien's encyclopedia. He needed this done fast, but he also didn't want too many people accessing the notebooks. He knew that the pages in every notebook were handwritten and very densely packed. Most of the time the handwriting was also hard to understand.

'How many agents would you like me to get, sir?' Jensen asked.

Kennedy figured that reading a couple of pages from one of Lucien's notebooks would not give that much away about the entire body of work. He consulted his watch – forty-three minutes until he had to call Hunter back.

'Can you gather a group of twenty-four, excluding you?' he asked.

Twenty-four plus Kennedy and Jensen themselves would give them twenty-six pairs of eyes. That would mean that each person would be responsible for only two pages in the space of forty minutes or thereabouts – not an impossible task.

'Twenty-four it is, sir,' Jensen replied. 'I'll see you in the library in three minutes, four max.'

'Daryl,' Kennedy said before Jensen ended the call. 'If you are going for cadets, make them young recruits who will follow orders and ask no questions.'

'Understood, sir.'

Thirty

Special Agent Daryl Jensen, together with sixteen FBI young recruits and eight special agents, had met Kennedy at the NCAVC private library within four minutes of ending their call. Without giving too much away, even to Jensen, Kennedy explained the task to everyone as best as he could.

'If you are in doubt,' Kennedy had said to the group. 'Add it to your list. Don't hesitate. Don't dwell on it for long. We don't have time to play around. If you think you've come across something that should make the list – *put it on the list*. Don't underline it or highlight it on the source so you can come back to it later. This is not a high-school exam. Under no circumstances are any of the notebooks to be marked, and I mean *no circumstances*. Is that understood?'

Everyone nodded.

Kennedy checked his watch. 'We have about thirty-eight minutes to get this done ladies and gentlemen, and time is absolutely crucial, so let's do it. Everyone grab two volumes and let's get to it.'

But it seemed that Kennedy had underestimated the difficulty of the job at hand. The first thing he had forgotten to take into account was that none of the pages in any of the notebooks were numbered. Lucien had never bothered with it, which meant that every agent/cadet had to manually count page by page until they reached page one-thirty-three. To avoid making a huge mistake, everyone did the count twice over, but the counting immediately raised the first question – was a page counted as two (front and back), like in a paperback book, or was it supposed to be counted as an individual page?

Kennedy's face went ghostly white when a young female cadet asked the question just seconds after picking up one of the notebooks.

Director Kennedy was no stranger to responsibility, but that was a call that he wasn't prepared to make alone.

'Give me just a moment,' he said, quickly exiting the library.

Hunter wasn't expecting a call back from Kennedy so soon. It had been less than eight minutes since he had called the NCAVC director to tell him about Lucien's question, but just like Kennedy, Hunter had also completely forgotten about the fact that Lucien had never numbered any of the pages in any of his notebooks. When Kennedy exposed the problem to him, Hunter tried to put himself in Lucien's shoes.

Lucien was a sneaky sonofabitch; there was no question about that. For that reason, Hunter considered the possibility of Lucien adding a twist to the first part of his charade and going against the norm, which would be to count the pages individually, not front and back like a regular book, but Hunter saw absolutely no point in Lucien making the first hurdle even harder than what it already was. No, Hunter thought, if Lucien was going to try to trick them, he would do it in the riddle, not in the question, simply because Lucien would want to stretch his game as far as he possibly could. There would be no fun for Lucien if his competitors struck out on the first half. Lucien would want his opponents to play a full game; he would want Hunter to get to the riddle because that would be where the fun, at least for Lucien, would really begin.

'Count it as two,' Kennedy told everyone as he walked back into the library. 'Front and back.'

It had been thirty-one minutes since the group had begun their task, which meant that Kennedy had only seven minutes left before he had to call Hunter back with the accumulation of all the individual lists. Kennedy himself was just about to get to the end of his second page. His list so far consisted of only three entries – the word 'heart', which he had been in doubt about, but it could mean that Lucien wanted to extract someone's heart out of their chest – the words 'fatal' and 'shock' not together, but in the same sentence, and since no one really knew what they were actually looking for, Kennedy decided to add 'fatal shock' to his list. His final entry was the word 'bloodbath'.

'Sir.' An agent interrupted Kennedy, coming up to the table he was sitting at. The agent had one of Lucien's notebooks in his hands. His right index finger was being used as a placeholder between two pages. 'Sorry to disturb you, but I just came across an entry here that sort of gave me the creeps. I thought that maybe you'd like to have a look at it straight away.'

'What is it?' Kennedy asked, putting down his pen.

'This.' The agent placed the volume he had with him down on Kennedy's desk, before indicating the eleventh line from the bottom of the page. 'Right here, sir.'

As Kennedy leaned forward and read the line, a bottomless pit opened up in his stomach.

'Holy fuck!'

Thirty-One

Lucien ended his call to Hunter, returned the phone to his pocket and calmly made his way toward the 7th Street Metro Center Station, just a few yards away from where he was standing. The walk took him about forty seconds and by the time he reached the station's entrance, Lucien could hear sirens approaching somewhere in the distance, which he was already expecting.

Despite making the call from an anonymous pre-paid cellphone without GPS technology, signal triangulation was still very much possible. As long as Lucien had stayed on the line for long enough, which he had done on purpose, the location where his call had originated from would have been triangulated by the US Marshals Office, who he was sure would be monitoring Hunter's cellphone by now. Lucien would've liked to have stayed and watched as LAPD officers, FBI agents and US Marshals wandered aimlessly around the corner of South Flower Street and Wilshire Boulevard looking for a ghost. That would've been worth a ticket, but Lucien had to get going. He had places to be and schedules to keep.

Down at the fairly busy 7th Street Metro Center Station platform, Lucien had to wait less than thirty seconds for the next subway train to arrive. He used that time to walk all the way to the far end, where the crowd of passengers was at its thinnest. Not surprisingly, when the train arrived, it was almost full. In Lucien's passenger car, two empty seats were all that was left. An elderly man, who boarded the train together with Lucien, took the one closest to the car's sliding doors. The second seat, the one Lucien took, was sandwiched between a mother, with her four-year-old kid on her lap, and a hipster with a bushy beard and a pompadour haircut, which had been smoothed out with enough wax to make a church candle.

Lucien kept his rucksack on the floor, wedged between his feet. As the doors slid shut and the train began moving again, he adjusted his fake glasses on his nose and sat back, his gaze moving around the crowd of passengers. Lucien loved observing people. He could learn a lot about them just by studying their mannerisms, their facial expressions, their movements. The more he watched, the more he picked up.

The kid fidgeted on the woman's lap, who was sitting directly to Lucien's right, and his eyes settled on the boy for a quick instant before moving to the mother's face. She was young – early to mid-twenties – with a peculiar face that not everyone would find attractive. Lucien himself couldn't decide if he thought she was pretty or not. Her eyes seemed to be too far apart, but the green in them was simply stunning.

The kid fidgeted again and the mother placed a hand on his arm to try to contain him. Most of her nail varnish had peeled off, revealing pitted fingernails. Her palms looked a little too pale and streaky, which straight away told Lucien that her diet was heavily deficient in iron, making her borderline anemic. There was a small inflation under her eyes, not due to an illness, but from lack of sleep and sunlight, probably because as a single mother – no wedding band on her finger – she had to work two jobs to make ends meet and most of the money she made went to the kid. Lucien figured that out because she wore the cheapest-looking pumps he had ever seen, which were about to fall apart on her, but the kid had on brand-new Nike sneakers.

Lucien's attention moved from the mother and kid to the elderly man who had boarded the train with him. He was easily in his late sixties or early seventies, with a peaceful face that looked as if it was held together by a crisscross of capillaries. The wrinkles on his forehead and around his eyes were deep, no doubt made worse by excessive sun exposure. His hands carried even more prominent wrinkles and they were dotted by liver spots. His fingers looked like small sausages. The knuckles furthest from his palms were knobbly and his nails brittle. Lucien didn't have to speak to him to know that he was a man who had spent most of his life working outside as a laborer and that probably was why he had developed psoriatic and osteoarthritis of the hand. Both conditions together would cause the old man significant pain, restricting his hand movements.

Lucien smiled internally. What an amazing coincidence. Who could predict that in the same passenger car he would find two different types of victims still missing from his research? That was why he loved big cities.

The train began slowing down as it approached the next stop, and Lucien turned to consult the Metro line map on the wall directly above his head. They were approaching Pershing Square Station. Lucien sat tight and observed.

As the train finally came to a full stop and the doors slid open, the old man got to his feet and exited the car. His steps were short, his posture half curved. His arthritis wasn't restricted only to his hands.

The kid next to Lucien fidgeted on his mother's lap once again, which prompted Lucien to think that they were also getting off at that stop, but mother and son stayed put.

Decisions, decisions, he thought. *Do I stay or do I get off?*

Lucien looked left, then right. That was when his stare finally met the boy's mother's for the first time and she gave him a shy but truthful smile.

And just like that, a decision was made.

Lucien stayed on the train.

Thirty-Two

Garcia didn't really go looking for a coffee shop once he left his office. Instead, he simply went down to the PAB cafeteria and sat alone at a table in the far corner, staring out the window, trying to think of absolutely nothing at all. All he really wanted to do was get away from the situation he could see developing upstairs. He was sure that Hunter was right – Lucien had planned this whole thing to the last detail – the frustration, the helplessness, the waiting, the psychological pressure . . . all of it. There was really absolutely nothing anyone could do about it except sit, wait and hope that Adrian Kennedy and his team got it right. Speculating about all the ifs, hows and whys would not help. On the contrary, all it would do would be to frustrate them even further, which was something everyone could do without at the moment.

By pure coincidence, Garcia walked back into his office just seconds before Hunter's cellphone rang again.

West and Holbrook were still there.

West had taken the seat behind Garcia's desk and Holbrook was standing by the window, ferociously texting away on his smartphone.

Garcia's look settled on West. 'Comfortable?' he asked with a sarcastic nod.

'Not quite,' West replied, half stretching his back. 'You need a better chair, buddy, but it's still better than the fold-up ones you have for your visitors.'

Before Garcia could hit back, Hunter's cellphone rang on his desk, sending everyone's attention to him and the entire room into a deep silence.

West immediately jumped to his feet.

Holbrook stopped typing.

Hunter checked the display screen – *unknown number*. He froze as his eyes moved to the clock on the wall. There were still fourteen and a half minutes left before Lucien's deadline. Hunter lifted his index finger, signaling the room to wait while he answered the call and placed it onto speakerphone.

'Hello.'

'*Robert, it's Adrian.*'

Everyone inside Hunter and Garcia's office breathed out in relief.

'Adrian?' Hunter queried, leaning a little forward on his chair. 'Where are you calling from? My phone didn't recognize the number.'

'*It wouldn't,*' Kennedy replied. '*It's unlisted. I'm using the library's landline.*'

'All right,' Hunter accepted it, but the concerned look went nowhere. Kennedy was also four and a half minutes ahead of his deadline. 'You're early, have you got the list?'

'*Forget the list, Robert.*' Despite the tiny speakers on Hunter's cellphone, Kennedy's hoarse voice powerfully filled the room.

'Forget the list?' West jumped the gun, approaching Hunter's desk. 'Why?'

The interruption earned him severe looks from everyone, including Special Agent Holbrook.

'*Who the hell is this?*' Kennedy asked. He also didn't sound too pleased.

'This is US Marshal Tyler West, Director Kennedy,' West replied, undeterred. 'As you know, I'm leading this manhunt operation. So? Why forget about the list? What have you found?'

'*Robert,*' Kennedy replied, clearly preferring to speak to Hunter than to West. '*You were right when you told us to count the pages as front and back, just like any regular book. We've been doing the best we can, blindingly trying to come up with this absurd list. We have added everything we thought could be relevant, until about a minute ago, when one of our cadets came across a specific entry toward the bottom of page one-thirty-three.*' Kennedy coughed to clear his throat. '*And this has got to be it, Robert.*'

'OK,' Hunter said before West could take the lead again. 'We're listening. What is it, Adrian?'

'*I'll read the entire passage so you can understand my concern,*' Kennedy said.

There was a quick pause, followed by the sound of Kennedy taking a deep breath.

'*After so many years,*' Kennedy read from Lucien's notebook, '*I can safely say that my research so far has taught me much about the mind of a psychopath, more specifically, those dubbed "serial killers" – the highs, the lows, the indifference, the desire – the list is long and complex, but there are still certain . . . taboo lines, shall I say, that I haven't yet crossed, one of which I simply lacked the materials to do so. But today I have finally acquired something that I've been searching for for some time. Something that will now allow me to cross that line and venture into a whole new realm . . . a whole new mindset.*'

'*And here it comes, Robert,*' Kennedy commented, before reading the final part.

'*Because I now have in my possession a full kilo, maybe a little more, of military grade C-4.*'

Thirty-Three

Located between Little Tokyo and Chinatown, in the northeastern corner of downtown Los Angeles, was Union Station – the largest railroad passenger terminal in the Western United States, servicing an average of 110,000 passengers every day. The station was as architecturally stunning as it was grand – the ceilings inside the ticket concourse were sixty-two feet high and though they appeared to be finished in wood, they were made of solid steel. The terracotta floors inside the station's large rooms carried a fascinating central strip of veneered marble and travertine. There were enclosed garden patios on both sides of the majestic waiting room, where an inlaid cement-tile floor reproduced the pattern of a Navaho blanket. Unfortunately, most passengers passed through it in such a hurry that they never really took the time to stop and appreciate the sheer beauty of the place.

Union Station was also just three stops away from where Lucien had first boarded the Metro train once he disconnected from his call to Hunter, and that was exactly where he got off. From there, the choice of where to go was almost infinite. He could take another Metro train to just about anywhere inside Los Angeles – from San Fernando Valley to Pasadena – East

Los Angeles to Long Beach and South Bay. If he so wished, he could also board an Amtrak train to wherever he wanted in the USA, but Lucien had no intention of leaving LA, at least not for the time being.

At Union Station, he sat by one of the garden patios inside the waiting room, studying the digital Metro-Line departures board. While he waited, he observed passengers as they rushed through the concourse in every possible direction. Despite the seemingly chaotic mood of the station, Lucien found it fascinatingly calming.

Two benches away from him, a grandfather sat with three of his grandchildren – two boys and one girl. The girl looked to be about sixteen, the boys, who were twins and had clearly inherited some of their grandfather's features, were a year or two younger than the girl. The grandfather appeared to be in his seventies, with a hairless head, bushy eyebrows and kind-looking blue eyes tucked away behind thick glasses. He sat with his hands on his lap, his right leg crossed over his left. His grandchildren sat on the bench opposite him, not because there were no spaces next to the old man, but apparently because they simply didn't wish to.

All three grandchildren had their smartphones firmly in their grip. The girl seemed concerned with just one thing – snapping selfies of herself from a variety of angles and then posting them onto some social-media site.

The first of the two twins had his smartphone sideways – landscape position – and he was moving it around as if it were a steering wheel, clearly fully engaged in some sort of racing videogame. The other boy was simply looking at pictures – at least that was how it seemed to Lucien. All he was doing was staring at his screen for a second or two, then either nodding or making a disapproving face before using his index finger to either swipe right or left.

Every now and then, the grandfather would try to interact with one of his grandchildren by either asking a question, which most of the time would go unanswered, or saying something, which at best would get a nod or a headshake as a reply. Sometimes, when one of the kids smiled at his or her screen, the old man would smile with them, once again, just trying to bond with the younger generation, but he wouldn't even get a look back from any of the kids. The old man's sad eyes would then refocus on his hands and he would sit in silence for another minute or two before trying again, only to be ignored in the exact same way. If he tried to show any sort of interest in what his grandchildren were looking at on their screens, they would quickly lean back and twist their phones out of visual reach.

No, Granddad, nothing for you to see here.

The entire scene was fascinating and terribly sad at the same time.

You only live once, Lucien thought. In his head he was talking to the three kids. *So please, by all means, spend twelve hours a day sucked into the Internet, searching for validation from people you barely know, and while you're at it, don't forget to ignore the few people who actually care about you and your pitiful existences.*

Lucien spent around fifteen minutes observing the old man and his grandchildren and the exercise filled him with an impulse Lucien knew only too well – the desire to teach those kids a valuable lesson – 'the importance of life . . . or lack of it as a matter of fact' – but as the thought began to take shape inside Lucien's head, he caught a glimpse of the Metro departures board once again. He'd been so engrossed in watching the sad family scene that he had forgotten to check the board. The train he'd been waiting for would depart in less than two minutes and the platform it was leaving from was all the way on the other side of the station.

Lucien seized his rucksack and quickly got to his feet. Coincidently, so did one of the old man's grandchildren – the boy who'd been swiping left and right. The boy began making his way in the direction of the public washrooms, still checking photos on his smartphone. Lucien followed him with his eyes for a couple of seconds, just enough for a very familiar feeling to clinch his body, like an embrace from an invisible evil being, who would first grab hold of him before whispering in his ear. A whisper that ran through Lucien's veins like pure poison, corrupting everything inside and taking him into a place in his mind where everything was dark.

Lucien checked the board once again – one minute twenty seconds before his train left. He watched as the kid disappeared into the washroom.

The feeling inside of him grew stronger . . . the place inside his mind darker still.

One minute.

Decisions, decisions.

Thirty-Four

It was no wonder that the last line Director Kennedy read to Hunter over the phone sent fear flying around his office like a crazy colony of bats.

Composition 4, or C-4, as it was popularly known, was a type of plastic explosive – and a favorite of the United States Armed Forces. It was referred to as 'plastic bonded explosives' because the compound was actually a mix of plastic binder and explosive material. The advantage of that was two-fold. One: the plastic binder coated the explosive material, making it less sensitive to shock and heat. Consequently, it made it a lot safer to handle. Plastic explosives could be dropped, kicked, slammed, thrown, punched, shot at with a firearm, or even exposed to microwave radiation, and it still wouldn't ignite. Explosion could only be initiated by a shock wave from a detonator. Two: the plastic binder made the explosive material highly malleable, very similar to modeling clay, so it could be molded into different shapes to actually change the direction of the blast.

US Marshal Tyler West's eyes came close to popping out of their sockets as he heard that Lucien could be in the possession of a PBX compound. He was an ex-marine and he knew only too well the sort of destruction C-4 was capable of.

'Did you just say C-4?' he asked Kennedy, leaning over Hunter's right shoulder. 'As in plastic explosive C-4?'

'That's exactly what Lucien has written into his notebook,' Kennedy replied.

'How the hell did he manage to grab hold of C-4?' West queried. 'That's military stuff.'

'First of all,' the answer came from Garcia, 'what does it matter how he got hold of it? He's got it and that's final, but this is the United States of America – the land where money talks and bullshit runs the marathon. As long as you've got enough money and the right contacts, you can buy just about anything you like.'

'God bless America,' Special Agent Holbrook commented.

'This has got to be it, right, Robert?' Kennedy asked. *'This is what Lucien meant by an avenue he hadn't yet explored. He was talking about mass murder. He's going to build a bomb.'*

Hunter had his eyes closed and his head low, his chin almost touching his chest. He nodded at his phone.

'Yes,' he replied. 'This will be it. That's what he wanted us to find.'

'Are you certain that this passage occurs on page one hundred and thirty-three?' West asked. The tone of his voice was getting more and more agitated with every sentence.

'Positive,' Kennedy confirmed. *'I counted the pages myself.'*

'Fuck!' West said. The agitation in his voice had spread to his limbs.

'So what's the plan, Robert?' Kennedy asked.

'The plan,' West jumped the gun once again, 'is that we need to get every bomb-disposal team available to us on stand-by.'

Hunter lifted a hand to ask West for a moment. 'We don't

have a plan just yet, Adrian, because we don't actually know what Lucien will do. Right now, all we can do is wait for his call and for him to give us his riddle. As it stands we have no idea of what that could be.'

'*I understand,*' Kennedy said. '*I need you to keep me in the loop on this one, Robert, and if you need anything from the FBI, just ask.*'

'I'll call you back as soon as I hear from Lucien again,' Hunter said, consulting his watch. 'Which should be in around ten minutes.'

'*I'll be waiting.*' Kennedy said before ending the call.

'No matter what happens,' West started again, 'we will have to alert every bomb-disposal team available to us and put them on stand-by. I was in the military before becoming a US Marshal. Do you have any idea what kind of damage one kilo of C-4 can do, Detective Hunter?'

'It depends what it's attached to,' Hunter replied.

West frowned. 'What? What do you mean by "It depends what it's attached to"?'

Garcia curbed the smile that tried forcing its way onto his lips. *Oh, you're going to get schooled now,* he thought.

Hunter took a deep breath. 'When detonated, C-4 has a double release of energy. The first detonates outward at a velocity of just over eight thousand meters per second. That's about seven times the nominal muzzle velocity of a nine-millimeter bullet. The second blast, which detonates at around the same speed, moves inward, toward the epicenter. That said, and despite the fact that it will produce a very big bang, C-4 alone, unless it's packed in large quantities, won't cause that much destruction. For example, one pound of C-4 would blow away the door of a cheap safe, or punch a basketball-size hole on a concrete wall, that's about it. But let's say you combine that pound of C-4 with broken glass, nails, metal pallets or whatever you like to create a dirty bomb, the explosion will transform the pieces into hyper-velocity bullets, propelling them far and wide and in all directions. In a close environment, like a room full of people, absolutely no one in a fifty-feet radius would be safe. No one would probably even survive.'

West's eyes stayed on Hunter. The frown was still there, but it was now a surprised one.

'Combine that same pound of C-4 with let's say . . . a gallon of flammable fuel,' Hunter continued, 'and taking into account that when detonated C-4 quickly decomposes to release nitrogen and carbon oxides, which are extremely flammable and travel at a velocity greater than the speed of sound, and the explosion will basically double its power of detonation. Since fire has now been added to the equation, the blast will work like a highly powerful multi-directional flamethrower. Everyone in a fifty-feet radius would most probably be torched alive.' His stare met West's. 'So like I've said, Marshal West – the kind of destruction C-4 can create depends on what the compound is attached to.'

West blinked once.

'I read a lot,' Hunter explained, reading the US Marshal's confused look.

West blinked again.

'And I retain a lot of what I read,' Hunter added.

'You don't say,' West replied.

'But you're right about alerting bomb squads,' Hunter said. 'If Lucien is really planning something with C-4, we'll have to have them ready to move at the drop of a hat.'

'I'll make the call,' West said, letting out a heavy breath and reaching for his cellphone. 'How long before Lucien calls again?'

'About seven minutes.'

Thirty-Five

At Union Station, Lucien rushed down the escalator and into the Metro train carriage just seconds before the doors slid shut. As they did, he stood there, half out of breath, rucksack slung over his right shoulder, watching as the platform was slowly left behind. He was still thinking about the old man, his grandkids and how the boy who had gone into the washroom would never really know how lucky he had been.

Count your blessings, kid, he thought. *Because you were just saved by a subway time schedule.*

At first, Lucien tried to deny himself the reason why the scene back at the station's waiting room had affected him the way it did, but deep inside he knew full well why. The old man reminded Lucien of his own grandfather – the only person in his family whom Lucien had ever got along with.

Lucien had been born into money. His father, Charles Folter, was a lawyer who ran his own very successful firm in Denver, Colorado. His mother, Mary-Ann Folter, was the daughter of one of the richest farmers in Wyoming, but despite all the money, all the luxury, Lucien's upbringing had been far from a happy one.

Lucien's father never really cared for family life, spending almost all of his time at work, or so he claimed, and that included weekends. In the mornings, he would leave the house early, before Lucien was even up, and if he did come back home that same day, which didn't happen very often, it would be late at night, way past Lucien's bedtime. As a child, Lucien would go through whole weeks without ever seeing his father.

Once, a very young Lucien did ask his mother why his father was almost never at home.

'Because your father is a very important man with a very important job, darling,' his mother had replied, but to Lucien what that really meant was that neither he nor his mother were as important to him as his job. That filled Lucien with such a feeling of worthlessness that he had never, ever forgotten that day, but he still had his mother . . . at least for a little while.

Lucien's early memories of her were of a very attractive, happy and caring woman, who would do anything for her family, but the time came when she too began to change.

Mary-Ann Folter had always loved life, she took tremendous pride in her appearance, she loved tending to her home and garden, and she adored spending time with Lucien, but all of a sudden, as Lucien hit his early teens, his mother started drinking heavily. The alcohol seemed to awaken a completely different person inside of her. Mood swings, punctuated by angry fits of yelling, became the norm in the Folter household. Her interest in everything she used to love slowly evaporated and she began spending more and more time locked inside her bedroom, only coming out during the hours she didn't expect Lucien to be home. When she did venture out of her bedroom, she would look a mess, with dark circles under her eyes, blotchy skin, disheveled hair and unwashed clothes. Soon after the alcohol came the visits to the doctor and the prescription drugs, and with them came the numbness, the indifference, the total lethargy.

At first, Lucien couldn't really understand what had happened. How could someone who used to be so full of life, so beautiful, so dedicated to her family, suddenly slide into such a dark downward spiral?

The answer to that riddle, funnily enough, came late at night on one Friday the thirteenth. Lucien was sixteen at the time.

Maybe it had been the odd situation at home that had caused him to become a reclusive introvert, or maybe it was the fact that most of the other kids around his age couldn't keep up with his intellect and, for that reason, they bored him. Either way, Lucien didn't have many friends back then, in fact, for many years he had none, but that had never really bothered him. Lucien actually enjoyed being by himself. That way, he didn't have to deal with the stupidity of others.

On that particular day, Lucien had left school late and gone to the Denver Art Museum, on 14th Avenue Parkway, which for one night only – Friday 13th – had stayed opened until midnight, displaying a special photographic exhibition on its seventh floor. The exhibition was titled 'Real Life Horrors (what you won't see in the movies)' – and it displayed over seven hundred real crime-scene photographs, which the FBI had lent the museum. Lucien wouldn't have missed that night for anything in the world.

Sure, entry to the exhibition was restricted to visitors who were eighteen years of age or older, but Lucien was a regular at the museum. At least twice a week he would go over after school and spend hours walking around. He knew most of the museum's staff, including the security guards, and all it took for one of them to look the other way while he sneaked in through the back door was a small bribe.

The exhibition was, if nothing else, troubling. Most of the images could easily be considered traumatizing, especially for a sixteen-year-old, but Lucien's fascination with death had begun years earlier, before his thirteenth birthday. His father, on one of the very rare occasions when he had spent time with Lucien, had taken him hunting up in the mountains in Colorado. At first, Lucien didn't think that he would enjoy it. Taking the life of an innocent animal for pure pleasure and vanity was something that at the time didn't really appeal to him, but there was something about the waiting, about the stalking, about looking straight into the animal's eyes just before ending its life, that simply captivated Lucien. That was the first time he realized that there was something about 'death' that made him feel . . . powerful.

On the night of the exhibition, Lucien stayed in the museum until just before closing time. He studied every single photograph displayed; the more gruesome they were, the more excited he got. When he left, he was in such a high state that he didn't feel like going home, so instead, he decided to go for a walk.

Lucien had no particular destination in mind, all he wanted, really, was just a walk. It was then, as he approached the intersection of California Street and 15th, that he saw his father exit a small restaurant just around the corner. The problem was, he wasn't alone. Hanging from his arm was a tall, young and very attractive blonde woman.

It was as if Lucien had been shot though the heart. His legs lost most of their strength and he had to hold on to a wall so as not to fall down.

Just before Lucien's father and the young blonde got into the cab that had pulled up in front of the restaurant, they kissed ... passionately. Lucien had never seen his father kiss his mother that way.

It was then, standing at a street intersection, that Lucien finally understood what had caused his mother to change so suddenly. Why the heavy drinking. Why the prescription drugs. Why the debilitating depression. She knew. Lucien was certain she knew, but for some reason, she couldn't bring herself to leave her husband.

Lucien never confronted his father.

His mother passed away from liver cirrhosis in the same year that Lucien was accepted into Stanford University. His father died a year later from a heart attack, while sitting in his office, on the top floor of his law firm.

Lucien's maternal grandfather used to visit the house often when Lucien was young. He adored Lucien and Lucien idolized him. Unfortunately he too passed away just months after his daughter.

Maybe it had been the kind eyes behind the thick glasses, or maybe it was the way in which he looked at his grandkids, but the old man at the waiting room inside Union Station had reminded Lucien of his grandfather.

The Metro train began slowing down as it approached the next station – Little Tokyo/Arts District. That was Lucien's stop. He didn't want to stir too far away from Union Station. It was all part of his plan.

As Lucien stepped out of the subway train and onto the busy platform, he checked his watch. Two minutes until he had to call Hunter again.

Now the fun would really start.

Thirty-Six

Inside Hunter and Garcia's office, no one had said a word for the past five minutes; as a matter of fact, people had barely moved. The atmosphere felt so tense, breathing became almost an effort.

Both detectives were at their desks and though their eyes were focused on their computer screens, their minds were somewhere else completely.

Tyler West was standing by the window, staring down at the street below. He was dying to go for a cigarette, but with time ticking away fast he didn't dare leave the office until Lucien's call had come through.

Peter Holbrook was sitting by the coffee machine, arms crossed in front of his chest, eyes down on the floor, thoughts wondering like a lost soul.

Hunter's gaze flipped to his cellphone, which was resting on his desk, a little to his left. The moving digital clock on the screensaver told him that there were less than two minutes before Lucien's deadline. He placed his elbows on his desk, laced his fingers together and rested his chin on his knuckles. The waiting was agonizing.

By the window, West also checked his watch.

All of a sudden, and without knocking to announce her arrival, Captain Blake pushed open the door to Hunter and Garcia's office and stepped inside.

'Has he called yet?' she asked in an anxious voice.

'No, not yet,' Hunter replied. 'But according to his own deadline, he should be calling in . . .' Another quick peek at his cellphone. 'Forty-three seconds.'

Captain Blake didn't yet know about the C-4.

'And did you get the list from Director Kennedy?' she queried. 'Do you have any idea what Lucien was referring to when he talked about "new avenues"? Have you all agreed on an answer to his question?'

West chuckled. 'Yes, we're pretty sure we have it.'

Captain Blake waited a few seconds but nothing else was forthcoming.

'So what is it then?' she pushed.

Before anyone had a chance to reply, Hunter's cellphone rang on his desk, sending four very uneasy pairs of eyes his way. *Unknown number.*

Lucien had called exactly on time. Not a second before. Not a second later.

Hunter signaled everyone to stay quiet before quickly answering the call and immediately initiating his phone conversation recording application before switching the call to speakerphone.

Everyone moved closer, surrounding Hunter's desk.

'*Hello, Grasshopper,*' Lucien's voice came through the tiny cellphone speakers loud and clear. '*Well, your sixty minutes are over. Do you have an answer for me?*' Hunter picked up an underlying amused pitch to Lucien's tone. He was no doubt enjoying this to the maximum. '*What is *missing from my research, Robert? Which dark path have I not explored yet?'*

'Lucien,' Hunter said. 'You don't have to do this. If you have a score to settle with me, do it with me. You don't . . .'

'I don't have to do what, Grasshopper?' Lucien cut Hunter short. *'You haven't answered my question, so I have no idea what you're talking about. What don't I have to do? I want to hear you say it, Robert.'*

As Hunter had anticipated, Lucien would play no game other than a psychological one and he would want to stamp his superiority over Hunter every chance he got. Hunter had no option but to play the game.

'Kill any more people, Lucien,' he replied. 'In whichever way that might be.' He kept his voice calm, his tone non-aggressive. 'You don't have to do it. You want to settle a score with me . . . let's do it . . . you and me . . . no one else needs to get involved. You tell me where and when and I'll meet you there. No back-up. No tricks. I give you my word.'

Hunter immediately raised his hand in the direction of West, halting him. He knew that the US Marshals Office would never approve or allow a private meeting between Hunter and Lucien. As West locked eyes with him, Hunter mouthed the words, 'I want to keep him talking.'

West accepted it by lifting both hands in a surrender gesture, but Hunter could see that he was getting agitated again.

'But of course I have to do it, Grasshopper,' Lucien replied. *'That's what my entire life is based on – my research into the minds of psychopaths.'*

'Oh, that's rich, coming from someone like him,' West whispered, and Hunter quickly halted him again.

'I've lived for it since the whole idea began solidifying in my

mind. Unfortunately, as you well know, that study was hastily interrupted around three and a half years ago, but now I can finally continue it, and continue it I will. Did you search page one hundred and thirty-three?' Lucien thought better of what he'd just said and rectified it. *'Well, not you, since I'm sure my work wasn't just sitting somewhere in your office, but you know what I mean, right? Did you get that douchebag, Kennedy, and his pack of ass-licking dogs to search it for you?'*

Everyone's eyes, except Hunter's, moved to Special Agent Holbrook, who didn't seem at all offended by Lucien's remark.

'But of course you did, Grasshopper.' Lucien answered his own question. *'So please, stop stalling and give me an answer. I want you to give me at least one avenue that has been missing from my research, Robert, and if you stall again, this call is over and you won't get to hear my riddle. No chance for you to save some innocent lives.'*

West looked at Hunter and his eyes widened before he gave the detective a firm nod.

Hunter wasn't sure if anyone else had picked up on it, but Lucien had just used the word 'lives', not 'life' as he had before – and Hunter was certain that he hadn't done that by mistake.

'What is it, Grasshopper? I want your answer, and I want it now.'

'Mass murder,' Hunter finally replied, but offered nothing else, and neither did Lucien. For several seconds, both sides of the call went silent.

Inside Hunter and Garcia's office, concerned looks were exchanged in all directions. Then, everyone heard the sound of hands clapping coming from Lucien's side.

'Very good, Grasshopper. I knew you wouldn't disappoint

me. Mass murder is indeed a path I haven't yet ventured down, and one that I have been thinking about a lot … but you could've figured that one out by yourself, Grasshopper. You didn't have to call Mr. Douchebag and ask him to check my notebooks for that answer, did you? But since you did, do tell me, what did he and his army of zombies find on page one-thirty-three? I'm curious, you see? For curiosity keeps the mind hungry and the heart young.' Lucien laughed. *'Did you see what I did there, Grasshopper?'*

Uncertainty masked the faces of everyone around Hunter's desk. It seemed like no one, except Hunter, had picked up on Lucien's little joke – 'I'm curious, you "C"? "4" curiosity keeps the mind hungry and the heart young.'

'So let me ask you this in a different way, Grasshopper – how am I about to enter into the world of mass murder?'

Hunter stayed silent, while fidgeting moved around the room's occupants like a Mexican wave.

'C'mon, Grasshopper, I've just opened the door for you to hit me with the best punchline ever. Are you really just going to leave me hanging like this?'

Captain Blake looked half lost, but everyone else recognized the sarcasm.

'How am I about to enter into the world of mass murder, old friend?' Lucien insisted.

Still nothing from Hunter.

'Could it possibly be with a … ?' Lucien held the expectation for five seconds: *'… bang?'* He then immediately broke into an animated laugh.

Captain Blake made a face as if she'd just heard not only a terrible joke, but one that made no sense at all.

'What?' Her lips moved but no sound came out.

'It's true, Grasshopper,' Lucien continued. 'I have in my possession two pounds, maybe more, of military grade C-4.'

Captain Blake's heart dropped to her stomach as her eyes exploded in size.

'No fucking way!' This time her vocal cords did come into action.

Hunter closed his eyes and brought a hand to his face.

'Oh!' Lucien said, sounding entertained. 'I was wondering when the audience would make themselves known. So with whom do I have the pleasure of speaking now?'

Hunter shrugged at his captain.

'This is Captain Barbara Blake of the LAPD Robbery Homicide Division,' she replied. Her voice was firm and authoritative.

'Delighted to make your acquaintance at last, Captain Blake. I'm Lucien Folter. Would anyone else like to make themselves known before I proceed?'

Once again, Hunter signaled everyone to stay quiet.

Lucien waited, but everyone else agreed with Hunter.

'The US Marshal in the room?' Lucien insisted.

No answer.

'Special FBI agent?'

No answer.

'Sheriff's department, maybe?'

No answer.

'C'mon, people, don't be shy.'

Silence.

'No one, really? OK, suit yourselves.' There was another very short pause. 'Mass murder, Grasshopper – that's right, which means that you have earned the right to hear this cool little riddle I made just for you. The answer to which will tell *you the name of the establishment where I have left a small present. It's small, but it packs one hell of a punch.'*

'Lucien, please listen to me . . .' Hunter tried, but he knew Lucien didn't care.

'I'm only going to tell you this once, Grasshopper.' Lucien cut Hunter short again. *'Later you can play the recording back to your heart's content, but do not interrupt me again.'*

From his own desk, Garcia quickly retrieved a notepad and a pen. West and Holbrook did the same.

'Just like before,' Lucien proceeded. *'You'll have sixty minutes to find your answer. Get it right and you can save the day, Grasshopper. Be a hero and all, you know?'*

He paused.

'Get it wrong and . . . boom.'

There was no sarcasm in Lucien's voice.

'Are you ready? Because here it is: You will find me in a place where people should be silent, but not here. Where verses should be found, but not here. Where students should come eager to learn, but not here. Instead of silent people, you'll find them to be loud, but you'll also find the quiet man. Instead of poets' laughter, you'll find writers' tears. Instead of eager students, you'll find cheap teachers. Look not for the obvious, but for the unorthodox, and you shall find something special. You shall find the exceptional.'

Garcia, West and Holbrook wrote as fast as they could. The more they wrote, the deeper their frowns became.

There was another short pause to indicate that Lucien was done with his riddle.

'Sixty minutes, Grasshopper. The clock is ticking.'

With that, the line went dead.

Thirty-Seven

Captain Blake was still having trouble wrapping her head around what she'd just heard.

'This psychopath has two pounds of military grade C-4 in his possession,' she asked, as soon as the call was over. 'In my city?'

Hunter nodded. 'We only found that out a little over ten minutes ago, Captain.'

'Jesus!'

'What the hell was that riddle all about?' West asked, his gaze bouncing from his notepad to every face in the room. 'Did anybody get all that?'

'Not all of it, no,' Garcia replied. 'He spoke too fast.'

'Yeah, same here,' Holbrook agreed. 'Didn't get much after "poets' laughter".'

Hunter was already calling up the recording application on his cellphone.

'Let me play it back,' he said.

It took him just a few seconds to find the correct spot. This time, everyone got Lucien's riddle down word for word, including Hunter.

You will find me in a place where people should be silent, but not here. Where verses should be found, but not here. Where students should come eager to learn, but not here. Instead of silent people, you'll find them to be loud, but you'll also find the quiet man. Instead of poets' laughter, you'll find writers' tears. Instead of eager students, you'll find cheap teachers. Look not for the obvious, but for the unorthodox, and you shall find something special. You shall find the exceptional.

'What the fuck does any of this mean?' West asked. His eyes were still on his notepad. The expression on his face was a picture of confusion.

'It's a riddle,' Garcia replied. 'It's not supposed to make obvious sense. It's not supposed to be easy to decipher.'

Hunter was sitting back in his chair, his elbows resting on the chair's arms, his fingers interlaced in front of his chest, his eyes reading every line over and over and over again.

Four minutes went by without a single word being spoken.

Holbrook was the first to make a suggestion.

'I think he might be talking about some old school building that's now used for something else,' he said, bringing everyone's attention to him. 'I've always been very good at riddles,' he added, before indicating the large magnetic board that was pushed up against the south wall. 'May I?'

'Please,' Garcia replied.

Holbrook quickly wrote the entire riddle on the board in large letters. He then drew two horizontal lines through it. The first after the first three sentences and the second after the next three, essentially dividing the riddle into three parts.

'As we know,' he began. 'The answer to this riddle will give us a location somewhere here in Los Angeles, right? But I think that what Lucien has done here is divide the riddle into three parts.' He indicated on the board. 'The first tells us what the location used to be. The second, what the location has become, and the third is some sort of clue on how to interpret the whole thing.'

Holbrook could see confusion starting to darken every face.

'Let me explain,' he said, pointing to the first three sentences on the board. 'This is what I call the first part: *You will find me in a place where people should be silent, but not here. Where verses should be found, but not here. Where students should come eager to learn, but not here.* Now, if we remove the tag ending to these sentences, which is exactly the same for all three, we end up with: *You will find me in a place where people should be silent. Where verses should be found. Where students should come eager to learn.*'

Holbrook turned to face the room.

'What he seems to be doing here is telling us what the location he's referring to used to be, but for some reason it's not anymore.'

He indicated each sentence as he clarified.

'A place where people should be silent – but not anymore. Where verses should be found – but not anymore. Where students should come to learn – but not anymore.'

He paused, giving everyone a chance to catch up with his line of thought.

'And to me, *A place where people should be silent. Where verses should be found. Where students should come to learn,* sounds like some sort of teaching environment, doesn't it? A classroom ... a school ... a university ... something along those lines.'

The mask of confusion slowly began to untangle.

'The second part of the riddle,' Holbrook continued, 'is the really tough part, because I think it's supposed to tell us what this "ex-teaching/learning environment", if that really is what Lucien means, has turned into.'

Once again he indicated on the board.

Instead of silent people, you'll find them to be loud, but you'll also find the quiet man. Instead of poets' laughter, you'll find writers' tears. Instead of eager students, you'll find cheap teachers.

Everyone went silent for a long moment.

'Any suggestions?' Captain Blake asked.

'But the riddle doesn't end there,' Garcia said before anyone had a chance to say anything. 'Lucien ends it with: "Look not for the obvious, but for the unorthodox and you shall find something special. You shall find the exceptional."'

'True,' Holbrook agreed. 'And that's the third part I was talking about – some sort of clue on how to interpret the whole thing. He's telling us that we should think outside the box – *Look not for the obvious, but for* the unusual – *the unorthodox* – which again will bring us back to the tough part of the riddle, the middle bit: what has this place become?'

'Look not for the obvious?' West asked. 'Is there an "obvious" to this crap? Because if there is, I can't see it. Which obvious place is it that: *Instead of silent people, you'll find them loud and you'll also find the quiet man. Instead of poets' laughter, you'll find writers' tears. Instead of eager students, you'll find cheap teachers*? Can anyone think of anything?'

Hunter kept his attention on the board. Holbrook had offered a very good analysis of how the riddle had been put together – three different parts. He had also offered a very plausible dilution of the first part of the riddle. It did seem that Lucien had begun his charade by referring to some sort of ex-teaching establishment – a place where people were silent, where verses were found, and students went to learn, but that wasn't the case anymore. Despite Holbrook's very good interpretation of the riddle, there was something in Lucien's use of words that somehow bothered Hunter. Something that he couldn't put his finger on.

'Anybody?' West pushed. 'Anything?'

Everyone in that room knew that in those sorts of situations, the best thing to do was not to overthink. Usually, the answers to such riddles were simpler than most people would expect. Overthinking had a tendency to sabotage the creative process, tricking the mind to let go of a correct answer exclusively because it sounded too simple. But simple or not, no one seemed to have anything to offer . . . not even a distant guess.

West ran an anxious hand over his military haircut and as his gaze met Hunter's, he nodded almost sarcastically.

'Yep, we're fucked.'

Thirty-Eight

As the sun began to tuck itself away behind the horizon line, the sky above Los Angeles became a labyrinth of colors. Orangey-red gave way to an odd shade of purple, which in turn gave way to a long dark sheet perforated by an uncountable number of sparkling dots, but all that natural beauty was under threat, as a small army of heavy gray clouds had begun gathering themselves at the east end of the sky.

Lucien finished his call to Hunter, extracted the SIM card from the prepaid cellphone he was using and dumped it in the nearest trashcan. With the night closing in fast, it was time to move on. He had a schedule to keep.

Lucien returned the cellphone to his pocket and began making his way back to the Metro station.

It had taken Lucien a couple of days to decide on the target location, but he believed that his decision had been a good one, especially considering that Los Angeles wasn't a city he was all that familiar with.

Lucien had no experience with explosive devices. He had never used or created one before, but he knew the theory and the physics of it and he knew it well. He had read countless articles and several books on the subject. He understood about velocity of detonation, density of compound mixture, maximum heat of ignition, pressure of explosion per cubic centimeter . . . all of it. He had made precise calculations to find out the optimum amount of C-4 he should use so that the blast would cover every inch of the location he had chosen, adding a little extra just for good measure. Though there was no way he could test his device, he was absolutely certain that if Hunter failed to decipher his riddle, no one at location X would survive . . . no one.

The riddle itself took Lucien quite a while to come up with, mainly because of all the research involved and the fact that he wanted to make it difficult, but not completely impossible. After all, what would be the fun in engaging in a game in which he already knew he would win? He needed to give Hunter and whomever else he was working with at least a sliver of a chance of getting it right, though he sincerely doubted that anyone would figure it out.

Lucien got to the entrance of the Little Tokyo Metro station and checked his watch. He had more than enough time to get to location X and plant his package. Yesterday, before getting back to his hotel room and immersing himself in the preparation of his device, Lucien had visited his chosen location for the second time in two days. He had furtively studied its layout and the movement of people, and he knew exactly where to hide his bomb. A place where no one would notice it. After that, all he had to do was wait. Once the sixty minutes he gave Hunter were up, a simple phone call to the cellphone attached to his device would trigger the detonation shockwave into the C-4.

The thought of that happening excited Lucien a lot more than he thought it would. To him, murder had always been a personal affair, a one-to-one engagement. What filled his soul with ecstasy was looking into the eyes of his victims as he drained the life out of them. He enjoyed savoring their fear. Being far away as they perished, unable to see the desperation and the pain taking over every atom of their bodies as they realized that their lives were ending, had never really appealed to Lucien. But now that he had created the murdering device himself, he had to admit that an odd tingle of excitement had been with him throughout the entire process, and that tingle was growing larger by the minute. Turning the whole thing into a game, especially against Hunter, only added to the excitement.

Before taking the escalator down to the train platform, Lucien looked up at the sky. The small army of gray clouds that had gathered at one end had seemingly given up on their fight, as they were fast dispersing, leaving behind another beautiful star-filled night.

Yes, Lucien thought. *This will be a great night for some fireworks.*

Thirty-Nine

Back inside Hunter and Garcia's office, US Marshal West's cellphone rang in his pocket and he reached for it as if his life depended on it. After listening for about ten seconds, he closed his eyes and breathed out pain.

'OK, thank you,' he said before disconnecting. 'They triangulated Lucien's call to an area just outside Little Tokyo Metro station,' he announced to the room. 'And I was informed that that's just one stop away from Union Station, which is supposed to be the busiest Metro station in the whole of LA, is that correct?'

Garcia and Captain Blake nodded at the same time. Hunter, on the other hand, kept his attention on Lucien's riddle on the board. There was something else that had started bothering him about the whole thing – the way Lucien had divided his charade.

'Do you think that Union Station could be his target?' West asked, his tone overflowing with worry.

'Right now,' Garcia replied, 'just about anywhere in this city could be his target. Until we come up with an answer to this crazy riddle, we won't have a clue.'

'Was the Union Station building ever a school, or a

college . . . any sort of educational establishment in a past life?' Holbrook asked.

'No,' Hunter replied with certainty. 'It has always been a passenger terminal since it opened its doors for the first time sometime in the late 1930s.'

'How about the surrounding area?' West this time. 'Is there anywhere near Union Station that could fit the first part of this riddle? A place where students used to go, but it has been transformed into something else, like maybe a shop, or a cinema, a nightclub . . . anything.'

'We can't go around trying to find an answer to this riddle that way,' Hunter said.

Everyone paused and looked back at him.

'Which way is that, Detective?' West asked.

'Looking for a place where students used to go – some sort of "ex-teaching/learning establishment".'

'And why not?' The question came from Holbrook. 'I thought we agreed that—'

'Because that's exactly what Lucien wants us to do,' Hunter cut Holbrook short.

Everyone waited, but Hunter stayed quiet.

'We don't need or have the time for another riddle from you, Robert,' Captain Blake intervened, knowing full well how Hunter's mind tended to work. 'So can you please clarify what you mean?' She consulted her watch. 'It's already been ten minutes since you've put down the phone with Lucien. We have fifty left.'

'I think Agent Holbrook's analysis of how Lucien has put his riddle together is right on the money,' Hunter began. 'The riddle has been divided into three parts – the first seems to be telling us what Lucien's target location used to be, the second what the location has become and the third how we should look at the whole thing.'

'Yes, we've already established that, thank you very much.' West's patience seemed to be running on fumes. 'What's your point, Detective?'

'My point is that there was no real need for Lucien to divide his riddle into three parts,' Hunter replied. 'It's another one of his psychological tricks.'

Hunter's last few words stopped everyone in their tracks.

'A psychological trick?' Captain Blake asked. 'How so, Robert?'

'Think about it,' Hunter explained. 'There was no need for Lucien to tell us what his target location used to be in the past, was there? All he had to do was give us the second part of the riddle – the part that is supposed to tell us what that location *is*, not *was*. What's the point in him telling us what that location used to be?' He shrugged. 'To help us out? To give us a better chance at finding the right answer? A better chance at stopping him? A better chance at getting to his bomb?'

Hunter saw everyone's expression change to a much more concerned and pensive one.

'Nonetheless,' he continued, 'Lucien begins his riddle by telling us three things that used to happen at this location, but not anymore.' He stood up and approached the board. 'Lucien knew that we would figure this part out first, for two simple reasons. One . . .' He made an 'obvious' face. 'It comes first in the riddle and two – it's noticeably easier than the second part, or so it seems.'

'So you think he's lying?' West asked, his voice a little less aggressive than seconds ago. 'You think he gave us a bogus first part of the riddle just to throw us off track? Like making us believe that this place used to be some sort of school or something, when in truth it was never anything remotely like it. Maybe the place never even had a past life?'

'Well, if that's the case,' Holbrook cut in, 'then what's stopping Lucien from lying about the whole riddle? All of it could be bullshit, specifically the part that's supposed to tell us what the place is.'

'It's not,' Hunter said with a shake of the head. 'Lucien would see no reason for doing that, but the first part of the riddle is definitely to throw us off track, just not in the way you're thinking.'

Confusion returned to the room.

'Lucien is a psychopath through and through,' Hunter clarified. 'He truly believes that he's superior to all of us, especially intellectually. He'll see no reason to have to resort to cheap tricks like lying, or creating a bogus riddle. The riddle is true.'

'But you just said that the first part of it was definitely to throw us off track,' West insisted.

'And it is, but not because it's false. Its purpose is to misdirect, to make us overthink.' Hunter lifted a hand to stop any forthcoming questions because he knew things were getting a little complicated. 'Let me explain.'

'Please do,' West said.

'Agent Holbrook came up with a very plausible answer for the first part of the riddle in what? Three minutes, maybe less?'

Holbrook nodded. 'Call me Peter, please.'

'So Lucien makes the first part of the riddle a little easier than the rest,' Hunter continued. 'But not too easy so it doesn't look too obvious, and what I mean by that is – Peter was able to come up with an acceptable *ballpark* answer to this first part, but not a specific one – if the answer to the riddle's first part really is some sort of "ex-teaching/learning establishment", then there's no way for us to say for sure that this place used to be a school, or a college, or a classroom, or whatever it was. From the riddle alone, the closest answer we can get to is a ball-park one – "some sort of ex-teaching/learning establishment".'

Hunter gave everyone a second.

'Are you still with me here?'

Thoughtful nods all round.

'By putting us on a clock,' Hunter carried on, 'Lucien has increased the pressure exponentially, and here's where the psychological trick I was referring to kicks in. Because we're on a timer, we'll automatically rush things, so as soon as we come up with a plausible answer to any of the three parts of the riddle . . .' Hunter pointed to the first part on the board. '"Some sort of ex-teaching/learning establishment" – we'll just go with it. We'll barely start looking for alternative answers because A: we don't really have the time, and B: our answer seems pretty good, so we stick with it. That will lead us to the second problem. What I would consider the trump card in Lucien's psychological trick.'

This time instead of head nods, Hunter was greeted by raising eyebrows.

'It's called subconscious suggestion,' Hunter announced, and quickly followed it with an explanation. 'Without even having an answer to the second part of the riddle and without knowing if our answer to the first part is correct or not, we're already trying to match both parts.' He nodded at West and Holbrook. 'Those were your questions just a moment ago, weren't they? If the building at Union Station was ever a school, or a college, or any sort of educational establishment in a past life. If there was anywhere near Union Station that could fit the first part of this riddle – a place where students used to go, but it has been transformed into something else.'

All of a sudden, Hunter's point became a lot clearer to everyone.

'By splitting up his riddle,' Hunter added, 'and making its first part seemingly easier than the rest, Lucien was hoping that we would come up with an answer to it first – and we did. What that does, without us realizing, is plant a suggestion seed into our subconscious.'

'And from that moment on,' Holbrook took over, now seeing where Hunter was going, 'we start referencing whatever answer we come up with for the second part of the riddle to the one we believe we've got right – "Some sort of ex-teaching/learning establishment" – and if the second answer doesn't match the first, we'll simply discard it.'

'Exactly,' Hunter agreed. 'The first part of the riddle sub-consciously pushes us to potentially overthink the second. Right now, just like Carlos said, the target location can be just about anywhere in this city, not just somewhere that used to be a school or something similar. Plus, we don't even know if we're on the right track with that answer or not. We accepted it straight away because it sounds very reasonable, but we haven't looked for a single alternative to it yet.'

'So instead of trying to look at the whole thing at once,' Garcia suggested, addressing Hunter. 'Why don't we split the riddle? You and West work exclusively on the first part. See if you guys can think of anything else other than – "some sort of ex-teaching/learning establishment". Peter, Captain Blake and I will tackle the second part and try to come up with an answer to it. We can then try to match whatever we have and see if we can come up with a location.'

'Sounds like a plan,' West agreed.

Hunter, Captain Blake and Holbrook nodded.

'OK,' Garcia said, checking his watch. 'We've got forty-six minutes until deadline. Let's find this goddamn target location.'

Forty

Night had finally arrived over Los Angeles, bringing with it a long blanket of shimmering stars and a natural full moon more impressive than any Hollywood werewolf movie CGI could produce. The temperature outside was just shy of seventeen degrees Celsius, but with no breeze to speak of, the air on the streets, especially around the concrete jungle that was downtown LA, felt warm and stale. Still, when compared to the temperature and the air inside Hunter and Garcia's office, the streets of downtown LA seemed like the Garden of Eden.

To avoid their eyes and minds wandering into portions of Lucien's riddle that they weren't supposed to, both teams had written down their respective parts on separate pieces of paper. Hunter and West were at Hunter's desk, while Garcia, Captain Blake and Holbrook surrounded Garcia's workstation. Both teams worked in silence and kept their backs to the large board where Holbrook had written the riddle in its entirety.

It was funny how the brain worked when it came to perception of time while under pressure. Both Hunter's and Garcia's team had been working on their individual parts of the riddle for what to them seemed like mere seconds, when in truth, they'd been at it for almost seven minutes.

Standing by Hunter's side, West had not only been dead silent for the entire time, which Hunter didn't actually mind, but his whole demeanor had also vaguely changed. He had become almost shy.

'Is everything all right?' Hunter asked in a voice barely louder than a whisper.

West nodded awkwardly, his eyes moving away from the piece of paper on Hunter's desk.

'Are you sure?' Hunter pushed. He understood that the sort of pressure they were under could easily alter a person's behavior, but despite not knowing West all that well, and regardless of him ever before dealing with a bomb threat or not, Hunter knew that, as a US Marshal, West was used to working under bone-crushing stress. It was part of the job package.

West finally gave in. He pressed his lips together, almost embarrassed, while shaking his head. His eyes met Hunter's.

'I'm not going to lie to you on this one, Detective,' he said. 'I one hundred percent suck at this kind of stuff. Always have, since I was a kid. Throw whatever you like at me and I promise you I'll beat it. Throw a riddle at me and my mind goes into lockdown mode. I don't know why. It just does.'

'Any new options over there?' The question came from Holbrook, who had just checked his watch again. 'We've now got around thirty-eight minutes to deadline.'

Hunter and West turned to face the other group.

'We've come up with two other contenders for the first part,' Hunter said.

'Really? What else have you got?' Captain Blake asked.

Hunter drew everyone's attention back to the entire riddle on the board against the south wall, but indicated only the first part of it.

You will find me in a place where people should be silent, but not here. Where verses should be found, but not here. Where students should come eager to learn, but not here.

'Other than some sort of teaching or educational establishment,' Hunter said, 'we think that Lucien could perhaps be referencing a library.'

The entire room went silent for a moment, everyone's eyes devouring the three first lines on the board as if they had never seen them before.

You will find me in a place where people should be silent – a library.

Where verses should be found – a library.

Where students should come eager to learn – a library.

One by one, the concerned expressions on everyone's faces quickly gave way to a look of acceptance. It made sense.

'What's the second option you came up with?' Holbrook quickly asked before everyone started discussing 'library' as an answer for the first part of the riddle.

Hunter looked at West, who almost shrugged back at him.

'We think that there's also a chance that Lucien could be talking about a church,' Hunter said.

This time Garcia, Captain Blake and Holbrook didn't direct their attention back to the board. Instead, they exchanged anxious looks among the three of them.

'Something wrong?' Hunter asked.

'I'm assuming Lucien isn't really a religious person,' Garcia said.

'Not even a little bit,' Hunter affirmed. 'On the contrary, he's always hated religion with a passion.'

Hunter's statement worried Garcia's team even more.

'By that do you mean Christianity?' Holbrook asked. 'Or religion in general?'

'The entire scope of religion,' Hunter came back. 'Why? What's the problem?'

'The problem is that we've been wrecking our heads over here, Robert,' Garcia said. 'And the only place, the only establishment, we could come up with that would maybe, in a skewed way, fit the second part of the riddle is a place of worship . . . a place of prayer . . . a church.'

Forty-One

This time it was Hunter and West's eyes that shot to the board and the second part of the riddle.

Instead of silent people, you'll find them to be loud, but you'll also find the quiet man. Instead of poets' laughter, you'll find writers' tears. Instead of eager students, you'll find cheap teachers.

Losing no time, Holbrook stepped forward to explain what they meant.

'Allow me to break this second part into separate sentences,' he said, 'and the sentences into sections. It makes it easier to understand.' He indicated on the board. '*Instead of silent people, you'll find them to be loud:* as we all know, churches have come a long way since the old days. Many of them doing their best to adapt to modern society. In some of these churches, prayer services go on almost like a party, with people dancing and singing as if in a carnival.'

West scratched the underside of his chin in a fidgety way. He'd never been to one of these churches, but he knew about them and he'd seen them on TV.

Holbrook moved on. '*You'll find the quiet man:* The "quiet man" here, could be Lucien referencing the priest, the pastor, whoever it is that presides over the service in the particular location he has in mind. Maybe, despite running the service, for one reason or another he does not partake in the party-like atmosphere. He's the "quiet man".'

Holbrook permitted Hunter and West a quick second to take all that in.

'Please also remember that we're talking about a place where Lucien has been before and we haven't,' he added. 'He knows if there are people in there who are quieter or louder than others and we don't. We are playing a blind man's game here.'

'Go on,' West instructed him.

'OK, next sentence. *Instead of poets' laughter, you'll find writers' tears.* Are either of you two familiar with the Bible?'

'Not to the point of remembering specific verses by heart,' Hunter replied, anticipating that that was what Holbrook was about to throw at them.

'I've read some of it,' West said, and simply left it at that.

'This could be a long shot,' Holbrook said. 'But then again, everything about this riddle is a long shot – but Psalm fifty-six, verse eight, says: "You have taken account of my wanderings; Put my tears in your bottle. Are they not in your book?"'

Hunter thought about it for a second. He knew that Lucien indeed despised every aspect of religion, but Christianity had always been his favorite target whenever he vocalized his feelings about the subject. Hunter was also certain that Lucien didn't know the Bible by heart – but with the help of the internet, it would have taken him no longer than just a few minutes to find a reference to Psalm 56:8.

'There are other ways of looking at this as well,' Garcia cut in. 'Correct me if I'm wrong, but I believe that most religious "playbooks" – the Bible ... the Torah ... the Quran, whatever – are mainly written in a verse format that resembles poetry.'

Hunter and West nodded.

'And though these books are supposed to . . . "elevate the spirit", "give us hope", "teach us the true meaning of life", whatever one choses to believe,' Garcia continued, 'all of them are heavily associated with pain, with sadness, with loss and death, with struggle and sacrifice for a better world . . . all of which would produce tears.' Garcia paused and indicated the board one more time. *Instead of poets' laughter, you'll find writers' tears.*

West's eyebrows lifted at Garcia.

'The last line in the second part of the riddle,' Holbrook said, taking over again, indicating on the board and wanting to move on as fast as possible. '*Instead of eager students, you'll find cheap teachers:* could be a reference to the ridiculous abuse of religion that we see everywhere today. Charlatans all pretending to be priests, pastors, reverends, gurus, spiritual leaders . . . whatever they need to be to con vulnerable people out of their hard-earned cash. Simple people . . . poor people . . . people who desperately need something to believe in.'

The room went quiet for a split second.

'If Lucien really hates religion in the way you've said he does,' Captain Blake addressed Hunter, 'especially Christianity, then I think that we might be on to something here. His target could very well be a place of worship – a church.'

'And have you noticed the time?' Holbrook spoke again.

Hunter looked at his watch. 'Seven forty-seven.'

'He's talking about how long we have left until Lucien's deadline,' West intervened.

'No, he's not,' Hunter countered.

'No, I'm not,' Holbrook confirmed.

West looked back at both of them a little confused.

'It's Sunday,' Hunter said. This time his words came out heavy with concern. 'The number of churches around LA and Greater LA that offer an eight o'clock Sunday service is almost unthinkable.'

West closed his eyes and threw his head back. 'Fuck!'

'The problem is,' Garcia jumped in, 'if we're right about all this, how the hell are we supposed to know which church Lucien is talking about here?'

'We need to connect what we have,' Hunter replied, 'and hope it leads us to a specific location.'

'That's right,' Holbrook agreed. 'We need to look for a church or place of worship that in a past life was maybe some sort of school or teaching environment, a library, or perhaps even a previous church.'

'Great,' Garcia said sarcastically, reaching for the phone on his desk. 'That sounds like a piece of cake.' He quickly placed a call to the UVC Unit research team.

Holbrook checked the time. They had twenty-eight minutes until deadline. 'I'll get an FBI team on it as well,' he said, also reaching for his cellphone.

Back sitting at his computer, Hunter had already started his own Internet search. Garcia was also at his machine, trying his best. Holbrook was hanging over his shoulder almost annoyingly.

Captain Blake was by Hunter's desk, but unlike Holbrook, she kept her distance. Hunter was much better at this than she was and she knew it.

West was back on the phone to Derek Tanner, the leader of the LAPD Bomb Squad. He told Tanner to have his team locked and loaded and ready to move at a second's notice.

The atmosphere inside Hunter and Garcia's office had now been upgraded to Defcon 1. With minutes going by like seconds, 'tense' was a huge understatement.

'How much time do we have?' Garcia asked Holbrook as he wiped beads of sweat off his forehead.

'Twenty-four minutes.'

'Shit!' Garcia sat back on his chair and ran both of his hands through his hair.

'Do you mind if I give it a try?' Holbrook asked, nodding at Garcia's computer.

'Knock yourself out,' Garcia replied, getting to his feet.

Holbrook took his seat and immediately began typing a new criterion into the search box. Once he hit 'enter', the first result page loaded in 0.49 seconds.

He had just started scanning the results when Captain Blake noticed the look on Hunter's face.

'Have you got something?' she asked, taking a step toward Hunter's desk.

Her question drove everyone's gaze to Hunter, who had his elbows on his desk, his eyes cemented to his computer screen and the look of a man who had just been mesmerized.

'What have you got?' West asked, quickly repositioning himself behind Hunter's chair.

'There's a spiritual ministry located near Memorial Park in Pasadena,' Hunter began. 'That specific ministry has been at that location for ten years, but the building they use is about thirty years old.'

'What was it before it became a ministry?' Holbrook asked.

'A Lutheran church,' Hunter replied.

Holbrook jumped to his feet and rushed over to Hunter's desk.

Garcia followed.

'But that's not all,' Hunter said. 'Have a look at this.' He clicked a link on the webpage he was on and a large photograph of the building used by the ministry filled his screen. The building's architecture was, in all respects, very unconventional. Its façade featured a combination of odd-shaped stained-glass windows and metal beams, which gave the tall structure – about forty-to-fifty feet high – a somewhat psychedelic look. From the outside, the building's steep-angled A-framed shape gave the impression that all one could see was its roof, as if the rest of the structure was hidden underground. As a final touch, the stairs that led up to the ministry's entry lobby were color-coded by neon lights – red, white and blue.

'*Look not for the obvious, but for the unorthodox*,' Holbrook said, quoting the last part of Lucien's riddle. 'If this isn't an unorthodox-looking building then I don't know what is, especially for a place of worship.'

'But there's still more,' Hunter added. 'Have you noticed the name of the ministry?'

Only then did everyone's attention shift toward the top of the webpage. The ministry was called – The Exceptional Love of Christ Ministry.

Even Captain Blake felt her skin turn into gooseflesh. 'You've got to be kidding me.'

Look not for the obvious, but for the unorthodox, and you shall find something special. You shall find the exceptional.

'This has got to be it,' Holbrook said, his voice lifting with enthusiasm, his gaze circling the room.

'It has to be,' West agreed. 'There's no way this is a goddamn coincidence.'

'Do they have a service happening tonight?' Captain Blake asked.

Hunter clicked the 'back' button to return to the ministry's home page.

'Yes,' he replied, reading from the service times that were listed on the top right-hand corner. 'They have one starting at eight o'clock.' He consulted his watch. 'That's in six minutes.'

'And how long until deadline?'

'Twenty-one minutes,' Holbrook answered. 'The bomb is supposed to detonate fifteen minutes into the service.'

'Where in Pasadena?' West asked, his cellphone already against his right ear.

'Corner of Holly Street and Marengo Avenue,' Hunter replied.

While West spoke with the leader of the bomb squad, Captain Blake reached for the phone on Hunter's desk and called the LAPD dispatch desk.

'This is Captain Barbara Blake of the LAPD Robbery Homicide Division,' she said into the mouthpiece as soon as the call was answered at the other end. Despite her urgent tone, her words came out clearly and paced. 'I'm calling with a code red. I need you to instruct Pasadena PD to send every available unit to the corner of Holly Street and Marengo Avenue. The location is a spiritual ministry called The Exceptional Love of Christ. The entire building is to be immediately evacuated, do you hear? *The entire building*. Once that's done, everyone is to be pushed back to a safe zone, which should be no less than thirty yards from the building itself. No one is allowed any closer ... *no one* ... with the exception of the bomb squad, which is already on its way.'

...

'Yes, I did say bomb squad, now focus. Pasadena PD has ...' She looked at Hunter.

'Twenty minutes to deadline,' he said.

'Fifteen minutes,' the captain told the police dispatcher, 'to get everyone out of that building and behind the thirty-yard perimeter line, did you get that? *Fifteen minutes*. Get it done ... now.' She put the phone down.

'Let's go,' West called from the door.

'How long to Pasadena from here?' Holbrook asked as everyone shot out of Hunter and Garcia's office.

'With sirens blasting and at this time on a Sunday evening,' Garcia replied, tilting his head to one side, 'we can probably make it in fifteen.'

West nodded. 'Fuck if that's not cutting it close.'

Forty-Two

Lucien paused before the odd-looking building and smiled at his own feat. Despite knowing how clever Hunter was, he had chosen well.

The riddle was true. Every line. Every word. And he knew that Hunter would not figure the whole thing out in time. Not in sixty minutes, no matter how smart he was.

The time was 7:56 p.m. – nineteen minutes until the deadline. Nineteen minutes before he could light up the Los Angeles sky with his own brand of fireworks. And what a display it would be. Sure, he wouldn't be able to look any of his victims in the eye. He wouldn't be able to see the panic in their faces or even savor their fear as life was blasted out of their bodies, but still, the knowledge that through a device that he had put together himself, he could bring death to so many at once, filled him with an almost inexplicable elation.

Inside, the place wasn't actually full, but people were still arriving.

Lucien decided to wait outside for a minute or two. He wouldn't be able to look his victims in the eye as they perished inside, but he sure as hell could look at some of their unsuspecting happy faces, full of hope and life, as they walked through the front door. Faces that in twenty minutes' time would be no more.

Two of those faces belonged to a young couple that had just crossed the road and entered the building – their arms rounding each other's waist, their lips adorned by satisfied smiles. As they walked past Lucien, he began wondering what their response would be if he actually tried to save their lives tonight. What would they say if Lucien walked up to them right then and told them not to go in there tonight? What would they do if he told them to turn around, go home and be happy with each other?

Would they take the advice of a complete stranger?

Would Lucien's request sound peculiar enough to make the two young lovers pause for thought, or would they just dismiss his words?

Just another street nutcase, probably looking for some change.

Inside, the two lovers took a seat at the far right and Lucien allowed his wandering thoughts to dissipate into thin air. He watched a few more people walk in before readjusting his glasses on his face and reaching for his rucksack, which was on the floor, by his feet.

It was time to go inside.

Maybe it was because in his mind, Lucien had already concluded that the two young lovers would not have listened to him, should he have tried to save their lives; or maybe it was because of the sickly-sweet way in which they looked at each other, but Lucien decided that he would place his rucksack as close as possible to the couple. They would be the first ones to go.

Indeed, Lucien thought. *Paradise awaits.*

Forty-Three

The two siren-blasting unmarked police vehicles shot out of the PAB parking lot like rockets on speed. Holbrook and West were in the first car, while Hunter, Garcia and Captain Blake followed directly behind. Garcia was at the wheel, not necessarily because he was a better or safer driver, but because he did have a more reliable and faster car than Hunter.

'Take North Hill Street instead of Santa Fe Freeway,' Captain Blake said from the backseat, as Garcia turned left onto West 1st Street. 'They've started roadworks on the freeway a couple of days ago. Traffic at anytime, any day, is a nightmare – sirens or no sirens.'

'I didn't know about the roadworks,' Garcia replied. 'But I was going to take North Hill anyway.'

'Well, they didn't,' the captain said, indicating West's black Camaro, which had sped ahead in the direction of the freeway.

Garcia turned right just before Stanley Mosk Courthouse and took the overpass in the direction of Chinatown, completely ignoring stop signs and traffic lights. Traffic wasn't a problem and he was able to hit 80 mph in a 55 zone with ease.

'How many people do you think might be attending the service tonight?' the captain asked.

'Your guess is as good as mine, Captain,' Garcia replied.

'But there will be kids there, won't there?' she pushed. 'Despite being an evening service, there will be kids inside that room.'

Neither Hunter nor Garcia replied, their silence speaking for them.

Through the police radio on Garcia's dashboard, they could hear the progress of Pasadena PD. The closest unit to their target location was still a couple of minutes away.

'How can they still be two minutes away?' Captain Blake asked. 'I called dispatch with a code red about four minutes ago.'

'This is the city we live in, Captain,' Hunter said. 'In LA, a pizza will get to you faster than an ambulance or the cops, and home-delivery cocaine will get to you faster than a pizza.'

'That's messed up.'

'One hundred percent,' Garcia agreed.

They joined Arroyo Seco Parkway and shot through the bridge over the Los Angeles River like a stock car. As they neared Sycamore Grove Park, they finally heard news about Pasadena PD units arriving at the Exceptional Love of Christ Ministry. The clock on Garcia's dashboard showed 8:02 p.m.

'They've got eight minutes to get everyone out of there and behind the perimeter line,' the captain said. 'Thirteen before the bomb goes off.'

The next news they heard was that the bomb squad was now less than a minute away.

'Eight minutes is easily doable,' Garcia said. 'We might not be able to save the building, but if Pasadena PD works fast, they'll get everyone out of there in time, no problem.'

'Let's hope,' Captain Blake said.

As they were approaching the end of Arroyo Seco Parkway, Hunter caught a glimpse of a twelve-foot billboard to his right, but it took him a full second to properly take the image in. It took the gears inside his brain another second and a half to start moving at full speed.

All of a sudden, Hunter twisted his body on the passenger's seat to look behind him, trying to catch the billboard again, which was now long gone. The movement was so abrupt and unexpected that it startled Captain Blake on the backseat.

'What the hell, Robert?'

Only then did she notice the look in his eyes and the expression on his face. Something wasn't right.

'Robert, what's wrong?' she asked.

Hunter didn't reply. Instead he immediately reached for his cellphone, called up his mobile browser, and typed something into the search engine. The result came back in 0.56 seconds.

Blood drained from his face.

He quickly typed in a new search – 0.53 seconds.

'Oh my God!' he said as he read the result.

'Robert, what the hell?' Garcia this time. 'What's going on?'

One more search, then another just to be absolutely sure.

'No, no, no . . . this can't be . . .' Hunter said before blinking once, his brain working double-time to once again navigate the dark labyrinth that was Lucien's riddle. This time, he found the exit without hitting any walls, and that was when his heart almost exploded inside of him.

'You've got to stop the car,' he said.

'What?' Garcia frowned at his partner. 'Robert, what the fuck is going on? What are you talking about?'

'We've got this wrong,' Hunter replied, looking back at

Garcia. 'We've got this whole riddle wrong. How the hell did I miss that?' He sounded angry at himself.

'Missed what, Robert?' Garcia again.

'All the clues in Lucien's riddle.' The vacant look in his eyes was gone, substituted by a fearful one. 'We're heading to the wrong place.'

'What?' Captain Blake's jaw dropped. 'What do you mean – the wrong place?'

'I know what Lucien is talking about in his riddle,' Hunter said. 'And it's not a ministry. We're heading to the wrong place.'

Forty-Four

Lucien entered the building and found a seat less than five feet away from the young couple he had seen outside. He placed his rucksack on the floor and pushed it under his chair to get it out of the way. Despite the gravity of what he was about to do, Lucien showed no signs of being nervous, looking as relaxed as a man sitting at his front porch on a Sunday afternoon.

After checking the time, Lucien allowed his eyes to slowly move around the place. He wanted to remember as many faces as he could, and he wanted to remember them just as they were right then – some happy, some serious, some sad, but all of them oblivious to what was about to hit them in just over ten minutes' time.

The place was filling up, the chatter of voices getting louder and louder. Lucien caught an earful of the conversation going on by the entrance door – a group of four men discussing last night's basketball game. None of them seemed happy. Apparently the LA Lakers had lost again, this time to the Minnesota Timberwolves and by twenty-one points.

The conversation going on five feet in front of Lucien sounded just as boring – the young couple was discussing which sort of paper they should use for their wedding invitations, which according to what Lucien had overheard, was less than three months away. The husband-to-be was arguing in favor of a cheaper paper. He was trying to convince his fiancée that they should save as much money as they could on the smaller things and then use those savings for a nicer honeymoon. The wife-to-be was advocating in favor of the most expensive option they'd been given. Her argument was that she didn't want her guests to think that they were cheap. The frivolity of that conversation was beginning to give Lucien a headache. It was time to refocus on the task at hand.

'Excuse me,' Lucien said to the couple, leaning forward on his seat. 'I'm so sorry to interrupt, but I was wondering if you wouldn't mind keeping an eye on my bag just for a minute while I zip to the restroom. The place is filling up and I don't want to lose my seat. I won't be long.'

'Sure, bud, no problem at all,' the man replied, giving Lucien a sympathetic nod.

The woman locked eyes with Lucien, offering him a shy but very charming smile.

'Thank you so much,' Lucien said, moving his rucksack from the floor onto his chair as a place keeper, before pushing the chair a little closer to the couple. 'I'll be right back.'

As Lucien walked away, the couple went back to discussing their wedding invitations. Neither of them noticed when, instead of turning right in the direction of the restrooms, Lucien turned left, past the group debating last night's game and out the front door.

Outside, he checked his watch again – four minutes until deadline.

Forty-Five

'Robert, what the hell are you talking about?' Captain Blake asked, her tone urgent, her voice half aggressive, half fearful.

'Carlos, pull up,' Hunter ordered, his phone already in his hand. 'Pull up now.'

'What the fuck, Robert?' Garcia said, quickly pulling up onto the side of the road. 'You better tell us something here, buddy. We've got eleven minutes until deadline.'

But Hunter wasn't listening anymore. He was already on the phone to the UVC unit research team with a whole new set of instructions. It took him about thirty seconds to explain to the team leader what he needed them to do.

Despite attentively listening to Hunter's phone conversation, Garcia and Captain Blake made very little sense of his words.

'What the hell was that all about, Robert?' Captain Blake asked as soon as Hunter disconnected from the call.

'Lucien's riddle,' he said. 'It's not talking about a ministry, or a church, or any place of worship like we thought. It's talking about a "bar" somewhere in Los Angeles. It's also not talking about an ex-church, or ex-library, or ex-teaching facility, or ex-anything else for that matter.'

'Yes,' Garcia responded. 'We've heard what you said to the research team. We just don't understand it. Where did that change of mind come from? And how did you figure all that out just like that?' He snapped his fingers.

'A few seconds ago,' Hunter began. 'We passed a large billboard right at the end of Arroyo Seco Parkway. That was where the change of mind came from. That was when I finally realized that Lucien's riddle is a goddamn play on words – and it's directed straight at me.'

'A play on words directed at you?' Garcia questioned. 'I'm lost.'

'The first mistake we made,' Hunter said, 'was that we misinterpreted the first part of the riddle, which consequently threw us off. That was exactly what Lucien wanted us to do.' Hunter immediately lifted his hand, indicating that he already knew that he should better explain what he meant. 'We believed that Lucien, in the first part of his riddle, was referring to a place that used to be something else, but it's not anymore, remember? The suggestions were that the place had maybe been some sort of teaching establishment, or a library, or even a church.'

'Yes, of course we remember,' Captain Blake said from the backseat. 'We were there.'

'The problem is,' Hunter continued, 'Lucien never used the phrase "not anymore". That was Agent Holbrook's interpretation, but because it sounded so plausible to all of us, we took it in and it stuck.'

'What?' Garcia looked at Hunter as if he were from outer space.

Hunter, who had committed the entire riddle to memory, recited the first part again.

'*You will find me in a place where people should be silent, but not here. Where verses should be found, but not here. Where students should come eager to learn, but not here.* Lucien doesn't say "not anymore", he says "not here".'

'And the difference is?' Captain Blake asked. She too looked a little lost.

'The difference is that "not anymore" indicates that something *did* happen at that location before, but it doesn't anymore,' Hunter clarified. '"Not here" implies that something *should* happen at that location, but it doesn't. It's a play on the name of the establishment, I'm sure of it.'

The confused looks on Garcia and Captain Blake's faces didn't lessen.

Hunter broke it down even more.

'What if there's a bar somewhere in LA called "The Church", or "The College", or "The Library"?'

Confused looks turned to thoughtful.

'People should be silent in a church,' Hunter carried on. 'But not here – not in "this" church.' He drew quotations in the air to emphasize his point. 'Because in this case, "church" is simply the name of the establishment. That's not saying that people used to be silent in that particular building, but they aren't anymore, which was what we believed the riddle meant.'

It took Garcia and Captain Blake a few seconds to wrap their heads around Hunter's new theory.

'Fine,' Garcia agreed, though he still looked half dazed. 'I sort of get the play on words with the name of the establishment. It does make sense, but why are you now saying that Lucien's target location is a bar? Why a bar?'

'That's where the billboard I was talking about came into play,' Hunter replied. 'It was an advertisement for a particular whisky. That got me thinking and that's why I was searching the Internet for answers.'

'Answers to what?' the captain shrugged.

Hunter recited the second and third parts of Lucien's riddle.

'*Instead of silent people, you'll find them to be loud, but you'll also find the quiet man. Instead of poets' laughter, you'll find writers' tears. Instead of eager students, you'll find cheap teachers. Look not for the obvious, but for the unorthodox, and you shall find something special. You shall find the exceptional*.' Hunter made a face as if he were angry with himself. 'Those are all whisky names. I've just checked.'

'What?' Total confusion was back masking Garcia and Captain Blake's faces. 'What are whisky names?'

Phone still in hand, Hunter brought back the result page to the first search he'd made just seconds ago and read the result out loud.

'The Quiet Man is an Irish single-malt whiskey,' Hunter explained before moving onto the next result page. 'Writers Tears is a copper-pot Irish whiskey. Teacher's is a blended Scotch whisky and when compared to most blended Scotch whiskies, is relatively "cheap".' He moved onto the third result page. 'Something Special is also a blended Scotch whisky that comes in quite an *unorthodox*-looking bottle.' He showed them the picture on his cellphone screen before continuing to the last result page. 'The Exceptional is a blended Scotch whisky that comes in three types – malt, blend and grain.' Hunter put down his phone and breathed out despair. 'They are all whisky names. The billboard I just saw was an advertisement for Teacher's whisky. That was what got my brain going.'

Garcia sat back against his seat and swallowed dry, his brain working double-time to connect all the dots.

Captain Blake simply looked mesmerized.

'Lucien knows how much I enjoy whisky,' Hunter continued. 'The riddle was tailor-made for me. Even though I've never even heard of three of those whiskies, his riddle is centered on a subject he knows I enjoy. A subject he knows I have knowledge of. It's his way of telling me that I was really the one who should've solved it, no one else.' He paused for breath. 'Do you remember the note that was found inside Lucien's infirmary cell?'

'Sort of,' Garcia replied. 'But not word for word.'

'I do – *You should've taken me out inside that plane when I gave you the chance, old friend. That chance is well and truly gone. Now it's my turn. Get ready, Grasshopper, because we're going to play a game.* This game he wants to play isn't against this task force. It's against me. He also told me over the phone, once we correctly answered his first question that I had earned the right to hear the little cool riddle he'd made "just for me".' Hunter shook his head angrily. 'How can I have been so damn stupid?'

'And so now you've asked the research team—'

'To find me any bars in LA,' Hunter explained, 'called either "church", or "library", or "school", or anything along those lines, but specifically whisky bars. With the exception of Teacher's, all the other whiskies Lucien has mentioned are terribly hard to find. They are really uncommon drams, which means that only specialist bars will have them, not every boozing hole in LA.'

'But what if Lucien was just being generic?' the captain asked. 'He could've searched for those whiskies on the Internet and used them because they served the purpose of his riddle.'

'Not Lucien,' Hunter disagreed. 'He would've been to the

bar and seen those bottles either on the shelves or in their drinks menu. He probably even drank them just for the fun of it.'

Garcia checked the time. 'We've got six minutes.'

That was when Hunter's phone rang again.

Forty-Six

Hunter snapped his cellphone from his lap without even looking at its screen, fully expecting it to be his research team with some news. It wasn't.

'*Did you guys get fucking lost or something?*' US Marshal West asked, his tone twenty percent confused, eighty percent angry. '*Where the fuck are you?*'

Hunter breathed out.

West did not wait for a reply. '*Pasadena PD has done a great job here. Everyone has been cleared out of the building and securely pushed behind the perimeter line. We still have just over five minutes till detonation and the bomb squad is in there right now looking for this bomb.*'

'You're in the wrong place,' Hunter said, his tone firm and severe.

'*I'm sorry,*' West replied. '*What was that again?*'

'We've made a mistake deciphering the riddle,' Hunter told him. 'Lucien's target location is not the Exceptional Love of Christ Ministry. You and the bomb squad are at the wrong location.'

'*Are you fucking joking? Because this isn't funny, Robert.*'

'It's not a joke,' Hunter came back. 'We've made a mistake.'

He paused and rephrased. 'I've made a mistake. The riddle isn't talking about a ministry, or a church, or whatever. It's talking about a bar.'

'About a what? A bar? What bar? What the hell are you talking about, Robert?'

'We don't know what bar yet,' Hunter said. 'And that's why I need to get off the phone. We don't have a lot of time left.' He pinned Garcia down with an odd look. 'Call Carlos and he'll explain everything to you.'

Garcia almost choked. 'You what?'

'I've got to go.' Hunter disconnected.

Three seconds later Garcia's cellphone rang. He checked the display screen – US Marshal West.

'Oh, that's just peachy,' he said, as he answered his phone.

Five seconds after that, Hunter's phone rang again. This time, the call did come from his research team.

Forty-Seven

'Please tell me that you've got something,' Hunter said, bringing his phone to his ear, his voice pleading.

'*We might,*' Shannon Hatcher, the leader of the research team, replied. Her voice sounded skeptical. '*But I can't say for certain.*'

'Just give me what you have,' Hunter told her.

'*That's the problem, Detective,*' Hatcher replied. '*I've got nothing for any whisky bars in LA named "Church, The Church, A Church", or any variations of it. The same was true for "library" and "school".*'

'Fuck!' Hunter whispered between clenched teeth.

'*But you did ask me to search for anything along those lines, right?*' Hatcher continued.

'Yes, sure, why?'

'*Because there's a bar tucked away in Hollywood called Whisky Athenaeum, and athenaeum, as you know, is a synonym for library.*'

Hunter's heart practically stopped beating and all his blood seemed to shy away from his skin for an instant, turning him ghostly pale.

Lucien's riddle's third and final part came back to him –
Look not for the obvious, but for the unorthodox.

'Lucien wasn't talking about an unorthodox-shaped bottle,'
Hunter whispered to himself, though Garcia and Captain
Blake heard him loud and clear. 'He was talking about the
name of the location. Shannon, you're a genius. That's it.
That's got to be the place. Do you have an address and a phone
number for it?'

'*Of course.*' Hatcher dictated both to Hunter, who immediately dictated it to Garcia and Captain Blake.

Garcia, who was still on the phone to West, passed the
address to him, before quickly turning his car around and
getting back onto Arroyo Seco Parkway.

Captain Blake also reached for her phone. She had to call
dispatch and give them the exact same orders she had given
them back in Hunter's office, this time with the new address.
The real problem was: if they were lucky, maybe one or two
police units could make it to Hollywood in four minutes. That
was all the time they had left, but there was no chance in hell
that a second bomb-squad team would make it there in time.
That bomb would go off no matter what.

'Shit!' Garcia said, as he stepped on the gas, bringing his
Honda Civic to 100 mph. 'Even with clear roads it will take us
fifteen, maybe twenty minutes to get to Hollywood from here.'

'Just do your best,' Captain Blake said.

Hunter had disconnected from his call to Hatcher and had
instantly dialed the number she had given him for the Whisky
Athenaeum.

'It's ringing,' he announced to everyone.

'C'mon, c'mon. Pick up,' Hunter begged.

Three and a half minutes to deadline.

'*Yo!*' A male voice said, as the call was finally answered. '*Whisky Athenaeum. How can I help?*'

Loud music blasted through Hunter's earpiece.

'OK,' Hunter replied, doing his best to keep his voice steady and composed. 'I need you to listen very carefully to what I'm about to tell you. My name is Robert Hunter. I'm a detective with the Homicide Special Section of the LAPD. I need you to get everyone out of your bar *right now*. Get everyone out of the building and to the other side of the road. Do you understand what I'm telling you?'

'*No, not really,*' the man replied, his voice getting louder, trying to overcome the music. '*You want me to do what?*'

'I need you to get everyone out of the building and to the other side of—'

'*I can't really hear you, buddy,*' the man cut Hunter short.

That's because the music is too damn loud, Hunter thought.

'*It's probably a bad connection,*' the man said. '*Let me put the phone down and you can try calling again, OK?*'

'No, don't hang–' Hunter began, but the man had already put the phone down. 'You've got to be kidding me!' Hunter said, already pressing 'redial' on his phone.

Two and a half minutes to deadline.

The phone rang once ... twice ... three times.

'Oh, for Christ's sake, pick it up.'

Through the police radio on Garcia's dashboard they all heard the news that the nearest unit to the bar in Hollywood was just over two minutes away.

'They're not going to make it,' Garcia said, letting out a completely defeated breath.

Finally someone answered the phone at the other end. This time it was a woman's voice.

Two minutes to deadline.

'*Whisky Athenaeum. How can I help you—*'

'Listen,' Hunter cut her short in a firm voice, but before he was able to say anything else, Captain Blake snatched the phone from his hand.

'I'll do this,' she said, bringing the phone to her ear. 'Listen up,' she told the woman at the other end of the line. 'This is Captain Barbara Blake of the LAPD's Robbery Homicide Division.' Her authoritative voice also carried a very high level of urgency in its tone. 'I'm not going to beat around the bush here. A fucking lunatic has planted a bomb inside your establishment. This bomb will detonate in—'

'*Bombs?*' the woman came back. She was just a hair shy of shouting. '*Of course we do them. We have Jager Bombs, Glitter Bombs, Dr Pepper Bombs, Irish Car Bombs ... you name it. We have a whole menu on bomb shots. Are you looking for something specific?*'

'No,' Captain Blake blasted back, her voice matching the woman's in decibels. 'You're not listening to me.' It was time to get graphic. 'In about a minute and a half everybody inside your bar will die, including you. Somebody has planted a bomb somewhere inside your workplace. It's real ... it's live ... it's happening ... and it will go off in ninety seconds. You need to get *everyone* out of there now. And I mean NOW.'

There was a short pause on the woman's side. '*Is this a joke?*'

'No, this is not a goddamn joke.' The captain's voice began losing its composure. 'This is as real as it gets and we're losing time here. You really need to get *everyone* out of there right–'

'*You need to speak to my manager,*' The woman interrupted the captain. '*Hold on.*'

'No ... there's no time to hold on. You're running out of—'

The woman had already put down the phone and walked away.

'Oh my God … arrrgh!' Captain Blake let out an overly frustrated growl. 'What's wrong with these people?'

'Nothing, Captain,' Hunter said. 'They're just being people.'

The seconds ticked away.

'*Hello, can I help you?*' A new male voice finally came to the phone. No doubt the bar manager. '*What is this about a bomb you're saying?*'

Thirty-five seconds to deadline.

'I'm the LAPD Robbery Homicide Division Captain,' Blake's voice was now pleading. 'You need to get everyone out of your bar *now*. This is not a joke and this is not a hoax. Someone has planted a bomb somewhere inside your bar and it will go off in less than a minute.'

'*A bomb?*' the man asked. '*Like a bomb bomb?*'

Captain Blake's eyes rolled into her head. 'Yes, a bomb bomb, the kind of bomb bomb that will blow everything to high heaven and kill everyone inside your bar, including you and your entire staff.'

'*Jesus!*' The bar manager finally got the picture. '*How long do I have?*'

Captain Blake checked her watch, as she did, she felt her blood run cold. 'Twelve seconds,' she replied in a voice that had clearly lost all hope.

'*Twelve … fuck!*'

Captain Blake heard a loud ruffling sound, as the man simply let go of the phone. Three seconds later the loud music came to a stop.

Seven seconds to deadline.

'*Everyone please listen up.*' Captain Blake heard the bar manager yell at the other side of the line. '*HEEEEYYYY.*'

Three seconds to deadline.

'*I need everyone to get out right—*'

There was a very loud bang, immediately followed by the line going dead.

All of a sudden, Hunter's cellphone beeped in Captain Blake's hand, announcing a new text message.

Hunter took it from her and checked the display screen.

Unknown number. He immediately opened the message. It contained only one word, which was followed by a smiling emoji face.

BOOM ☺.

Forty-Eight

Inside the Whisky Athenaeum bar in Hollywood, the young couple had finally come to an agreement in regards to which type of paper they would use for their wedding invitations. Actually, it was less of an 'agreement' and more of a 'surrender' on the husband–to-be's part. They'd been through similar scenarios before and he knew that there was no way he would ever win that argument, no matter how rational he sounded. If his fiancée wanted the expensive paper, then she would get the expensive paper. End of story.

'Another drink?' he asked, reaching for the menu on their table.

'And why not?' she replied, as she checked the time. 'It's still early.' She leaned over to kiss her fiancé. 'What are you going for this time?'

'Oh, I'm staying with whisky,' he replied, flipping the menu to the correct page. 'But I think I might try something a little different. Something less peaty. Maybe one of the Irish whiskeys. How about you?'

'Umm, I'm not sure,' she replied, turning to face the list of special cocktails on the board by the bar. 'I might go for a Tamarind Margarita, what do you think?'

He shrugged. 'Sounds good ... I guess. You're the one drinking it.'

'Yeah,' she convinced herself. 'I'll have one of those, please.'

'One Tamarind Margarita coming up,' he said, as he pulled his chair back to be able to get up. 'Honey,' he called, frowning. 'Have you seen that dude that left his rucksack here?' He quickly scanned the bar.

She had completely forgotten about that.

'No, I haven't,' she replied, stretching her neck to look around the place.

'He said that he was going to the restroom,' the husband-to-be said. 'But that was a few minutes ago. Do you think he's still in there?'

'I don't know. Do you want to go check it?'

'What, check the bathroom? I don't even know the dude. Do you think I should?'

'I'm not sure.' Her eyes moved to the rucksack on the chair by their table.

At that exact moment, the pre-paid cellphone tucked away inside the rucksack came to life. Its display screen lit up to announce an incoming call. A split second later, the Whisky Athenaeum was no more.

Forty-Nine

Zero point two seconds. Faster than a human eye can blink.

That was how long it took the cellphone that Lucien had placed inside the rucksack to send an electric impulse from its battery, down a thin pair of wires, and into a small alloy shell, located at the heart of the C-4 compound. That alloy shell, which had been filled with gunpowder, was the bomb's detonator.

Essentially, a detonator was nothing more than a little bomb sitting inside a big bomb.

As the detonator ignited, it produced intense heat, which pushed the temperature at the core of the C-4 compound to higher than necessary to detonate it.

BOOM!

And it really was a big boom.

The blast could be heard for miles – as far as Bel Air to the west and Glassell Park to the east – but the intriguing factor was, no one inside the Whisky Athenaeum heard it.

Lucien had placed his bomb inside a twelve-by-twelve-inch metal box. The box itself had been filled with a mixture of stainless-steel ball bearings, loose needle-rollers and diamond-point metal nails. Inside the rucksack, taped to the sides of the metal box, were two 1.5-liter bottles of ethanol, which carried a peak flame temperature of 1,920 degrees Celsius.

As the C-4 compound blew, it changed state, from solid to gas – highly flammable gas. The metal box, which had been sealed with impermeable sealant, instantly shattered into hundreds of different-sized fragments, which, in turn, joined forces with the contents of the box, creating an inescapable lethal cloud of flying metal, but that was only half of the deadly force packed by Lucien's bomb.

The detonation also displaced a significant mass of air, which due to its velocity turned scalding hot. As that hot air came into contact with the two bottles of ethanol, it created a second lethal cloud – this one made purely out of flames. Both clouds came together as one, expanding as they moved away from the epicenter of the blast, practically doubling in size with every half-a-foot they traveled.

What most people failed to realize was that the shockwave caused by a detonation worked similarly to a tornado, in the sense that it not only destroyed whatever it encountered in its path, but it also sucked into its nucleus all the debris that it had created as a consequence of that destruction – wood and metal shrapnel from destroyed tables and chairs, shards of glass from bottles and drinking glasses, concrete fragments from walls and columns, and pieces of bone and human matter from all its victims – adding it all to the detonation's already deadly and lightning-fast moving cloud.

Understandably, since they were the closest ones to Lucien's rucksack, the two young lovers were the first to be hit. By the time the shockwave reached the next table along, which was occupied by three college students, the ball of annihilation had grown to over ten times its initial size.

More deadly debris was sucked into the boiling fragment cloud before it hit the married couple who were sitting about five feet from the students' table. They were celebrating the fact that after three long years, the husband had finally beaten prostate cancer.

The cloud expansion carried on moving forward, and as it stretched to the group of four guys who were still discussing last night's basketball game, it had enlarged to cover the Whisky Athenaeum bar from wall to wall and floor to ceiling. Due to the distance it had already traveled – over twenty feet by then – and all the large obstacles that it had encountered along the way – tables, chairs, human bodies, etc. – the dynamic energy of the destruction ball had become uneven, which meant that each one of the four LA Lakers' fans got hit with a different deadly momentum.

The two people behind the bar – the bar manager and the woman who had talked to Captain Blake on the phone – were simply engulfed by the destruction cloud, now also heavy with blood and pieces of human flesh.

Less than a second after detonation, the blast finally hit the front of the bar, shattering every window and dispersing the last of its energy into the Los Angeles night air, but Lucien's mathematical calculation concerning the power of the explosion in relation to the square-footage of the place had been as close to flawless as possible. As soon as the blast reached the outside, the energy that was left in it was just enough to blow out half a dozen birthday candles, nothing more. Even the glass shards from the shattered windows didn't travel further than just a few feet.

The shockwave died down.

Its job completed.

Nothing else to destroy.

No one else to kill.

The ceiling just above the epicenter of the blast had collapsed. The bar counter had been ripped from the floor. Inside what used to be the Whisky Athenaeum bar there was nothing else left but rubble, debris and death. Fire had taken over the space, fueled not only by the scorching air produced by the velocity of the shockwave and the highly flammable ethanol that Lucien had attached to his bomb, but also by the contents of the target location. The average alcohol volume per bottle on most of the spirit bottles behind the bar was forty percent or more.

The shockwave destruction was over in zero point nine seconds, but the fire devastation had only just started.

At the time of the explosion, there were thirty-two people inside the Whisky Athenaeum. Zero point nine seconds later, twenty-nine of them were dead.

Three people had survived the initial blast – two female customers and one male member of staff – all three of them out of pure luck, though the two female customers turned out to be a lot luckier than the staff member.

The two customers didn't know each other, but they had gone to the restroom at just the right time.

The male survivor, who was part of the three-strong staff that had been working that night, had, ironically enough, gone to the cellar at the back to pick up a bottle of The Quiet Man whiskey, as they had just run out of it at the bar. The reason why the two female customers turned out to be luckier than the staff member was because the fire-escape door was located at the end of the hallway that led to the restrooms.

After the explosion came a very brief moment of realization, quickly followed by sheer panic. It took the two female customers over a minute to stop screaming. It took their brains another thirty seconds to be able to momentarily overcome the initial shock and figure out that they should exit the premises through the fire-escape door.

In the long run, the member of staff who had gone to the cellar hadn't been so lucky. In reality, the Whisky Athenaeum cellar was nothing more than a medium-sized storage room at the far end of the bar. Access came via a door on the back wall. Though the explosion didn't actually trap him in the cellar, the intense fire that followed did. There was simply no way that he could've exited the storage room and found his way through all the rubble to the outside of the bar without burning himself alive.

Despite using his shirt to protect his nose and mouth, he passed out from smoke inhalation in just under five minutes. Four minutes later, his heart stopped beating.

He was only twenty-one years old.

Fifty

Just like Captain Blake had feared, the first responders to the 'code red' dispatch call didn't quite make it in time. The police unit had just turned the corner when they saw the place blow up and immediately ignite in flames right in front of their eyes.

'Jesus!' Officer Jordan shouted, slamming on the brakes and swerving hard left.

'Oh my God!' That was all the reply Officer Prescott could muster before her trembling hands shot to her mouth. This was only her second month as a sworn police officer.

Within a minute of Officers Jordan and Prescott getting there, five other police units arrived. Though they all tried, there was very little anyone could do other than keep the chaos of curious onlookers at a safe distance, watch the place burn and wait for the fire department to get there, which also didn't happen fast enough.

The first fire engine only arrived at 8:26 p.m., eleven minutes after the bomb had gone off. The second and third ones arrived just seconds later. Twenty-one firefighters fought the blaze for exactly nine minutes and forty-nine seconds before the last of the flames was finally extinguished.

Smoke rose from the ashes in eerie plumes, sending a new,

frightening mist into the Los Angeles night air. With it, came a moment of bewildering silence. A moment of realization and extreme sadness. A moment of utter fear, as it was suddenly understood that what had happened there had been no accident. The explosion that had enveloped the Whisky Athenaeum bar hadn't come courtesy of a gas leak or an accident. This had unequivocally been the evil that men do.

The mist that rose from the torched drinking den also brought something else with it. Something that on that night, everyone who had gathered around had the displeasure of witnessing – a particular smell that savagely entered the nostrils and traveled through the nasal cavity like piercing shards of glass, scratching every internal wall until it finally reached the lungs. The power of the smell was so intense that it churned the stomachs of even the most seasoned of firefighters.

That was the smell of scorched human flesh.

Fifty-One

Hunter sat on the curb across the road from what once had been the Whisky Athenaeum. His legs bent at the knees. His feet flat on the ground. The fire had been extinguished a little over thirty minutes ago. Though he was looking straight ahead at the steaming pile of wet rubble in front of him, his eyes weren't really focusing on any of it.

Hunter, Garcia and Captain Blake had arrived at the scene as the fire brigade was still fighting the blaze. FBI Special Agent Holbrook and US Marshal West arrived six minutes after them.

Hunter had always been known for his game face. A face that no one could read. A face that would never give anything away. But that night, his expression could be read from a mile away. It showed a crude mash-up of desolation, anguish and helplessness. Neither Garcia nor Captain Blake had ever seen Hunter look so defeated.

He watched, powerless, as firefighters fought the blaze with everything they had. The press, national and international, had also descended on that stretch of Hollywood with all their might. Reporters were coming from everywhere, trying their best to get any sort of information from whoever would speak to them. Speculation was already flying high, with talks of dormant terrorist cells finally coming to life in Los Angeles, suicide bombers who had entered the USA via Mexico, and even a mention of a new and improved version of the Unabomber.

Hunter himself had been approached by at least three different reporters from three different networks, but neither his eyes nor his body language acknowledged their presence.

Camera flashes exploded against a backdrop of total destruction with so much frequency, it looked like a 1980s disco street party was going on. Every single onlooker, all of them being kept behind a safe-zone perimeter line, had their smartphones firmly in hand, filming and photographing everything. As a matter of fact, even before the fire brigade had arrived, the social-media pages of tens of regular people were already broadcasting live images of what was going on.

'Would you like some water?' Garcia offered, coming up to Hunter.

Hunter said nothing; his eyes watched the smoke lift from the ground, as if it contained the souls of everyone who had perished inside that building, moving from this world onto hopefully a better one.

Garcia sat beside his partner and placed a bottle of water on the ground by Hunter's feet.

'I wanted to help those people here tonight,' Hunter finally said, without breaking eye contact with the smoke ghosts. 'I should've figured out that riddle a lot earlier. It was all there . . . all the clues . . . all the hints. How could I have been so blind?'

'What happened here tonight was not your fault, Robert,' Garcia said. It wasn't that hard for him to see the dark hole Hunter was staring into. 'No one . . . absolutely no one would have figured that riddle out and you know it. You were the only one who could've done it, and you did it. We were just unlucky with the time. C'mon, Robert, sixty minutes to figure all that crap out? "The Quiet Man? Writers Tears? Something Special" and whatever else? "A place where people should be quiet, but not here? Look not for the obvious, but for the unorthodox?" You have got to be kidding me, right? It was an nearly impossible task. Lucien wanted this bomb to go off no matter what.'

Garcia followed Hunter's gaze before letting out an angry and frustrated breath.

'And if it hadn't been for the stubbornness of the staff working in there tonight, we could've saved lives. Two minutes, Robert. There were still two minutes on the clock when you called them. It wasn't that big a place. No kitchen, just a bar. If the barman had listened to what you and Captain Blake were telling him, he could've gotten everyone out of there in time.' He looked at his partner. 'I know how frustrating this is, but *none* of this is your fault, Robert.'

'I know this place, Carlos.' Hunter's voice was heavy with sorrow. 'I've been here once before, about three years ago. If you wanted to try Irish whiskey, this was the place to come to. I should've thought of it. When I figured out that Lucien was referring to some sort of bar, I should've thought of this place. Why didn't I do that?'

'Because you're human, Robert,' Garcia shot back. 'Not a fucking machine.'

'How the hell did you figure this out?' US Marshall West asked, coming from behind both detectives. He and Special Agent Holbrook had been busy talking to the firefighter operation leader until then. 'How, from that crazy riddle, did you come up with the name of this place?' West's tone of voice was far from aggressive. He was, in fact, genuinely intrigued.

'It doesn't matter how,' Hunter replied, without looking back at him. 'Because the outcome was exactly the same as if we hadn't figured it out.' He jerked his chin in the direction of the destroyed building. 'We didn't get here in time. We didn't manage to save anyone.'

'What a mess,' Captain Blake said as she joined the group. She too had been talking to the firefighter operation leader. 'What a goddamn mess.'

'It will take a few days until we get the official number of victims,' Holbrook said. 'If we do get an accurate number, that is. The site won't be cleared for inspection until tomorrow morning, that's when we can start looking for bodies, but this is a bombing site; depending on how many people were standing too close to the epicenter of the blast and how powerful the ignition was, some bodies might've been pulverized.'

Before Hunter could get to his feet, his cellphone rang again.

Unknown number.

He didn't have to say anything. From the look on his face, everybody knew whom the call was coming from.

Fifty-Two

'*Wow, that was quite a big boom, wasn't it?*' they all heard Lucien say, as Hunter had switched the call onto speakerphone as soon as he'd answered it. He and the entire group quickly put a little more distance between themselves and the noisy and chaotic back-and-forth of firefighters and police officers at the site of the explosion.

'*Oh, sorry,*' Lucien continued in a sarcastic voice. '*I forgot that you weren't there to see it, Grasshopper. But you're there now, right? So I guess that by having a look at the building . . . well, I mean, what's left of it, you can get a good enough mental image of how majestic the "big boom" was.*'

There wasn't even an ounce of remorse in Lucien's tone of voice. No sorrow either. He spoke of the bombing as if he were talking about a trivial movie scene, or a minor chapter in a book, not a real-life atrocity – one that he himself had masterminded and executed.

'You sonofabitch,' West blasted out, fire burning in his eyes. Hunter wasn't able to mute the phone in time. 'Wait until I get my hands on you.'

Hunter shook his head at West. 'Don't go there,' he mouthed the words.

'*Oh! Hello there,*' Lucien said, now sounding amused. '*It sounds like we have a newcomer to our party, Grasshopper, and an angry one at that, it seems. So who might this distraught individual be, may I ask?*' He didn't give them any time to reply. '*No, no, don't answer that. Please allow me at least one guess. Ummmmmmm . . . I think I'm going to go with . . . a member of the US Marshals Office. How's that?*'

'That's right, you piece of shit.' West was getting angrier by the second.

Hunter shook his head at him again.

West couldn't care less.

'This is US Marshal Tyler West. Did you get that, you scumbag? That's Ty-ler West.' He repeated his name very slowly. 'You better remember that name, because I'll be the one slapping the handcuffs on your wrists.'

'*Is that a fact?*'

'You bet your ass it is.'

Lucien laughed excitedly.

'*I am sincerely looking forward to that moment, US Marshal Ty-ler West. Did I get that right?*'

Before West could reply, Hunter muted the phone call.

'Are you done?' he asked West. 'Because this isn't helping. No matter what you say to him, you won't be able to faze him, but he's already getting into your head. Can't you see that? Let it go, Tyler.'

West lifted both hands in surrender.

'*The problem you have, US Marshal Tyler West,*' Lucien said. He certainly wasn't done yet. '*Is one of the main factors that really separates someone like you from someone like me, or even someone like Robert.*' He paused just to heighten the suspense. '*Your emotions,*' Lucien said at last. '*It's quite*

evident that you don't really have a firm grip on them, allow-
ing them to take over you, to affect your judgment, to guide
your words, and I'm guessing that sometimes they even guide
your actions. For a man in your position that is a huge, huge
flaw – one that if you don't remedy, it will one day inevitably
be your downfall.'

West looked at Hunter in total disbelief. 'Is this sack of shit
giving me career advice?' he whispered.

'Would you like to know why it is so easy for a person like
me to murder someone and simply walk away without feeling
any guilt, any regret, any sadness?'

Hunter unmuted the call.

'No, I actually wouldn't,' West replied angrily.

Lucien chuckled. *'See?'* he said. *'There you go again, US*
Marshal Tyler West, allowing your emotions to envelop your
thoughts, take over your brain and speak for you, because who
are you kidding here? We all know that the real answer to that
question is: "Of course you would." You're an officer of the
law and what I'm offering you here is privileged information.
The kind of information that might one day help someone
like you catch someone like me. I'm offering you the kind of
knowledge that you won't find in any books, or studies, or
anywhere else for that matter. This is the kind of knowledge
that only psychopaths carry locked deep inside their brains,
though I will admit that most psychopaths don't actually real-
ize it. But I'm a different kind of psychopath.'

It looked like West was about to cut Lucien short, but
Hunter, Garcia, Captain Blake and Holbrook all saw it coming
and gestured for him to stay quiet.

'I'm a scholar,' Lucien continued. *'A researcher, a scien-*
tist of the mind, if you will. I'm a psychopath who studies

psychopaths. I study their methods … their tricks … their thoughts … their actions … all of it, and that's why I have the knowledge I'm offering you right now. Like Robert once suggested – I'm a psychopath by choice, not by nature, and that makes me the most dangerous kind of psychopath there is, because I "want" to kill, I'm not driven to it by an internal uncontrollable urge, which means that all I do is planned.'

Lucien's words seemed to chill the Los Angeles night air.

'*So why don't we try this again, US Marshal Tyler West? And this is the last chance I'll give you. Would you like to know why it is so easy for a person like me to murder someone and simply walk away without feeling any guilt, any regret, any sadness?*'

Everyone nodded at West, who gritted his teeth in anguish, as if he'd just been stabbed in the back. To him, allowing the next few words to exit his lips was a defeat.

'Yes, I would.'

'*There we go,*' Lucien said, his voice steady. '*That's the spirit I'm looking for. Well, US Marshal Tyler West, since you've asked so politely, let me indulge you this once.*

'*The reason why it is so easy for some psychopaths to kill a man and then simply walk away devoid of all emotions is because as soon as the moment is done, we're already retelling the story to ourselves, transposing the murder.*'

West made a 'what-the-hell-is-he-talking-about' face.

As if Lucien could see him, he replied. '*What that really means, US Marshal Tyler West, is that all of a sudden, the act of killing isn't "our" act of killing anymore. It belongs instead to some fictional being … a character of our imagination … a monster that we cannot control.*'

He paused momentarily to allow those words to be fully absorbed by his phone audience.

'And how can one feel guilt for something one can't control? In our psychopathic minds, reality becomes fiction, a fabrication. The act of killing becomes just a game we play, a scenario, like Cowboys and Indians when we were kids, did you ever play that? It's not real. Once we walk away from it, it's gone. We're not an Indian, or a cowboy, or a killer anymore. It's all left behind in the playground.'

'Is he fucking serious?' Garcia whispered, placing his palm in front of his mouth so that his words wouldn't reach Hunter's cellphone.

'This technique,' Lucien continued, 'unsurprisingly, isn't restricted only to psychopaths. Far from it. It was and still is vastly used worldwide by governments and the military, especially during wartime. How do you think that all these war criminals all over the world – Chechnya, Syria, Iraq, Auschwitz, Congo, America, you name it – can walk away from murdering thousands of men, women, and children in the fields and concentration camps, and still sleep at night like a man after an orgy?'

No one ventured a reply.

'I'm sure that if you want, US Marshal Tyler West, Robert can later explain all the details to you, but it's a technique called "disassociation". You might've heard of it before.' The sarcasm was back in Lucien's tone. 'That's how they and we – psychopaths, murderers – make peace with ourselves after we've taken a life ... or many. We transmute the act of killing from reality to something that doesn't feel so real to us, like a story or an article in a newspaper. I'm sure you already know this, but human memory is very fickle and easy to deceive. We remember things the way "we" want to remember them, regardless of how they actually happened. We do this enough *times and we'll eventually get to a point where good and evil loses all meaning because we believe what we want to believe. Have I painted a pretty enough picture for you, US Marshal Tyler West?*

'And that is the world today.'

West's facial expression was somewhere between disgusted and thoughtful.

'*But I do have an extra trick,*' Lucien decided to add. '*This happens before the act. All I need to do before killing someone is close my eyes for a very brief moment. Would you like to know why I do that, US Marshal Tyler West?*'

Everyone nodded at West again.

'Yes,' he replied.

'*I didn't quite catch that. Can you repeat it for me, please?*'

West looked like he was about to explode with anger.

'Yes, I would like to know why you do that.'

Lucien laughed again, this time an irreverent and unconcerning laugh. '*But of course you would.*' The laughing continued. '*The answer is actually quite simple. I do it because inside of me there's a place where everything is dark ... where everything has died ... and all I need to do to go there is close my eyes.*'

West looked at Hunter as if he had finally figured Lucien out. 'He is completely deranged,' he whispered.

'*Maybe you should ask the FBI to allow you to read some of my research, US Marshal Tyler West. Vanity aside, it makes for pretty good reading. Anyway, class is over. I really think that we should get back to what's important here, and that will bring me to you, Grasshopper. I'm quite disappointed in you again. I thought that you would figure the riddle out in time.*'

Another pause.

'*Actually, I don't even know if you figured it out at all. Did you, or is it that the only reason why you and US Marshal Tyler West are at the explosion site is because once the bomb went off, the secret of the location was revealed?*'

Hunter kept quiet.

'*You didn't pick up on all those whisky names ... all those clues?*'

West and Holbrook looked at Hunter with question marks in their eyes. They still didn't know how he had figured the riddle out.

'*Or did you fall for the trick?*' Lucien asked.

Now everyone in the group looked doubtful.

'*The ministry, Grasshopper,*' Lucien explained. He guessed that the silence that had followed was due to no one really knowing what he was talking about. '*The Exceptional Love of Christ Ministry in Pasadena. Did you think that I had planted the bomb inside the ministry?*'

This time even Captain Blake closed her eyes, cursing through clenched teeth.

'*You did, didn't you? You fell for the trick.*'

Hunter felt a crater form in his stomach.

Another laugh. But this one sounded truthful.

'*Believe it or not, Robert, that wasn't planned. Not at first, that is. It all came to me right at the last minute. As I began writing the riddle, I realized that the first part of it could very easily be referring to a church, or something of the like. That gave me an idea.*'

Hunter saw that West was getting agitated again and immediately lifted a hand at him, just in case he was, once again, thinking about jumping the gun.

West swallowed his anger.

'*Did you know that there are close to three and a half thousand religious worshiping places in Los Angeles?*' Lucien revealed. '*That's a hell of a large number, don't you think? Which, in turn, gave me a hell of a large number of choices. All I needed to do was find one I could work with. It did take me a little while and I had to rewrite the riddle a few times to get it right, but in the end I think I did a great job, what do you say?*' Lucien waited a couple of seconds. '*What do you say, US Marshal Tyler West, did I do a good job? Did all of you head toward the Exceptional Love of Christ Ministry in Pasadena, while the real bomb was just behind this young couple, who looked to be very much in love, sitting at a table quite close to the bar inside the Whisky Athenaeum?*'

'You heartless sonofabitch,' West said, but Hunter had already muted his phone. He saw that West was about to explode.

'*Anyway,*' Lucien moved on, '*I think that's enough for today, isn't it? I'm sure that all of you have quite a lot in your hands right about now. All that paperwork to fill in . . . all those body parts to collect. Shame on you, Grasshopper. You should've figured this one out. You should've saved those people. This one is on you, my friend.*'

Hunter looked down at the ground, unable to meet anyone's eyes.

'*You're losing your touch, Grasshopper.*'

The line went dead.

'What he said right at the end was absolute bullshit,' Captain Blake said, standing directly in front of Hunter. 'You know that, don't you? This barbarism isn't your fault.'

As Hunter returned his phone to his pocket, everyone noticed three well-dressed gentlemen with sleek haircuts clearing security at the perimeter line. One of them asked the police officer at the line a question and they all saw when the officer pointed to their group.

'I guess it's "explaining" time,' Hunter said.

'Fucking great,' West commented.

'Who the hell are they?' Garcia asked.

'National Security Agency, ATF, and probably Homeland Security as well,' Hunter replied. 'They will be with the Counter-Terrorism Unit. A bomb detonation in a public environment is automatically looked at as a terrorist act,' he explained. 'And every terrorist act essentially threatens the security of the nation.'

'Fantastic,' Garcia said. 'This Lucien guy has managed to get the LAPD, the FBI, the US Marshals Office and now the NSA, the ATF and Homeland Security involved in chasing him. All he needs now is to step on the DEA's toes and he'll have a full house.'

'The NSA and Homeland Security won't get involved in chasing a fugitive,' West said. 'That's our job; but the ATF might want a piece of this. Robert is right – there will be a lot of explaining to do and from now on . . .' West's head tilted in the direction of the three newcomers. 'Big Brother will certainly be keeping an eye on how we're doing.'

'Those three won't be the only ones we'll need to explain this to,' Captain Blake added, before indicating a black Lincoln Navigator that had just pulled up outside the perimeter line. 'Here comes the mayor, and I bet that the Chief of Police and the Governor of California will be right on his heels.' She shook her head at Hunter. 'This is not going to be fun.'

Fifty-Three

The rest of the evening and most of the next day was spent on completing paperwork and trying to explain to high-powered officials, politicians and government figures why a terrorist-like act had been perpetrated against the city of Los Angeles, claiming a yet unknown number of civilian lives in such a grotesque manner. Hunter, Garcia, Captain Blake, Holbrook and West jumped from tense meeting to tense meeting, as absolutely everyone demanded immediate answers.

To help with the explanations and to ease the burden on the manhunt task force, Adrian Kennedy himself contacted the President of the United States and the US Secretary of Defense, who is the head of the US Department of Defense – the department under which the National Security Agency operated. He also had to set up a meeting with the United States Secretary of Homeland Security.

It didn't take Kennedy long to convince all three of them that, despite the bombing, this was a manhunt for a very dangerous and disturbed fugitive. What had happened in LA had been an isolated incident and not a terrorist act against the United States of America. Lucien Folter had no political agenda like terrorists do. He was no Unabomber either. His intentions weren't to use indiscriminate violence to spread terror among the population.

'So what are his intentions?' the President had asked.

Kennedy told them about Lucien's past and about Lucien's murder encyclopedia, which inevitably got him a round of disbelieving looks and raised eyebrows, but Kennedy was smart and he played the whole thing down several notches. He told everyone that 'encyclopedia' was just the word that Lucien liked to use, but in truth, it was nothing more than just a few loose notes.

'Twelve pages in total,' he had lied.

As expected, the press had started reporting on the case just minutes after the explosion had occurred, and they had been true to form, effectively doing what they do best – speculating on the reasons behind the blast and sensationalizing the story as much as they possibly could; the more dramatic the headlines, the more papers they would sell, the more viewers they would get.

To try to clarify some of the myths created by those headlines – the bombing being the work of a terrorist cell that had been dormant in Los Angeles since the 9/11 attack in New York being the most outrageous of them all – the US Marshals Office, the FBI and the LAPD were forced to call a joint press conference the morning after the blast. In front of the cameras, Hunter, Captain Blake, Holbrook and West stood awkwardly, as they practically recited a statement that had been agreed upon by the heads of all three law-enforcement agencies. No lies were told. What they did do was use the best trick they had in their arsenal when it came to talking to the press: selective information. Reveal only what the public needed to now, nothing else. With that in mind, not a word was mentioned about Lucien's riddle and the race against time.

'I almost forgot,' West told Hunter, as they walked out of another bureaucratic meeting. He then retrieved a small square box from his pocket. 'Check this out.' He pulled open the box lid. Inside was a round metal object not bigger than a quarter.

'OK,' Hunter said. 'Nice, what is it?'

'This, my friend, is your tracking device. Remember we talked about it?'

Hunter looked at West sideways.

'I told you that we could come up with something good.' West placed the round object on the palm of his left hand and showed it to Hunter. 'You'll see that at the back of it, there's a small metal clip. I remember that you told me that when you and that FBI agent had to follow Lucien to his hideout in New Hampshire, he not only figured out that your shirt-button was a microphone device, but he also made you leave behind your belt, watch, coins, keys, wallet, everything, right?'

Hunter nodded.

'So here's the thing with this,' West said, winking at Hunter. 'You can clip it to anything you like, but my suggestion is to clip it to your pocket, but on the inside of your trousers. Let me show you.' Right there, on the landing just outside the Robbery Homicide Division detective floor, West undid his belt then his trousers to show Hunter.

Awkwardly, Hunter looked around to check if anyone else could see what was happening.

West reached inside his trousers and pulled out his pocket before indicating. 'You clip it right here, see? At the very tip of the pocket, on the inside, and the reason for that is very simple.' He zipped up his trousers and tightened his belt before going back to Hunter's tracking device. 'To activate it, all you need to do is press it firmly at the center.' West pressed it once. 'You'll feel it click under your finger and then vibrate very slightly for just one second, but it will make no clicking or vibrating sounds and it will not turn on any lights. What this really means is that this tracking device won't give itself away, but the thing to remember is that when this is turned on, it's turned on. You cannot turn it off, so don't do it by mistake.'

Hunter's eyebrows arched at West. 'So you just turned it on?'

'No. It's not activated yet,' West explained. 'Operations will activate them later today, once all of them have been handed out.' He nodded at Hunter. 'Yes, we're all getting one. Since our faces have all appeared on TV, we're not taking any chances with this Lucien individual anymore. Anyway,' West said, handing the tracking device to Hunter, 'the inside of the pocket is just my suggestion.'

'I'll do it in a more private location,' Hunter said, placing the small box inside his trouser pocket.

'Just try to remember to unclip it from your trousers before putting it to wash, all right?'

'I'll do my best,' Hunter said.

'Can I ask you something?' West asked as they began walking again.

'Sure,' Hunter replied.

'Last time you were on the phone to Lucien, just after the bombing, he doubted that you had actually deciphered his riddle in time. He told you that you were losing your touch and all that crap – but you did figure the riddle out in time.'

Hunter nodded once.

'So why didn't you tell him that?' West questioned. 'Why did you give him another victory, however small? I would've rubbed it in his face. I would've made him understand that his riddle wasn't as hard as he might've thought it was ... that he isn't as clever as he might think he is.'

'I see your point,' Hunter began. 'But it wouldn't have achieved anything.'

'Yes, it would have,' West came back. 'It would've shown Lucien that he's not the "King-Ding-a-Ling" he thinks he is. It would've slapped the smirk that I'm sure he had across his lips, right off his face.'

'In other words,' Hunter retorted, 'it would've angered him further.'

West paused and fixed Hunter with an uneasy stare.

'We have no idea what Lucien's next move will be,' Hunter clarified. 'He might've enjoyed the riddle game to such an extent that he would like to do it again, and by that I mean create a whole new riddle for his next murder – because we all know he'll kill again. We're not sure if he'll stick with mass murder, but we all know that if we don't get to him soon, he will kill again.'

'Yes, I know that,' West agreed.

'If Lucien decides to play the riddle card one more time and we just made him believe that his first riddle wasn't hard enough for us, what do you think he will do?'

West's only reply had been to shift his weight from one foot to the other.

'On the other hand,' Hunter carried on, 'if we make him believe that his riddle was way too elaborate, way too intelligent for us, we feed his ego. It's a way of admitting that he's superior to all of us, which will please, not anger him.'

'So you think that by pleasing this nutjob,' West said, 'he might, if he decides to use another riddle for his next murder, cut us a little break and make it easier?' West didn't look too convinced.

'He might,' Hunter replied. 'But that wasn't my main concern. My concern was in not angering Lucien any further, because that would've almost certainly have prompted him into an "I'll show you all what I'm capable of" frame of mind. Out of anger, he could've decided to start murdering a person every day, or worse even. But if we massage his ego, there's a chance that that will soothe him for a few days, so instead of going out killing, he might just lay low and savor his victory for a while.'

West had to admit that he hadn't thought of it that way.

Fifty-Four

The official 'estimated' number of victims was only released forty-eight hours after the explosion. Forensic FBI and LAPD agents rummaged the site for hours, searching for every bone and fragment of bone they could find, but what they were really looking for were skulls.

In a blast site, where there was a high possibility that bodies could've been dismembered or torn apart, but not pulverized, it was common practice to use 'skull count' as the official method to achieve an 'as-accurate-as-possible' number of victims.

At the end of forty-eight hours, the FBI forensics lab released an official statement indicating that the number of people who had lost their lives during the Whisky Athenaeum bombing rested at thirty.

The LAPD, the FBI and the US Marshals Office came under extreme scrutiny by the press, the Mayor of Los Angeles and the Governor of California, though the US Marshals Office was really the agency at the thick end of it all, since legally, apprehending a fugitive was solely the responsibility of that office.

'Can someone please explain to me – how the fuck is this possible?' The angry question came from Eric Lombardi, the Mayor of Los Angeles.

He was standing by the window inside Captain Blake's office. Besides him and Captain Blake, also present in the meeting were Hunter, Garcia, Special Agent Peter Holbrook, US Marshal Tyler West and Los Angeles Chief of Police Roger Davidson.

'It's been eight days since this psycho bombed a public establishment and killed thirty people *in my city*.' The mayor's naturally deep voice sounded particularly menacing when he got angry. 'Eight goddamn days, and you're telling me that no one has a clue how to get to him?' He waited, but no one said anything in reply. 'Correct me if I'm wrong here, but I was told that this Lucien Folter individual isn't a terrorist. He's a fugitive, who escaped from prison . . . how long ago?' His eyes moved to West.

'Fourteen days ago,' the US Marshal said.

'Exactly. This freakshow has been on the run for fourteen days.' The mayor's heated stare circled the room. 'Fourteen . . . but he's not only on the run from the US Marshals Office. No, sir. This guy has also got the freaking FBI and the goddamn LAPD chasing him around.'

It was the Chief of Police, Roger Davidson, who got the laser stare this time.

'But that isn't all,' the mayor carried on. 'Because unlike most fugitives, who the US Marshals Office has to first track down, this guy's whereabouts is known. In fact, it's been known for days, isn't that right? He's here.' He used both of his index fingers to point to the floor. 'In Los Angeles. He's been here all along. And the reason we know that, is because *he told us – four days before he blew up that bar*.'

West scratched an itch at the top of his head. He was about to say something, but the mayor wasn't finished yet.

'So here are the facts,' he continued. 'We know what this Lucien Folter looks like. We know where he is – I mean, which city he's hiding in – and we also know that he has no known accomplices and that he tends to work alone. To top it all off, this guy has been in prison.' Up came the mayor's right hand. 'Wait, let me rephrase that. He's been in solitary confinement for three and a half years, with absolutely no contact with the outside world. No visitors. No phone calls. No letters. Nothing. Nevertheless, he's able to break out of prison, kill seven people as a starter, travel across the country, in a commercial airline, I might add, get his hands on some military grade C-4, call up the authorities to play a charades game with them, blow up a bar and *no one* can find him? And I'm not talking about just any "no one". This "no one" includes the US Marshals Office, the FBI and the LAPD. We're not chasing a ghost here, ladies and gentlemen. We're chasing a man . . . *one* man. We have his picture, we know who he is and we know that he's here in this city, yet we don't have him in custody. So please allow me to ask again – can someone in this office please explain to me – how the fuck is this possible?'

'Because that's how Lucien has lived most of his life.' After several silent seconds, Hunter was the only one to offer a reply.

'Excuse me?' The mayor turned to face him.

'Before being arrested three and a half years ago,' Hunter said, 'Lucien Folter wasn't Lucien Folter.'

The mayor frowned at him. 'Are you going to start making sense any time soon, Detective, because I don't have all day?'

'Since his college days,' Hunter began, 'Lucien hasn't been Lucien.'

'Really?' the mayor questioned. 'So who has he been?'

'Whoever he wanted to be,' Hunter replied and immediately

moved on to an explanation. 'Lucien is no idiot – on the contrary, he's highly intelligent. Once he began his killing spree, which would take us back all the way to his college days, he knew full well that what he was doing was extremely risky for him.'

Hunter saw no reason in mentioning anything about the true reason behind Lucien's murders – his encyclopedia. All that that would do would be to instigate a whole new avalanche of questions.

'Lucien knew that one mistake,' Hunter continued, 'one slip-up was all it would take for him to have the police on his heels. So he devised a plan very early on. That plan was to never use his own identity. The way he executed that plan was by searching for victims who he could, at a later date, take over their identities, if he so needed to.'

'Sorry,' Mayor Lombardi paused Hunter. 'Can you run that by me again? Take over their identities if he so needed to? How?'

'Lucien began searching for male victims whose appearance resembled his,' Hunter explained. 'And that resemblance didn't even have to be very pronounced. All he really needed was the right height and the right body type – not too thin, not too fat, everything else he could adapt, including age.'

Lombardi and Davidson looked a little confused.

'Over the years,' Hunter clarified, 'Lucien became an expert in how to alter his appearance. He knows all there is to know about makeup, prosthetic foam, liquid latex, wigs ... you name it. He can make himself look whichever way he needs to look. Not only that, but he can also alter his voice, his accent, his intonation, his posture, his walk, his mannerisms ... everything. Lucien's plan consisted of him finding male victims who would be around his same height and have a similar body type. Once he did, he would befriend them, get to know everything he could about them, and then finally take them.'

'By "take them",' Mayor Lombardi said, 'I assume you mean kill them.'

'That's correct,' Hunter confirmed. 'Once they were dead, Lucien would take possession of every documentation he could find – passport, ID card, driver's license . . . anything. That person's name would then go onto a list of identities Lucien could take over if he ever needed to. And he would make himself look exactly like that person's document photograph.'

'Did you say that that person's name would go onto a list?' the mayor asked.

Hunter nodded. 'When Lucien was finally arrested three and a half years ago, we discovered a box of identity documents in one of his hideout locations. All of them male. All of them around the same height and body type as Lucien.' He paused so the mayor could process his words.

'He was giving himself a list of options?' Mayor Lombardi asked.

Another nod from Hunter. 'That's the kind of person Lucien is – a sort of modern-day urban survivalist, with absolutely no ties to anyone or anywhere, which allows him to get up and go at the drop of a hat and become whoever he wants to become – and he's exceptionally good at it.' Hunter indicated a photograph of Lucien that was sitting on Captain Blake's desk. 'Within a few hours of escaping, Lucien would already look nothing like that. Two weeks after his escape . . .' Hunter shrugged. 'He could be walking around this city as an old-age pensioner, or an African American, or even as a woman.'

It was Mayor Lombardi's turn to scratch a nervous itch at the back of his head.

'You've said a moment ago that we're not chasing a ghost here, sir,' Hunter said in a tired voice. 'You're right. Lucien isn't a ghost. He's more like a mutant, someone who can assume whatever identity he wants, whenever he wants. Add that to the fact that he has lived like a ghost for most of his life – no friends, no family, no home, no place or person who we can put under surveillance in the hope that he will one day soon turn up or contact them – and you have someone a hell of lot scarier than a ghost.' Hunter locked eyes with the Mayor. 'Are you starting to get the picture of why *no one* can find him?'

Fifty-Five

'That was tough,' Garcia said, as he and Hunter finally walked out of the meeting with Mayor Lombardi and Chief of Police Davidson.

Hunter agreed in silence.

It had been eight days since the bombing and with each passing day the task force grew more and more frustrated as they just didn't seem to find any way to progress with their manhunt. But what really terrified everyone was that with each passing day, they were just that little bit closer to a new phone call from Lucien, and they all knew that he wouldn't call just to say 'hello'.

'Are you OK?' Garcia asked. He could clearly see how tired his partner looked.

'Yes, I'm fine,' Hunter replied, not very convincingly.

'I could ask you if you're getting any sleep,' Garcia said. 'But that would be one stupid question, wouldn't it?'

This time there was no reply from Hunter.

'Anna is cooking bacalhoada tonight.' Garcia tried a different approach. 'Why don't you come over and have some dinner us?'

Bacalhoada was a Portuguese dish made with salty dry cod and vegetables. The dish was also very popular in Brazil and one of Garcia's favorites. He had been the one who, a few years back, had introduced Hunter to it. Hunter was converted with the first forkful.

'I don't have as much Scotch at home as you do,' Garcia added. 'But I do have some good stuff.'

Hunter checked his watch. It was coming up to half past six in the evening.

'I'd love to,' Hunter replied. 'But I've made plans to see Tracy tonight.'

Hunter's reply surprised and pleased Garcia at the same time. 'Oh, that's great. How's she doing?'

'She's fine, I guess. We've talked on the phone, but I haven't seen her since before the bombing.'

Garcia wasn't at all surprised, considering their workload.

'You know that you can always bring her along, right?' he said. 'Anna and I love her. She's good fun.'

'Thank you, I appreciate it, but Tracy managed to get a last-minute reservation for an *Alice in Wonderland* themed bar and restaurant in Alhambra.'

'Oh, I know the one. We've driven past it a few times.'

'Yes, it's called the Rabbit Hole,' Hunter said. 'To be truthful, I thought about canceling it, but it would've been the third dinner cancelation in eight days.'

'Yeah, no, don't do that, Robert,' Garcia urged him. 'Two things: one – you really do need a break from all of this.'

Hunter pulled a face at Garcia.

'Yeah, look, I know it's hard,' Garcia agreed. 'I know that you tend to take things a lot more personally than anyone. This case in particular, but you know just as well as I do that you need to disconnect, Robert, even if only for a few hours. If you don't, you'll melt down.'

The sideways look dissipated.

'And I know that if there's anyone that can make you disconnect,' Garcia continued, 'Tracy is that person.'

Hunter wouldn't disagree with that.

'What's number two?' he asked.

'Sorry?'

'You said that there were two things,' Hunter reminded him. 'Disconnecting is one, what's number two?'

'Number two is – don't cancel stuff on women, man.'

Hunter laughed.

'No, man.' There was no play in Garcia's tone. 'This is no joke. This is serious stuff. Canceling anything on a woman is already a very bad move. Canceling a dinner date on the day – especially when she's the one who made the booking – is a definite "hell, no". Trust me, Robert, that sort of thing pisses them off no end. No matter what they tell you. Yeah, they might hit you with something like ...' He put on his best feminine voice. '"It's OK. No problem at all. Of course I understand. Of course I don't mind. We can reschedule it for another day".' Garcia shook his head vigorously. 'Don't fall for that crap. They might tell you that everything is OK. They might even look like everything is OK, but inside her, the gates of hell will unlock.'

Hunter laughed again.

'Trust me on this one, Robert. I'm a married man. This is probably the only thing I'm more experienced at than you. Don't cancel the dinner date.'

'I won't,' Hunter said. 'I said that I thought about canceling, but decided not to.'

'Good move.' Garcia smiled at his partner. 'So, are you guys now officially dating?'

'I wouldn't say that,' Hunter replied. 'We see each other every now and then, that's all. It works for us.'

By choice, Hunter had always lived alone. No wife. No girlfriends. No kids. He'd never been married and the few relationships he'd had had never lasted longer than just a few months, sometimes a lot less. Not because he was a difficult person to be with – at least he didn't think so – but because of the pressures and the commitment that came with being the head of the LAPD's UVC Unit. Very few could really under-stand and cope with the demands of such a job – the late nights, the early mornings, the constant danger, having to cancel things right on the last minute – but worst of all was the kind of constant darkness his mind lived in. Dealing with evil on an almost daily basis really wasn't for everyone, but Hunter had to admit that Tracy Adams was different. She did understand the pressures and the commitment attached to Hunter's job better than anyone he'd ever met. Maybe it was because she was also a criminal psychologist, or maybe it was just down to her per-sonality and character, but none of it seemed to ever affect her.

'C'mon, man,' Garcia said, sensing a slight hesitation on Hunter's part. 'It's obvious to everyone that you really like her, and she likes you back just as much. I also know that you haven't seen anybody else since you met her. Just admit that you guys are now properly dating.'

'Yeah . . . we're not, though.'

'You are one stubborn man, do you know that?'

Hunter began walking in the direction of the stairs.

'There goes one stubborn man,' Garcia called out. 'One stubborn man, who now has a girlfriend.'

Without looking back, Hunter waved goodnight.

'Yeah . . . you've got a girlfriend.'

Fifty-Six

Tracy Adams was born in Albany, Oregon, the only child of simple, middle-class parents, George and Pamela Adams. George was a schoolteacher – English and history – and Pamela ran her own small clothes shop in Arbor Hill, an eclectic and historic neighborhood just north of downtown Albany.

Tracy was born in July, under the sign of Cancer, and according to her mother, who was a great believer in astrology, being a Cancerian was the main reason why Tracy was always so calm, unpredictable and highly intuitive. Tracy herself had never believed in any of it, but just to please her mother, probably the kindest soul Tracy had ever met, she would every day at breakfast time, just before leaving for school, read the horoscope column with Pamela.

Tracy's father, who came a very close second on her 'kindest souls' chart, also had never really cared for the silly horoscope predictions his wife would throw at him at least once a day, but just like his daughter, George would indulge Pamela just to see her happy.

In Tracy's eyes, George and Pamela Adams weren't just kind souls, but also the most understanding parents any kid could ever hope for.

As far back as Tracy could remember, she was never like most other girls. As a child, instead of playing with dolls or throwing pretend tea parties with other girls her age, her interest lay in reading books – especially old American classics like *The Scarlet Letter*, *The Great Gatsby*, *To Kill a Mockingbird*, *Little Women*, *Flowers for Algernon* and several others, but nothing fascinated her more than the stories and poetry crafted by the hands of Edgar Allan Poe – who coincidently, was also Hunter's favorite American poet.

Tracy loved the way Poe's words always seemed so dark, but at the same time so full of wisdom and sometimes even hope, but Tracy's fascination with the obscure didn't end with her preference in literature. It went way beyond that, touching most aspects of her life as she was growing up. She preferred darker clothes, gloomier songs, scarier movies, and as soon as she started wearing makeup, in her case at the age of twelve, the darker, gothic look came as an automatic no-brainer for her. But just as with so many young teenagers in America and all over the world, the real 'style-defining' factor for her had been music – or more precisely, a music genre.

It was at the age of fourteen that Tracy heard *Pretty Hate Machine* for the first time, the debut album from an Ohio-based band called Nine Inch Nails ... and an undying love affair was instantly generated. The band's dark music style, together with its unconventional rhythms and strong lyrics, spoke to her with almost the same intensity as Edgar Allan Poe's poetry. She fell in love with the album, the band, and the music genre – industrial rock. Soon she discovered other bands in the same style, such as Ministry, Skinny Puppy and others, which led her to also discover gothic rock and much older bands such as Bauhaus, The Sisters of Mercy, Fields of the Nephilim, and The Killing Joke.

Not surprisingly, Tracy's newfound love for her recently discovered music styles and the bands that defined those genres began to heavily influence the way she dressed, styled her hair, painted her nails, wore her makeup ... everything, and if she already felt different before, music also made her look different, which for a girl of fourteen, living in a mainstream society and attending a somewhat conservative school, would undoubtedly turn into a problem.

As soon as her look changed, the bullying began.

From night to day, Tracy was cast aside by all the other kids. She was called names, made fun of ... all the horrible things that bullying encompassed. Even girls she believed to be her best friends, didn't want anything to do with her anymore.

One spring afternoon, back when Tracy was a freshman, Pamela, who had taken the day off work because of a stomach bug, saw her daughter storm through the front door, say nothing to her, not even 'hello', which was completely unlike Tracy, and immediately go upstairs to her room. Mother-mode kicked in instantly and a couple of seconds later, Pamela was knocking at her daughter's door.

'Tracy, honey, what's the problem?' Pamela asked from just outside her room.

'Nothing, Mom,' Tracy replied without opening the door. 'Everything is fine.'

Pamela had promptly detected not only an angry but also a hurt quality to Tracy's tone of voice.

'Yes, that's ... obvious.'

'Seriously, Mom, everything will be fine.'

Despite asking, Pamela had a pretty good idea of what had

upset her daughter so much. She knew that not only kids, but people in general, could be very reluctant in accepting change, especially when they didn't understand it.

'OK, if you say so.' Pamela knew her daughter well, so she tried a different approach. 'Oh yes, honey, I wanted to ask you for a favor, if I could. Doesn't have to be now. Whenever you have some time, OK?'

Tracy said nothing in reply, so Pamela carried on.

'I love the way you did your hair and makeup this morning, honey. Can you show me how you did that? Maybe before the weekend, if you could? Your dad and I are going out for dinner on Saturday and I'd love to try something similar.'

Silence.

Pamela waited.

A couple of seconds later, Tracy opened her bedroom door. The way she looked at her mother asked a silent question.

Pamela saw no signs that Tracy had been crying, which was a good thing, but she sure looked angry.

'Seriously, honey,' Pamela said. 'The way you did your eye shadow, the blending . . . it all looks amazing. Where did you learn how to do that?'

Tracy held her mother's stare for a short while.

'You're only saying that because you're my mother.'

'No, I'm not.' Pamela looked a little hurt. 'Like you don't know me better than that, Tracy. I really do like it, and I wouldn't mind trying something similar come the weekend. Can you give me a few pointers?'

'Well, you're the only one who likes it then, Mom, everyone else thinks I am a whore.'

And there it was.

'I see,' Pamela said, her tone concerned.

'Even Debbie and Wendy think so,' Tracy said. They were her best friends.

'Did they say that?' Pamela asked, sincerely surprised.

'Not in so many words, Mom, but I could see it in the way they were looking at me. They don't even say "hi" to me anymore. If I try to approach them, they walk away. They've even moved seats in class so they wouldn't be sitting next to me. It's like I embarrass them.'

'Let me ask you something, darling,' Pamela said, her voice understanding. 'Do you like it? Your makeup, your hair, your clothes, your whole new style? Do you really like it, or are you just doing it because you want to look like the people in the bands you enjoy?'

Tracy didn't even need to think about it.

'I do, Mom. I really like it. I think it suits me. It suits my personality. It reflects the way I am inside. Yes, sure, the look is inspired by my favorite bands, but I really do think it suits me.'

'And do you think you're going to stick with it?' her mother asked. 'Or go back to the way you looked before, just because others don't approve of your new style?'

'No way. I'm sticking with it.' Tracy sounded one hundred percent sure. 'I'm sorry, but screw them if they don't like it. It's my look, not theirs.'

'So there's your answer, honey,' Pamela said, giving her daughter a proud smile. 'If you like it and you're comfortable with it, that's what matters, and I couldn't be more proud, because what you're doing is one of the hardest things for anyone to do out there, especially someone your age.'

'And what's that, Mom?'

'You are being you.'

Tracy frowned at her mother.

'Come, let's have a seat,' Pamela said, stepping into Tracy's bedroom and indicating her bed.

'Tracy,' Pamela said, taking her daughter's hand into hers as they sat down, 'one thing that you might not realize now, but I'm sure that you will in time, is that very few people on this God-given earth are who they really want to be, or do what they really want to do. The truth is: to be ourselves . . . to really be ourselves, it takes courage, confidence and a lot of character. A great number of people out there, and I really mean a *great number* of people, don't dress like they would really like to dress, or wear their hair the way they would really like to wear it, or their makeup, or anything. Most people do what is expected of them, not what they really want.'

'Expected?' Tracy asked.

Her mother nodded.

'By who?'

'By others,' Pamela replied. 'By their parents, by their friends, by their teachers, by their bosses, by society . . .' She shrugged and smiled at Tracy. 'I wasn't expecting to have to give you this pep talk until much later. Graduation day, perhaps, but nevertheless here we are – so let's do this.'

She adjusted herself into a more comfortable sitting position.

'Being an individual, a lot of the time, isn't as easy as it sounds,' Pamela explained. 'As we grow up, we all go through different phases in our lives, honey. Sometimes new movements are created, new music genres, new styles, new beliefs . . . something that speaks to us in such a different way that we want to be part of it, and not everyone will understand that. I was a hippie when I was younger, and so was your father.'

'No way!'

'It's true,' Pamela confirmed with a pleased smile. 'I'll find some pictures later to show you. But when I became part of the hippie movement, not only most of my so-called friends hated the way I looked and dressed, all of them leaving me for dead, but so did your grandparents. In fact, they hated it so much that they told me that if I wanted to look like a hippie, then I should also be prepared to live like a hippie and get out of their house.'

Tracy's eyes widened. She knew nothing of this.

'For real?' she asked. 'They told you to leave?'

'Uh-huh.'

'So what did you do?'

'I left. I packed a few things and I hit the road, and I did it because I was comfortable with the way I was back then. I liked the way I dressed. I liked the way I looked. I liked what I stood for back then and I loved the music. Everything was so . . . liberating. I was being me. I was being myself. And it felt good.'

'But you're not a hippie now,' Tracy said. 'So do you regret it? I mean, leaving Grandpa and Grandma's house, losing all your friends?'

'Not even for a second,' Pamela replied. 'Because I was being true to myself. I was doing what I wanted to do. I was living my life for myself, not for my parents, not for my friends . . . I was living my life *for myself*. But I remember thinking that apart from the way I looked, nothing had really changed. I was still the same person. Different hair, different makeup, different clothes, but I was still the same person. If that was all it took to make my so-called best friends decide to not be my friends anymore, then I don't think that there was much of a friendship there to start with anyway.' She smiled at her daughter. 'And it was because I left home that I met your father. I would've never met someone like your dad if I had stayed home.' Pamela paused and ran a hand through Tracy's hair. 'All I'm trying to say, honey, is that being yourself is the best thing you can do . . . always.'

That was not the last time Tracy heard those words. What she never knew then was that being herself would, just two weeks later, save her life.

Fifty-Seven

That morning, Tracy had walked to school, just like she did every weekday. To try to avoid some of the name-calling, she used to time her walk so she would get to school just seconds before the first-class bell rang, but still, avoiding all of it was almost impossible.

'Here comes the weirdo!' she heard someone say as she walked past a group of girls.

'You forgot your coffin, Morticia,' someone else called out, before they all ignited in laughter.

Tracy never let any of it really bother her, but that morning, as she made it through the school gates, she was stopped by Trevor Darnell, a very shy and quiet freshman, who always sat at the back of the class, ate lunch by himself and barely spoke to anyone.

'Hey,' he said, as Tracy was just about to get into the main school building. They had never properly spoken to each other before.

'Hey,' Tracy said back, giving Trevor a subtle nod.

Despite being only fifteen years old, Trevor Darnell was already six feet tall, which made him a giant next to Tracy, who at the time was five-foot-four.

'I like your new style,' Trevor said, his tone of voice subdued. 'I like what you've done with your hair and your makeup. Very cool.'

Tracy was genuinely surprised, not only by the compliment, but by the fact that Trevor was actually talking to her.

'Thank you,' she said. 'That's very nice of you to say. I really appreciate it.'

'I've seen you around,' Trevor continued. 'You didn't used to dress like this.'

Tracy didn't know how to reply.

'It suits you. It really does – the hair, the makeup, the clothes, all of it – but the best thing about your whole new look is that you're being yourself.'

Tracy frowned at those words. That was exactly what her mother had told her just a couple of weeks earlier.

'I like that.' Trevor added. 'I like that very much. Very few people around here have the guts to be themselves – to really be themselves, me included. I wish I had the courage to do the same as you, but my parents would never allow it.' He looked away for an instant before locking eyes with Tracy one more time. 'I've also noticed that your friends have sort of pushed you aside since you've changed your look.'

Tracy began to feel uncomfortable.

'Don't worry about that,' Trevor said. 'It's their loss. It really is.' There was a sincerity in his tone that Tracy wasn't expecting to hear. There was also an odd creepiness to it that made Tracy shiver in place.

At that exact moment, to Tracy's relief, the first-class bell rang.

'We'd better get going,' Tracy said. 'We're late.'

But as she tried to move past him, Trevor stepped to his side and blocked her way.

'Please don't,' he said.

Tracy looked back at him, confused.

'Please don't what?'

'Please don't go to class,' Trevor replied. 'Not today. You don't want to be in class today. Trust me.'

Tracy couldn't figure out what she saw right then inside Trevor's eyes, but she knew that she had never seen anything like it before.

'Go home,' Trevor practically begged her. 'Today, you really are too cool for school.'

Tracy didn't really know what to do. Her legs seemed to be paralyzed.

'And please don't ever change,' Trevor said. 'Don't ever stop being yourself, no matter what other people say . . . no matter what other people want. Be you. Always be you.'

With that, he turned and entered the school building, his heavy rucksack hanging from his left shoulder.

Tracy stood still for a short moment while a multitude of crazy thoughts began exploding inside her head, but one in particular led them all.

She felt her hands clam up, her heartbeat triple in speed and a knot tighten somewhere between her chest and her throat. The air around her became dense, almost impossible to breathe.

All of a sudden, and Tracy never really knew how she found the strength for it, she ran. She ran like the wind, but not back home. She entered the school building and took off down the corridor like a maniac; her destination – one of the seniors' first-period class, US History, a class her father taught.

George Adams was three quarters of the way through his class roll call when Tracy swung open the door to his classroom as if a hurricane had hit it, startling everyone, including her father.

'Tracy?' he said, tilting his head slightly forward so he could look over the rim of his reading glasses. 'Why aren't you in class, young—' That was when he noticed the look on her face. A look of pure fear. 'Tracy, what's wrong?'

As Tracy took in a breath, just before words could reach her lips, the first automatic-weapon shots rang out down the corridor.

Fifty-Eight

Lucien hadn't contacted Hunter in eight days, but that didn't mean that he'd been idle, on the contrary. The morning after the blast, Lucien was already busy organizing his next move – and this time he intended to do something very different.

Lucien hadn't liked the way he had felt after the bombing. Despite the atrocity being his way of saying a big 'fuck you' to Hunter, the FBI and the US Marshals Office, it was still categorized as murder and, as such, it fell into the realms of his research into understanding the emotions and the psychological effects that murder could have on the mind of an aggressor.

True to the way that he had always conducted his 'studies', once the murder act had been completed, Lucien would catalogue his feelings as soon as possible, preferably while they were still fresh in his mind – while the images still meant something to him. That evening, after calling Hunter after the explosion, Lucien went back to his hotel room. Once there, he returned to his notes, writing down every thought, every emotion, every memory related to the incident he could recall ... and what he found out completely surprised him. If Lucien pushed aside the ecstasy of personal victory over Hunter and the authorities, the way he felt immediately after the bombing displeased him to a level he wasn't expecting.

Lucien had been excited about the whole experience beforehand, he would not deny that; but on reflection, he had to put that excitement down to the feeling of accomplishment he felt once he had finished constructing his dirty bomb. Dealing with C-4 and building a bomb from scratch was something he had never done before, and for a first-timer he knew he had done an outstanding job. His calculations had been as precise as a mathematician's, and his delivery had been nothing less than perfect. But once he thought about the act itself – and Lucien had witnessed it all; he was standing across the road from the Whisky Athenaeum when he called the detonation cellphone – he felt no pride . . . no exhilaration . . . no soothing satisfaction.

Despite having been inside the target location just minutes before the explosion, despite memorizing as many faces as he possibly could, the feeling of elation that he usually experienced during and directly after a murder act never really hit him. It all felt too impersonal, too detached, too surreal.

That night Lucien wrote:

Watching that building blow up before igniting in flames didn't feel anything like I thought or expected it would. Let me be clear here, I knew that this would be like nothing I'd done before. For me, it was a different concept, a different approach – killing from a distance. It wouldn't feel the same, I knew that, but still I was hoping to get some sort of joy – a lesser version of the godlike feeling perhaps – but I got none of it.

From across the street, I pictured the bodies inside that bar being ripped apart by the blast's shockwave, sending body parts flying through the air like missiles, and showering the room with blood. I imagined how satisfying it would have felt to have witnessed their flesh being burned and torn from their bones by the velocity of the air displacement. It wasn't difficult. In my mind, I could clearly see those images because I could remember their faces ... all of them ... and it brought me no satisfaction. In the end, I felt ... cheated. I felt as if I had done all the prep work, all the research, but the murder itself had been committed by someone else.

Understand this – murder is a very personal act. It is perhaps the most personal of all human interactions. What electrifies the blood inside a killer's veins, what makes the heart of a killer beat faster and faster, is the direct contact with the victim and the God-divine connection it creates. Looking into the victim's eyes, sensing his/her fear, smelling it, savoring it, owning it ... there is nothing like it. It's a feeling so powerful that it changes you. It alters your perception, your brain, your being. Tonight, even though I have murdered more people at once than I have ever done before, I experienced none of that feeling. There was no shiver up and down my spine, no speeding heartbeat, no dilation of the pores or pupils, no goosebumps ... nothing.

The experience was valid from a research point of view, but to me this was a cowardly act, one that I'm ashamed of. One that I will not be doing again.

Despite his disappointment, Lucien wasn't one to dwell on the memory of any of his murders for longer than just a few hours, if that. By the time he closed his notebook, the bombing already felt like an alien act. By the next morning, it was nothing more than just some sad newspaper headline.

Fifty-Nine

Lucien usually took a break between murders, or – as he liked to call them – 'research topics'. In the past, those breaks had varied anywhere between thirty days and one whole year, during which time Lucien would decide on what his next 'topic' would be and in which state/city/town he would conduct his research. Once those points had been decided on, he would choose his victim – sometimes carefully, sometimes not – and gather as much information on that victim as he possibly could; but this time there would be no lengthy break in between murders. There was no need for it.

For the past three and a half years, Lucien had spent every minute of every day thinking about his revenge, thinking about what he would do once he got out. All the planning had already been done, all that was left for him to do was fill in the blanks on a few minor details and he would be ready to strike again – and ready he was.

On the morning after the bombing, Lucien had walked out of the run-down hotel where he'd been staying in Lynwood. His destination – a new hideout location that he had come across a couple of days earlier.

Usually, Lucien would've cleaned the room he had stayed in

to a biohazard-lab standard, leaving absolutely nothing behind, not even a fingerprint or a single hair strand, but this time there was no need for it. He didn't have to hide his identity.

Unlike before, when Lucien was unknown to the authorities and had never been considered a suspect in any murder investigation, he was now a fugitive. His identity wasn't a secret anymore. The police, the FBI and the US Marshals Office knew exactly who they were looking for, they just couldn't find him.

Lucien's new hideout was an abandoned and dilapidated building on the outskirts of Altadena – a tiny neighborhood fourteen miles north of downtown LA, located between Pasadena and the Angeles National Forest.

Several days ago, Lucien had spent hours navigating Google maps, looking for a suitable location for what he had in mind. He knew that he needed to find a new hideout site sooner rather than later, one where he could be alone and work undisturbed, one with no neighbors, where no one would witness his comings and goings, one where he could keep a victim captive if he so desired; and from the images he saw, the structure he'd found tucked away at the very end of a quiet non-residential road looked absolutely perfect.

The building, a disused storage warehouse, was flanked on one side by an empty plot of land and on the other by dense vegetation, leading up to the Angeles National Forest itself. The heavy iron-mesh fence that surrounded the property was still in place, but a couple of sections had been kicked in and breached, which would allow the structure to be accessed without great difficulty.

On the inside of the fence, grass and weed had sprung through the cracks and along the joints of the warped and uneven concrete slabs that made up the ground.

Being an ex-storage facility, there were very few windows, all of them small, glassless and high off the ground – too far for anyone to reach. Judging by how damaged they all were, Lucien guessed that kids had probably used them as target practice for rock-throwing.

The outside walls had once been white in color, but the strong Californian sun, aided by LA's famous downpours, had long ago damaged the paint, causing most of it to crack and peel off. Not that it mattered, anyway. Most of the building had been completely redecorated with graffiti, which funnily enough, also looked old and faded.

Lucien took note of the address and, a couple of days before the bombing, in the very early hours of the morning, he had decided to go check the property for himself.

The building, which was about thirty-five yards in length by twenty-five wide, had the look of an airplane hangar, with a metal Gambrel-style roof and enormous sliding front doors. The doors were rusty and heavy, but they were still on their rails, and despite the loud screeching noise, with a little 'stronger than normal' push they had worked just fine, and Lucien had encountered no real problems getting through them and into the property.

Outside, the sun had just begun cracking the night sky. Rays of light had slowly poured through the broken windows at the top, creating an interesting crisscross of light beams, populated by an eternity of moving dust particles that seemed almost alive.

The place smelled just like it looked – old and abandoned, with the added bonus of strong mold, dust, urine and stale sweat. It was an odor that would make most people gag, but Lucien had also picked up another smell. Something not so intrusive. Something a little more familiar. Something he couldn't quite identify.

For a moment, Lucien had stood by the front doors, adapting to the smells and allowing his eyes to slowly take in the surroundings.

Just like he had expected, the inside of the old storage hangar consisted mainly of a large open-plan area, easily capable of storing at least three monoplanes, but right at the back of the structure, on the left-hand side, a sizable section had been partitioned off into what looked to have been the facility's main office. That office had a second floor, accessible via an external spiral staircase on its right-hand side.

'Now, that could be very handy,' Lucien had said to himself.

Something else that Lucien had expected to find on the inside was a considerable amount of trash and debris. Well he did, but not nearly as much as he thought he would. Other than some broken glass from the windows at the top, Lucien had found several sheets of cardboard, a few dirty and soiled rags, used condoms, discarded syringes and a vast number of different-sized solid wood planks – some broken, some not. That was when it dawned on him. The familiar smell he was having trouble recognizing was sawdust and wood. That hangar-looking building had been a wood storage warehouse. Through the marks on the floor, Lucien was able to easily identify where the shelving units and the industrial table saws had once been.

At the back of the hangar, Lucien had had no problems getting into the old main office. In there, the gagging smell from outside gained a new, sour attribute before shifting up several gears, forcing Lucien to drag his shirt collar up to cover his nose and mouth. Though the trick had helped a little, it didn't manage to stop his eyes from watering.

'I'm going to have to do something about this smell,' he had told himself. 'Fully matured in here.'

The former office room was comfortably spacious, with large squared windows that faced the open-plan floor – all of them glassless. The owners had left behind a lot of their office furniture – two desks, six chairs, three different-sized filing cabinets and a large metal shelving unit that pretty much took up an entire wall. One of the desks and three of the chairs were damaged – not enough legs. One of the filing cabinets was missing a couple of drawers, but everything else seemed fine.

Upstairs, demountable composite partitions had been used to divide the large office space – identical to the one downstairs – into four different working cubicles. Some more furniture had also been left behind, together with two landline telephones, a large wall-mounted corkboard, a broken coffee machine, and two old Remington typewriters. The floorboards were a bit squeaky, but still very solid.

Back down on the main warehouse floor, Lucien had paused for a moment. He could barely believe that he had found such a perfect place and that as far as he could tell he wouldn't have to fight anyone for it.

In a large city like Los Angeles, abandoned structures, especially large ones like that disused storage warehouse, tended to attract their fair share of hobos and homeless people, but apart from the used condoms and discarded syringes, Lucien had seen no signs to indicate that the location was in constant use by vagrants.

'This is perfect,' he had said as he'd walked out of the large building and slid the doors shut behind him.

Lucien only needed the place for a couple of weeks, maybe less, just until he finalized his plan . . . his revenge. After that, he would disappear and no one would ever hear from him again.

Sixty

The old storage warehouse was indeed perfect for what Lucien had in mind; the only problem was that geographically it was a bitch to get to via public transport or on foot. Lucien needed a vehicle, one big enough to transport some material and a few pieces of machinery. Nothing excessively heavy. Nothing a regular-sized van couldn't carry, but he needed the vehicle immediately, he needed to pay for it in cash and he needed no questions asked – something that wasn't too hard to find in the City of Lost Angels.

On the morning after the bombing, Lucien spent about an hour sitting in an Internet café in Lynwood, browsing the web for a vehicle that met his needs. He found a few close by, made three different appointments, and ended up purchasing the second one he saw – a white 1998 Dodge Ram Van – not because it was in better condition than the other two, but because the owner, a very sweet seventy-six-year-old Hispanic lady who lived in Paramount, never asked to see an ID document and had offered to wash the van for Lucien if he decided to take it.

That had made Lucien laugh out loud and won him over.

'There's no need,' he told the lady. 'I'll take it just the way it is. I like it dirty.'

'Yeah, me too,' she replied, which made Lucien laugh even harder.

Lucien paid the lady, signed nothing, picked up the van keys and drove off a happy man.

On the way to his new hideout location, he stopped by a few shops to purchase the equipment and materials he would need to proceed with the last phase of his revenge plan. He could've gotten everything from one single store, but there was no need to risk raising eyebrows, especially on the morning after the bombing. Splitting the purchases between five different stores seemed like the most logical and safe thing to do.

Once he got to the abandoned warehouse, Lucien parked the van around the back, totally hidden from view, and went to work.

Topping his task list was: 'Get rid of that damn smell in the office enclosure'.

For that, Lucien had bought two gallons of strong antibac-terial floor cleaner, a couple of heavy-duty industrial brooms, a heavy-duty industrial mop, a pair of rubber rain boots, a few disposable mouth and nose masks, and thick rubber gloves.

After moving all the furniture out of the old office and onto the main warehouse floor, Lucien began scrubbing.

He had gone for a scented floor cleaner instead of regular thick bleach because all he really wanted to do was to get rid of that sickening sour smell. Thick bleach would simply substitute one stomach-churning odor for a headache-inducing one.

It took Lucien almost three hours to scrub clean both office floors, but once he was done, instead of the nostril-ripping smell that had brought tears to his eyes just a few days ago, a subtle and quite pleasant lime scent lingered in the air.

Next on Lucien's list was the remodeling of the entire office space. For that, he made use of the demountable composite partitions from upstairs, together with the large number of wood planks that had been left behind in the old warehouse. From the stores, Lucien had purchased a few different mechanical saws and three portable, fuel-run, high-powered generators, which made cutting the planks to size the easiest of all his jobs. After several long hours, the glassless windows had been boarded up, the door reinforced, and both office floors re-divided.

The third job on Lucien's list was by far the most complicated and laborious of them all. A task that in order to compensate for the lack of extra hands – ideally a two-man job – Lucien had had to improvise and adapt. It took him almost two days to finish it, but at the end of it all, he finally achieved the result he wanted.

With his hideout task list completed at last, Lucien was free to begin what most criminal psychologists called the Murder Phase, thought Lucien himself preferred to call it the Ecstasy Phase.

According to criminal psychologist Joel Norris, who conducted a lengthy study of convicted brutal murderers back in 1988, there were seven different stages a serial killer went through in his/her mind – the Aura Phase, the Trolling Phase (victim and location), the Wooing Phase, the Capture Phase, the Murder Phase, the Totem Phase and the Depression Phase.

Lucien's own 'research' contradicted Norris's study by arguing that in a killer's mind some of those phases played very differently than how Norris had described them, or even not at all. In Lucien's case, the Murder Phase had always filled him with exhilaration, it made his heart beat faster, it filled his veins with adrenaline and his brain with endorphin, dopamine and serotonin. It was like a magical drug rush. From the killer's point of view, Lucien's 'research' renamed that particular stage the Ecstasy Phase, and this time, for what Lucien had in mind, he was anticipating the Ecstasy Phase to fill him with more pleasure than ever before.

If Hunter had thought that the bombing of a public place and the death of thirty innocent people had been a monstrous act, then what Lucien had in store for him would feel like Satan himself had come alive.

Sixty-One

Joel Norris's study into the stages of a serial killer had identified seven phases, but through his own research Lucien
had found out that in many instances, an extra stage would
manifest itself – the Stalking Phase. It could either appear
by itself, creating eight stages in total instead of seven, or be
interchangeable with Norris's third stage – the Wooing Phase.

According to Norris, a large number of serial killers would
move from the Trolling Phase – where the killer chooses a
victim – into the Wooing Phase – where the killer tries to win
the victim's confidence before luring him/her into a trap. Norris
did rightly add that not every serial killer would go into the
Wooing Phase, only the more organized and confident ones,
which was also true for Lucien's Stalking Phase. Some serial
killers – the more organized ones, Lucien included – tended
to, right after choosing his/her victim, spend a period of time
observing their target. The advantage that that gave them
was twofold. One: in the cases where the killer would move
from the Stalking Phase into the Wooing Phase, it could give
them a better idea as to how to gain the victim's confidence
before luring them into a trap. Two: in the cases where the
killer substituted the Wooing Phase for the Stalking Phase,

it would give the killer a better understanding of the victim's movements and habits throughout his/her day, which would help the killer make an informed decision as to when would be the optimum time to move into the Capture Phase – the taking of the victim. Did the victim live alone? If not, was the victim ever alone at home during a portion of the day or night? Did the victim have the habit of going out for a run, or a bike ride, for instance, at a specific time of the day or night . . . anything that could reduce the risk of the killer being spotted as he/she moved into the next phase. Lucien, whenever possible, would always embark on the Stalking Phase before taking a victim. This time it would be no different.

He had already decided who his next victim would be, and now that the bombing was out of the way and he had found a suitable hideout location, he could finally move on to his Stalking Phase.

Lucien spent the next five days tailing his chosen victim for at least eighteen hours a day. He had taken tens of photographs and noted down absolutely everything he could about the victim's daily routine. By the third day, Lucien had already identified several repeating patterns. By the fifth day, he knew exactly how he would move onto the Capture Phase.

Sixty-Two

After five long days of stalking his victim, Lucien had decided that the best time to make his move would be on a weekday, anytime between one and six in the afternoon. He had discovered that during those hours, the victim would usually be alone in her home; while the neighboring houses would be practically empty, which severely reduced the risk of him being spotted. His approach plan was as simple as they came – he would knock on her door.

The victim's house was located halfway down a short and somewhat remote street in Downey, thirteen miles southeast of downtown Los Angeles and known for being the birthplace of the Apollo Space Program. The house itself was modest when compared to the other properties on the street – single-story, driveway but no car garage, no swimming pool, small backyard and, best of all, no protective fence or alarm. The victim also had the habit of leaving her bedroom window unlocked during the day, sometimes even at night. If Lucien had decided to break into the victim's house instead of using the visitor's approach, he would have no problems doing so, but when he saw the 'for sale' sign three properties away on the same road, a plot very quickly took shape inside his head.

With an approach plan formulated, all that was left for Lucien to do was to pick the best day to execute. He chose Monday, eight days after the bombing.

That morning, Lucien spent some time developing a whole new persona, someone who would match the particular kind of resident a neighborhood such as Downey would attract – a well-dressed, well-spoken, upper-middle-class, successful, career-orientated individual. As a profession, Lucien decided that this time he would pose as an attorney. The name, James Mitchell, he borrowed from one of his old professors back at Stanford University. His back-story was uncomplicated – born and raised in Manhattan, New York. After leaving high school, he was accepted into Columbia University, where he graduated in the top five percent of his class. He had spent the last fifteen years working for the same law firm in New York City – Latham & Watkins LLP. After his divorce, the Big Apple quickly turned into Sour Apple and he began looking for opportunities elsewhere. Along came a very hard-to-refuse offer from Gibson, Dunn & Crutcher LLP, one of the top law firms in the country, whose headquarters was located in the famous Wells Fargo Center in downtown LA.

Lucien was certain that he wouldn't have to go into any of those details with his victim, but they helped him prepare for the role and better visualize the character he needed to be. They also added to the overall excitement of the Capture Phase.

Just like he'd done countless times before, Lucien stood in front of a mirror, trying different looks, different postures, different mannerisms ... gluing everything together until he had come up with the perfect character for the job. This time, it took him just over an hour to get there.

Lucien's accent was neutral, typical New Yorker, but he

spoke eloquently, as a Columbia Law honors graduate would. His tone of voice was calm, soft, but at the same time confident. For appearance, Lucien went with what he considered the 'average lawyer' look – short, dark brown hair, light brown eyes, a trendy moustache, hooked nose, pointy chin and thin-framed glasses that gave him a slightly intellectual look. For the eyes, Lucien once again used contact lenses. The nose and chin were expertly altered using prosthetic foam. The moustache didn't quite fit the original image Lucien had in mind, but he took inspiration from his memory of the real James Mitchell, professor of Cognitive Neuroscience at Stanford University.

Once Lucien was finally done, he slowly checked himself in the mirror – left profile, right profile, straight ahead, head up, head down, and mouth wide open. There were no flaws, no cracks in his makeup. All that was missing was the right attire and the look would be completed, and Lucien had just the thing.

While tailing his victim around town, he had seen a couple of different outfits in the window of a second-hand shop that he was sure would come in handy sooner or later; best of all, they fitted him perfectly. One of those outfits was a light-blue, double-breasted suit with a dark bowtie. He matched it with a white shirt and black shoes before checking himself in the mirror one last time.

Lucien had vanished. Staring back at him was James Mitchell, attorney at law for Gibson, Dunn & Crutcher LLP.

Sixty-Three

The late morning sky above Los Angeles was crisscrossed with isolated, thin white clouds that served to enhance its pure blue. The temperature at 11:00 a.m. stood at eighteen degrees Celsius, but the forecast predicted that the day would get warmer as it progressed, with the possibility of it reaching twenty-three degrees by three o'clock.

Lucien – or rather, James Mitchell – left his hideout by the Angeles National Forest at 12:47 p.m. On a Monday afternoon, an uninterrupted drive from Altadena to Downey would take him around forty to forty-five minutes, but he needed to make a quick stop before his final destination.

The small, family-run bakery was located next door to a Chinese restaurant, at a neighborhood center in Alhambra, just south of Pasadena. James Mitchell pulled up outside, entered the shop and purchased a box of three handmade artisan cupcakes. Thirty-eight minutes later, he was parking his van in front of a church in Downey, a couple of streets away from his target's house.

As he exited his vehicle and locked its door, *Mitchell* took a moment to contemplate the modest place of worship before him. On the brick wall, high above the wide entrance doors, was a white and gold effigy of a crucified Christ. *Mitchell* looked up at it and smiled.

'How're you doing up there?' he asked the effigy. 'Comfortable?'

He waited a second, as if he was truly expecting some sort of reply.

'So,' he carried on with his one-sided conversation. 'If you were real, you would stop me right now, wouldn't you? Send a lightning bolt to strike me dead or something, because since you're supposed to know all, it stands to reason that you would know damn well what I'm about to do . . . and it will be messy, that I can promise you.' *Mitchell* shrugged carelessly. 'But you're not going to do anything about it, are you? No lightning bolt is coming down from the skies to strike me dead, or anything like it, is it?'

Once again he waited a moment, but this time *Mitchell*'s eyes moved to the blue sky, as if searching for something.

'Yep, no lightning bolt.' He chuckled. 'Is that because you're a lie and you've never existed, or is it because you're just like me – a sadistic fucker – who likes to watch me doing what I do, because you like to watch them suffer. Is that the deal with you? You allow people like me to exist because you like to watch me hurt them – you like to watch them suffer?'

He waited briefly for another moment.

'Well, if that is the deal, then by all means just keep watching, because you will like what's coming next.'

From behind the church building, a Hispanic-looking man appeared, pushing a wheelbarrow filled with turf. As he got to the gates, he took off his hat and wiped the sweat from his forehead. His stare crossed *Mitchell*'s and he greeted him with a nod.

Mitchell returned the gesture, adjusted his bowtie, winked up at the effigy and calmly began making his way toward his target's house.

Sixty-Four

It was coming up to two in the afternoon when *James Mitchell* finally paused before the blue-fronted, single-story house two streets away from where he had parked his van. The thin white clouds that had decorated the sky during the morning had all vanished, leaving behind a clean, unperturbed bright blue sheet high above Los Angeles.

'It's a beautiful day to die,' *Mitchell* said as he adjusted his glasses and checked up and down the street. Everything looked absolutely still – no kids playing anywhere, no car movement, no one looking out their windows, no one tending to their front garden, and no passers-by.

Cupcake box in hand, *Mitchell* walked up the cobbled pathway that led to the house's front door. Once he got there, he drew in a deep breath, dusted his suit jacket with his left hand and rang the doorbell. A few seconds later, he heard footsteps tentatively approaching the door.

Mitchell straightened his posture.

The door's peephole darkened for a moment before he heard the sound of the security chain being slid onto its latch and the door being unlocked. It was then pulled back the length of the chain and half a woman's face appeared at the gap. She was about five inches shorter than *Mitchell*. Her striking green eyes, which sat behind black-framed glasses that perfectly suited her heart-shaped face, quickly studied the man standing there.

'Hello, can I help you?' Her voice was soft and comforting – the kind of voice that should belong to a documentary narrator.

From inside, *Mitchell* picked up the subtle scent of lilies and vanilla, mixed up with freshly brewed coffee.

'Oh, hello there, ma'am,' *Mitchell* said. His tone was composed and cordial. 'I'm terribly sorry to disturb you this afternoon. I actually just wanted to say "hello" and introduce myself. My name is Mitchell, James Mitchell, and I'm your new neighbor.' He paused while his eyebrows lifted. 'Well, three houses over, I mean. Number fifteen.'

'Oh! Really?' the woman said, truly surprised. Instinctively her eyes darted to her left, in the direction of house number fifteen. 'That was a very quick sale. Joanna and Albert only moved out about a month ago.'

'Oh!' *Mitchell* said in reply, injecting a very convincing amount of surprise into his tone. 'I didn't know that, but yes, you're right. It was indeed a very speedy deal. I fell in love with the house on my first viewing, which was fantastic for me because I didn't have much time to shop around, so I straight away offered the asking price and my offer was accepted the same day.' *Mitchell* smiled at the woman. 'I'm an attorney, you see? So ... perks of the job, I was able to get all the paperwork moving a lot faster than normal and the contract was finally signed two days ago.'

'Wow, that *was* quick,' the woman agreed. 'I bet Joanna is delighted. She was quite worried that it would take them a while to find a buyer. Apparently, at the moment, the market isn't as strong as it used to be.'

This was going much better than *Mitchell* had anticipated. The woman was engaging in conversation out of her own free will. *Mitchell* played along.

'That's very true, ma'am,' he confirmed. 'And to be honest, I was also quite worried that it would take me a while to find a place I liked. I'm moving over from New York, and since I didn't have that much time to look around – two, maybe three days on each trip – I did think that I would have to settle for something that wasn't quite what I wanted, just for the time being, but I got lucky. The house is absolutely beautiful and just what I was looking for.' *Mitchell* looked down at the box of cupcakes he was holding. It was time to move on to step two. 'By the way, these are for you.' With a smile, he offered the woman the box.

'Oh!' Surprise dotted her face for the second time. 'Hold on a second.'

She quickly undid the security chain before pulling the door fully open.

Her features were delicate, with a youthful plumpness in her cheeks that only added to her attractiveness. Her red hair was long, falling in waves to her shoulders. She wore a light blue dress with a row of fabric-covered buttons that stretched from between her breasts all the way down to her navel. A silver heart-shaped pendant hung from a matching chain around her neck.

'It's just a small gift to introduce myself,' *Mitchell* added.

Returning the smile, the woman took the box and her eyes moved to the man's face. 'That's so kind of you. Thank you so much. I really appreciate it.'

Right then, *Mitchell* knew that he had won the 'trust' battle. The initial apprehension that had surrounded the woman as she first opened her door was all but gone. All he had to do now was wait for her to invite him in, and he had no doubt that that would happen soon enough.

'It's a pleasure,' he replied. 'But as you can see, I didn't bake them myself.' A new, shy smile. 'I'm trying to get my new neighbors to like me, not hate me for the rest of their lives. I'm a terrible cook,' he admitted. 'I'm even able to mess up micro-wavable popcorn.'

The woman laughed. 'It can't be that bad.'

'Oh, it is. Trust me. I'm hopeless in the kitchen.'

'You're not married?'

Mitchell's face contorted slightly. 'Once upon a time. That's actually one of the reasons for the cross-country move.'

'Oh, I'm so sorry. I didn't mean to pry.'

'Oh no, please don't be,' *Mitchell* said, trying to sound positive. 'It was for the best. That much I'm very sure of, plus that's not the only reason for the move. I was offered a dream position at the headquarters of Gibson, Dunn & Crutcher, in downtown LA.'

Third serving of surprise. 'Oh! They're one of the big boys, aren't they?'

Mitchell nodded, offering the woman an animated smile. 'Yes, they are one of the really big boys.'

'So I'd say that congratulations are in order.'

Mitchell gave the woman a gentle head bow. 'Thank you very much.'

The woman's eyes moved to the box of cupcakes she had been given and she quickly shook her head in disapproval. 'Oh Jesus, I'm so sorry. Where are my manners? Would you like to come in? I've just finished making some coffee and it would go perfectly with these.' She nodded at the cupcakes.

He shoots. He scores.

Mitchell hesitated for a moment. 'Are you sure? I really wouldn't like to impose.'

'Of course I'm sure,' the woman replied with confidence. 'Please, do come in. I insist.'

'In that case, I accept your invitation with great pleasure.'

Mitchell followed the woman into her house. She never noticed the sneaky smile on his lips as she closed the door behind them.

Sixty-Five

From the front door, the woman led *Mitchell* straight into an ample living room where the curtains had all been drawn, keeping the afternoon sun down to a filtered shadowy glow. It was a beautifully decorated space, with gleaming hardwood floors and stunning antique furniture that included a gorgeous oxblood leather Victorian suite – two armchairs and a three-seater lounger – an Edwardian bookcase, an Ellenborough coffee table and a six-seater dining table. The walls were all adorned with framed bucolic and still-nature oil paintings in a variety of sizes, but the room's main feature was unquestionably the towering stone and black-granite fireplace on its north wall.

'Wow,' *Mitchell* said as he followed the woman past the dining table and onto the Chesterfield set. 'This is a beautiful room.'

'Thank you so much,' she said, indicating one of the armchairs. 'You really are very kind.'

While *Mitchell* took a seat, the woman stood.

'No, I'm serious,' he replied, his tone as sincere as it could be. 'I'm not saying it just to be courteous. It's exquisitely decorated. Very pleasant, and that fireplace is simply stunning.'

The woman smiled. 'That is indisputably the main reason why I chose this house.'

'I can certainly see why.'

The woman placed the box of cupcakes on the coffee table in front of *Mitchell*.

'So,' she asked. 'How do you take your coffee?'

'Black, please. No sugar. No milk.'

'That's easy.' She smiled. 'I'll be right back.'

Mitchell watched as the woman exited the room and disappeared into the kitchen. Once she was gone, his eyes moved to the picture frames on the first shelf of the bookcase. They were all of her together with members of her family, or at least that was what *Mitchell* assumed. She seemed happy in all of them and there was no denying that the woman had a charming, disarming smile.

Less than a minute later, the woman re-entered the living room, bringing with her a wooden tray containing a pot of coffee, two mugs, two side plates, two dessert forks and a small knife.

'Would you like some help?' *Mitchell* asked, getting to his feet.

'No, no. It's all under control. Thank you.'

The woman sat the tray down on the coffee table, next to the cupcake box.

As *Mitchell* sat back down, the woman poured coffee into both mugs before handing him one.

'I also take mine black,' she said.

'It helps us appreciate the true flavor of coffee,' *Mitchell* commented. 'Or so they say. I'm not really a connoisseur.' He had a tiny sip and felt the hot liquid burning the roof of his mouth. Funnily enough, *Mitchell* welcomed the pain. 'In saying that,' he added, 'this is very nice.'

'Colombian,' the woman explained. 'Some sort of special brew, I was told. Probably just a marketing ploy, but it really is nicer than your normal supermarket stuff.'

Mitchell nodded and had another small sip.

'Shall we try these?' the woman asked, reaching for the box of cupcakes and pulling open its lid. 'Which one would you like?'

'Oh no, none for me, thank you.'

'Oh, c'mon,' she insisted. 'Let's at least share one . . . please?'

'OK.' *Mitchell* gave in. 'Let's share one.'

'Great! So which one shall we go for?'

Mitchell gave the woman a subtle shrug. 'The blue one?'

'Blue one it is.' The woman took it out of the box, placed it on one of the side plates and sliced it in half. After moving one of the halves to the other side plate, she offered it to *Mitchell*.

Mitchell put down his mug and took the plate. They both had a forkful.

'Wow,' the woman said, nodding approvingly. 'This is very nice. Thank you so much again.'

Mitchell had to agree. That really was one of the best-tasting cupcakes he had ever had.

He washed it down with another sip of his coffee before allowing his attention to move to the bookcase directly behind the woman.

'That's quite a collection of books you have there.'

'Reading has always been a passion of mine,' she admitted.

'Mine too. Do you mind if I take a look?'

'By all means. Feel free.'

Mitchell put down his plate, got to his feet, placed his hands inside his trouser pockets and walked over to the bookcase. The shelves were packed with American and international classics, as well as a vast number of books on psychology and, oddly enough, criminal psychology, which brought a smile to *Mitchell*'s lips. As he turned to look at the next section of books, he was careful to position himself a little sideways, so that through the corner of his right eye he could still see what the woman was doing.

Her stare did follow him to the bookcase, but that lasted only a few seconds before it reverted back to her side plate and the last of her cupcake.

The man standing by the bookcase closed his eyes for an instant, searching for the darkness inside of him. It took him only a split second to find it.

All of a sudden, *James Mitchell*, attorney at law, vanished from the room. He didn't have the guts or the knowledge to do what needed to be done ... but Lucien did, and he was back. From his left pocket, he quickly retrieved a heavy-duty, see-through plastic bag. From his right, a double-loop zip tie.

As the woman lifted her hand to bring her fork back into her mouth, Lucien stepped forward and in one lightning-fast move, wrapped the plastic bag over the whole of her head and immediately pulled it back as tightly as he could, promptly ceasing her oxygen intake.

Total panic took over instantly. Her plate fell to the floor, crashing into several pieces as it came into contact with the wood surface. Her fork hit her foot and disappeared under the sofa. Her desperate hands, guided by raw fear, automatically shot up toward her face, as the most animalistic of all human reactions took over her entire being – the fight for survival. Impulse superseded thought – whatever it took to stay alive. But Lucien was already waiting for that precise reaction.

That wasn't the first time that he had used the plastic-bag approach and understandably, due to sheer panic, every victim's reaction was always the same – reach for the air obstruction; try to get rid of it.

Knowing that, Lucien had used only his left hand to hold the plastic bag in place. His grip was similar to that of a cowboy pulling back on the reins of a horse.

As the woman tried to grasp the bag, Lucien's right hand met hers in mid-movement. He grabbed her by the wrist in such an expert way that as he did, he slid her hand through one of the zip-tie loops before swinging her entire arm around, pulling it toward him and consequently around the back of the armchair she was sitting on.

The twisting of her right arm seemed to momentarily send her left one into complete confusion and instead of reaching for the plastic bag, it followed the pain that had suddenly exploded in her right shoulder.

With that, her panic intensified and her legs kicked out in total terror. Her feet planted firmly against the floor and she tried to pull herself up, but the position Lucien had placed her arm around the back of the armchair made it extremely awkward and severely painful for her to stand up. Her body slumped back down onto her seat.

The woman began desperately coughing against the plastic bag, filling it with foaming spit and misting its inside. Her nose began running and her eyes blinked urgently as she shook her head from side to side in an attempt to free herself. Her left hand finally decided to get back in the game. It let go of her right shoulder and immediately reached once again for the plastic bag – but once again, Lucien was waiting for it. His left hand let go of the plastic bag and in another flash move, grabbed hold of her left wrist, pulling it around the back of the armchair, just like he had done with her right arm. As both arms met behind the chair's backrest, Lucien hooked the second zip-tie loop over her left hand and pulled it tight.

Game over.

Sixty-Six

Lucien had a profound understanding of the human brain, its physiology and how it reacted when it was faced with the greatest of all fears – the fear of death. He knew which hormones the brain would produce and the sort of neurological impulses it would send to the rest of the body as it realized that life was about to be extinguished.

With most people, except for those who had been specifically trained for those types of situations, all logical thought ceased to exist, substituted by nothing more than simple electrical impulses. For that reason, human reactions became basic and very predictable. For example: Lucien knew that since the woman's brain had sensed the imminent threat of death and recognized its vehicle as 'lack of oxygen', it would immediately force the stem (the part of the brain at the back of the neck that controls basic functions, like breathing and being awake) to produce an outpour of two basic stress hormones – norepinephrine and cortisol. It would also send a 'basic panic' electrical impulse to the body's respiratory system, telling it to obtain more air in whichever way possible. The body's first instinct, guided by that 'panic' impulse and fueled by the stress hormones, would be to try to take deeper breaths to obtain more oxygen, which would of course fail, due to the plastic bag obstruction.

In the mathematics of survival, less oxygen equaled increased panic. With that, the woman's brain would then increase the outpour of stress hormones and send an even more urgent electrical signal out, which would force her heart to beat faster and her diaphragm to contract more rapidly. Deeper breaths would instantly become shorter and infinitely more desperate, but since the obstruction was still in place, they would bring no better results and with that, her panic would turn blind.

What that meant was that her oxygen-starved brain would begin to lose track even of its panic impulses, and that was why Lucien knew that he could let go of the plastic bag for a moment – while he secured both of her arms behind the armchair – without losing his power over her. It would take her brain and her body several seconds to finally realize that the obstruction hadn't been removed, but it had been greatly relaxed against her nose and mouth, allowing her lungs to take in a lot more oxygen.

With her arms firmly secured and immobilized, Lucien rounded the armchair and stood before the woman.

Her head was still flinging from side to side, which served to loosen the bag around her head even more. Air quickly found its way back into her lungs, but that did not lessen her panic.

'Breathe,' Lucien ordered her in a firm voice.

The plastic bag obstruction, together with fear and blind panic, kept her from hearing him.

Lucien reached for the plastic bag and pulled it from her head.

'Breathe,' he ordered again.

Her brain finally realized that the obstruction was gone.

'Breathe.'

Her short, desperate breaths at last became deeper and a lot steadier.

'That's it, nice and slowly ... in through your nose ...' Lucien took a deep breath as an example while motioning with his hands. '... And out through your mouth. You know how to do it.'

The woman complied. Her wide, confused and terrified eyes looked up at him. No matter how much her brain tried to, it just couldn't understand what was happening.

'I'm sure that right now you would like an explanation, wouldn't you?' Lucien asked.

The woman was so petrified, she couldn't reply. She couldn't even nod. All she was able to do at that moment was breathe, her chest rising and falling in a rapid and very odd rhythm.

'But of course you do.' Lucien answered his own question, paused, then began his explanation. 'What's happening to you right now is very simple. As soon as I blocked your oxygen intake' – he lifted his right hand, showing her the plastic bag – 'your brain sensed danger, the worst kind of danger there is: "threat to life". With that, a collection of neurons in your brain's stem immediately began producing norepinephrine and cortisol – two fear hormones. Those two hormones together are commonly known as "adrenaline". These brain neurons I'm talking about have long fibers, known as axons, and they extend their tentacles throughout the brain, releasing adrenaline everywhere and all at once.'

The fear in the woman's eyes was shrouded with even more confusion.

What is this psycho doing, giving me a biology lesson?

Lucien noticed the doubt in her eyes, but carried on nonetheless. He liked explaining either what he was about to do to his victims, or what was happening to them physically and psychologically. It inevitably increased their fear, and increased fear heightened his satisfaction.

'What adrenaline really does is – it gets in the space between one neuron and the next, called synapse. It then grabs the next neuron and asks for help. That neuron will ask the next neuron for help, which in turn will ask the next one and so on. So basically, adrenaline is a chemical messenger, alerting the brain of a present and imminent danger. The brain then sends the rest of the body nerve signals, which in a flash reach pace-maker cells within the heart walls, making it pump faster and getting the body ready for action. The adrenal glands, above your kidneys, are then triggered, also releasing adrenaline, but this time in much, much greater quantities and directly into your bloodstream. When adrenaline reaches your lungs, it attaches itself to cell receptors. Its function there is to expand the airways to provide more oxygen to power your muscles and brain, so you can either fight or run, and that was where the big problem was.'

The woman's breathing had almost come back to normal.

'Even though your airways had expanded,' Lucien said, 'they were unable to take in any more oxygen. In fact, they were taking in less, because I had blocked your oxygen pathways. What that did was confuse your brain, because it expected an increased amount of oxygen, but instead it got less. Your brain then realized that it was losing the battle for life.'

That sentence sent a new dagger of fear straight into the woman's heart.

Lucien regarded the woman. 'But what am I doing, giving you all this worthless explanation? You already know all this, don't you?'

The woman was still unable to reply, her terrified brain trying to make sense of the absurd scenario she was in.

'At least you should, taking into account the large number of psychology volumes on your bookcase. But anyway, this isn't the explanation you're looking for, is it? What you really want to know is – why am I here? Why am I doing this to you?'

Crashing through her fear, the woman was finally able to nod. She did it once very tentatively.

'Well,' Lucien replied, bending forward to whisper into her ear. 'I'm here for one reason and one reason only. The sweetest of them all . . . revenge.'

Her brow furrowed.

'Yes, I know,' Lucien said. 'And I don't blame you. You've got every right to be confused, because the truth is: my revenge has nothing to do with you, really. You're just an unfortunate by-product. Nevertheless . . . a killer's got to do what a killer's got to do, don't you agree?'

Tears welled up in the woman's eyes, but before panic could take over her body again, Lucien slapped her across the face so hard her head jolted back and slammed against the armchair's backrest, disorienting her completely. From her upper lip, blood flew up in the air. A few drops landed on Lucien's forehead and right cheek. While she screamed in pain and horror, Lucien used his left index finger to slowly collect the blood, before bringing it to his lips. Like a snake's tongue, his wiggled out of his mouth, its tip licking his finger clean.

'Your blood tastes sweet,' he announced, before grabbing both of her feet and zip-tying them together. He then turned his head to look in the direction of the kitchen.

'I bet that you have some incredible knives in there, don't you? Maybe even a meat cleaver? Those are my favorites.'

The woman looked back at Lucien and he could see her pupils dilating from fear. From his inside pocket, he retrieved a long, see-through plastic coverall.

'This is the only suit I have,' he explained as he slipped into the coverall. 'I wouldn't want to get it dirty, do you know what I'm saying?'

The woman's lips began to part to allow the scream that had been stuck in her throat for the past minute to finally come out, but Lucien had been waiting for it. Before her vocal cords could produce any significant sound, his right fist struck the upper portion of her stomach with incredible power and precision, completely winding her. Instead of a scream, what came out of her mouth was vomit. The cupcake she'd just eaten, now in liquid form, splashed itself onto her dress, the armchair and the floor. Lucien also got some of it, but the plastic coverall kept it from dirtying his suit.

'I wouldn't advise screaming,' Lucien told her. 'It can be extremely painful for you.'

Contorted in agonizing pain, all the woman could do was cough.

'Now, let me go find out about those knives.' He smiled. 'Don't go anywhere. I'll be right back.'

Sixty-Seven

It was no secret that Los Angeles nightlife was one of the most exciting in the world. From luxurious and trendy nightclubs where A-list celebrities liked to hang out, to obscure and sleazy underground clubs (where, funnily enough, some A-list celebrities also liked to hang out, albeit usually in disguise). There were themed bars and lounges scattered all over town, not to mention the many pop-up drinking dens that would spring up from night to day, only to disappear without a trace a few months later. In LA, you could have a drink in a crystal-meth mobile-cooking lab, identical to the one used in the *Breaking Bad* TV series, where cocktails would be served inside graduated beaker flasks, together with a line of blue snorting sugar, or in a hospital ward, where cocktail waitresses ran around in skin-tight latex uniforms. To attract punters, anything could be used as a theme – the more bizarre or iconic the better. The Rabbit Hole lounge and restaurant in Alhambra was one such place.

Hunter had driven past that particular bar/restaurant a couple of times before, but he'd never been inside. Due to the trendy crowd that such places inevitably attracted, he tended to avoid them like the plague, but *Alice in Wonderland* was

Tracy's favorite novel and when she found out about the Rabbit Hole, she just had to go. She begged Hunter to go with her.

As he parked his car on West Main Street, just across the road from number twenty-four, Hunter checked his watch – it was eight-thirty in the evening on the dot. Tracy Adams had made a reservation for a table for two for 8:30 p.m.

Hunter smiled as soon as he stepped out of his car. On the sidewalk, just outside the themed cocktail bar, a cartoon-looking makeshift pole had four very colorful wood plank signs nailed to it. Each one pointed in a different direction. Starting at the very top they read: 'The Rabbit Hole', followed by 'Mordor', 'Hogwarts', and finally 'Narnia'. Hunter liked their sense of humor straight away.

Not surprisingly, and despite opening its doors less than an hour ago, the Rabbit Hole Lounge was already packed; after all, happy hour, which saw its cocktails cut down to half of their normal price, went from 8:00 to 9:30 p.m.

As Hunter walked through the entrance door, he was greeted by a striking decorated hallway, where neon lights brought two floor-to-ceiling murals in fluorescent paint to life. They depicted several characters from *Alice in Wonderland*, including a white rabbit carrying a melting clock, Tweedledee and Tweedledum and, of course, Alice herself.

Once he cleared the corridor, Hunter found himself on the main lounge floor, which was lit only by dim purple and green lights. The bar area was to the left, where a shelved mirrored back wall displayed an impressive selection of bottles. The colored lights reflected off the mirrored wall and through the liquid inside the bottles to create a somewhat engrossing psychedelic effect that Lewis Carroll would've been proud of.

The ceiling was made to look like an inverted house garden.

It was lined with synthetic grass and everything hung upside down – flowers, white rabbits, lamps, two wooden park benches and even a small pond.

On the crude brick wall opposite the bar, a selection of framed and unleveled paintings also hung upturned.

Dance music poured out of the strategically positioned ceiling speakers, but what really filled the crowded bar room with deafening noise were people's voices.

Hunter skipped the bar and walked over to the next room along – the restaurant – where a very attractive hostess, dressed as the Queen of Hearts, stood behind a wooden podium. There was a small line of people waiting to be seated.

Hunter joined the line behind two blonde women and a man who looked like he took being a hipster very seriously. His hair was classically undercut and slicked back with what seemed like half a pot of hair gel. His bushy beard came down past his shirt collar, and the edges of his long moustache twirled up in a full loop. He wore a black and white checkered shirt, with red braces and a black bowtie. His blue jeans were rolled up just past his ankles, revealing no socks and severely worn, brown chukka boots. He was chatting away about something that neither of the two blonde women seemed very interested in, which didn't surprise Hunter. The hipster looked to have the charisma of a library card.

One of the two blondes smiled at Hunter.

Hunter smiled back. 'Very busy here,' he said, politely.

'Always,' the woman replied, her smile brightening. 'Is this your first time?'

Hunter nodded.

'It's an awesome-looking place,' she said. 'And the food isn't bad either.

The hipster king looked Hunter up and down. He clearly didn't appreciate the interruption. The slight twitch of his left eyebrow also told Hunter that he didn't approve of the detective's clothes.

It didn't take long for the hostess to get to Hunter.

'Hello,' she said in a cheery voice. 'How can I help?'

'I'm supposed to meet someone here for dinner,' Hunter replied, unable to curb the smile that came to his lips, courtesy of the hostess's attire.

'Do you have reservations?' she asked.

'Yes. It's booked for eight-thirty, under the name Adams, Tracy Adams.'

The hostess checked the computer screen in front of her.

'Yes, of course,' she said after a couple of seconds. 'Party of two, correct?'

Hunter nodded.

'You are the first to arrive,' she informed Hunter. 'I can either show you to your table, or if you prefer, you can grab a drink at the bar while you wait.'

'Are you sure?' Hunter asked, frowning slightly at the Queen of Hearts lady after consulting his watch. It was 8:37 p.m.

Tracy was the most punctual person he had ever met. She was always on time, if not a few minutes early. Not once, since they'd started seeing each other, had she ever been late to anything.

The hostess consulted her computer screen again before taking a step back to look inside the restaurant area.

'Positive,' she replied. 'You are the first to arrive.'

'OK.' Hunter accepted it, turning around to look back at the crowded bar. 'I think I'll take the table option, if you don't mind.'

'But of course,' the hostess replied, grabbing a couple of menus. 'Please follow me.'

She guided Hunter to a table by the south wall.

'Here we are,' she said, setting down the menus. 'Would you like to have a drink while you wait? Perhaps one of our cocktails?'

'Just water will be fine for now,' Hunter replied, taking a seat. 'Thank you.'

'I'll get that for you right away.'

As the hostess walked away, Hunter consulted his watch one more time: 8:39 p.m. He checked his cellphone: no messages – no missed calls.

A waitress came up to his table bringing a jug of iced water and two glasses.

'Can I get you anything else?' she asked.

'No, thank you. I'm fine for now.'

'If you need anything, just give me a shout. My name is Julie and I'll be your waitress for this evening.'

Once Julie walked away, Hunter had a sip of his water and allowed his eyes to circle the busy restaurant area. Every table was taken. To kill time, he read the food and the drinks menu. The Rabbit Hole did indeed have some very interesting cocktails and dishes.

Hunter had another sip of his water and checked his watch again: 8:47 p.m.

No Tracy yet.

Another look at his cellphone: no messages – no missed calls. He looked up to check the entrance to the restaurant area. The Queen of Hearts hostess was informing a couple that they had no tables available at the moment.

No Tracy.

All of a sudden, Hunter got a horrible feeling inside. Something that started deep down in his gut and quickly spread through every atom in his body. He had no real idea what it was, but the feeling was telling him that something was wrong. Tracy was never late. She should've been there by now. If something had delayed her, she would've called.

Hunter grabbed his cellphone and dialed her number, but as he was about to press 'call', he saw Tracy walk around a group of people and come up to the restaurant hostess.

The most relieved of smiles graced Hunter's lips and for a moment he felt silly.

You worry too much, he told himself, as he returned his phone to his pocket and got to his feet.

What neither he nor Tracy noticed was the well-dressed gentleman who had walked into the Rabbit Hole Lounge not long after her.

Sixty-Eight

Lucien had been following Tracy since she left the staff parking lot at the UCLA campus in Westwood. The drive, via I-10 West, had taken them around an hour. Lucien was sure that a criminal psychology professor had no reasons to suspect that she was being followed; nevertheless he kept his distance, always allowing five to six vehicles between her car and his van.

Truthfully, Lucien thought that he was following Tracy back to her apartment in West Hollywood, as he had already done a couple of times, but as soon as she turned right instead of left on Sunset Boulevard, Lucien knew that Tracy Adams wasn't heading home.

His surprise was magnified by a factor of 'X' when, just as he was parking his van, Lucien clocked Hunter's old Buick LeSabre parked just across the road from a cocktail lounge in Alhambra called the Rabbit Hole.

'Now this is turning out to be a much better day than I had expected,' he said out loud, as he watched Tracy lock her car, cross the road and enter the cocktail lounge.

Lucien was glad that he was still dressed as James Mitchell.

He found a parking spot a few yards away from where Hunter had parked his car and checked his face in his rear-view mirror. After readjusting his wig and his glasses, he exited the van and made his way into the Rabbit Hole.

Inside, Lucien smiled when he saw the upside-down garden on the ceiling.

'Nice touch,' he said, pausing at the end of the hallway that led to the main lounge floor. He checked the busy bar. Three bartenders were mixing drinks and pouring cocktails as fast as they could. Lucien scanned the crowd, but saw no sign of Tracy or Hunter. That was when he noticed the entrance to the restaurant area, at the other end of the lounge floor.

'But of course,' he said to himself. 'Dinner with the girl-friend, what else?'

Lucien grabbed a drinks menu and made his way over to the other side, pausing just a few feet from the Queen of Hearts hostess. Pretending to read the menu, he probed the restaurant tables. It took him just three seconds to find them sitting at a table by the wall. In situations like these, Tracy's long bright red hair worked like a beacon.

'Oh, there you two are.'

Lucien lowered the menu just a touch, so he could better observe his targets. Tracy had her back to the restaurant entrance, but because he was standing at an angle, he had a completely unobstructed line of view to Hunter. He saw the smiles, the facial expressions and the undeniable shine inside his old friend's eyes as he and Tracy kissed.

Lucien felt an exciting tingle grab hold of him. He had once seen that same look, that same shine inside Hunter's eyes ... and he knew exactly what it meant.

'Oh, Robert ... you soft-hearted idiot. You are making things way too easy for me.'

'I'm sorry?' the Queen of Hearts hostess asked.

Lucien had gotten so excited that he hadn't noticed that his last comment to himself had come out a little louder than he had meant.

'Oh no, nothing,' Lucien said. 'I apologize. I was just thinking out loud.'

The hostess smiled at him before turning her attention back to her computer screen.

Lucien put down the menu and exited the bar. Outside he returned to his van and reached for his phone.

'Let the fun begin, Grasshopper.' He dialed a number he had memorized. 'Let the fun begin.'

Sixty-Nine

'I'm so, so terribly sorry,' Tracy said to Hunter, as she got to their table. 'A student of mine caught me just as I was leaving campus,' she explained before leaning forward and kissing him on the lips. 'What are you smiling about?'

Hunter hadn't noticed that he had held on to the relieved smile.

'Just happy to see you, that's all,' he replied.

Tracy smiled back. 'Wow,' she said, kissing him again. 'That's very nice to hear.' She decided to try her luck. 'Did you . . . miss me?'

'I did,' Hunter revealed, to Tracy's total surprise.

Her smile brightened. 'That's even nicer to hear, and I really am sorry I'm late. I should've called, but I really thought I would still be able to get here in time. Total fail.'

'It's OK, really,' Hunter reassured her. 'Don't worry about it.' He walked over to the other side of their table and pulled the chair for Tracy.

'Always a gentleman,' she said, as she took the seat.

'So?' Hunter asked, returning to his chair. 'How are things at UCLA?'

'Oh, you know . . . same old, same old, but exams are coming up in a couple of weeks, which means that some students are now starting to panic, and when they panic, they mob me.'

'Yes, I can imagine,' Hunter said, handing Tracy the drinks menu.

She took it and at the same time narrowed her eyes at Hunter's glass.

'You're drinking water?'

'I just didn't want to start without you,' Hunter replied.

A new smile from Tracy. 'Yep, always a gentleman. So, what would you like to go for tonight?' She quickly scanned the first two pages of the menu. 'Wow, they do have some exciting combinations here. The Off With Their Heads sounds really good, and so does Alice's Laughter.'

'I think that I will just stick with Scotch instead of a cocktail,' Hunter said. 'Not really in the mood for an overly sweet drink.'

'Always a good choice,' Tracy agreed.

She too was a huge fan of Scotch whisky, with the knowledge to rival any aficionado. She turned the pages until she came to the Rabbit Hole's whisky selection.

'The choice isn't vast,' she explained, 'but they do have some nice drams here. How bad a day have you had?'

The reason for the odd question was because, after a few dates, Tracy had picked up that sometimes Hunter chose his Scotch according to how tough a day he'd had. The worse the day, the smokier he would prefer his whisky.

Hunter's reply was a simple eyebrow lift.

'That bad, huh?' Her eyes went back to the list. 'Well, they do have Caol Ila and . . . bingo. They have Caol Ila Moch.'

Hunter was pleasantly surprised. 'Problem solved then.'

'Yes, I would have to agree.'

Caol Ila was a Scotch whisky distillery on the isle of Islay. Islay whiskies were well known for being heavily peated and quite dark in color, but Caol Ila was probably the island's lightest offer – paler than most, but still fantastically smoky and peppery, with a somewhat sweet finish.

Julie, the waitress, returned to their table to take their drinks order. As she walked away, Hunter's cellphone rang inside his pocket, making his core shiver.

He gave Tracy a look that begged for her forgiveness.

Her only reply was a defeated chuckle, which was followed by a slump of the head, her eyes avoiding Hunter's. She could barely believe that this was happening again.

More often than not, their dates were interrupted by an unexpected phone call, which meant that in a few seconds, Hunter would probably rush out of the restaurant. It was terribly frustrating, but Tracy understood that that was his job and there was nothing that she or he could do about it.

Hunter's display screen confirmed his suspicion – 'unknown number'.

He accepted the call and brought the phone to his ear.

'*Hello, Robert!*' Lucien said in a cheery voice. '*Sorry it took me so long to get back in touch with you. I had a few things that needed sorting out.*'

Hunter not only didn't care to, but he also didn't know how to answer. He stayed quiet.

'*Anyway,*' Lucien continued. '*It's about time we got back to our little game, don't you think?*' There was a deliberate long pause. '*I've got a new question for you, Grasshopper.*'

Hunter's eyes lifted to find Tracy now attentively staring at him.

'*How do you kill someone without actually killing them?*'

Lucien asked, but to Hunter's surprise, Lucien didn't give him a chance to reply. *'It's easy, Grasshopper. You empty their soul, only to refill it with pain ... you take away what they love the most.'*

Hunter frowned at Lucien's words.

'Don't worry if you're not sure what I mean, Grasshopper. You soon will.' Another pause. *'Let's say – fifteen seconds.'*

The line went dead.

Hunter looked at his cellphone screen completely confused. Immediately and subconsciously, a countdown began inside his head.

Fifteen ... fourteen ...

Tracy kept her eyes on Hunter, fully expecting him to simply get up and go, but he didn't move, his attention still on his phone.

'Robert, are you all right?' she asked.

No reply from Hunter.

Twelve ... eleven ...

'Robert?'

Ten ... nine ...

'Robert, what's going on?'

Hunter finally looked at Tracy.

'I'm not sure.'

Six ... five ...

'What do you mean?' Tracy asked. 'Was that headquarters on the phone?'

'No.'

Three ... two ...

'Who was it then?'

One ... zero.

Tracy's cellphone rang inside her handbag.

Seventy

As a rule of thumb, Hunter didn't believe in coincidences, especially not ones like this, down to the exact second. His eyes jumped from his cellphone to Tracy and something began brewing inside his stomach. Something he didn't like at all.

Tracy didn't seem to care for the rings coming from her handbag.

'Who was it on the phone then?' she asked.

Hunter disregarded her question. 'Your phone is ringing,' he said.

'Yes, I know. It's probably just another student in the middle of another pre-exam panic.'

'Your students have your personal number?'

'Some do.'

Hunter nodded. 'You're not going to answer it? It could be important.'

Tracy studied Hunter for a few seconds. The phone call he'd received had surely made him start acting a little strange.

'Sure.' She unzipped her handbag and took out her phone. 'Unknown number, see?' she said, showing her display screen to Hunter. 'Definitely a student.'

The waitress came back with their drinks and placed them

on the table. 'Two Caol Ila Mochs.' Her pronunciation was one hundred percent off track.

As she walked away, Tracy finally accepted the call.

'Professor Adams,' she said into her phone before listening for about five seconds. 'I'm sorry . . . who is this?'

Hunter's frown deepened.

Tracy listened for a few more seconds.

'What?' she asked, pulling a face. Her stare moved to Hunter. 'What are you talking about?'

'What's going on?' Hunter mouthed the words.

'Who is this?' Tracy asked again. 'If this is your idea of a joke, then you're a very sick individual. You should seek help.'

Hunter could tell that Tracy was trying her hardest to keep her voice as calm as she possibly could, though anger had clearly taken over her demeanor.

'And if you so happened to be one of my students,' she continued. 'I swear I will find out who you are. You will then be dismissed from my class and reported to the board at UCLA, do you hear me?'

Hunter saw the expression on Tracy's face go from angry back to confused. Then fear started to creep in.

'What? Who?'

. . .

All of a sudden, the look she was giving Hunter acquired a whole new determination.

'You are sick . . . you—' Tracy broke eye contact with Hunter and looked at her cellphone screen.

The call had obviously ended.

'What happened?' Hunter asked.

'Some sick prankster,' Tracy replied, visibly shaken from the call. 'Who I know must've been one of my students . . . or ex-students.' She shook her head. 'I can't believe anyone in their right mind would think that this could be a funny joke.'

'This what? What did he say?' Hunter leaned forward to place his elbows on the table, being careful to keep his voice low and steady.

'Just stupid stuff. None of it funny. None of which I'd like to repeat.'

'Tracy ...' Hunter's voice was pleading. 'Tell me exactly what the caller said.'

Tracy looked at Hunter. She was touched by how much concern he was showing. She drew in a very deep breath, reached for her whisky and drank half of it down in one take.

Hunter waited.

'He said that he had just ...' She paused for another deep breath. '... Murdered my parents.'

Seventy-One

Tracy's words carved a black hole into Hunter's stomach, which sucked the blood off his face and the words from his mouth. All he could do for the next few seconds was fix her with a stare she had never seen before. At least not coming from Hunter.

'What a sick and stupid joke,' Tracy continued. 'I don't even know why I've let myself get so upset by it. Maybe it was because of his voice. It was just . . . cold, no emotion at—'

'Tracy,' Hunter interrupted her. 'Please, try to remember exactly what it was that the caller told you, word for word if possible.'

Hunter's new tone of voice filled Tracy with even more worry.

'Why? It's a prank, Robert. A very distasteful one. Let me show you.' She reached for her phone again. 'Let me call my mother and you'll see.'

'Tracy, please, before you call your mother, tell me exactly what the caller said.'

Tracy's eyebrows lifted at Hunter, but she gave up after a second or two. It took her just one gulp to finish the rest of her Scotch.

'All right,' she began. 'He told me that this afternoon he had visited my parents in their house and murdered them.'

The black hole in Hunter's stomach began swallowing his soul.

'He said that it had been a very messy affair and that there was a hell of a lot of blood.' Tracy paused, her eyes now fighting tears. 'He even knew my parents' address, can you believe that? When I told him that this was a sick joke, his reply was to recite my parents' home address to me, as if that would validate his stupid prank.'

'Where do your parents live?'

'In Downey.'

'Was the address the caller gave you correct?'

'Yes,' Tracy confirmed before relating the address to Hunter. 'What kind of sick bastard does something like that, Robert?' She was getting angry again. 'Believe me, I will find out who this person is, and when I do, he will be in so much trouble he will never stop regretting this day.'

'What else did he say?' Hunter asked.

Another stern look from Tracy.

'Please, Tracy.'

She sat back on her chair. 'He told me not to forget to tell "Grasshopper" about the call.'

Hunter closed his eyes.

Tracy shrugged. 'No idea what the hell that means, and he ended the call by giving me a bogus name.'

Hunter already knew the answer, but he had to ask. 'What name did he give you?'

'It doesn't matter, Robert, because it's obviously a false name. Unless this guy is as stupid as he is sick.'

'Tracy, what was the name he gave you?'

Tracy breathed out anger. 'He said his name was Lucien.'

Seventy-Two

Hunter got to his feet while reaching for his phone.

'What are you doing?' Tracy asked.

'I have to call this in,' he replied.

Tracy Adams was no stranger to police protocol. She knew how the gears of bureaucracy turned and she knew what made them turn. She had just told the head of the LAPD's Ultra Violent Crimes Unit about a phone call confessing to a possible double homicide. Hoax or not, as a law enforcement officer, Hunter would have to follow protocol. He would have to call this in so that a black-and-white unit could be dispatched to her parents' home address to either prove or disprove the veracity of the call.

'You don't need to do that, Robert,' she said, also reaching for her phone, but Hunter was already halfway through giving the dispatch operator Tracy's parents' home address. He lifted a hand to ask Tracy for a moment.

She didn't give it to him.

'Robert, I understand protocol, but please, before you waste police time, let me first call my parents and you'll see that there's no need for you to call this sick prank in. Someone is just being an idiot.'

Her attention skipped over to her display screen and she began dialing her parents' home number.

Hunter ended his call by asking the operator to immediately inform Detective Garcia and FBI Special Agent Peter Holbrook. He returned the phone to his pocket and reached for Tracy's arm.

'Don't,' he said, interrupting her.

'What?'

Tracy glanced back at Hunter while confusion and uneasiness collided inside her eyes.

'I have to, Robert,' she said, her voice just a little shakier than moments ago. 'So we can clear this whole thing up. This has really upset me and now we're getting the police involved. I just need to talk to my mother, OK? I just need to hear her voice.'

Hunter's grip tightened on Tracy's arm ever so slightly and it was his turn to break eye contact with her. As he looked away, the black hole in his stomach threatened to erupt and he felt his throat constrict. For an instant, he considered allowing her to make the call. The phone would probably ring unanswered until she gave up, which would just add to how tense she already was. She would then probably try either her mother or her father's cellphone, and that was what really worried Hunter. He knew that Lucien was indeed evil incarnated. He would have anticipated that Tracy's first move would be to call her parents to check on them. What if Lucien had taken their cellphones? What if he answered Tracy's call? What if he had recorded their screams and played that back to her?

'Robert, what's wrong?' Tracy asked, not only because she saw the apprehension in Hunter's face, but also because she felt his hand tremble against her arm.

He looked back at her and she saw sadness in his eyes.
'Robert?'

'I can't lie to you, Tracy,' Hunter finally said, his voice uneven.

'What?' She pulled her arm away from his hand. 'Lie to me about what, Robert? What are you talking about?'

Hunter's heart tightened inside his chest because he knew that this was all his fault. Lucien had somehow found out that Hunter and Tracy were seeing each other, despite Hunter meeting her only once since Lucien's escape.

'*How do you kill someone without actually killing them?*' That had been Lucien's question to him. '*It's easy, Grasshopper. You empty their soul, only to refill it with pain ... you take away what they love the most.*'

That was exactly what Lucien was doing. He was taking away not only what Hunter loved the most, but also what Tracy loved the most. He was emptying their souls and refilling them with pain – never-ending pain.

Once all was revealed, and it would be revealed, as Hunter wouldn't be able to lie to her, she would know that the only reason why her parents had lost their lives ... the only reason why they had been brutally murdered – and Hunter knew they would have been brutally murdered – was for no fault of their own, but because their daughter, Tracy, was 'dating' Hunter. That was it. That had been the fatal factor in their lives: their daughter meeting Hunter ... falling for him ... dating him. Once Tracy learned the truth, she would hate him with all the strength she had. Hunter was absolutely sure of that.

As Hunter tried to reach for his glass of water, he finally realized that his hands were shaking. Despite how terribly hard this was, he had to look her in the eyes.

'Lucien is real,' he told her, trying his best to keep his voice from failing him.

'Lucien is real?' Tracy asked. Her voice, on the other hand, gained in volume and fright. 'What the hell is that supposed to mean, Robert?'

Hunter held her stare. 'Can we go outside? Please?'

'No, Robert, we can't go outside.' A pinch of anger joined the cocktail of emotions swimming around in Tracy's tone. 'I want to know what the hell you're talking about, and I want to know now.' Her eyes teared up. 'This isn't funny, you know?'

'Come outside with me, please,' Hunter begged, reaching for her hands again, but once again Tracy pulled her arms away.

'No.' She looked at him almost in disgust. 'Tell me what you mean.'

Tracy's voice reached the surrounding tables, which prompted the couple to their right to look at Hunter disapprovingly. They had clearly assumed that he was to blame for whatever was happening between him and Tracy.

Hunter needed to get going. He couldn't stall any longer. He had to tell her.

'The person we're chasing at the moment,' he began, 'the same person who bombed the Whisky Athenaeum a week ago. His name is Lucien Folter. He is real.'

Only then did it dawn on Tracy.

Hunter hadn't seen her since before the bombing. Sure, they had talked on the phone, but Hunter never really discussed any of his investigations with anyone not linked to the case, not even Tracy, but she'd seen him on TV after the incident at the Whisky Athenaeum. She had watched the news and she had read the papers. She remembered when the FBI agent, who Hunter was standing next to during the televised press conference, reassured the citizens of Los Angeles that what had happened hadn't been the work of a terrorist organization, but of a single individual. Not a terrorist, but a fugitive who had escaped from prison a few weeks ago and had decided to go on a revenge rampage. The FBI agent never mentioned who or what the revenge was against, but he did mention the name of the fugitive – Lucien Folter. Tracy had been so shaken up by the phone call she had received that she had failed to make the connection until now.

'What?' Anger turned into total sadness, as tears finally broke through the dam in Tracy's eyes. 'Is this a joke?'

Hunter gave Tracy an almost imperceptible headshake. 'Lucien doesn't make jokes.'

'So what are you saying, Robert?' She breathed in, but oxygen didn't seem to reach her lungs. Her voice faltered. 'That my parents have really just been murdered in their own house and their killer just called me on the phone . . . for fun?'

Other tables were beginning to take notice of them.

Hunter could now feel most of his body trembling. Seeing Tracy like that was shattering his heart and there was nothing he could do about it. The worst of it was, he knew that that was only the beginning of her pain. It would get worse. Much worse.

'Why?' Tracy asked. 'Why would this lunatic who bombed a bar last week go after my parents. Why would he murder them? It doesn't make any sense, Robert.'

Hunter looked away for just an instant. When his eyes returned to Tracy's face, the white in them had turned a light shade of red. He could practically feel his soul dying inside of him.

'Because of me.' As soon as Hunter said those words, his throat went desert-dry.

Tracy kept her attention on Hunter, but he could see it in her eyes that her brain was still struggling to understand what those three words actually meant. Then, all of a sudden, the struggle vanished from them.

'The revenge,' she said, with tears now streaming down her face. 'In the press conference ... the one on TV a week ago. The FBI agent you're working with mentioned that the reason why this Lucien character blew that bar to dust and claimed all those innocent lives was because he was hell-bent on some revenge mission, but the agent never mention against who or what.' She had to pause and swallow down her tears before speaking again. 'His revenge is against you?'

Hunter blinked. The knot in his throat tightened. He nodded at Tracy. 'Yes.'

'So what you're telling me right now is that my parents are dead because of some stupid grudge someone's got against you?'

There it is, Hunter thought. The anger in her voice. The hate in her eyes. The execution of his soul.

'But ... why?' Tracy looked away with unfocused eyes, searching for an answer somewhere around her. 'Why would he go after *my parents* if his revenge is against you?'

Hunter could try to explain it, but what good would that do?

'No,' Tracy said, shaking her head. This was way too absurd to be real. 'No ... no ... no. This isn't happening. This is some stupid joke and I bet that one of my students is behind this. How can you confirm something like this when you've been sitting here with me this whole time? You can't be that sure, Robert.' The tears that had been streaming down her face began drowning her voice. 'You just can't. Go on if you want, send a black-and-white unit to their house and you'll see.' She reached for her phone again. 'I'm calling my parents and I will prove to you that you're wrong. This really isn't funny, Robert. I can't believe that you're doing this to me.'

Tracy dialed her parents' home number.

This time Hunter didn't fight her.

Seventy-Three

The phone in Tracy's parents' house rang once ... twice ... three times ... then kept on ringing. The more it rang, the more tears Tracy cried. She gave up after the twelfth ring.

'I'm going to call my mom's cellphone,' Tracy said in a voice as full of fear as it was of sadness. She didn't look at Hunter.

Hunter quickly checked his cellphone screen for any messages from Garcia – nothing. All he could do was hope that Lucien hadn't taken Tracy's parents' phones.

Tracy brought her phone to her ear and waited. At the other end of the line, her mother's cellphone rang five times before the automatic answering service picked it up.

'Mom? It's me. Please give me a call as soon as you get this, OK? I love you.' She disconnected. 'Let me call my dad.'

Hunter waited. His heart was dying inside of him a piece at a time.

Tracy dialed her father's cellphone number and waited for him to pick it up. He didn't. Just like with her mother's, the phone rang five times before the answering service took the call.

'Dad, where are you guys?' Tears almost kept her words from coming out. 'Please call me the second you get this message, OK? I just want to know that you and Mom are all right. Please, call me. I love you.'

'Tracy,' Hunter said, keeping his voice down. What he really wanted to do was to reach for her hand ... he wanted to hug her ... to comfort her, but he wouldn't dare try again. 'I have to go.'

'What? Go? Go where?' She began looking around. Confusion and denial was one of the first stages of shock. Tracy was reaching it fast.

Hunter didn't want to use the term 'crime scene'.

'To your parents' house,' he replied. 'I have to go.' He reached into his pocket and placed enough money on the table to pay for their drinks.

'How can you go to my parents' house when you don't know where they live?' Tracy asked.

Confusion had definitely settled in.

'If you are going,' Tracy said, getting to her feet. 'Then so am I.'

Hunter didn't have to explain crime-scene contamination protocol to Tracy, but until her parents' house had been officially declared a crime scene, there was nothing Hunter could do to stop her from going there. After all, it was her parents' house.

'OK,' he agreed. 'You can ride with me.'

'No,' she replied. Though her voice sounded mainly sad, Hunter could clearly hear the anger in it. 'I'll drive myself. I've got my car with me.'

'Tracy, you're too distressed to drive right now. Come with me, please.'

'No. I'm all right. I can drive.' She grabbed her handbag and rushed out of the restaurant.

Under condemning looks from all the surrounding tables, Hunter followed.

Seventy-Four

Police officers Brian Stone and Pedro Ramos were each nursing a freshly brewed cup of strong coffee, while sitting inside their black-and-white unit, which was parked by a late-night coffee shop on Firestone Boulevard in Downey.

'I think I'm going to go get a donut,' Ramos said, running a hand over his thick horseshoe mustache. 'Would you like one?'

'No, man, not for me,' Stone replied, looking down at his waistline. 'Yesterday we're all having lunch at Dal Rae, in Pico Rivera – Debra, the kids and me. We finished our food and I asked, "OK, so who wants some ice cream?"' He paused and stared back at his partner with a displeased look on his face. 'Debra looks at me with that "dead" look of hers and says, "Not you, honey. Maybe you should stick to fruit for a few months." And taps me on the stomach.'

Ramos let out a full-bodied laugh. 'I think she might have a point there, balloon boy!'

'Yeah, screw you, you Village People wannabe ... "Y.M.C.A."' Stone began singing the famous song, while using his arms to create letters.

'So that will be no donut for you then,' Ramos said, opening the passenger's door. 'Do you want me to get you a ... banana?'

Before Stone could reply, the police radio on their dashboard came alive.

'All units on the vicinity of Albia Street, off Marble Avenue, we have reports of a possible double 187. This is a code-two high priority that requires OOCI.'

OOCI stood for 'out of car investigation'.

'Double homicide?' Ramos said, closing the door again. His eyes lit up. 'Marble Avenue is just a couple of blocks from here.'

'We're on it,' Stone said, quickly securing his cup of coffee into the cup holder and switching on his engine. While he backed up out of the parking spot, Ramos reached for the radio.

'This is Unit B7602, we're about three minutes away from Marble Avenue. Requesting full address?'

The dispatcher quickly replied.

'Ten-four,' Ramos confirmed. 'We're on our way. Any info on the perpetrator? Is there a chance that he might still be in the house?'

'That's a negative on the info. No more is known at present, so proceed with extreme caution.'

'Always.'

A code-two high priority meant no lights or siren, so Ramos returned the radio to the dashboard and buckled up.

Stone did turn on the lights and siren just so they could get through two red lights without having to stop. It took them exactly two minutes and twenty-one seconds to reach the address they were given.

'That's the house,' Ramos said, indicating a single-story building with a short driveway but no garage. From the front, they could see no lights on.

'Let's go,' Stone said, exiting their black-and-white unit with his weapon already drawn.

Ramos followed suit.

Moving as carefully and as quietly as they possibly could, both officers approached the house's front door.

'Oh shit!' Ramos whispered under his breath, as they got to just a few feet from the door. It had been left ajar about half an inch.

They each placed their backs flat against the wall to the left and right of the door. Ramos on the left. Stone on the right.

In silence, Ramos signaled his partner to indicate that he would push the door open.

Stone acknowledged the instruction with a head movement.

Ramos readied his weapon on his right hand before extending his left arm and slowly pushing the door until it was fully open. He then bent his torso forward just enough to be able to peek inside – too dark to see anything – he shook his head at Stone.

From inside, a horrible, almost disorientating smell assaulted their nostrils.

Immediately, both officers pulled their faces away, as if they'd been slapped.

Ramos had to bring a hand to his mouth to stop him from coughing.

Neither had any idea of what that awful smell could be, but whatever it was, they knew it wouldn't be good.

Stone signaled Ramos that he would enter the house first. He used his fingers to countdown from three . . . two . . . one.

On zero, he rotated his body one hundred and eighty degrees to his right. With his feet shoulder-width apart, both arms extended in front of him and his weapon held in a firm double handgrip, he paused at the door, his eyes searching frantically for a target.

He saw nothing, except for a faint light that seemed to be coming from behind another door that had also been left ajar at the far end of the room he found himself in.

Ramos repeated his partner's movement, but rotating left instead of right. The movement positioned him just behind Stone. He too could see no movement inside the shadowy room.

Stone took a tentative step forward. Time to announce their presence.

'LAPD,' Stone called out in a firm voice. 'Anyone in here?'

Nothing.

'Do you see a light switch on the wall?' Stone asked without looking back at Ramos.

'Yep,' Ramos replied before reaching for it and flicking it on.

The room stayed dark.

Ramos moved the switch up and down a couple more times just to be sure.

'Nope,' he said. 'No lights.' His right hand came back to his weapon and his left hand reached for the flashlight on his belt.

Stone did the same.

'I don't like this, Brian,' Ramos whispered. 'I don't like this one bit. And this smell is about to make me puke.'

Their flashlight beams crisscrossed each other several times, as they moved their torches around the room, trying to get a better idea of the space they were in.

It looked to be a nicely decorated living room, with shiny wooden floors.

'LAPD,' Stone called again. 'If there's anyone in here, you need to show yourself, nice and slowly, with your hands high above your head where we can see them. Do it *now*.'

Nothing. No movement anywhere.

'Be advised,' Stone continued. 'If you don't show yourself, we're authorized to use lethal force.'

Both officers waited, their flashlights moving back and forth around the room.

No movement anywhere.

'Light at the other end of the room,' Ramos said.

'Yep,' Stone replied. 'I see it. Let's go.'

With each forward step they took, their flashlights, eyes and aim moved from right to left and left to right, covering the length and the width of the room. It took them twenty-three steps to finally cross it.

The light that came through the break on the door flickered inconsistently, indicating that its source was most probably candles. As they neared the room, the sickening smell got stronger and stronger.

Officers Stone and Ramos assumed the same position as they had at the front door – Ramos to the left of it and Stone to the right. Ramos signaled that he, once again, would push the door open and peek inside. Stone nodded once.

Ramos proceeded with the move just like moments before, but as he bent his body forward enough to be able to peek inside the next room, he paused. His gag reflex tightened and his mouth was flooded with saliva.

Stone, who kept his attention on his partner, ready to move into the room beyond, saw Ramos's eyes become the size of two donuts and his jaw drop open.

'Pedro, what's wrong?' he asked.

Ramos's right hand left the double grip he had on his weapon so he could cross himself . . . twice.

'*Santa Madre de Dios.*' The words escaped Ramos's lips

without him even noticing them. Something dislodged inside his stomach.

Stone was through asking, so he once again rotated his body to position himself in front of Ramos and at the center of the now-opened door. In a split second, the expression on his face was a mirror image of the one on his partner's.

'Jesus Christ!' His eyes moved around the room in complete and utter terror. His voice came out shaking. 'Who the fuck would do something like this to anyone?'

'*El Demonio,*' Ramos replied, his voice also unsteady. 'The Devil himself, that's who.'

Seventy-Five

Outside the Rabbit Hole lounge and restaurant, Hunter tried one last time to reason with Tracy.

'Tracy, please, leave your car here and come with me, or at least let me call you a cab. Please don't drive. Not in the state you're in.'

But Tracy wasn't listening anymore. She stormed past him, crossed the road and jumped into her car.

It was obvious that Tracy's emotional state would put her and possibly others at risk if she got behind the wheel. Her entire body was shaking, her vision was blurred from all the tears and it didn't take an expert to know that her attention would not be on the road or on her driving. Knowing that, and despite being in a hurry to get to the crime scene, Hunter did the only thing he could do to at least keep an eye on her – he got into his car and followed directly behind Tracy.

From across the road, not that far from where Tracy had parked, Lucien watched the scene unfold with a quirky smile on his lips.

'Oh no, Robert,' he said to himself, as he watched Tracy and Hunter drive away. 'She seems very angry at you, is that possible? Is it possible that she will hate you for the rest of her life? Is it possible that she will blame you for her parents' death? Is it possible that she will forever curse the day the two of you met?' He laughed out loud. 'Yes, Grasshopper, I think it's very possible.' He got back into his van.

Lucien would've loved to be able to watch what would happen next, once Hunter and Tracy got to her parents' house. He would've loved to watch their reaction to the work of art he had left them, but following them and watching from the crowd of onlookers that would no doubt gather at the police perimeter would be way too risky.

'No,' Lucien said, as he turned on his engine. 'My job here is done.' His eyes moved to the item on the passenger's seat and he smiled. 'For now at least.'

Seventy-Six

At that time of night, a drive from Alhambra to Downey should've taken Hunter and Tracy around twenty-five minutes, perhaps a little longer depending on traffic, but Tracy's absent-minded mental state pushed her into making three wrong turns, including one onto the wrong freeway. All in all, Tracy's erratic driving added at least an extra eighteen minutes to their journey, which in Hunter's eyes, wasn't at all a bad thing.

Hunter didn't want to be the one who would have to stop Tracy from rushing into her parents' house, which would be exactly what he would have to do if they got there too soon – before a crime scene had been declared and a police perimeter had been established.

As a detective, even though they already knew the identity of the perpetrator, Hunter couldn't allow a crime scene to be contaminated.

Hunter also knew what Lucien was capable of and the most horrible of gut feelings was telling him that Lucien had gone overboard this time. To Lucien, this wasn't research anymore. This was revenge, and Lucien would've wanted to teach Hunter a lesson.

To protect Tracy from walking into the most grotesque and

nightmarish of scenes, a scene that would certainly leave irreversible mental scars, destroy her psychologically and haunt her for the rest of her days, Hunter would do everything in his power to stop her from entering that house, even if it meant that she would hate him forever.

As they neared Tracy's parents' home address, Hunter called Garcia.

'Carlos,' Hunter said once Garcia answered his phone. 'Are you there yet?'

'I'm about five minutes away,' Garcia replied. 'I live in North Hollywood, remember?' There was a quick, thoughtful pause. 'Wait a second – am I there yet? So you're not at the scene?'

'No, I'm about as far as you are, maybe a little less.'

'I thought you were having dinner with Tracy somewhere in Alhambra.'

'I was.'

'But I got the call around forty minutes ago.' There was confusion in Garcia's tone. 'From Alhambra to Downey . . . you should've been there way before me. What's going on?'

Hunter took a deep breath before speaking. The gagging knot returned to his throat. 'The victims,' he said. 'They're Tracy's parents.'

'The victims are who?' Uncertainty turned into pure shock.

'They're Tracy's parents,' Hunter repeated, struggling to keep his voice steady. 'To get to me, Lucien went after Tracy's parents.'

'I . . .' Garcia struggled to find the words. 'Are you sure?'

'Lucien called Tracy. We were at the restaurant. I just got confirmation from dispatch that two bodies were found at Tracy's parents' home address.'

'Lucien called Tracy? How the fuck did he . . . ?' Garcia thought better of his question. 'Shit! Is she with you?'

'No. She's in the car in front. That's why I'm not there yet. It's a long story. How about West and Holbrook, are they at the scene?'

'Maybe, I'm not sure. I haven't heard from them yet.'

'OK. Listen, whatever happens we can't allow Tracy to go into the house. I don't know what Lucien's done, but ...' Hunter was unable to finish the sentence.

'Yeah, that goes without saying,' Garcia agreed. 'I'll be there in just over three minutes.'

'If we don't make another wrong turn, we should be there at about the same time.'

They disconnected.

Seventy-Seven

As they finally turned right into Marble Avenue, Hunter noticed flashing blue and red lights coming from behind a cluster of houses. Tracy's parents' street was the first on the left and Hunter was relieved to see that a police perimeter had already been set right at the entrance to their road. As Tracy tried to turn into the street, she was flagged down by a uniformed police officer. Hunter pulled up right behind her.

'She's with me,' he said, sticking his head out of his window, as he displayed his detective badge.

The officer shone a flashlight on Hunter's credentials before nodding at him. 'You're the boss.'

The officer signaled his partner to lift the black and yellow crime-scene tape so Hunter and Tracy could drive through.

Three police vehicles were blocking the driveway to Tracy's parents' house, so Tracy hastily parked half on the street, half on the sidewalk.

Hunter parked on the road and as he did, he saw Garcia's Honda Civic clear the police perimeter just behind them.

Tracy jumped out of her car as if it were on fire and dashed in the direction of her parents' house.

Hunter went after her.

Tracy got as far as the front lawn before two LAPD Officers blocked her path.

'Sorry, lady,' the tallest of the two said, lifting a 'stop' hand. 'You can't go in there. This is a crime scene.'

'This is my parents' house,' she replied, in between sobs. Her eyes were cherry-red and puffy from all the crying.

The two officers exchanged a quick and very concerned look.

'I understand,' the taller officer replied. 'And I'm terribly sorry, but I can't let you through.'

'IT'S MY PARENTS' HOUSE!' Tracy yelled back, trying to force her way past them.

It didn't work.

'I'm sorry,' both officers said as they held her back.

Tracy turned around to look for Hunter. He was just a couple of steps behind her. Her pleading eyes found his and in a voice bathed by tears she begged.

'Please . . . tell them to let me in . . . please.'

'Tracy, I can't,' Hunter replied. His tone was overflowing with pain. 'Not right now.'

'Please . . .' she pleaded one more time. Her whole body began shivering again. 'I need to see them. I need to see my parents.'

Garcia joined them on the front lawn.

Tracy's attention moved to him. 'Carlos, please help me. I need to see my parents.'

Garcia peeked at Hunter before approaching Tracy.

'Tracy, we can't,' he said. 'You know we can't. It's a crime scene, and you know protocol just as well as we do.'

'Let us go in first, Tracy,' Hunter said. 'And we'll come and get you.'

'I need to see them.' Tracy's sobs intensified. 'I need to see them.'

At that exact moment, Hunter and Garcia saw FBI Special Agent Peter Holbrook walk out the house's front door. He was wearing white shoe covers, latex gloves and a light blue, surgical-style hairnet. Holbrook paused just outside the door, pulled the hairnet from his head and used it to wipe away the sweat from his forehead. The look in his eyes was vacant, distant and lacking belief. It took him a few seconds to notice Hunter and Garcia standing with the two Police Officers. He used the hairnet to dab the sweat from around his lips and approached the two detectives.

'Jesus!' he said. 'You guys are not going to . . .' He then saw Garcia shake his head at him ever so slightly, while his eyes darted in Tracy's direction.

Holbrook paused.

Tracy's full-of-tears eyes rested on him. 'This is my parents' house.' Her voice was failing. 'I need to go inside. I need to go see them. Please help me.'

Holbrook saw the sadness in Hunter's face. He turned to address Tracy.

'I'm Special Agent Peter Holbrook with the FBI,' he introduced himself. 'I'm terribly sorry, but unfortunately I can't allow you to go inside, Ms. Adams. Not at this point in time. Right now your parents' house is officially a crime scene and there's a protocol to be followed.'

'Screw protocol,' Tracy countered. 'This is still my parents' house. You can't do this to me. I need to see them.' She looked back at Hunter. 'Please help me, Robert. Please don't do this to me. I am begging you. '

It was Holbrook's turn to pin Hunter and Garcia down with

horrified eyes as he shook his head. His lips moved in silence: 'Whatever you do, don't let her in there.'

A white forensics van cleared the police perimeter at the top of the road.

'Ms. Adams,' Holbrook again. 'Please come with me.' He placed a gentle hand on her shoulder. 'Let's have a seat for a moment.' He indicated one of the black-and-white units parked on the road.

Tracy shook his hand off of her. 'I don't need to have a seat. What I need is to go see my parents.'

'Please, Tracy,' Hunter pleaded. 'I promise I'll come back for you, but you have to give me five minutes. Even if I wanted to, right now, I can't clear you to get in there because this is officially a US Marshals and FBI investigation. Five minutes and I'll come for you. I promise.'

Holbrook's puzzled stare bounced from Hunter to Garcia then back to Hunter. Both detectives read between the lines: *You really don't want to let her see what's in there.*

Tracy finally gave in and allowed Holbrook to take her to one of the police units.

'I'll stay with her,' Holbrook said.

Hunter and Garcia left Tracy with Holbrook and quickly made their way to the house.

'Have you met them before?' Garcia asked. 'Tracy's parents?'

'No, never,' Hunter replied.

They cleared the second set of crime-scene tape, which was at the front door, and stepped into the house's dark living room. A stomach-churning smell immediately hit them as if they had run into a wall.

'Whoa!' Garcia said, his left hand rushing to cover his nose and mouth.

Hunter closed his eyes for a quick instant, as if that would help his nose acclimatize to the pungent scent.

'This is not the smell of rotten flesh,' Garcia said.

Hunter agreed by slowly shaking his head. He knew exactly what that smell was.

In silence, they crossed the room toward the open door at the other end of it, where the light had been turned on. Twenty-three steps until they got to the door.

Garcia's hand let go of his nose and mouth and dropped by the side of his body. His eyes moved around the room aimlessly, trying to make any sense of what they were seeing.

'What ... the actual ... fuck?'

Seventy-Eight

Standing at the door, Hunter felt his strength abandon him.

There was so much blood inside that dining room it was hard to believe that there were just two victims, but the incredible amount of blood, which covered most of the floor before stretching to the walls, the furniture, the curtains and even the ceiling, was only a fraction of the horror that stood before them.

The room was centered by a six-seater dining table, with two chairs on either side of it and one at each end. Tracy's parents occupied the two end chairs. Lucien had positioned them sitting down, as if they were having their last ever supper together. The mother, wearing a silky red dress, sat at the north end of the table, while the father, who wore a dark pinstripe suit, sat directly opposite his wife.

At first glance, their attires were what helped identify who was sitting at what end, because neither body had a face ... neither body had a head.

George and Pamela Adams had both been crudely decapitated, leaving behind a grotesquely butchered neck stump at the top of each torso, where muscle tissue, arteries, veins and their severed spinal cords had been left exposed. Their bare flesh had begun acquiring a dark brown quality as oxidation took place, but it still looked a little moist, revealing that the wound had occurred sometime in the past six hours.

From the sheer amount of blood everywhere, especially the ceiling splatters, Hunter and Garcia both knew that Tracy's parents had not only been beheaded inside that room, but Lucien had done it pre-mortem – while they were both still alive.

'This is beyond . . .' Though he tried, Garcia was unable to find the words.

On the table, in front of each headless body, there was a dinner plate and a wine glass, and that was where sick and evil collided. Lucien had served their heads to each other.

In front of Mrs. Adams, at the center of a plate that was overflowing with blood, was her husband's totally unrecognizable head. The reason why it was unrecognizable was because his head had been burned to such an extent, his facial skin had completely blistered before roasting into a crispy texture with a charcoal color, which explained the sickening smell that had taken over the house. It was the same smell Hunter and Garcia had picked up at the site of the bombing several days ago – the smell of burning human flesh.

Both of Mr. Adams' ocular globes had also burst inside their sockets, resulting in two ominous dark craters where his blue eyes had once been.

Across the table, on the plate directly in front of Mr. Adams' headless torso, Mrs. Adams' head sat facing him, but unlike his, hers hadn't been burned at all.

Mrs. Adams' red hair, which was very similar in color to her daughter's, had been brushed back and was sprawled around the plate on the blood-soaked tabletop. Her once-beautiful green eyes had gone milky and had begun sinking deeper into her skull, but they were wide open and staring straight ahead at her husband's lifeless torso.

As if her eyes had somehow photographed her very last breathing moment, they had frozen in a look of unadulterated fear and horror, but Lucien's resolve to shock did not end with the serving of the heads. He had given both decapitated bodies cutlery – a fork on the left hand and a knife on the right. Both forks had been driven deep into the left side of the respective heads in front of them. The knives, on the other hand, had been shoved into each of the heads' mouths. From the door where Hunter and Garcia were standing, it looked like the headless bodies were just about to cut a slice of their partners' head.

'Lucien roasted one of the heads?' Garcia asked, his voice just a whisper, his tone lacking conviction. 'Why would he do that?'

Hunter had no answers ... no voice. He felt completely empty inside. All he could do right then was stare at the horrible scene before him. The only thought inside his head was ... Tracy.

'Peter is right,' Garcia said, referring to what Special Agent Holbrook had tried to tell them outside. 'There's no way we can allow Tracy to come in here, Robert. This cannot be the last image she has of her parents. It will destroy her.'

'So what have we got here?'

The question came from behind them and both detectives knew exactly who that voice belonged to: Dr. Susan Slater, one of the best lead forensics agents California had to offer. She had worked with Hunter and Garcia on several past cases.

'From the smell alone,' she continued, 'someone got burned ... and very badly.'

Hunter turned to face the doctor. Their eyes met and the desolation she saw in him, she had never seen before. Not coming from Hunter.

'Robert, are you OK?'

'Susan,' he said in reply, as his gaze moved to her briefcase. 'I need a favor.'

Seventy-Nine

Just like he had promised, after almost exactly five minutes, Hunter exited the house and walked over to the police unit that Tracy was sitting in.

'Tracy,' he said, offering her the glass of water he had with him. 'Please drink this. It's just sugary water.'

Tracy almost slapped the glass out of Hunter's hand, but he moved it out of the way in time.

'I don't need any sugary water, Robert.' Her voice was still unsteady, but it had regained its angry tone. 'What I need is to get into my parents' house.' She got back on her feet. 'You asked me to give you five minutes. Well, those five minutes are up. You promised me. I'm going in.' She tried to get past him, but Hunter stood his ground.

'I know I asked you for five minutes.' Hunter's voice was full of sorrow. 'But I need just a little longer.' His eyes darted in the direction of the house. 'Forensics have just arrived and you know this just as well as I do. They need to contain the scene, set up the lights, collect evidence, and photograph everything *in situ*. They can't risk contamination or anything being moved.'

'Robert's right.' Holbrook tried to help.

'Please, Tracy,' Hunter insisted. 'Have this and give me just a few more minutes.' He nodded at Holbrook and this time it was the FBI agent's turn to read between the lines.

He did.

'Once forensics has finished photographing everything,' Holbrook said, addressing Tracy. 'I'll walk you in there myself. How does that sound?'

A new barrage of tears began running down Tracy's cheeks. It broke Hunter's heart and he knew that she would never forgive him for what he was about to do, but he would rather pay that price than allow Tracy to see what Lucien wanted her to see.

'Please!' He offered her the glass one more time. 'It's just sugary water.'

Tracy finally gave in, took the glass and drank all of it down in small sips.

It took only three minutes for the strong sedative Dr. Slater had mixed in with the sugary water to take effect. When Tracy woke up, ten hours later, she was back in her apartment in West Hollywood. Hunter had taken her home and stayed with her all the way until the morning, when she finally came to again.

Thanks to the residues from the sedative, blinking the stupor of sleep away from her eyes took a lot longer than normal, with confusion setting in with the first eyelid flutter. It took Tracy a couple of minutes to be able to discern her surroundings. Only then did she realize that she was back in her bed.

Hunter had brought her a glass of milk and a sandwich, which he'd left on her bedside table.

Another two minutes went by before Tracy was able to sit up, and that only happened because Hunter helped her. As her sleepy eyes slowly danced their way around her bedroom, the fog that enveloped her memory finally began to dissipate.

'Why am I here?' she asked, her voice weak. 'Why am I in my bedroom?'

'You were sedated.' The answer didn't come from Hunter, but from Amber Webster, Tracy's best friend. Hunter had called her the previous night and asked her to come over.

'Amber?' Tracy hadn't noticed that her friend was in the room until then. 'What ... what are you doing here?' She paused as realization hit her at last. As it did, Hunter saw hope die inside her eyes.

'This wasn't a dream.' Her voice gained in volume. 'My parents, where are they?'

'You were sedated,' Amber explained again, approaching Tracy's bed and placing a hand on her shoulder. 'Robert brought you home.' Amber began crying. 'I'm so sorry, Tracy.'

Tracy glanced at Hunter and everything came back to her in an avalanche. Her eyes filled with tears and her tears with anger.

'You ... lied to me.'

Guilt cloaked Hunter, but he didn't look away.

'I'm sorry, Tracy. I had to.' His voice was weak ... defeated.

'Why didn't you let me see them?'

'He was trying to protect you, Tracy.' Amber tried to help, but Tracy wasn't listening.

'I need to go to their house,' she said. 'I need to go see my parents.' Tracy tried to stand up, but dizziness forced her to sit back down again.

'They are not there anymore, Tracy,' Amber said.

'What? Why? Where are they?'

Amber looked at Hunter.

'Their bodies have been moved to the coroners' office,' he explained.

Tracy exploded in sobs.

Hunter took a step toward her, but Tracy halted him with a stare that was full of disbelief and rage.

'This is all because of you?' she asked.

Hunter stayed quiet, as he felt his legs weaken under him.

'My mother is gone . . . my father is gone . . . and this is all because of you? Because of some stupid revenge thing?'

There was absolutely nothing Hunter could say.

Tracy looked away. 'Please, Robert, just go.' She lifted a shaky hand and pointed to the door.

Amber tried again. 'Tracy, please listen—'

'No, I don't want to listen.' For a moment, Tracy looked like she was about to be sick. 'I just need you to go, Robert. Please just go, OK? Just go.'

'I'm so terribly sorry, Tracy,' Hunter said as he turned to leave her room. 'If I could have given my life for your parents', I would have.' He looked at Amber. 'Please look after her,' he whispered. 'And please let me know if she needs anything.'

As he stepped outside her room, Hunter heard Tracy's sobs become almost hysterical.

Outside her apartment block, Hunter got back into his car, but didn't turn on the engine. Instead, he buried his face in the palms of his hands.

How do you kill someone without actually killing them? It's easy, Grasshopper. You empty their soul, only to refill it with pain . . . you take away what they love the most.

Eighty

'I'm sorry I'm late,' Hunter said, as he finally joined the 'task force' meeting that was being held inside Captain Blake's office.

The captain, who had just finished spreading last night's crime-scene photos over her desk, checked her watch. Since Hunter was less than five minutes late, she decided to cut him some slack.

'Nice of you to finally grace us with your presence, your highness,' she said in a firm voice, but left it at that.

'Are you OK to be here?' Garcia whispered, as Hunter joined US Marshal West and FBI Special Agent Holbrook by the captain's desk.

'Yes, I'm fine.'

'Now that you're finally here, Robert,' the captain said, her tone now a lot more concerned than angry. 'Let me ask you something – does any of this madness have any sort of special meaning to you?' She uneasily dragged his attention to the photographs. 'The beheadings? The burning of one of the heads, but not the other? The dinnertime scene? The decapitated bodies supposedly feeding on each other's heads? Any of it?'

Hunter looked back at his captain with vacant eyes.

'The reason I'm asking,' Captain Blake continued, 'is

because none of this makes any sense to any of us, but as we've learned with that absurd riddle that Lucien gave you prior to blowing away thirty innocent lives, most of what he does seems to be a direct dig at you, all part of this crazy revenge game he wants to play.' She held Hunter's stare. 'Does any of this fall into that category?'

Hunter looked at Garcia, who understood the silent question and replied with a very subtle headshake, indicating that he hadn't revealed anything to anyone yet.

Hunter proceeded to explain to everyone who the victims really were, before telling them about the phone calls Lucien had placed first to him then to Tracy.

'Jesus!' Captain Blake was the first to break the awkward silence that had followed Hunter's explanation. 'That's a whole new level of insanity.'

'But why the ridiculous, over-the-top display of violence?' West asked. 'Not to mention the crazy cinematic scene?' He lifted a hand at Hunter. 'I understand everything you've said – Lucien's intention was to make Tracy, the person who you're in love with, hate you, but he could've easily achieved that by just murdering her parents and making sure that she understood that you were to blame for that. He didn't have to decapitate them, or roast one of their heads, or even stage the scene in the way he did. Are you sure that there are no hidden meanings behind any of this? Maybe something that goes all the way back to your college days?'

'I'm sure,' Hunter confirmed.

'So Lucien did all this just for the hack of it?' Captain Blake asked.

'No,' Hunter replied. 'He did it because all of that was meant for Tracy's eyes, not ours.'

The room went silent with doubt.

Hunter explained.

'I don't see how Lucien could've known beforehand that Tracy and I were having dinner together yesterday evening. Tracy only managed to get a booking for last night because of a cancelation that came in in the middle of afternoon. Not enough time for anyone to pull all that off, not even Lucien.'

'So what was Lucien's plan then?' West pushed.

'A very simple one,' Hunter replied. 'To murder Tracy's parents in a very horrific way ... a way that he knew would completely destroy her mentally and psychologically. Once that was done, he would stalk Tracy's movements, waiting for the optimum moment to place his call.' Hunter paused, giving everyone a chance to chew on his words.

'So you think that Lucien followed her to the restaurant?' Holbrook asked.

'I have no doubt he did,' Hunter replied. 'In fact, I'm sure that he followed her inside. When he saw her sitting with me, Lucien just couldn't resist. Just imagine his satisfaction in being able to call Tracy, tell her about her parents' murder and then make sure that she understood that the person sitting directly in front of her at that precise moment, the person who she believed that she was in love with, was to blame for everything.'

'Fuck!' West said, picturing the scene in his head. 'Lucien was probably inside the restaurant, watching the two of you as he made the calls.'

'Probably,' Hunter agreed. 'But I'm glad that he called Tracy when he did.'

Doubt returned to the room.

'What do you think would have happened,' Hunter asked,

'if, for example, Tracy was sitting at home alone when she got the call from Lucien?'

The penny finally dropped for everyone.

'Tracy would've probably called her parents,' Holbrook said. 'Once she got no answer, she would've gone straight to their house.'

'Did you read the police report?' Hunter again. 'Lucien left the front door unlocked, probably because he couldn't be sure if Tracy had a key to her parents' house or not. He *wanted* her to walk in on that scene. He wanted her to see what he had done to her parents.'

For a beat, everyone's attention returned to the crime-scene photos.

'Lucien could've staged that scene in a number of different ways,' Hunter proceeded. 'It really didn't matter to him, as long as it was shocking enough to fracture Tracy's mind . . . and Lucien knows exactly what it takes to devastate one's mental state. That's why he approached it from two sensory angles – visual and smell – to make sure that she would never recover from entering that house . . . to make sure that her subconscious would forever associate any burning smell with what had happened to her parents.'

Hunter saw Garcia instinctively cup a hand over his nose and mouth just like he had done at the crime scene.

'Tracy might blame me for her parents' death,' Hunter accepted it. 'She might hate me for the rest of her life, which was Lucien's primary objective, but she won't be haunted by those images and she'll never be tormented by the smell that lingered in that house.' Hunter shook his head. 'No fracture of the mind. No devastation of her mental state. I can live with that.'

'So in a very bizarre way,' West said in conclusion, 'keeping Tracy from entering that crime scene was a victory over Lucien.'

Hunter wouldn't call it a victory, but he was trying his best to sound positive. 'I guess.'

'So what do we do now?' Captain Blake asked.

Though everyone knew there was nothing anyone could do other than wait for Lucien to call again, no one dared reply. The thought of a new call from Lucien was enough to frighten everyone to their core, except Hunter. He feared the exact opposite – the possibility that Lucien would never call again.

Lucien Folter had come to Los Angeles for one reason and one reason only – to take revenge on Hunter – and if Hunter were honest with himself, Lucien's job was done. Hunter felt defeated, empty and broken. Lucien had won the war. There were no more battles to be fought, and with no more battles, there was no reason for Lucien to stay in LA.

Hunter's fear came from the knowledge that if Lucien decided to disappear, no one would ever hear from him again.

Eighty-One

Four days had passed since Tracy's parents' murder and not an ounce of progress had been made on Lucien's whereabouts. The task force's only real success had been their ability to keep the press in the dark. The fact that the double homicide in Downey had been perpetrated by the same person who had bombed the Whisky Athenaeum in Hollywood was never discovered, which in all fairness was a huge achievement, considering that they were dealing with the United States press – arguably the most intrusive and resourceful press in the world.

On the subject of Tracy's parents' murder, the coroner had confirmed that both victims had been decapitated while they were still alive. The instrument used had been a meat cleaver, which was found in the kitchen. It belonged to the house. The autopsy had also revealed that the decapitation job hadn't been a smooth one. Lucien had hacked at each of their necks three to four times, which explained the incredible amount of blood splatters and arterial spray found at the crime scene.

Hunter had to call in a few favors to keep most details of the autopsy report hidden from Tracy, especially the fact that the beheadings had happened pre-mortem, not post-. That sort of knowledge, Hunter knew, was much more destructive than helpful, and he would do anything in his power to lessen Tracy's pain, whose progress so far had been as expected – very slow.

Hunter had respected her decision not to see or talk to him again, but he kept in daily contact with Amber, Tracy's best friend. She had told Hunter that when awake, Tracy spent most of the time either crying or catatonically staring out the window or at a photograph of her parents. Sometimes she would cry herself back to sleep, others she would grow hysterical and the only way to calm her down again would be to sedate her.

Back in their office, Garcia had just finished typing an email when he heard a loud growl coming from Hunter's stomach, who was sitting at his desk.

'Damn, man,' Garcia said, his eyes widening in surprise. 'Was that your stomach?'

Hunter stayed quiet.

'I thought it was another earthquake. It practically shook the building, Robert. When was the last time you ate? And I know you haven't had lunch yet because you've been in this office all day.'

'I had a big breakfast.'

'I'm sure you did. What was that, a super-duper-deluxe protein shake?'

No smile from Hunter.

Garcia got to his feet. 'You know what? Thinking about it, I'm quite hungry myself. How about we go get something to eat before that dinosaur in your stomach decides to eat the two of us?'

Hunter looked back at his partner unamused.

'Oh c'mon, that was a decent joke,' Garcia argued before taking on a serious tone again. 'For real, Robert.' He checked his watch. 'It's past five in the afternoon and you haven't eaten yet. No wonder your stomach sounds pissed off. C'mon.' Garcia's head gestured toward the door. 'Let's go grab a bite and call it a day. We're both obviously hungry and I'm sick of staring at my computer screen all day. We've been doing this for four days now without an inch of progress and to be honest, I wouldn't mind getting home before nine in the evening for once. So c'mon, get your stuff and let's go. I'm buying.'

Hunter sat back on his chair. 'Where do you want to go?'

'You pick,' Garcia replied. 'You know me, I can eat anything. We can go local if you like – the Blue Cube, Senor Fish, Redbird . . .'

Hunter looked a little unsure.

'How about the Five Star Bar then,' Garcia suggested. 'You like that place, don't you? They play good music and their burgers and sandwiches aren't bad either.'

Hunter did enjoy the atmosphere at the Five Star Bar.

'Seriously, Robert, let's go,' Garcia pushed. 'It's not like we have that much to do in here. We've been sitting on our asses for four days now, and we're not achieving anything other than frustration. Plus, you look like a man who hasn't eaten in a week. I'm surprised that no one has walked up to you on the streets, handed you a sandwich and a cup of coffee and said, "Here you go, buddy, stay positive".'

Garcia waited but once again got no response from Hunter.

'Nothing? Not even a ghost of a smile on that one?'

'It wasn't funny?'

'The only reason why it wasn't funny is because it's true. No jokes now, Robert, let's go get some food. Don't make me call Anna and put you on the phone with her about you not eating.'

Hunter smiled, as he finally reached for his jacket.

'Wow,' Garcia said. 'Out of all the jokes I made, the one about my wife was the one that made you smile?'

Hunter shrugged. 'That one was funny.'

Eighty-Two

The Five Star Bar was located at number 267 South Main Street, a mere block away from the Police Administration Building. As the clock struck five-thirty in the afternoon and people began leaving work ready for the weekend ahead, the place was just starting to fill up when Hunter and Garcia got there. A tall, dark-haired waitress, with nose and lip piercings, sat them down right at the back, three tables from the stage.

'Are you guys here to see the band later on?' she asked, as she handed them a couple of menus each.

'Who's playing tonight?' Hunter asked.

The waitress looked first left then right, as if she was worried that someone else would overhear her. When she spoke again, she kept her voice quiet. 'It's a secret gig from a band called Demotional.'

Hunter's eyebrows lifted. 'The Swedish band?'

The waitress didn't hide her surprise, as Hunter looked nothing like the kind of person who'd listen to death metal. 'Have you heard of them?'

'Yes, of course,' Hunter replied. 'I've got a couple of their albums.' He noticed the look on the waitress's face and decided to explain. 'I'm old school. I prefer albums to CDs and CDs to digital, whenever possible.'

The waitress smiled. 'Me too.'

'So Demotional are playing a secret gig here tonight?' Hunter asked, nodding at the compact stage.

'Yeah.' The waitress sounded very excited. 'They're on at ten.' A new smile. 'You should stay. I heard them sound-check earlier today and they blew the roof off. I can barely wait. Anyway, I'll give you guys a couple of minutes to have a look at the menus and I'll be right back.'

'De-motional?' Garcia asked, as the waitress walked away.

'Yes,' Hunter nodded. 'They're a death metal band from Sweden. They're really good.'

'Death metal? Is that very different from . . . "life metal"?'

Hunter didn't laugh.

'My jokes are just wasted on you,' Garcia said. 'OK, so what are you drinking?'

'Water, I think.'

Garcia put down the menu and scowled at Hunter. 'Water? Are you kidding? It's Friday night, Robert, at the end of one hell of a week. You need a drink almost as urgently as you need food. How about Scotch?' he suggested, knowing that Hunter wasn't a fan of beer. 'They've got some decent stuff in here.'

'Scotch doesn't really go well with burgers,' Hunter replied.

'Fair enough,' Garcia accepted. 'Pick something else then. Something that could at least help you relax a little.'

'All right.' Hunter gave in. 'I'll have . . . a glass of wine.'

'Better,' Garcia said. 'Red or white?'

'Red.'

'Red it is.'

The waitress came back to their table. 'So, have you decided yet?'

'I'll have a beer,' Garcia replied. 'Any beer will do, but he's thinking about red wine.'

'Good call,' she said, sending another smile Hunter's way. 'Any preference? We've got a pretty good selection from Napa Valley, including Malbec, Zinfandel, Cabernet Sauvignon, but my favorite is a Pinot Noir we got just last month. Light, but at the same time very flavorsome and amazingly smooth.'

'Sold,' Hunter said.

The waitress also took their food order – cheeseburger and fries for Garcia, just a cheeseburger for Hunter.

'How's Tracy doing, do you know?' Garcia ventured the question.

Hunter looked away for an instant.

'As expected,' he replied. 'Psychologically it will take her a while to heal. She was very close to her parents, especially her mom, but she will heal. She's a very strong woman. It will just take time, but the good news is – she will do it without those images playing around in her nightmares.'

'Which is a good thing.'

Hunter agreed with a nod.

The waitress came back with their drinks. As she left, Garcia had a swig of his beer, while Hunter allowed his wine to rest in the glass.

'Robert,' Garcia said, noticing the sadness in his partner's eyes, 'I've told you this before and I'll tell you again one thousand times. None of this is your fault, you know that, right?'

'Yes, I know,' Hunter replied, before finally having a sip of his wine. 'Even if I'd tried to anticipate Lucien's move, the clear winner in my head would've been Lucien going after someone close to me ... someone who I cared about – my best answer would've been Tracy, not her parents. As I've told you, I had never even met them before. I would've never factored them into the equation. And even if I had managed to anticipate that specific move, Lucien would've found another way to get to me.'

'Tracy isn't just a strong woman, Robert,' Garcia said. 'She's also very intelligent and her head is firmly on her shoulders. Sure, she's hurting right now, but that's understandable. She'll come around soon enough, and when she does, she will place no blame on you. She's too smart for that. Just give her time.'

The tall dark-haired waitress showed an African American gentleman to the next table before turning to face Hunter. 'So, how's the wine?'

'Fantastic,' Hunter replied. 'Thank you for the suggestion.'

'Order up.' They all heard the call from the kitchen window.

'I think that's you guys,' the waitress said. 'I'll be right back.' She was back less than thirty seconds later. 'Here we are, cheeseburger and fries and a cheeseburger on its own.'

'Why don't you come hang out with Anna and me tonight?' Garcia asked as they tucked into their food. 'We're probably just going to watch a flick or something, but it's better than being on your own.'

'Another time, maybe,' Hunter said, putting down his burger after just two bites. 'But I might come back here for the gig.'

Garcia nodded. 'Demotional, right? Death metal?'

'That's right. I've never seen them live before and they're a great band. Plus, like I said, they're from Sweden and they don't tour the US that often, so this is a great opportunity. I'll probably go back to the office or shoot home first. The gig isn't until ten.' He consulted his watch. 'Just over four hours from now. Too long to just hang around.'

'I see your point,' Garcia agreed. 'And I think that a gig is a great idea.'

Garcia took care of the bill once they had finished their food and they walked back to the Police Administration Building in silence.

'Let me ask you something,' Garcia said as they got to the PAB's parking lot. 'Do you think that Lucien might still go after Tracy?'

Hunter looked up at the sky. The sun was nearing the horizon in preparation for its daily disappearing act.

'There's no telling with Lucien,' Hunter said in response. 'But I really don't think so. What would be the point in putting himself through all the risk, all the trouble that he put himself through to make Tracy blame me for her parents' death and to completely break her, if he intended to kill her just a few days later anyway?'

Garcia accepted Hunter's reasoning with a thoughtful nod. 'It makes sense.' He unlocked his car door, unclipped his handcuff and flashlight holsters from his belt, and threw them in the backseat. 'But I know you. You have put surveillance on her anyway, haven't you?'

'I've called in a few favors,' Hunter admitted.

Garcia smiled as he got behind the wheel. 'I'll see you in the morning. Have fun at the "death metal" gig.'

Hunter smiled back. 'You don't really know what style that is, do you?'

'Nope, but I'm going to Google it as soon as I get home. I'm also going to look up this Demotional band.'

'You can always come and check them out for yourself,' Hunter suggested. 'Bring Anna. She might like it.'

Garcia pulled a face at Hunter. 'Death metal? Yep, I'm sure

she'd love it.' He chuckled. 'Her favorite band when she was younger used to be NSYNC. No jokes here. Death metal will be right up her street, I'm sure.'

As Garcia drove away, Hunter paused for a moment, trying to decide if he should go home first, or just go back to his office for a few hours. He was serious about going back to the Five Star Bar to catch the gig later on, but before making a decision, Hunter wanted to call Amber and check on Tracy. As he reached for his cellphone, he heard it ring inside the left outside pocket of his jacket, which made him frown.

There were two problems with that.

One: Hunter always kept his cellphone in the inside pocket of his jacket, never the outside ones. Two: it was not his ringtone.

Eighty-Three

Puzzled, Hunter immediately looked left, checking the ground around him to see if anyone had maybe dropped their phone in the parking lot. Nothing.

The phone rang again, putting an end to Hunter's doubts. The ring was definitely coming from his left pocket.

Hunter reached into it and, to his surprise, his fingers wrapped around a Nokia 5160.

'What the hell?' Instinctively, Hunter looked down at his jacket, mildly concerned that he had grabbed someone else's jacket as they left the Five Star Bar. His mind had been distracted enough for that to have happened, but no, the jacket he had on was indeed his.

The phone rang in his hand one more time. The display screen showed: 'unknown number'.

That was when it dawned on Hunter.

'No way.'

His worried eyes searched the vicinity. There were police officers and civilians coming and going from the Police Administration Building. Hunter tried to examine their faces, but everyone seemed to be in a hurry, moving way too fast.

Outside the main entrance, a short woman was smoking a

cigarette and talking on her phone, but she was too short to be Lucien.

The phone rang again . . . and again . . . and again.

Still searching the faces that he could see from where he was standing, Hunter pressed the 'answer' button and brought the phone to his ear.

'*Hello, Grasshopper,*' Lucien said. Once again, he was using his real voice. '*Surprised by the phone-in-the-pocket trick?*'

A police officer, standing by a black-and-white unit across the parking lot, had his phone in his hand, but he was texting, not making a call.

'*So sorry about the ancient cellphone,*' Lucien said. '*Do you remember those? The particular model you have in your hand is from 1998.*' He chuckled carelessly. '*Back then Nokia used to be the world leader in cellular phones . . . and by a clear mile. Whatever happened to them?*'

Lucien insisted in talking to Hunter in a polite manner, as if they were still good friends, as if nothing had ever happened between them. It was an old psychological trick that tended to infuriate one of the parties, but Hunter knew much better than that.

'*I'll tell you what happened,*' Lucien continued. '*They were crushed by a smarter and stronger opponent. An opponent with better ideas and a much stronger game plan; does that ring any bells, Grasshopper?*'

Hunter stayed silent, his stare still bouncing from face to face.

Nothing.

He began slowly making his way out of the PAB parking lot, toward West 1st Street, his mind quickly skipping through all his options. There weren't many.

'You're right, Lucien,' Hunter said. He saw no point in doing any of this anymore and his lack of fight showed in his voice. 'You won. I lost. There are no two ways about it. So what do you say we end this once and for all, since I've got nothing else for you to take?'

There was a short, pondering pause from Lucien.

'*OK, I'm listening. What do you have in mind?*'

'You and me,' Hunter replied. 'Face to face. No one else. No US Marshals. No FBI. No one. Your revenge is against me and you've already hurt plenty of innocent people. There's no need to hurt anyone else. Let's get this done and over with, Lucien. You and me. You name the place and the time and I'll be there . . . alone. You have my word on that.'

Lucien laughed. '*And I'm just supposed to trust your word on this?*'

'It's all I have left, Lucien.' Hunter got to West 1st Street and paused just outside the entrance to the PAB parking lot. He looked left then right before simply shaking his head. There were too many people walking up and down the road for Hunter to be able to spot Lucien, if Lucien was even there.

Once again, there was a pause from Lucien's side, as if he were weighing his options.

Hunter still searched the street.

'*I name the time and the place?*' Lucien asked.

'Yes.'

'OK,' Lucien agreed. '*Let's do it now. Right now.*'

Eighty-Four

Garcia checked his dashboard clock as he exited North Broadway and joined Hollywood Freeway heading northwest – 6:12 p.m. Traffic was as expected for a Friday evening in the City of Angels – slow. At that pace, he would probably make it home sometime between 6:40 and 6:55, which compared to most days was definitely a winning situation.

His thoughts reverted back to Hunter. In all their years as partners, Garcia had never seen Hunter so hurt; but then again, Garcia had never seen evil like Lucien Folter. The Devil himself, Garcia imagined, would probably be scared of Lucien.

As his thoughts wandered from Hunter to Tracy, Garcia felt an awkward chill finger-walk the back of his neck and all of a sudden he was thinking of Anna. His heart seemed to tighten inside of him and something told him that he needed to check on his wife, and he needed to do it now.

Just as Garcia reached inside his jacket for his phone, it began beeping. It sounded like an alarm, but not quite. The coincidence was such that it startled Garcia.

'What the hell?'

He knew that he had no alarms programmed into his cell-phone and he had never heard that specific alert sound coming from his phone before – two high-pitched beeps, immediately followed by a single, lower-pitched one. It played on a loop with the added bonus of the phone's vibrating feature.

Garcia's fingers finally grabbed hold of his cellphone. Traffic was slow, but moving, so he quickly peeked at its screen before his attention went back to the truck in front of him. The application message read: 'USM TRAC AC'.

'What the hell is this?' Garcia called out, his entire forehead creasing. He placed his index finger on the phone's fingerprint reader to unlock his screen and checked it again.

'US Marshals Tracking Activated.'

It took the neurons inside Garcia's brain a full second to deploy. What he was looking at was the tracking application that US Marshal Tyler West had installed on everyone's smartphone. Its function was to track the device West had handed Hunter in case Lucien had gone for him. That application was only supposed to come alive if Hunter had activated his tracking device by pressing it.

'What the fuck?' Garcia checked the dashboard clock again. He had left Hunter at the PAB parking lot less than ten minutes ago – the *Police Administration Building* parking lot. There was no way that Lucien had grabbed Hunter from that location. Hunter must've pressed the button on the tracker by accident.

Garcia immediately dialed Hunter's number and heard his partner's phone ring once ... twice ... three times. After the fifth ring, the answering service picked up the call.

'What the hell is going on?' Garcia disconnected, turned on his police lights and began moving over to the freeway hard shoulder, but before he got there, his cellphone rang. The call was coming from US Marshal West. He and Special

Agent Holbrook had the same application installed on their cellphones.

'Tyler,' Garcia answered his phone, as he pulled up onto the hard shoulder.

'*Carlos, are you with Robert? He's not answering his phone.*'

'Yes, I know. I just tried calling him too and no, I'm not with him. Not anymore. But I was, about ten minutes ago.'

'*So the tracker is real?*'

'I'm not sure.'

'*Shit! It's moving,*' West called out. '*The tracker is moving.*'

Garcia checked his cellphone screen. The tracker application consisted of a map, a red dot and a blue dot. The red dot was the tracker in Hunter's pocket. The blue dot showed the location of the phone running the app, in this case, Garcia's cellphone. On his screen, the red dot had just turned from West 1st Street into North Broadway.

'I'll be goddamned,' Garcia whispered.

'*We've got to assume that this is live and Lucien's got Robert. You said that you were with him just ten minutes ago. Where are you now?*'

'Hollywood Freeway heading northwest, approaching exit 5A.'

A pause.

'*All right. Stay put for a few seconds, there's a chance he might take the North Broadway exit onto Hollywood Freeway. If so, he'll head toward you.*'

'How about you, Tyler?' Garcia asked. 'Where are you?'

'*That's the problem,*' West replied. '*I'm in Santa Barbara.*'

'Santa Barbara? What the hell?'

'*I was in court,*' Tyler explained, '*giving testimony on an older case. Anyway, I'm on my way now, but it will take me over two hours just to get to downtown LA.*'

A new beep from Garcia's phone announced a new incoming call – Special Agent Holbrook.

'Tyler, hold on,' Garcia said. 'Peter is on the line. Let me switch this into a group call.

Two seconds later.

'*Carlos, what the hell is going on?*' Holbrook asked.

'*This is real, Peter.*' The answer came from West. '*Robert isn't answering his phone and is on the move. We have to assume Lucien's got him.*'

'*All right,*' Holbrook replied.

Garcia told Holbrook where he was.

'*Shit!*' Holbrook replied. '*I'm about forty-five minutes from you, but I'm on my way.*'

'Don't disconnect,' Garcia told everyone. 'We can coordinate while we move.'

'*Understood,*' West and Holbrook said in unison.

Eighty-Five

'OK, *let's do it now. Right now,*' Lucien said.

Hunter wasn't expecting that answer. His best guess was something like: 'I'll call you back'.

'Now?' Hunter asked.

'*What? Too soon for you?*'

Hunter breathed in. 'No, now is fine.'

As Hunter began making his way from the PAB parking lot to West 1st Street, he innocently placed his left hand inside his left trouser pocket. From inside his pocket, he clicked the tracking device on.

'*If we're doing this, Robert, we're doing it by my rules. You break any of them and this call is over and you'll never hear from me again, but I promise you that before I leave Los Angeles, what I've done in this city will look like kindergarten stuff compared to what I have in store. Are we clear?*'

Hunter knew that he had no other option.

'*You suggested this, Robert.*'

'Yes, we're clear,' Hunter agreed. 'Your rules.'

'OK,' Lucien said after several deliberating seconds. '*So listen up. Rule one: you do not disconnect from this call for any reason. You keep the phone against your ear until we meet. No exceptions.'*

'Will the battery last?' Hunter asked.

Lucien laughed. *'It's a 1998 phone, Robert. That was when the batteries used to last a whole week, remember? It will last. Trust me. Rule two: I say, you do. No questions. Nor arguments. Rule three: if I even suspect you're being tailed by anyone this call is over and you know what happens next, right?'*

Hunter saw a sixteen-year-old kid on his phone at the end of the street. No way that that was Lucien.

'Yes, I do,' Hunter replied.

'Good. Are you ready?'

No, Hunter wasn't ready, but what choice did he have?

'Ready as I'll ever be, I guess.'

'So let's play, Grasshopper. Your detective's badge?' Lucien asked. *'Is it clipped to your belt?'*

Hunter looked down at his waist. 'Yes.'

'Unclip it and put it in your jacket pocket. Do it now.'

Hunter followed his instructions.

'Your wallet, where is it?'

Hunter frowned at the phone. 'Inside my pocket.'

'Trouser or jacket?'

'Jacket.'

'Using your left hand, take it out nice and slowly ... and yes, Robert, I can see you – black jacket, black jeans, dark blue shirt, standing on West 1st Street, right in front of the entrance to the LAPD Headquarters, looking up and down the street as if you would be able to spot me.'

A lump came to Hunter's throat. Automatically, his eyes searched the street one more time and he soon heard Lucien laughing down the phone.

'*C'mon, Grasshopper, give it up. The only way you would spot me would be if I wanted you to. You know that.*'

Hunter did know that.

'*The wallet, Robert. Take it out nice and slowly.*'

Hunter took his wallet out of his jacket pocket and held it up above his head.

'*Open it and take out all the cash you have. You'll need it, but bills only. No coins. No money clips. As you take each note out of your wallet, hold it up.*'

Hunter frowned at the instructions, but followed them anyway. He had a total of ninety-seven dollars.

'*Put the money in your trouser pocket.*'

'What's this about, Lucien?' Hunter asked, as he once again followed Lucien's instructions. 'You ran out of money? Need a loan or something?'

'*You'll see. Now return the wallet to your jacket.*'

Hunter did.

'*Your cellphone, where is it?*'

'Jacket as well.'

'*Using your thumb and index finger, show me. Again, nice and slowly.*'

Hunter reached into his pocket, pulled out his phone and held it above his head.

'*Good. Put it back in your pocket.*'

Once again, Hunter followed Lucien's instructions.

'*Now let's get rid of everything, shall we? The jacket, the phone and your weapons,*' Lucien ordered. '*I take it that you have a holster under that jacket, right? Get rid of it as well.*'

Hunter had to swap the phone from one hand to the other to take off his jacket and his gun holster.

'*Back-up weapon as well,*' Lucien said.

'I don't have one.'

'*Am I to believe that?*'

'I don't.' Hunter lifted both of his arms above his head, while slowly turning to show the small of his back.

A mother, holding on to her eight-year-old daughter, frowned at the crazy man with his hands in the air doing a slow pirouette on the street. She crossed the road just to avoid walking past Hunter.

'*Ankle holster?*' Lucien asked.

Hunter lifted both of his trouser legs to show both of his ankles. No weapon.

'*A detective without a back-up weapon,*' Lucien said. '*Since I know that you're far from being dumb, this must mean that you're very sure of yourself, Grasshopper.*'

Hunter found the comment rich, given that it was coming from Lucien.

'OK.' Lucien sounded satisfied. '*Let's leave the jacket and the holster behind. Drop it on the floor.*'

Hunter shook his head. 'I can't drop my weapon on the street.'

'*You'd better do as you're told or this call is over, Robert.*'

'Not on the street, Lucien. A kid could find it.' Hunter turned to look behind him. 'Look, behind me, just inside the headquarters parking lot, on the right. Let me put it on the hood of the black-and-white unit. That way a cop will find it, not a civilian.'

Silence.

'C'mon, Lucien, this is not a trick.'

'*Fair enough.*' Lucien finally agreed. '*Just get rid of it.*'

Hunter wrapped his jacket around his weapons holster, walked back into the PAB parking lot and placed everything on the hood of the police car. 'Now what?'

'*Now we're going to move, but you're not taking your car. Flag down a cab.*'

Now Hunter understood why he needed the money.

On West 1st Street, it took him just a few seconds to get a cab – a yellow Toyota Camry.

'OK,' Hunter said. 'So where am I going?'

The cabdriver, a Jamaican American man in his mid-forties, peeked at Hunter through the rear-view mirror.

'Yuh asking me, mon?'

Hunter pointed to the cellphone against his ear.

'Hah, mon.' The cab driver laughed, looking at Hunter's cellphone. 'That ting is oooolllldd.'

Hunter completely disregarded the comment.

'Where to, Lucien?'

'*Well, let's see …*' Lucien replied. '*How about … Echo Park. I like that place.*'

Echo Park was a heavily populated neighborhood centered around a lake of the same name. It was located just north of downtown LA.

Hunter nodded before instructing the driver.

'Any particular place, mon?'

Lucien heard the question.

'*Anywhere in that neighborhood works. I'll give you new instructions once you get there.*'

The driver turned right on North Broadway.

Less than half a mile later, he took another right to join Hollywood Freeway, heading northwest, in the direction of where Garcia was parked.

Eighty-Six

Parked on the hard shoulder on Hollywood Freeway, a mile and a half ahead of Hunter's cab, Garcia watched the red dot move against the map on his cellphone screen with tremendous anticipation.

'It's coming my way,' Garcia said into his phone.

'*Stay put,*' West replied. '*If it reaches you, let it go past. There's no need to follow him too close behind. We've got him on the tracking app, so he isn't getting away. If he goes past you, allow fifteen, maybe twenty cars between the two of you. The last thing we want right now is for Lucien to realize that he's being tracked, but keep an eye out. See if you can spot which vehicle they're in.*'

'I'll try,' Garcia said. 'How far are you, Peter?' he asked Holbrook, knowing that West was too far away to count on.

'*I'm still over thirty-five minutes away,*' Holbrook said.

Garcia sat back in his seat, let go of a deep breath and kept his eyes on his cellphone screen. The tracking application also showed the actual distance between the red and the blue dot – one point two miles.

He rotated his body on his seat to look behind him. At that time in the evening, the traffic on Hollywood Freeway was as slow-moving as ever, which considering the situation they were in, wasn't a bad thing. His eyes returned to his cellphone screen. The red dot was a mile away from him.

Garcia's heart began beating faster and he felt his hands clam up.

'*Eyes open, Carlos,*' West said again. '*Try to spot the car.*'

'Yes,' Garcia replied. 'I haven't forgotten.'

Zero point eight miles.

'I've got you, Robert,' Garcia said under his breath. 'I've got you.'

Right then, he saw the red dot veer right and take exit 4A, moving north toward Echo Park and Hollywood.

'Oh fuck!' Garcia said out loud.

'*Was that before your location?*' Holbrook asked, not being that familiar with the streets in LA.

'Yes,' Garcia replied, slotting his cellphone into his dashboard holder. 'Over half a mile from me. I can't turn back on the freeway, but I can take exit 5A, which is just ahead of me. That will get me to North Rampart Boulevard. I can head east from there toward Hollywood. I'll follow them from there.'

Garcia turned on his siren and rejoined Hollywood Freeway. Less than two minutes later, he took exit 5A.

The red dot on his cellphone screen kept moving north on Echo Park Avenue until it reached Sunset Boulevard. It then swung left.

'Where the hell are you going, you crazy fuck?' Garcia's words were spoken through gritted teeth. 'Where the hell are you going?'

Eighty-Seven

The sun had finally dipped behind the horizon when Hunter's cab joined Hollywood Freeway – four lanes practically solid with vehicles.

'Sorry bout dis, mon,' the cab driver said with a quick shrug. 'I should've taken North Beaudry Avenue. The freeway is a nightmare at dis time. Are you in a rush?'

'Am I in a rush?' Hunter's question was meant for Lucien.

'*No, not really,*' Lucien said. '*Tell the driver he can take as long as he likes. You're paying.*'

'No, no rush,' Hunter replied.

'Exit 4A is just ahead, mon,' the driver said. 'We'll be out of dis hell soon.'

'That's fine,' Hunter agreed.

'*Don't be so quiet, Grasshopper,*' Lucien said. '*Keep talking, so I know that you're not trying anything.*'

'What could I try, Lucien? I'm in the back of a cab. No phone . . . no weapon . . . what could I try?'

The driver heard the word weapon and quickly peeked over his shoulder at the passenger in his backseat.

'*You've always been a very smart and resourceful person, Grasshopper. I'm not taking any chances.*'

'I gave you my word, didn't I?'

'*Forgive me if I'm not one hundred percent sold on that, Grasshopper.*'

'All right,' Hunter said. 'So what would you like me to say?'

'*Let's see . . .*' Lucien paused as if trying to think of something. '*Oh, I know. Repeat after me . . . ready?*'

Hunter waited.

'*You are my fire.*'

'I'm sorry?'

'*Repeat after me, Grasshopper – You . . . are . . . my . . . fire.*'

Hunter shook his head as he repeated Lucien's words.

'*My one desire.*'

'My one desire.'

The cab driver looked at Hunter through the rear-view mirror with an odd frown.

'*Believe me when I say.*'

'Believe me . . .' Hunter paused. His frown was even more pronounced than the driver's. 'Are those the lyrics to a Backstreet Boys song?'

Lucien laughed out loud, as if he had heard the best joke in the world. '*There's no fooling you, is there, Grasshopper?*'

The cab driver simply shook his head before returning his attention to the road.

'*Do you remember Ghost?*' Lucien asked. '*He was the one who shot your FBI partner last time we met.*'

Memories of that fateful day came rushing back to Hunter like a sucker punch to the stomach and he saw the whole scene play before his eyes in slow motion.

'Yes,' he replied, his voice solemn. 'I remember Ghost.'

'*That used to be his favorite song.*' Lucien was still laughing.

'*If you know it, you can sing it to me. C'mon, Grasshopper, I'll count you in.*'

'I don't,' Hunter countered.

The cab took exit 4A.

'*OK, I know what you can do,*' Lucien came back after a few silent seconds. '*I remember how fanatical about books you used to be. I bet that hasn't changed at all, has it, Grasshopper?*'

'I still read, yes.'

'*And one thing that I remember well from our college days, is that you used to know most of Edgar Allan Poe's poems by heart.*'

'All of them,' Hunter replied. 'I know all of Poe's poems by heart.'

'*That's right, now I remember. You told me that you began reading Poe and others to keep your mind from going back to your mother's death, isn't that right, Robert?*'

Hunter said nothing. Instead, he allowed his stare to focus on the traffic outside his window. The car to his left had two occupants – the driver, a short-haired brunette woman in her mid-thirties, and a young boy sitting next to her in the passenger seat. The boy looked to be around seven or eight years old and his attention was solely on the hand-held videogame device he had in his hands.

'*I bet that those morbid poems go down really well with the ladies, don't they?*' Lucien said before breaking into another laugh.

They came to a stop at a traffic light, and as they did, the boy in the neighboring car looked up from his videogame device, turning his head to his right. His eyes locked with Hunter's and the boy smiled a truly innocent smile before giving the detective a shy wave.

Hunter waved back.

'*So I guess it's problem solved,*' Lucien said, dragging Hunter's attention back to the call. '*If you don't want to sing, then you can recite Poe's poems to me. How about we start with "The Raven"? That's his most famous one, isn't it?*'

Hunter stayed silent.

'*Go, Grasshopper. I'm all ears.*'

Hunter caught the eyes of the driver in the rear-view mirror again and his eyebrows bobbed up and down as if saying, "What can I do?" A second later, he began reciting 'The Raven' by Edgar Allan Poe.

Eighty-Eight

Sitting at the wheel of his van, twelve vehicles behind Hunter's cab, Lucien watched as the taxi driver exited Hollywood Freeway, taking exit 4A toward Echo Park and Hollywood. The maneuver would add at least an extra ten minutes to their journey and Lucien did think about mentioning something to Hunter over the phone, but why give out his position unnecessarily? Lucien was in no rush. Safe a few minor adjustments, everything was already in place and ready to go. There would be no real harm or advantage in getting to the final destination later rather than sooner.

Since Tracy's parents' murder, Lucien had spent the last four days making sure that every detail of his elaborate plan would run as smoothly as possible. He had tested and re-tested everything several times over and only when he was completely satisfied did he decide that it was time to execute.

'Everything one day comes to an end, Lucien,' he had told himself, as his final plan took shape inside his head. 'Everything . . . no matter how good or important it may seem. You always knew this. From the day you began your research . . . from the day you decided to go down this path . . . you knew that the end would one day come.'

Lucien was more than prepared for what he had to do. He had considered a multitude of scenarios and possibilities on how his plan would roll out and so far, everything was going exactly to plan.

Lucien remembered that when he had called Hunter days ago, asking for the answer to his riddle, Hunter had begged him not to use the C-4 and offered to meet him face-to-face, so that they could put an end to all of this.

'You want to settle a score with me,' Hunter had said. 'Let's do it ... you and me ... no one else needs to get involved. You tell me where and when and I'll meet you there. No back-up. No tricks. I give you my word.'

Lucien knew that Hunter would come back to that. He knew that Hunter would once again try to level with him, so that they could end this once and for all.

Lucien never took anything or anyone for granted, especially a person like Robert Hunter. For four years, while at Stanford University, Hunter and Lucien were the best of friends and practically inseparable. Though many years had passed since their college days, Lucien knew his friend's nature well. He understood his principles and he knew what Hunter stood for. Those were personality qualities that rarely changed with time, and that was why Lucien was counting on Hunter putting his offer forward once gain.

And Hunter didn't disappoint, but there was something in his tone when he proposed that they met – a true sadness that seemed to come from deep within. A sadness that suggested that Hunter had given up on the fight and had simply accepted his fate.

Everything one day indeed comes to an end.

Eighty-Nine

'*Tell the driver to go past Echo Park itself,*' Lucien told Hunter, interrupting him mid-poem. '*Until he gets to Sunset Boulevard, just ahead of you.*'

The hairs on the back of Hunter's neck stood on end. As he looked left, he realized that they were level with the park. Immediately, he swung his body on his seat to look behind him. Lucien had to be following them. There was no other way he would've known their position so precisely.

But the effort was fruitless.

Traffic behind them was solid and in a single file, which meant that Hunter could really only see the driver sitting inside the car directly behind them – a Mercedes Benz driven by an old lady who looked to be in her mid-sixties. Instinctively, Hunter scooted left on the cab's backseat, then right, trying to see past the Mercedes Benz.

No good.

'Everyting OK, mon?' the driver asked, noticing Hunter's agitation in the backseat.

'Yes, everything is fine,' Hunter replied, facing forward again. 'Can you please go all the way up to Sunset Boulevard?'

'Sure ting, mon.'

Ninety

By the time Garcia was finally able to veer off onto exit 5A, the red dot on his cellphone screen had driven past Echo Park and turned left on Sunset Boulevard. A broken-down truck on the outer lane had slowed him down considerably, despite his siren and flashing lights.

'How are you doing, Peter?' he asked Holbrook, after informing everyone of his very slow progress.

'*I'm gaining on him,*' Holbrook said. '*But also very slowly. I'm now maybe about half an hour away.*'

Garcia was holding on to his steering wheel so tightly, his knuckles were starting to go white. He was the closest to Hunter and, even with clear roads, he was still at least eighteen to twenty minutes away. If Hunter's life depended on them getting to him, and Garcia was pretty sure it would, that was nowhere near good enough.

'Does anyone think that we should dispatch a couple of units to intercept?' he asked. 'We're still way too far out and I've got a bad feeling about this.'

'*No, we can't.*' West was the first to reply.

'Why not?' Garcia queried, as he used his horn to get the

attention of a yellow Mustang in front of him that didn't seem to notice his flashing blue and red lights.

The Mustang finally pulled over to one side.

'*Because we have no visual confirmation that Robert is with Lucien at this point,*' West replied. '*They might not be together in the same vehicle, Carlos.*'

Garcia's eyes narrowed, as he thought about it.

'*What if Lucien is giving him instructions over the phone or in some other way?*' West continued. '*Do we even know if Robert is in his own car or not?*'

Garcia had been so surprised by Hunter's tracker coming alive, so worried about his partner, that he hadn't thought of that.

'No, we don't know,' he replied. 'But I can find . . .'

Garcia was interrupted by another incoming call. This time it was Captain Blake.

'Hold on,' he said. 'The captain is on the line.' He took the call.

'*Carlos, what the hell is going on?*' She sounded concerned rather than angry. '*Is Robert with you? An officer just found his jacket, together with his phone, car keys, wallet, badge and his weapon lying on the hood of a black-and-white unit down in the parking lot. What the hell?*'

That clearly answered the question of whether Hunter was driving his own vehicle or not.

Garcia quickly explained what had happened before adding Captain Blake to the conference call.

She too immediately suggested dispatching a couple of units to the location of the red dot so they could intercept.

West gave her the same answer he gave Garcia.

'*We now know that he's not driving his own*

car,' the captain replied, '*which clearly suggests that Lucien's got him.*'

'*Not necessarily,*' West came back. '*Lucien could've forced Robert to commandeer a vehicle and follow his instructions,*' he explained. '*He could've forced him to take a cab or even a police car. Have they all been checked and accounted for?*'

Captain Blake's silence answered West's question.

'*Lucien could've also enlisted the help of a third party,*' West continued. '*Sending a vehicle to pick Robert up – a cab or a chauffeur company, I don't know – but there are way too many possibilities that put Lucien and Robert in separate vehicles, or even separate locations. We just can't risk it. Not at this point.*'

West took a breathing pause.

'*Look, Captain,*' he moved on, his tone sympathetic. '*You and Carlos have a much more personal relationship with Robert than Peter and myself. I understand that and I understand your concern. Yes, I'm not going to lie to you – his life is in very great danger, but Robert is the head of the LAPD's Ultra Violent Crimes Unit. His life is in danger every time he gets out of bed and goes to work. The same goes for all of us. It's the nature of the job we do and we all took an oath to protect and to serve.*'

Neither Garcia nor Captain Blake could argue with West's reasoning.

'*Since Lucien's escape, eighteen days ago,*' West added, '*we've all been working for this exact moment – the moment that we could somehow get close to him, because like Robert said before, Lucien is the closest thing to a ghost we'll ever see. If he had chosen not to contact Robert in the first place . . . not to come looking for revenge, I don't think that we'd ever stand a chance of catching him again. This is the only opportunity we've had so far and if we blow this . . . something tells me that we'll never get a chance again.'*

After clearing the yellow Mustang, Garcia began making great progress, but he was still about twelve minutes away.

On his cellphone screen, he saw the red dot turn left on Sunset Boulevard then left again on Lemoyne Street. As Lemoyne Street joined Park Avenue, the dot stopped moving.

'It's stopped,' Garcia announced. 'The tracker's stopped moving.'

'*Where?*' Captain Blake asked. She was the only one who did not have the tracker app installed on her cellphone. '*Where has it stopped?*'

'North entrance to Echo Park,' Garcia replied. 'By Echo Park Lake. It's in the parking lot.'

Everyone went silent for a moment.

'*Wait a second,*' Holbrook said. '*It's moving again . . . onto the grassy area. He's on foot.*'

Garcia's attention began jumping from the road in front of him to his cellphone, as if he were witnessing the fastest tennis match in history.

'Peter is right,' he said. 'It's moving across the grass, in the direction of the lake itself.'

Garcia's attention returned to the road. He swerved past a motorbike and stepped on it with everything he had.

He was about ten minutes away.

Ninety-One

'*Tell the driver to swing left and take Lemoyne Street,*' Lucien instructed Hunter, who was just about to start reciting another poem over the phone to Lucien. They'd covered only two blocks on Sunset Boulevard.

Hunter did as he was told and once again turned to look behind them, still trying to spot Lucien somewhere. Still too many cars following in a single file.

'*Directly at the end of Lemoyne Street,*' Lucien continued, '*across Park Avenue, it's the entrance to the north car park in Echo Park. Tell the driver to drop you there.*'

Less than a minute later, the yellow cab was pulling into the car park.

'*Now pay the driver and get out,*' Lucien ordered Hunter, who followed his instructions.

'You want to meet in the park?' Hunter asked.

'*You'll see,*' Lucien replied.

As Hunter stepped out of the cab, he turned and faced the parking lot entrance, his eyes searching everywhere, but no other vehicle had followed them inside. He tried searching the road outside, but the distance and darkness posed a problem. He could see cars driving by, but there was no way that he would be able to identify anyone at the wheel.

'*From the parking lot,*' Lucien instructed, '*start making your way toward the lake itself. You can see it from there. It will be on your left.*'

Hunter moved from the parking lot onto the grass, bearing southeast.

'I know this park well, Lucien,' he said, as he walked past an old man walking his dog. 'You can just tell me where you want me to go and I'll get there. You don't have to guide me by the hand.'

'*Oh why? Are you growing tired of my voice? Already? I can change it for you if you prefer. How about this?*'

Just like that, Lucien's voice altered completely. In a split second it assumed a tone about half an octave above his real voice and it gained a heavy Russian accent.

'*Is this any better?*'

Hunter shrugged as he walked. 'Whatever you prefer, Lucien.'

Lucien reverted back to his real voice. '*If you keep on walking due southeast, in just a few seconds you'll come to the northeast tip of Echo Park Lake. It's the only portion of the entire lake that has an island.*'

'OK, and . . . ?'

'*There are several trees on that island.*'

'Yes, I know,' Hunter replied. He could see it directly in front of him. Five paces later, he was by the edge of the lake, facing the small central island that Lucien was referring to. 'You're not going to tell me that you're hiding behind one of those trees, are you?'

Lucien laughed again.

'*If I could've pulled that one off, that would've been something, wouldn't it?*'

'It would, indeed.'

Hunter had a look around. Despite being night time, the park was still open and there were still several people around – some jogging, some walking their dogs, some just enjoying a pleasant Los Angeles evening surrounded by trees and green fields. No sign of Lucien.

'So *what about the central island?*' Hunter asked.

'*I left you a present there,*' Lucien replied. '*Behind one of those trees.*'

A 'present' sounded way too ominous for Hunter's liking.

'What do you mean by "a present"?'

'*You'll see. You have to go get it, but here's the trick. As you have probably noticed, the pedestrian bridge that allows punters to get to the island is shut.*'

Hunter looked to his right and saw that the small bridge entrance was indeed blocked. A large black-and-yellow "workmen" signed read – "DANGER. Bridge shut due to structural work. Do not cross." Hunter looked down at the water. The distance between him and the central island was about thirty-five feet, and at that point the lake was at least six and a half feet deep.

'You want me to swim across?'

'*That's the idea, Grasshopper, but here's the thing – before you get into the water, strip.*'

'Excuse me?'

'*My rules, remember?*' Lucien reminded Hunter. '*I want you to get to that central island, but your clothes stay where you are. And please don't forget that I can see you, but you can't see me. One unexpected movement from you and this ends right here.*'

Hunter knew exactly why Lucien was asking him to get rid of his clothes and get into the water. He was making sure that

Hunter had no electronic devices with him – no microphones, no cameras, no trackers.

Hunter looked around again. There were enough people in the vicinity of the lake to notice him getting undressed.

'You want me to jump into the water naked?' he asked.

'*Is that a problem?*' Lucien asked. '*Don't worry, Grasshopper. I'm sure that there isn't much to see anyway.*'

'I'm going to get arrested,' Hunter said, looking around one more time.

'*For your sake, let's hope you don't. Now strip, then throw all of your clothes into the lake – shirt, trousers, underwear, shoes, socks … all of it. Do not leave anything by the water's edge, am I clear?*'

'How about the phone?' Hunter asked.

'*Into the water.*'

Surprise took over the detective's face. 'How are we going to communicate, Lucien?'

'*Trust me, Grasshopper. Now, phone, clothes, everything … into the lake and make sure they sink. If you don't reach the central island in thirty seconds and find the package I've left you, this is all over, is that understood?*'

'It's nuts, but yes, it's understood.'

'*Do it now.*'

Right there, by the water's edge and before several pairs of shocked eyes, Hunter got completely undressed and jumped into the water, taking with him all of his clothes, which he had wrapped around his shoes and the phone he'd been using. He made sure that everything had sunk down to the bottom of Echo Park Lake before swimming over to the small central island.

Ninety-Two

Garcia cut through Silver Lake, heading east toward Echo Park. Due to the red dot on his cellphone screen slowing down to a snail's pace, he gained on it, but still not fast enough.

'*It's stopped again,*' Holbrook announced. '*Right by the northeast edge of Echo Park Lake.*'

Garcia peeked at his cellphone. 'What the hell is it doing?'

'*It looks like he's either appreciating the view,*' West replied, '*or he's talking to someone.*'

'*Lucien?*' Captain Blake asked.

'*Possibly,*' West answered. '*But if so, Lucien picked one hell of a public spot to meet up with Robert. How close are you, Carlos?*'

'Seven minutes . . . maybe a little less.'

'*Code-two high priority on this, Carlos,*' Holbrook warned him. '*No sirens, no lights. Approach with extreme caution. We cannot give out that Robert is being tailed. The tracker is still holding at the same location, but we have no idea of what Robert is doing. Like Tyler said, he might be just standing there waiting for something, or he might be talking to someone. We don't know. We need visual confirmation before deciding on a plan of action.*'

Do they think this is my first time doing this? Garcia thought, but kept it to himself. 'Understood.'

As soon as he joined Glendale Boulevard, Garcia switched off his flashing lights. Fifteen seconds later he swung left onto Park Avenue. Five seconds after that, he was pulling into the same car park where the cab had dropped Hunter.

'I'm here,' he informed everyone as he parked his car, grabbed his cellphone and exited his vehicle.

'No movement from Robert yet,' West announced. *'He's still by the water's edge.'*

'Yes, I see that,' Garcia replied, checking his cellphone. He took a deep breath to steady himself and as calmly as any citizen having a leisurely night stroll through the park, began making his way toward the lake. Fifteen paces later he paused by a young couple sitting at a bench smoking a spliff.

'What's happening, Carlos?' Captain Blake asked.

'I can't see him,' Garcia replied, staring straight ahead. On his screen, the red dot was still blinking just a few yards directly in front of him. He looked left then right. No sign of Hunter.

'What do you mean, you can't see him?' West asked. *'Is he behind a tree or something?'*

'No, no trees. No obstacles whatsoever. I have a clear, direct-line view to the tracker location. Clear view of the water. There's no one there.' Garcia took a few more steps toward the lake.

'Carlos, what's happening?' Captain Blake insisted in an urgent voice.

'Give me a sec, Captain,' Garcia said, quickly tracking back to the spliff couple sitting at the bench.

'Sorry,' he said, interrupting them. 'Did you happen to see a tall, sort of strong-looking individual, standing by the lake just a moment ago by any chance?'

'Naked, ripped dude?' the woman replied with a smile. Her voice was dragging, a consequence of what she was smoking. 'Yeah, man. Dude got butt-ass naked right there.' She pointed to where Hunter had been. 'Then just jumped into the water and swam off to the island.'

'He jumped naked into the water and swam to the island?' Garcia's face was made of surprise.

'That's right, man,' the woman confirmed. 'He was probably tripping, but damn was he ripped? Wanna hit?' She offered Garcia her spliff. 'It's good stuff, man.'

'No thanks. I'm OK. Did he swim back from the island?'

'Not that we saw.'

Garcia thanked them and went back to his phone.

'He jumped naked into the water and swam up to the central island,' he told everyone.

'*He did what?*' Captain Blake, Holbrook and West all asked at the same time.

'I've just talked to some people who have been sitting at a bench facing the lake,' Garcia explained. 'They told me that they saw this guy, who fitted Hunter's description, get butt-naked, jump into the water and swim up to the central island you can all see on the map.'

'*Swim to the island?*' the captain asked. '*Why didn't he use the footbridge?*'

'It's blocked,' Garcia replied, turning to look in the direction of the bridge. 'Structural work.'

'*And then what?*' West asked. '*Did he swim back? Did he swim off to the other side? Is he still on the island? What did he do?*'

'I don't know,' Garcia came back, rushing back to the side of the lake. 'The people I talked to said that they didn't see him swim back.' From the water's edge, he began rounding the island. At its widest point, it measured around sixty-five feet, at its longest one hundred and thirty. It was a little hard to see through the darkness and the trees, but Garcia saw no sign of Hunter anywhere, not on the island nor on the other side of it.

'He's gone,' Garcia confirmed, his heart sinking. 'Robert is gone. I've just circled the entire island. I've looked everywhere. There's no trace of him.'

'*But have you checked the island itself?*' Captain Blake pushed. '*On the ground, behind a tree. He could have been knocked unconscious or . . .*' She thought of worse, but kept herself from saying it.

'Captain,' Garcia reassured her, 'he's not here.' The lump that came to his throat almost gagged him. 'Robert isn't here. We've lost him. Game over.'

Ninety-Three

It took Hunter mere seconds to swim from the water's edge to the small island at the northeast end of Echo Park Lake. The water was positively cold and as he pulled himself onto the awkwardly shaped piece of land packed with trees and shrubs, the hefty breeze that the night had brought with it chilled him to the bone. Shivering from head to toe, he frantically began looking around, searching for whatever it was that Lucien had left for him there.

'What the hell am I looking for here?' he asked the trees, and funnily enough, they replied.

As Hunter took a few steps into the island to look behind a high bush, he heard a phone ring. Instantly, he stopped moving and looked back in the direction he had come from. Maybe the ring was coming from the other side of the water.

It rang again, not from the other side, but from somewhere to his right. He held steady and waited, his eyes searching everywhere. The ring came again, identical to the one he'd heard coming from his pocket about an hour earlier. This time, it was coming from behind a short, leafy tree.

Hunter moved to it.

One more ring.

Darkness made it all a little difficult, but after the next ring, Hunter finally saw it. Behind the tree, another cellphone, this time a 2001 Samsung SCH-N300, had been left on top of a heavy-duty plastic bag.

Hunter reached for the phone.

'Lucien.' He answered the call in an unsteady voice.

'*I knew that you wouldn't disappoint me, Grasshopper. How's the water?*' He laughed.

Hunter wrapped his left arm around his body and began rubbing his hand against his torso to try to produce some heat.

'So,' Lucien continued. '*Let's move to the second phase of our face-to-face meeting, shall we? The one with no trackers, or microphones, or cameras, or anything else you might've had with you, Robert.*'

Hunter waited.

'*Inside the plastic bag, you'll find an old tracksuit.*'

Hunter bent down and picked up the bag. The tracksuit was pink.

'*You'll also find a pair of flip-flops. You will love them, I'm sure. Everything should fit you fine.*'

Hunter was so cold that he was about to rip open the bag, but Lucien stopped him.

'*Now you have to swim back to shore,*' Lucien told him. '*So if I were you, I wouldn't put those clothes on just yet.*'

The wind picked up in strength and Hunter let go of a frozen breath.

'*The plastic bag should be good enough to protect the clothes,*' Lucien explained, '*if you are intending to jump back in the water with everything in the bag, or you can just toss everything across the lake to the other side, but here's the catch – you're not turning back west, where you just came*

*from. You're moving east. You're jumping into the water at
the other side of the island. Got that?'*

'Yes, I got it.'

*'Your choice what you want to do with the clothes – in the
bag or toss it, but you've got twenty seconds to make it there,
and the clock starts ... now.'*

Bag in hand, Hunter quickly moved past the trees and
bushes to get to the east side of the small island. The distance
across the lake from the island to the shore on the east side was
very similar to that on the west side – about thirty-five feet. It
was a lot easier for Hunter just to toss the bag across and then
jump back into the water, but his concern was the phone. If he
threw it across the lake, chances were that it would break. Even
if he placed it inside the bag with the pink tracksuit, there were
no guarantees that the phone wouldn't smash when it hit the
ground on the other side.

Hunter decided that he couldn't risk it. He got to the edge of
the island and with his right hand, tossed the plastic bag with
the tracksuit and the flip-flops to the other side. It covered the
distance with no problem and Hunter watched as it hit land
about sixteen feet clear from the water's edge.

Now all he had to do was swim with the phone without
allowing it to get wet.

Piece of cake, he thought.

At that end, Echo Park Lake was about six and a half feet
deep. Hunter was exactly six feet tall, so if he held the phone in
his right hand and extended it high above his head, he would be
able to get into the water without getting the phone wet. From
there the rest was easy.

That was exactly what he did. Nine seconds later he was at
the other side.

As Hunter pulled himself out of the water, two women, both in their early twenties, cycled past him and almost collided with each other.

'Damn,' one of them said, 'I didn't know that there were Chippendales in the water. I threw that wish coin in there years ago. You took a while to materialize.'

'If you're cold, honey,' the other shouted out, 'I can warm you up.'

They both laughed.

'OK,' Hunter said into the phone, getting to the plastic bag and ripping it open. 'Now what?'

'*Now I'd suggest that you get dressed,*' Lucien replied. '*Inside the trouser pocket of your tracksuit, you'll find some cash. Get yourself to Echo Park Avenue as fast as you can and flag down another cab. I'll give you more instructions then.*'

Ninety-Four

It took Hunter four tries to finally get a cab to stop for him. In a city like Los Angeles, an old pink tracksuit didn't really put in a good word for anyone. The flip-flops, one size too small and decorated with a large pink rose on the toe-strap, didn't do Hunter any favors either.

'Where to?' the cab driver, an African American woman in her thirties, asked, turning on her seat and looking at Hunter a little intrigued.

Hunter waited. He knew Lucien had also heard the driver.

'*Tell her to go in the direction of Altadena.*'

Hunter instructed her.

'Are you going to a party or something?' the driver asked, fixing Hunter down through the rear-view mirror.

'No, not really.'

The driver nodded. 'So that really was *your* choice of clothes for this evening? Because ... damn.' She shook her head vigorously. 'That tracksuit is nasty. And those flip-flops ... uhm, uhm.' She carried on shaking her head. 'I mean *uhm, uhm.*'

'I didn't have much of a choice tonight,' Hunter replied.

'*I like her,*' Lucien said. '*She's funny.*'

After Echo Park and all the precautionary measures he had

taken, Lucien didn't have to follow Hunter's cab anymore to know exactly where he was.

It had taken him a few days to find it, but the phone that Hunter was now using – a Samsung SCH-N300 – was one of the first ever commercial mobile phones to have a GPS system integrated into it. Lucien could now follow Hunter's movement through the electronic map on his own smartphone, which was a great advantage to him, because he needed to get to his warehouse at least ten minutes before Hunter.

'OK, *which poem were you on again?*'

'Poem?'

'*Yes, Grasshopper. Poe's poems, remember? I was really enjoying that and you still have quite a few to go, don't you?*'

With no other alternative, Hunter sat back in his seat and began reciting poems again.

The driver took them through Glassell Park and Pasadena before finally taking North Lake Avenue heading toward Altadena.

'Sorry to interrupt your very creepy telephone serenade,' the driver said. 'But we'll be getting to Altadena very soon. Any specific location you would like me to drop you off?'

Lucien instructed Hunter, who passed the information to the driver. Five minutes later, a very relieved cab driver dropped Hunter off at a remote, non-residential area in the north part of Altadena.

Still taking no chances, Lucien kept Hunter on the phone, making him walk for another five minutes, until he finally guided Hunter to the correct location.

'*The last property on the left, right at the top of the road, Grasshopper,*' Lucien said. '*The hangar-looking building.*

There's a breach in the fence just a few yards from the front gate. You can get in through there.'

Despite the darkness, Hunter studied the building from the outside. It was clearly another business hit by recession. There were so many of these disused structures scattered all over Los Angeles, that he wasn't at all surprised that Lucien had chosen to use one of them.

Hunter followed Lucien's instructions and got through the fence. At the other side of it, he followed the cracked and warped concrete slabs that once led visitors from the fence gates to the warehouse main entrance doors.

'The doors to the warehouse are open,' Lucien informed Hunter. *'Hanging from one of its handles you will find a headlamp. I suggest you put it on and switch it on. It's dark in there.'*

Hunter got to the door and found the headlamp. Once again he followed Lucien's instructions.

The inside of the warehouse carried an odd mixture of scents – wood, antiseptic cleaner, something floral and something definitely stale.

Hunter paused just a few paces inside the door and looked around. With no windows and no artificial light, the darkness inside was almost absolute, except for the weak beam of light that shot out of Hunter's forehead, strong enough to illuminate only about ten feet in front of him. The floor, just about everywhere, was littered with broken glass.

'Watch your step, Grasshopper. I don't want you to start bleeding yet.'

Hunter took slow and cautious steps forward.

'That's right, keep on walking straight ahead. Soon you'll come to an internal, two-story structure. The place's old head

office. On its right-hand side, you'll find a spiral staircase that'll take you to the second floor. Get up there. The door is unlocked.'

Hunter found the staircase and made his way to the second floor. At the top, he reached for the door handle and pushed it open.

More darkness.

More odd smells.

But this time he picked up a scent that really bothered him – the scent of fuel.

Hunter paused just outside the door and looked around. Just like downstairs, the floor inside the office was littered with broken glass.

'Don't stop now, Grasshopper.'

Hunter turned to look back at the entrance to the warehouse. Lucien still had eyes on him.

'How's this poss—'

That was when things finally began making sense inside his head.

Since this whole ordeal had started, back at the PAB parking lot, Hunter had never really had any time to think. Lucien never allowed him to, keeping him active all the time, reciting poems from memory and making him rush from one place to another. Always on the phone. Constantly talking. But now, finally at Lucien's hideout place, Hunter's brain found time to re-engage.

Hunter had been the one who had suggested that they met ... that they put an end to all of this, but Lucien had it planned all along. That was why he'd planted a phone inside Hunter's jacket pocket. That was the reason why he'd called. If Hunter hadn't said anything about meeting up, Lucien would've probably suggested it himself. How else would he have had everything already in place? The second cellphone, the clothes inside the plastic bag, the island at Echo Park Lake, the headlamp at the door to the old warehouse . . . everything.

Lucien clearly had eyes on him when he placed the call. He knew that Hunter was alone at that precise moment. By forcing him to start moving immediately, Lucien was making sure that Hunter wouldn't have time to alert anyone.

I've been played all along, Hunter thought, cursing how stupid he had been.

'*What are you waiting for, Grasshopper?*' Lucien asked, bringing Hunter's thoughts back to reality. '*Too late to turn back now, don't you think?*'

Hunter finally stepped into the room. With each step he took, he heard and felt the crunch of broken glass under his feet.

'OK. *That's far enough,*' Lucien told him after about eight paces.

Hunter stopped moving.

'*Now, please remove your flip-flops and throw them to your left.*'

Hunter looked down at the floor to make sure that he wouldn't be stepping on shards of glass before complying.

'You won't need that phone anymore either.' This time Lucien's voice didn't come from the phone in Hunter's hand. It came from somewhere directly in front of him.

Hunter's stare shot in the direction of the voice.

Slowly, at the furthest reach of his headlight, the shape of a person ominously began to materialize.

Hunter narrowed his eyes to recalibrate their focus and as the shape finally stepped out of the shadows and into the weak head-beam light, Hunter was instantly swept by doubt.

'Hello, Grasshopper,' Lucien greeted Hunter. Instead of a phone, he had a gun in his right hand.

Though the voice belonged to Lucien, the person standing before Hunter looked nothing like him, but what really made Hunter's skin crawl with disbelief was the fact that Hunter had seen that person before.

And he had seen him less than two hours ago.

Ninety-Five

Darkness made it hard for Hunter to see every detail, but he would be lying if he didn't admit that he was mesmerized by Lucien's incredible transformation. His hair, his skin, his nose, his eyes, his lips, his hands, the shape of his face . . . everything seemed to belong to someone else. It was as if Lucien had not only taken over someone else's body, but someone else's entire persona as well. The man who stood ten paces before Hunter could've sat right next to him in a restaurant and Hunter wouldn't have known any better.

And that had been exactly what had happened.

It took Hunter less than three seconds to match the face to the memory, and it almost choked him.

The man standing before him was the African American gentleman who had taken the table next to theirs at the Five Star Bar.

Lucien smiled proudly as he noticed the look on Hunter's face.

'How is this for "losing my touch", Robert?' he said before turning his face left then right to allow Hunter to admire his feat. 'Fascinating what one can do with the right skills, don't you think?'

Voice aside, Hunter still searched the face of the man before him for any traces of the real Lucien.

He couldn't find any.

'Yes,' Lucien confirmed, leaning a little to his left and switching on a small table lamp on top of a wooden crate. 'It's really me, old friend. I was the one sitting next to you in that bar.'

With his left hand, Lucien pulled off his wig and let it drop to the floor, displaying his completely shaved head. He then grabbed the bridge of his false nose and ripped the whole thing off his face before doing the same to his lips, ears, chin and forehead.

'Boy,' he said, as he cleared his face of the last piece of latex. 'These things can get really uncomfortable after a few hours, you know?' He opened and closed his mouth a couple of times to stretch his jaw muscles.

Hunter watched as the man in front of him slowly transformed back into Lucien.

'Before you get any ideas, Robert,' Lucien said, 'could I remind you that we're about ten paces apart. In between us and all around you, there's more than enough broken glass to completely lacerate both of your bare feet, so if I were you, I'd stand exactly where you are.'

Once again, Hunter looked at the floor. He really was completely surrounded by hundreds of pieces of broken glass. Dashing toward Lucien was definitely out.

Lucien took a moment to study his old college friend. When he spoke again, there was no play in his voice anymore.

'For the past three and a half years, Robert, I've yearned for this moment every second of every minute of every hour of every day. The moment when you and I would be standing face-to-face again.'

'Funny,' Hunter said in reply. 'I haven't thought about you at all in that time.'

Lucien shrugged. 'I didn't expect you to.'

He reached inside his coat pocket for a cleansing tissue and began wiping his face clean of the dark makeup he had used.

'By the way, how is the lovely lady you were seeing? Have you talked to her much in the past few days? Does she hate you yet?'

Hunter kept a steady face. He would not give Lucien the satisfaction.

'I'll level with you, Robert,' Lucien continued. 'My original idea did not include her parents. When I began planning my revenge against you, locked inside a cage barely large enough to be called a cupboard, I had no idea if you were seeing someone or not. I hoped you would be, but I wasn't counting on it. Not in the least. Since I took Jessica and your unborn child from you all those years ago, you never really had another significant relationship, isn't that right?'

It took every ounce of Hunter's willpower for him to show no emotion once he heard Jessica's name.

'That's why I wasn't counting on you having a girlfriend. Yes, my plan was to once again take someone from your life,' Lucien explained. 'Someone who you cared about – your police partner, maybe, a good friend ... I didn't really know who. That was a detail that I knew I would only find out once I made it to LA, so you can imagine my surprise when, on my first night in this city, I saw Tracy.'

Lucien paused, reached for a second cleansing tissue and carried on wiping his face clean.

'Finding your home address from your cellphone number wasn't that hard,' he explained. 'Yes, I had help, but in this city, that sort of help can be found on any corner. You know that, don't you?'

Hunter knew that to be true.

'So that night,' Lucien continued, 'my first night in LA, actually, I checked out your address. I was just standing there, running through a few thoughts in my head, when I saw you arrive. A couple of minutes later, I saw you appear at your window.

'I began wondering how long I would have to stalk you for until I found out who I would take from you, when I saw this beautiful redhead appear out of nowhere and stop just under a lamppost.' Lucien chuckled. 'Not in my wildest dreams would I have imagined that she had anything to do with you. Her beauty was why she got my attention in the first place.' Lucien nodded. 'I have to hand it to you, Robert. She's absolutely stunning.'

Hunter felt his mouth go dry, but his poker face stayed solid.

'Then I see her take out her phone, and while she's making a call, her eyes move to your building. I followed her stare and *voilà* – at your window, I saw you answering your phone.' Lucien let out a pleased laugh. 'The rest you can imagine, right?'

There was nothing Hunter could say.

'The idea of taking her did cross my mind,' Lucien admitted. 'But I'd already done that when I took Jessica from you all those years ago, and one of the premises of my entire research is to try different approaches, different methods.' Another careless shrug from Lucien. 'This was not supposed to be part of my research. This was revenge, pure and simple, but when I thought about it, I saw no reason why I couldn't join revenge and research together.'

Lucien finally finished cleaning his face.

'My plan was always to bring "guilt" into your life, Robert.

The kind of guilt that would consume you from inside. The kind of guilt that you could never get rid of and you'd carry with you until the day you died. So I followed Tracy for a couple of nights. One of those nights she visited her parents in Downey and that was when the idea came to me. After that, all I had to do was put a plan together and execute it.'

Lucien lifted his left hand in a half-surrender gesture.

'I'll admit that I had no idea that she would be having dinner with you that night. That was just a bonus.'

Hunter's eyes moved to the gun in Lucien's hands. Lucien seemed to be holding it quite unconcernedly.

'If you'd had the chance,' Lucien asked, 'you would've given your life for theirs, wouldn't you?'

Hunter didn't reply. He didn't have to.

'Of course you would have,' Lucien accepted it. 'You've always had a big heart, Robert. The problem with a big heart is – it will only be broken into more pieces. Haven't you learned that by now?'

Despite being nighttime, the temperature inside that second-floor office must've been in its mid-twenties. Hunter began wondering why was Lucien wearing such a heavy coat.

'Now let me ask you something else,' Lucien continued. 'Let's say that there was a way in which you could stop me, a way in which you could really put an end to all this . . . but the catch was, you would have to give your life for it. Would you do it, Robert? Would you die just so you could stop me?'

'Yes,' Hunter replied without hesitation and with supreme conviction.

'Really?' Lucien asked as he nodded. 'Would that be because you really want to stop me, or because you don't want to live with the guilt that you should've deciphered that riddle and saved all those people in that bar that night? The guilt that you are the reason why Tracy's parents are dead.'

Hunter saw the fact that Lucien believed so firmly that his acts had indeed filled Hunter's heart with suffocating guilt as an advantage. There was no reason for him to make Lucien believe otherwise. He purposely allowed sadness to creep into his eyes before answering.

'Both,' he lied.

Lucien took a few seconds, as if deliberating on Hunter's answer.

'Interesting,' he said. 'And maybe this is your lucky day, Robert, because I have a present for you.'

Lucien held the suspense for a beat.

'Tell me what you think of this.'

Ninety-Six

Every muscle in Hunter's body tensed almost to the point of cramping. He knew that Lucien would have a plan in place, and if Lucien had a plan then some sort of twist was to be expected, but Hunter had never imagined that it would be something like this.

Lucien let go of his gun and, in one smooth movement, pulled open the heavy coat he had on to show Hunter his present.

Underneath it, Lucien was wearing a suicide vest.

Hunter blinked, incredulous.

There were five makeshift front pockets at around chest height, each containing a small cylindrical lump of plastic explosive. Different-colored wires jumped from one lump to the other, connecting them all together. A sixth pocket had been sewn just underneath the first five. It contained a cellphone. The same wire that connected the five lumps of explosive ran down to the sixth pocket, making the phone the final part of Lucien's bomb.

Lucien saw the blood drain from Hunter's face.

'Oh, c'mon, Robert,' he said, giving Hunter a sarcastic smile. 'Did you really think that those two pounds of C-4 was all I had?' He made a face as if he was having a conversation with a naughty child. 'How naive of you.'

Hunter was still studying the vest Lucien had on.

'If you're wondering if this is real or not,' Lucien said, 'trust me, this is as real as it gets and it's as powerful as the one I used in Hollywood, but much deadlier. Look around.'

Hunter stood still.

'Go on,' Lucien insisted. 'Look around.'

Hunter finally turned his head to look first to his right, then his left, his head-beam creating a narrow corridor of light. As it slowly moved around the office space, Hunter finally understood what Lucien was referring to. On the floor, pushed up against the walls, there must've been at least fifteen one-gallon plastic containers. They were all full and they were the reason for the fuel smell Hunter had picked up as he entered the room, but that wasn't all. Also scattered around the room were a vast number of wood planks and cardboard sheets. If Lucien's suicide vest went off, that entire office would become one huge fireball in the blink of an eye, which would burn at super-high temperatures. Nothing and no one would survive.

Hunter looked back at Lucien with an unspoken question in his eyes.

Lucien read it loud and clear.

'You're wondering if I'm ready for this?' he asked. 'What's with all this naivety, Robert, is it age?' He laughed. 'You know that I don't believe that there's a God, right?' Lucien clarified. 'I don't believe in afterlife, or paradise, or fate, or that we are all part of some stupid master plan, or any of the bullshit humanity has been fed for centuries.' He pointed at Hunter. 'But I'll tell you what I do believe, Robert. I believe that we all should find our own reason to live, our own reason to make our lives worthwhile, whatever that reason may be. Something that drives us forward. Something that makes us want to brave this fucked-up world we live in. Something that inspires our minds and feeds our souls, that's what I believe, Robert . . . and that's what I did. I found something that gave my life purpose and filled me with excitement. My research was my life.'

Lucien paused and looked around for an instant.

'Fine,' he agreed without much care. 'In the eyes of most it was a dirty job, but who the hell are we kidding, Robert? This world is full of dirty and disgusting jobs and you know it. Government jobs, law enforcement jobs, big corporation jobs, pharmaceutical jobs . . . all of them entities whose greed seems to have no end. The world is being brainwashed and monopolized by just a handful of companies, which are run by the biggest megalomaniacs, psychopaths and sociopaths of all time, and you are giving *me* dirty looks.' Lucien chuckled as he shook his head. 'Compared to them, Robert, I'm a spit in the universe. Yes, I did what *I* chose to do and maybe I would've continued doing it, if you hadn't showed up three and a half years ago.'

Hunter saw fire flash inside Lucien's eyes.

'Back then,' Lucien explained, 'no one knew I even existed, Robert. I approached every single one of my experiments differently – different MOs, different signatures, different levels of sadism, different locations. The authorities, whoever they were, never once connected any two of my acts to the same perpetrator. I was never, not even once, inside anyone's radar. I could walk the streets unconcerned, safe in the knowledge that my research was secure . . . but not anymore. I am now a wanted man, a fugitive. No matter where I go, I will never walk the streets unconcerned again. Forevermore I will be looking over my shoulder, wondering if the person standing on the corner reading a newspaper is a government agent or not.

Despite how good I am at transforming myself into a different person, I will never have peace of mind again . . . and that's not a life, Robert. I refuse to spend the rest of my life running, and I will *not* spend the rest of my life in a cage, being studied like a lab rat by that sick fat-fuck, Adrian Kennedy.'

Determination oozed from every word Lucien uttered.

'My research is done, Robert,' Lucien admitted. 'Maybe there are a few things here and there that I would've liked to have tried, but that's fine. I have achieved what I set myself out to achieve. I have lived my life the way I wanted to live my life, no matter what. How many people in this world can say that, Robert?' Lucien jerked his chin in Hunter's direction. 'Can you?'

Before Hunter could answer, his headlamp blinked unsteadily for a moment before going off. The room became darker still. The weak table lamp to Lucien's left was now the only light source inside the office space.

'Everything one day comes to an end, my friend,' Lucien said, and for the first time ever Hunter detected a hint of pure sadness in his voice. 'Everything, including you and me.'

Another overly tense pause.

'So to answer your wordless question, Robert – yes, I am ready for this. I'm ready to die right here, right now. Are you?'

Hunter needed to stall Lucien. His plan depended on time.

'Yes,' he replied.

'Really? OK!'

Under Hunter's watchful eye, Lucien placed his gun by the table lamp on the wooden crate before reaching inside his left jacket pocket and retrieving another cellphone. He quickly dialed a number, but stopped short of pressing the 'send' button. He then threw the phone over to Hunter.

'Here, catch.'

Hunter caught it mid-flight.

Lucien picked up his gun again.

'The host cellphone number is cued in,' Lucien informed Hunter, indicating the cellphone in his suicide vest. 'All you have to do is press "send", Robert, that's all.'

Hunter's stare moved to the phone.

'And if I don't?' he asked.

Lucien laughed. 'Having second thoughts already, are we? I thought that you were confident in your decision just a second ago. I thought you were ready for this.'

Keep stalling, Hunter thought. *Keep stalling.*

'I know you, Lucien,' he replied, his voice still calm. 'You've never been the sort to have no plan B. I'm sure that you've factored in the possibility of me not detonating that vest. Then what?'

Lucien laughed again. 'That's why I like you, Robert. You've always been too clever for your own good. Of course I've considered that possibility.'

'Of course you have. So what is the option?'

'The option is that you can also press the red button and cancel the call.'

'And what happens then?'

'Then there will be no big bang,' Lucien explained. 'No fireworks. Both of us will be able to walk out of here alive, but the difference is, I have a quick escape route and, as you can see . . .' Lucien pointed to his feet. 'I'm wearing some pretty heavy-duty boots. You, on the other hand, will have to find your way out of here barefoot, through a sea of broken glass, and in pitch-black darkness.' He shrugged at Hunter. 'Not a high price to pay when considering the alternative, right?' A cheeky smile. 'But you won't get off that easily, old friend.'

Somehow, Hunter knew that there would be a twist.

'This is the only opportunity I will ever give you to stop me,' Lucien continued. '*Ever*. If you choose not to, the only logical conclusion is that you don't want me to stop . . . so I won't.' Lucien allowed those words to float in the air for a moment. 'Once I get out of here, Robert, I'll disappear and you'll never see me again, old friend, ever . . . but you'll certainly hear from me again. I can promise you that.'

Hunter didn't need an explanation to know what Lucien meant, but Lucien wasn't one to leave things unexplained.

'In every city, every town, every village I stop, I'll claim a new victim.' Another careless shrug. 'Maybe more, who knows? And every time I do, I'll make sure you know that the reason why they died is because you were too chicken-shit to press that "send" button. How's that for a new concept of a guilt trip? The guilt trip that will keep on giving.'

'You really have thought of everything, haven't you?' Hunter was still trying to stall.

'Oh yes,' Lucien replied. 'I have indeed, old friend. And I guess that now it's the moment of truth. It's time you made a decision. You have five seconds.'

As Hunter's eyes scanned the room one last time, his heart sank inside of him. He knew that he had run out of options. Lucien was standing ten paces in front of him and he was holding a weapon. Even if Hunter had his shoes on and the floor wasn't completely littered with broken glass, he would've never been able to cover that distance in time. Lucien would shoot him dead before he'd made it halfway.

'Five . . .' Lucien began the countdown.

Hunter looked at the phone in his right hand, his thumb hovering over both buttons. His plan hadn't worked. No one was coming for him.

'Four . . .'

Hunter felt his entire core shake.

'Three . . .'

His eyes moved to Lucien and his grip tightened around the phone.

'Two . . .'

Everything one day comes to an end . . . everything.

'One . . .'

Dashing toward Lucien would undoubtedly mean certain death . . . so would pressing that 'send' button. The difference was, either Hunter died alone, or he died for a cause.

'Zero . . . time's up, Robert.'

Hunter wished that he could've said goodbye to Garcia.

He wished that he could've said goodbye to Tracy.

His only comfort was that Lucien would *never* kill again.

Hunter locked eyes with his old college friend for the last time and took in a deep breath.

'I'll see you in hell, Lucien.'

Ninety-Seven

The explosion was heard by all of the neighboring streets. In fact, the blast noise reached just over a quarter of a mile in all directions. Just like he had done before, Lucien had calculated everything to the last detail and with analytical precision – the amount of plastic explosives needed, the number of fuel gallons, the distance between Hunter and himself, how fast the fuel would burn, the velocity of the shockwave ... everything.

Lucien wanted the place to blow up and immediately ignite in flames, but he also wanted to restrict the destruction mainly to the warehouse and the office inside it. In his eyes, there was no need to make a huge spectacle out of it. This was between Hunter and Lucien, nothing else and no one else mattered. Not to Lucien.

Once the host cellphone in the suicide vest was activated, it took only zero point two seconds for it to send an electrical signal to the detonator embedded into one of the five plastic explosive lumps in the vest. The electrical signal ignited the detonator, which in turn produced more than enough heat to push the core plastic explosive temperature to what was needed to detonate the compound.

And it all blew up just like Lucien had planned.

The solid wood boards that Lucien had nailed over the old internal windows were savagely ripped from the walls and blown across the entire warehouse. The roof directly above the epicenter of the blast was blown high up in the air, showering the outside of the warehouse with a significant amount of blazing tiles and metal debris, which served to set some of the surrounding vegetation on fire. But it was inside the office space where Hunter and Lucien stood that Lucien's precise calculations and unparalleled evil brilliance became evident.

Due to the proximity between the explosives and the fuel, the heat produced by the blast's shockwave instantaneously melted the plastic containers, reaching the liquid fuel inside them faster than a bullet would. The result was the entire upstairs office being homogeneously engulfed in a single, gigantic wall of fire, hot enough to melt steel.

Hunter was right – no living thing could've escaped from that office.

Ninety-Eight

Lucien wasn't the kind of person who would leave anything to chance, so of course he had factored the possibility of Hunter canceling the call instead of putting it through. That was why he had a contingency plan in place for that too.

Despite knowing Hunter well, despite Lucien's certainty that his old college friend would do the noble thing and try to put an end to Lucien's murderous reign by pressing the 'send' button, Lucien also knew that Hunter could be just as unpredictable as Lucien himself.

Maybe Hunter also had a plan in place, something that Lucien had somehow failed to anticipate, and that was why he had lied to Hunter.

When asked, Lucien had told Hunter that if he canceled the call instead of putting it through, there would be no 'big bang', no fireworks.

That wasn't true.

Lucien wanted that warehouse to blow up.

He wanted the fireworks.

And that was why he had rigged the phone that he had given Hunter so that both buttons – red and green – would carry the exact same function.

It didn't matter which button Hunter had pressed. The call would have been put through to the host phone in the suicide vest regardless. That warehouse would blow up no matter what, and Lucien couldn't have been more pleased.

Everything had paid off – the lengthy rehearsals, the almost endless calculations and re-calculations, the meticulous planning, all of it – but the real stroke of genius came with the blast itself.

Yes, Lucien had practiced everything so many times, he could've run through all of it back to front and he still wouldn't have missed a step, but the explosion itself couldn't be rehearsed, couldn't be practiced, and it couldn't be tested. He had to get every inch, every tiny calculation absolutely right if he was to stand any chance of walking out of that warehouse alive.

And he did.

Ninety-Nine

The suicide-vest idea had begun taking shape in Lucien's head about three years ago, once he realized that escaping from a FBI Federal Prison wasn't as impossible as he thought it might be. From that moment on, Lucien began running through different scenarios in his head, looking for a plan that could be pulled off.

The idea itself wasn't that complicated. First, he needed to get Hunter alone inside an isolated, dimly lit room, preferably somewhere out of town or thereabouts. The lack of light inside the room was essential for the plan to work. Then came the speech. Lucien's eyes, demeanor and words had to be convincing enough for Hunter to believe that he was ready to die, that he was satisfied with his work on this earth, that he would not spend the rest of his life running and that he would never, ever go back into a cage. And if there was one thing Lucien knew that he excelled at, it was sounding convincing.

The final and most important part of all was, of course, the blast. Lucien needed to calculate the velocity, the intensity and the travel distance of the blast shockwave with as much precision as possible so he wouldn't be hurt, and that depended solely on one thing – the distance between Lucien and the bomb.

The bomb was not strapped to Lucien's body. That was a dummy suicide vest. The phone on it was real, but the plastic explosive lumps were made out of modeling clay. The real suicide vest was located across the room from him, about five paces behind Hunter's position and fifteen paces from where Lucien was. It had been strapped against someone else's body, a 'John Doe', who Lucien had taken from the streets a couple of days back. That John Doe matched Lucien in height, weight, body shape, age and ethnicity, though none of that was really essential. As long as Lucien had been correct with his calculations concerning how hot the flames inside that office space would burn and for how long, no DNA would be able to be extracted from whatever bone fragments were found in the aftermath of the explosion by any CSI team. Lucien knew that for a fact.

The blast, together with the intense heat produced by the shockwave and the burning fuels, would completely obliterate all of John Doe's soft tissue – skin, muscle, flesh, gray matter . . . everything. All that would be left behind, since the bomb was in actual physical contact with the body, would be fragments of hard tissue (bones and teeth), but just to be on the safe side, Lucien had already extracted all of John Doe's teeth.

The accuracy of DNA extracted from burned bone fragments depended exclusively on the fragments' stage of fire-induced destruction. When it came to human hard tissue, five stages existed – well preserved, semi-burned, black burned, blue-gray burned, and blue-gray-white burned With the two last stages – blue-gray and blue-gray-white burned – the accurate amplification of genetic markers became practically impossible, as the fragments would lose most of their characteristics and become extremely prone to contamination.

All that Lucien needed to do was make sure that John Doe's bone fragments burned hot enough and for long enough for them to be categorized as either blue-gray or blue-gray-white burned. That was the main reason for all those gallons of fuel scattered around the room.

With all that calculated and in place, Lucien was left with his final problem – how would he get out of that room alive? How would he escape the inferno that that second-floor office would become?

The answers to those questions could be found in a simple premise – Lucien was the one getting out of that room, not Hunter. That was why Hunter and Lucien's positioning inside that office was so important. That was also why Lucien needed to keep most of the office hidden in shadow and why he told Hunter to stop when he told him to stop. Hunter had reached the exact position Lucien needed him in.

About six paces behind Lucien and a little to his left, hidden behind a few cardboard boxes, was the office fire exit. Lucien didn't have to build it. The exit was already there because fire exits are a government safety regulation. If that warehouse had a two-story office located deep inside it, it would've only been allowed to operate if government safety regulations were met, and they indeed had been.

The external metal fire door behind Lucien led to a fire escape staircase at the back of the warehouse. The door had a fire-rate integrity level of 30. That meant that it had been built to resist heavy fires for thirty minutes. Lucien had calculated exactly how much plastic explosive he had to use and in which direction he had to shape them, so that the blast shockwave would've lost most of its power by the time it reached the fire door – twenty-one paces away from the epicenter of the blast.

As long as he was on the other side of that fire door when the suicide vest blew, Lucien would not be harmed, but how could he get to that door if he was facing Hunter and Hunter was the one initiating the suicide-vest detonation?

Once again, the answer wasn't so hard to come by, because who said that the suicide-vest detonation needed to occur immediately with the press of that 'send' button?

Five seconds – that was all Lucien needed to be able to turn around, cover the distance between him and the fire door, get to the other side of it, and close it behind him. He had practiced enough times to know.

With that knowledge, programming a delay between the host cellphone on the suicide vest receiving the call and it initializing detonation wasn't a hard thing to do.

In a nutshell, the whole idea was simple – Hunter would press the 'send' button (no explosion). Lucien would instantly turn around and run to the door. Five seconds later, he would've made it to safety.

BOOM!

Everything else was not Lucien's concern anymore.

One Hundred

The heart-stopping excitement of this being for real and not just another practice run overflowed Lucien's body with more than enough adrenaline to, for a brief moment, power his muscles with almost superhuman strength and speed. By the time John Doe's suicide vest detonated, Lucien had not only made it past the fire door and closed it behind him, but he had also cleared most of the external fire-escape staircase.

Despite his precise calculations, the blast was powerful enough to rattle the entire building structure and shake the immediate ground outside the warehouse with the strength of a mini-earthquake, forcing Lucien to grab hold of the handrail at the bottom of the stairway with everything he had.

'Holy shit!' he gasped, as he looked up.

Behind him, the office space he and Hunter had been in just seconds ago had been completely swallowed by a ferocious and unforgiving flame monster, whose ugly tongue was licking the night sky through the large hole that the blast had punched through the roof.

For an instant, Lucien paused and marveled at what he'd just accomplished. He could barely believe that he had actually pulled this off with such immaculate precision.

Now it was time to disappear.

Lucien had left his van hidden behind a cluster of bushes at the back of the warehouse, and that was exactly where it would stay. The abandoned van would add legitimacy to his plan because the police would no doubt find all the tire tracks that the van had left inside the property grounds. Tire tracks and no van would certainly instigate a few unanswered questions and that was never a good thing.

Yes, the van was staying right there, but the old van wasn't the only vehicle that Lucien had acquired in the past few days. He had also purchased a beat-up moped, which he had parked several streets behind the warehouse, by the Angeles National Forest. Lucien had timed his run. Three and a half minutes was all the time he needed to get to it. After that, Lucien Folter would cease to exist.

Before disappearing forever, Lucien faced the warehouse one last time.

'Goodbye, Robert,' he said to himself, as he was taken by a melancholic feeling that surprised him. 'This might sound funny, old friend, but I will miss you. I really will.'

Lucien was about to turn around and begin his run to freedom when he heard the unmistakable sound of a 9mm pistol being cocked just inches from the back of his head.

'If you even think about moving,' the voice said, angrily. 'I swear to God that I will blow your head clean off your torso and tribal-dance around your headless corpse.'

One Hundred and One

Echo Park, Los Angeles, less than an hour before

'*Directly at the end of Lemoyne Street,*' Lucien had told Hunter. '*Across Park Avenue, it's the entrance to the north car park in Echo Park. Tell the driver to drop you there.*'

Less than a minute later, the yellow cab was pulling into the car park.

'*Now pay the driver and get out,*' Lucien ordered Hunter, which immediately set several alarm bells ringing inside his head.

This is wrong, Hunter thought. *There's no way that Lucien is meeting me in such an open and public place. It would be way too risky for him. This is either a diversion or another precautionary measure.*

Lucien might've had eyes *on* Hunter's cab, but not inside it. Hunter was certain of that. He would have to act fast.

Before paying the driver, Hunter quickly retrieved the small tracker that was clipped to the inside of his trouser pocket and hid it between the phone and his right palm.

'*Now strip,*' Lucien had told Hunter moments later, once he'd reached Echo Park Lake. '*Then throw all of your clothes into the lake – shirt, trousers, underwear, shoes, socks . . . all of it. Do not leave anything by the water's edge, am I clear?'*

'How about the phone?' Hunter had asked.

'Into the water.'

'How are we going to communicate, Lucien?'

'Trust me, Grasshopper. Now, phone, clothes, everything . . . into the lake and make sure they sink.'

Hunter needed to improvise, and he needed to do it fast. He hadn't asked, but he suspected that if that tracker got wet it would be the end of it.

As Hunter undressed, he expertly kept the tracker palmed in his right hand, but just before jumping into the water, he brought his hand to his face to hold his nose. In a quick, sleight-of-hand movement, Hunter transferred the tracker from his palm into his mouth – the only place he could think of where he could protect it from water damage.

Hunter used his tongue to wedge the tracker between his teeth and the inside of his left cheek before finally jumping into Echo Park Lake. As he hit the water, he prayed that this would somehow work.

One Hundred and Two

Garcia had driven into the parking lot at the north end of Echo Park exactly six minutes and forty-seven seconds after Hunter had jumped into his second cab.

'He's gone,' Garcia had confirmed through the phone. 'Robert is gone. I've just circled the island. I've looked everywhere. There's no trace of him.'

'*But have you checked the island itself?*' Captain Blake pushed. '*On the ground, behind a tree. He could have been knocked unconscious or . . .*'

'Captain,' Garcia reassured her. 'He's not here. Robert isn't here. We've lost him.'

'*Fuck,*' the captain yelled. '*We should've dispatched a couple of black-and-whites to intercept him. We've might've lost Lucien, but we would've saved Robert. We now have noth—*'

'Hold on a second,' Garcia interrupted her again, his stare back on his cellphone screen, his voice wavering with excitement. 'It's moving again. The tracker is moving again.'

'*What?*' Captain Blake asked. '*What do you mean, moving? Moving where?*'

'*He's right,*' West said, clear surprise altering his voice. '*The tracker is back on, but it all of a sudden jumped from Echo*

Park to Montana Street . . . no, wait . . . it jumped again . . . it's now on North Glendale Boulevard.'

'What the hell is going on?' the captain asked. *'Is that Robert or is that a trick?'*

'No idea,' Garcia replied.

'Wait,' West spoke again. *'You said that Robert jumped into the water, right?'* he asked Garcia.

'That's what I was told.'

'So maybe the tracker got wet or something and it's malfunctioning, but somehow it's still transmitting.'

'Possible,' Holbrook agreed. *'It would explain the crazy jumping from one location to another.'*

'Whatever it is,' Garcia said, already running back to his car. 'It's all we've got, so I'm going after it.'

'It jumped again,' West announced. *'It's now on Glendale Freeway.'*

'Shit,' Garcia said, checking his cellphone screen as he got to his car. 'That puts him at around fifteen minutes ahead of me again.'

'Peter, where are you?' West asked.

'Golden State Freeway,' Holbrook replied. *'About twenty-two minutes out.'*

'I'm going to send a unit to intercept,' Captain Blake said. *'I'm not running this risk again.'*

'Don't!' West shouted. *'Nothing has changed here, Captain. We still have no visual confirmation of Robert or Lucien, which means that we're still playing a blind man's game. I'm sure that I don't have to remind you that Lucien is a federal fugitive, which makes this, above all, a US Marshals' operation, not a LAPD one.'* He paused to calm himself down. *'I really don't want to, so please don't make me pull rank on this,*

Captain, but "I" am running this show. No one is intercepting that red dot until I give the green light.'

Garcia had gained considerable ground as he followed the tracker through Eagle Rock, Pasadena, and Altadena, managing to reduce the distance between him and the red dot to just over five minutes, but as he drove past Washington Park, he saw the red dot slow to a complete stop. Fifteen seconds later, it began moving again, this time a lot slower.

'He's back on foot,' Garcia said, following the red dot's slow progress on his screen.

'Yes, but where the hell is he going?' Holbrook asked. *'Please don't tell me that there's another park with a lake somewhere around there.'*

'No,' Garcia replied. 'No lakes around there whatsoever, but if I'm not mistaken, there are quite a few large warehouses and storage hangars around that area. Many of them disused. He could be heading to any of them.'

'Or to the National Forest itself,' Captain Blake added. *'He's certainly within walking distance of it.'*

Garcia stepped on it. Four minutes later, he saw the red dot turn left and slowly walk up a dead-end street.

'That's got to be where he's going,' Garcia said, pulling up to the side of the road. 'I'm less than a city block away from him, but I've got to go the rest of the way on foot. There's absolutely no traffic around here. If I haven't been spotted yet, I certainly will if I drive any closer.'

'Be careful on those empty streets, Carlos,' Captain Blake told him. *'This could all be a trick.'*

'Yes, I know.' Garcia agreed. 'Peter, where are you?'

'Getting closer, but I'm still about ten minutes behind you.'

Garcia checked his cellphone screen again. The red dot

was just about to get to the top of the road. 'Sorry, but I'm not waiting.'

'*Don't worry,*' Holbrook came back. '*I'll catch up.*'

It took Garcia less than a minute to reach the same dead-end street that Hunter had walked up moments earlier. As he got to the bottom of it, the red dot turned and entered the last property on the left. Garcia missed visual confirmation by mere seconds.

'*That's got to be the place,*' Captain Blake said. '*Nowhere else to go from there.*'

'*It's got to be,*' Holbrook agreed.

'*Carlos, I'm sending back-up your way right now,*' Captain Blake informed her detective.

'*Not yet, Captain,*' West said, stopping her again. '*Like I've said – not until we have visual confirmation.*' He took in a worried breath. '*Get them on stand-by, if that makes you feel any better, but no unit is to approach that location until I say so.*'

While West argued with Captain Blake, Garcia had made his way up the road as fast and as stealthily as he could. Once he got to the last property on the left, he found the same outer-fence breach that Hunter had walked through and, with the utmost caution, he approached the old and disused warehouse. He got to its doors just in time to see a feeble directional light disappear at the top of what could've been a stairwell.

'I'm going in,' Garcia said, after describing the entire scenario over the phone to the rest of the group.

'*No goddamn way,*' West shot back. '*Are you crazy? You just told us that you can't see two inches in front of your own nose in there, Carlos. How are you going to navigate a floor, which you have no idea of its layout, in pitch-black darkness?*'

If you make a sound in there by kicking something on the ground that you can't see, you're busted. If you light a match in there, you're busted. If you bump into a wall, or a box, or anything, you're busted.'

Garcia stayed quiet.

'*If Lucien is really in there with Robert,*' West continued, keeping his voice as calm as he could muster, '*what do you think he'll do once he finds out that Hunter was being tailed?*' West didn't wait. '*I'll tell you what, Carlos – he'll either kill Robert straight away, or first use him as a bargaining chip and then kill him.*'

'So what do you want me to do, nothing?' Garcia whispered.

'*I can get a SWAT team out there in eight minutes flat,*' Captain Blake said, clearly addressing West. '*They are on the other line and ready to go. All they need is the green light.*'

Everyone went quiet, waiting for the US Marshals' decision. It took him only a second to make up his mind.

Holbrook was still five minutes away.

'*OK, Captain,*' West finally agreed. '*Tell your SWAT team that they can move.*'

Garcia checked his watch. Eight minutes was an eternity in this sort of situation, and he wasn't about to just wait there.

'I'm going to search round the compound and check for a back door somewhere,' he said.

West said nothing because he knew that he wouldn't be able to stop Garcia.

'*Be careful,*' Captain Blake said.

'Always.'

Two minutes later, the place blew up.

One Hundred and Three

With a gun aimed at the back of his head, Lucien stood absolutely still. The loud noise as the fire consumed the warehouse before his eyes had kept him from hearing anyone approaching from behind.

'Hands up where I can see them, you sack of shit,' Garcia commanded.

How? Lucien tried to think back to when and where he could've made a mistake. His plan had been perfect. He was sure of it. *How did he get here? How did Robert tip him off? Even if Robert had some sort of tracker on him, unless it'd been implanted under his skin, it would've stopped working once he'd jumped into Echo Park Lake.*

'I'm not going to tell you again.' The determination in Garcia's voice was undeniable. 'Put your hands high above your head, or I'm blowing your head off.'

'Should you be out here?' Lucien asked as he slowly complied. He had recognized Garcia's voice from the Five Star Bar earlier that evening. 'Or should you be in there trying to save Robert, your partner?'

Just moments ago, Garcia had found Lucien's van hidden behind some trees. He was just examining it when he saw

Lucien step through a fire-exit door at the top of a metal staircase at the back of the warehouse. As he cleared the staircase, the whole place blew up.

Garcia dropped his phone and felt his heart stop beating for a moment when he saw part of the roof fly up in the air and fire immediately engulf the top part of the warehouse.

Not even he knew how he managed to keep his voice caged in his throat once he realized that Hunter had never made it through that fire door. That blast – that entire inferno – was meant for Hunter, and if Hunter was in there . . .

Garcia felt everything inside him constrict. No one was getting out of there alive.

'Or should you be in there trying to save Robert, your partner?' Lucien's words were still ringing in Garcia's ears, but he knew that that was a lie. It had to be.

Even without facing him, Lucien sensed Garcia's hesitation.

'He's not dead, you know?' he said, his hands above his head.

Despite all his experience, Garcia's weapon was trembling in his hands. Not because he feared Lucien, but because he couldn't conceive the idea that Hunter was gone.

'I'm telling you the truth,' Lucien pushed. 'Robert, your partner, he's not dead . . . not yet . . . but he *will* be soon enough if you don't help him.' A short pause. 'It will take a person anywhere between two and ten minutes to perish from smoke inhalation,' Lucien explained. 'Depending on the density and heat of the smoke. Well, I created what you see in front of you, and I can tell you with absolute certainty – that smoke is pretty dense . . . pretty hot.'

Reflexively, Garcia's gaze bounced from Lucien to the burning warehouse, then back to Lucien.

'You're lying,' he said. He wanted to believe, but he had to trust his eyes. 'If Robert was anywhere in that second floor with you, and I saw him get up there, the blast alone would've killed him.'

'That was the beauty of my plan,' Lucien boasted. 'Despite what you saw, Robert wasn't on that second floor when the bomb blew.'

One Hundred and Four

Lucien hadn't lied. Hunter was not on that second floor when John Doe's suicide vest blew up.

Yes, that had indeed been Lucien's initial plan – blow Hunter out of existence, then disappear forever, but when he entered that warehouse for the first time and saw that two-story office deep at the back of it, an entirely new idea began taking shape inside his evil mind – why kill Hunter?

Lucien checked the infrastructure of the office, calculated all the logistics and came to the conclusion that his madness – and it *was* madness – was achievable. That was when he began refurbishing the place and making all the necessary modifications.

It took Lucien about twenty hours of solid work to get it all finished and working exactly how he wanted it to, but at the end of it all, he couldn't have been more proud.

'This is a work of genius,' he said to himself as he tested the entire mechanism for the umpteenth time. All that was missing was Robert Hunter.

One Hundred and Five

'The host cellphone number is cued in,' Lucien informed Hunter, while indicating the cellphone in his suicide vest. 'All you have to do is press "send", Robert, that's all. You said that you wanted to put an end to all this. Here's your chance, old friend.

'I'll see you in hell, Lucien.'

Hunter locked eyes with Lucien, took in a deep breath and pressed the 'send' button.

No big bang.

No explosion.

No bomb went off.

The cellphone that Hunter had in his hand did connect to a different cellphone, but not the one in John Doe's suicide vest. It connected to a cellphone linked to the trapdoor mechanism that Lucien had devised and crafted. A trapdoor that Hunter hadn't seen, but was standing right on top of it.

And it all happened in the blink of an eye.

As Hunter's thumb pressed down on that 'send' button, the floor beneath his feet vanished, creating an instant drop. In a flash, Hunter disappeared through the trapdoor and crashed hard onto the floor ten feet below him. His left ankle twisted awkwardly and very painfully as his feet came into contact with the cement floor.

Above him, Lucien calmly walked over to the large gap created by the trapdoor and looked down at Hunter.

'I'm impressed by your resolve, Robert. You would really have put an end to your own life just to stop me killing again, wouldn't you?' Lucien looked as if he was deliberating about what had just happened. 'Did you really think that I wanted you to die?'

Hunter reached for his left ankle. The pain was so intense, he was starting to shiver.

'No, Robert,' Lucien answered his own question. 'I don't want you to die. I want you to live. I want you to live with the present I've given you – the guilt of allowing thirty innocent people to die and the hate of the woman you love. I want you to keep that locked inside of you, allowing it to eat away at your soul little by little, day by day . . . until it consumes you.'

Another deliberating pause.

'But I'll admit that we were once good friends, Robert,' Lucien accepted. 'In fact, you were the only real friend I've ever had, and as a sign of respect to those long-gone days, I'll give you another chance to choose, but this time it won't be as easy as just pressing a button.'

Hunter looked left then right, but impenetrable darkness seemed to be all around him.

'The suicide vest is real,' Lucien continued. 'Very real – and so are all these gallons of fuel up here. The vest *will* blow up in less than a minute from now. The blast's shockwave has been precisely calculated and it shouldn't kill you down there.' Lucien made a dubious face. 'But just to be on the safe side, I would roll that way a couple of yards if I were you.' He pointed to Hunter's right. 'Like I said, the blast shouldn't kill you, but the smoke and the fire certainly will.' Lucien rotated his neck from one side to the other to get rid of some stiffness. 'So the choice is yours, Grasshopper. If you want to live, all you have to do is brave the smoke, the fire, all that broken glass out there, and drag yourself out of here, but you'll have to go the long way, as this end of the warehouse is bound to get pretty hot.'

Hunter could feel that the fall had caused some real damage to his left ankle. That, together with bare feet, a sea of broken glass, fire and smoke, didn't sound like great odds to him.

'But if you really want to die,' Lucien carried on, 'then just lie back, wait for the smoke to reach you, which won't take long at all, and take a few deep breaths.' He smiled. 'Either way, I'm out of here. Our paths will never cross again, Grasshopper.' Lucien winked at Hunter. 'Who knows? Maybe I *will* see you in hell someday. It really was a pleasure knowing you, my friend. I hope you make the right choice.'

Lucien's face disappeared from the gap in the ceiling above Hunter.

Seconds later, the entire second floor blew up.

One Hundred and Six

At the back of the burning warehouse, Lucien could practically taste Garcia's uncertainty, he could sense his uneasiness. Lucien knew that he had to capitalize on it.

'Robert wasn't on that second floor,' he reassured Garcia.

'Bullshit.'

'It's true. Just think about it,' Lucien argued. 'Why would I go through all the effort, all the risk, all the tremendous work I went through to bring so much pain and guilt into Robert's life, if I intended to kill him only a few days later. Where's the sense in that?'

'Sense or no sense,' Garcia said. 'How could Robert ever have survived this?'

'Because I wanted him to,' Lucien replied, before quickly explaining about the trapdoor he had created.

Garcia's stomach knotted. He didn't know what to think.

'You're losing time here,' Lucien told him. 'The smoke in there is getting thicker and thicker, and the fire ...' Lucien chuckled. 'Just look at it. Robert either twisted or broke his ankle when he fell. I saw it happen. Even if he wants to, getting out of there with that ankle will be a struggle.'

Garcia was almost sure that Lucien was lying, but was he

willing to risk it? They were talking about Robert, his best friend, his partner for over ten years, and the person who had saved his and Anna's life more than once before.

Lucien was right – time was ticking away fast.

'Robert is dying in there,' Lucien pushed again, his voice calm.

Screw this, Garcia thought, and reached for his handcuffs.

That was when his stomach danced a jig inside of him.

When he'd got into his car, back at the PAB parking lot, he'd done what he always did when he was going home – he'd unclipped his handcuffs and flashlight holster from his belt and threw it all on the backseat.

'Shit!'

'It's OK if you don't go to Robert's rescue,' Lucien said. 'After all, if he dies you get to take over his job, don't you? Head of the LAPD Ultra Violent Crimes Unit. That is some title, isn't it? Listen, if you don't tell anyone that you didn't even try to save your partner, I promise that I won't either.'

It was completely against police protocol to leave an arrested subject alone. No matter who that subject was, no matter the circumstances . . . but the loophole right there was that technically, Garcia had never placed Lucien under arrest. He had told him to stop and put his hands up, but he had never officially placed Lucien under arrest. So if Lucien wasn't under arrest, then Garcia wouldn't be breaking protocol.

Lucien still had his arms high above his head, his eyes forward, watching as the warehouse burned before him. Garcia was three paces behind him, his weapon aimed directly at the back of Lucien head.

Unlike Hunter, Garcia didn't have a degree in psychology, but he didn't really need one to understand how psychological blackmail and manipulation worked, which was exactly what Lucien was trying to do. The problem Garcia had was – without handcuffs; he had absolutely nothing, no sort of device on him with which he could immobilize Lucien.

But who said that he needed some sort of device?

'Fuck it,' he said out loud. A split second later, he rammed the underside of his right boot as hard as he could, into the back of Lucien's right knee.

Lucien felt his knee dislodge. His leg buckled under his weight before going totally limp, sending him crashing to the ground. The painful scream he let out could've woken the dead.

On the ground, shivering with pain, he finally turned to face Garcia.

'Motherfucker!' he yelled out, as his hands grabbed at his right knee, angry spit flying from his lips. 'You broke my fucking leg.'

Garcia shook his head. 'No, no, you seem to be a little confused here. What happened was – you fell while trying to escape and hit your knee.' He paused and smiled. 'Oh yes, you also hit your head.'

In a super-fast and very powerful movement, Garcia slammed the handle of his 9mm pistol into the back of Lucien's head.

Lights out.

One Hundred and Seven

It took Garcia twelve seconds to make it back to the front door of the warehouse. The interior of the building, which just moments ago lay hidden under a thick cloak of darkness, was now completely lit up by a wave of flames that was quickly consuming everything in its path.

At the large double doors, Garcia had to use his right arm to shield his eyes and face from the heat and brightness that came at him with incredible ferocity. Instinctively, his left hand shot to his nose and mouth, immediately cupping over them, but the smoke was too powerful, too intrusive, forcing Garcia into a coughing frenzy.

The coughing caused his eyes to water; the heat and brightness caused them to narrow to the size of two tiny slits.

To recompose himself, Garcia took a few steps back and used the palms of both hands to dry his eyes. He then grabbed the collar of his shirt and brought it up to his face, hooking it against the bridge of his nose to create a makeshift smoke mask. That in place, he tried looking inside the warehouse once again. Flames and smoke seemed to be everywhere, but he was finally able to see.

The first thing Garcia noticed were the odd shining sparkles coming from the ground, as if the floor had been littered with different-sized diamonds.

His eyes narrowed again.

Two seconds went by before he finally figured out that what he was actually looking at was broken glass, reflecting light from the flames. They covered the entire floor like a carpet.

His eyes moved from left to right as he tried to identify the least dangerous route that would take him to the office enclosure at the back. There wasn't one. Trying to reach that internal office structure through the inside of the warehouse looked like suicide.

Garcia's eyes watered again, but not from the heat or smoke – this time his tears came from pure emotion.

'FUUUUCK! FUUUUCK!'

The flames seemed to consume even his angry shouts.

Garcia's hands shot to his head in total desperation. There was nothing he could do.

At the back, another burning roof chunk came crashing to the ground, sending new sparkles flying in the air like fireworks and dragging Garcia's attention toward it.

That was when he finally saw him.

Hunter was lying face down on the floor to Garcia's right, about forty-five feet in front of him. His arms were idle by the side of his body, his legs lifeless.

Garcia blinked to make sure that the smoke wasn't making him see things.

Then he saw Hunter move. Just a tiny lift of the head, nothing else.

Garcia felt a new shiver begin at the core of his soul and gain momentum like a rocket. That momentum moved straight to his legs and without a second thought for the fire or the smoke,

Garcia took off toward Hunter. Four seconds later, he was standing over his partner.

Smoke had caused him to start coughing again, but his improvised smoke mask did provide him with just enough protection to keep him from going dizzy and losing his balance.

Garcia's 'fight or flight' defense mechanism kicked in with everything it had, speeding his heart, tightening his muscles and flooding his whole body with an incredible cocktail of hormones, which was exactly what he needed to fuel him through this desperate situation.

In one swift move, Garcia bent down and picked Hunter off the ground as if Hunter were half of his own body size and weight.

'Hold on, Robert,' he said as he threw his partner over his right shoulder. 'I've got you, man. I've got you.'

Holding his breath so he didn't have to breathe in any more smoke, Garcia carried Hunter out of the burning warehouse. This time, he covered the distance in eight seconds.

One Hundred and Eight

Outside, several feet away from the inferno that the warehouse had become, Garcia finally placed an unconscious Robert Hunter on the grass. He could barely believe the state his partner was in.

Hunter had no top on, having taken it off, ripped it into two pieces, and wrapped them tightly around both of his feet for protection against the endless carpet of broken glass. As he'd tried to escape the fire, he tripped and fell several times, causing different-sized shards of glass to lacerate his hands, arms, chest, shoulders, back, knees and legs, transforming most of his body into a mess of blood, cuts and glass. The improvised shoes had partially worked, but a few larger shards had managed to cut through the fabric on Hunter's right foot and embed themselves deep into his flesh. His left ankle had swollen to the size of a grapefruit.

The unforgiving fire had also done its job on Hunter, scorching his arms, legs, back and chest.

'You'd better breathe, Robert,' Garcia said in a quivering voice. 'Because I really don't want to have to give you mouth-to-mouth.'

No movement from Hunter.

'Robert?' Garcia's voice gained in strength.

Nothing.

'Robert?'

No reply. No movement.

'Shit!'

Garcia immediately swung his body around and placed the heel of his right hand just above Hunter's breastbone. He then placed his left hand over his right one and started chest compressions.

'One ... two ... three ... four ... five ... c'mon, Robert, don't do this, breathe, man, please breathe. Twelve ... thirteen ... fourteen ... fifteen ...'

Garcia stopped with the compressions and tilted Hunter's head back ever so slightly before lifting his chin – a maneuver used to lift the tongue from the back of the throat to open the airwaves. Garcia then pinched Hunter's nostrils shut and bent forward to give his partner mouth-to-mouth.

Hunter smiled.

'Gotcha.' His voice was barely a whisper.

Too shocked to say anything back, Garcia paused and stared at his partner wide-eyed, his whole body shaking.

Suddenly, Hunter's entire torso jerked up, as he began coughing desperately – his lungs trying their hardest to flush out all the carbon monoxide, cyanide and whatever else combination of combustion products he had breathed in.

The crazy surge of adrenaline that had powered Garcia in and out of the burning building was finally gone, depleting him of all energy. Like a stringless puppet, he collapsed to the ground right beside Hunter, his muscles finally feeling the exhaustion brought on by the exceptional effort they'd made.

Several seconds went by before Garcia was finally able to

turn his head to look at Hunter, their breathings labored, their faces colored by soot.

'Holy crap, man!' Garcia said between deep breaths and coughs. 'Don't ever do this to me again.'

Hunter's completely bloodshot eyes locked with Garcia's. He then used all the strength he had left in him to extend his bloody right hand in Garcia's direction.

Garcia met him halfway, taking his hand.

'Thank you,' Hunter said, his voice weak. 'Thank you.'

Garcia nodded back and smiled. 'I have to ask you something, though . . . what the hell are you wearing, Robert?' His eyes moved to Hunter's tracksuit trousers.

'What the fuck happened here?' The question came from Holbrook, who had finally made it to the warehouse. His eyes were wide with shock, his breathing strenuous from all the running.

Garcia looked at Hunter and shrugged.

Finally the sound of sirens could be heard in the distance.

'Lucien . . .' Hunter said amid heavy coughs, '. . . had a suicide vest on.'

'What?' Holbrook's gaze moved to Garcia, then to the warehouse, then back to the two detectives on the ground. 'Lucien blew himself up?'

Garcia allowed his head to slump to one side, before slowly bringing it back around to look at Holbrook.

'Not quite,' he replied. 'But I think that was the effect that he was looking for – suicide.'

Holbrook looked around for a moment, clearly searching for Lucien.

'So he managed to escape?' Holbrook asked in a heavy tone. 'Again?'

It was Garcia's turn to cough a couple of times.

The sirens were getting closer.

'Not quite,' he said, before smiling and gesturing with his head. 'He's at the back ... he's not going anywhere.'

One Hundred and Nine

'So Lucien wanted to convince you that he really was blowing himself up?' Adrian Kennedy asked Hunter, after hearing the whole story.

'No, not me,' Hunter explained from his hospital bed. 'Before blowing up the warehouse he told me that he was getting out of there and disappearing forever. The plan was devised to convince everyone else.'

Kennedy, who had flown over from Washington in the early hours of the morning, had joined Garcia, Holbrook, West and Captain Blake inside recovery room 2B on the second floor of the famous Ronald Reagan medical center complex, located inside the UCLA campus in Westwood.

Hunter was lying on an adjustable bed, his back bandaged and propped up against the headspring, which had been lifted to a fifty-degree angle. His feet, arms, hands, and torso had also been bandaged. Thirty-seven lacerations in total, but Hunter had been lucky. Despite the intensity of the fire, the burns to his arms, legs and back had all been first- and second-degree only.

'Once forensics are finally done with fine-combing through the site,' Hunter continued, 'I'm very sure that they will find severely burned hard-tissue fragments.'

'From who?' Captain Blake asked.

'From some unlucky soul, who Lucien had probably murdered before hiding the body in that warehouse,' Hunter clarified.

'All right,' the captain accepted. 'But he must've known that any bone fragment found in the aftermath of the fire, especially that one, would've been tested for DNA. His plan wouldn't work.'

'Of course Lucien knew that,' Hunter agreed. 'But he also knew that it wouldn't have been possible to extract any relevant DNA from any of the bone fragments that might've been found inside that warehouse.'

'What?' West frowned. 'Why not?'

Hunter quickly explained about the accuracy of DNA testing on bones and bone fragments according to their stage of fire-induced destruction.

West looked at Hunter sideways.

Shrugging hurt his shoulder, so Hunter simply nodded. 'I read a lot.'

'But he told you that he was getting out of there alive,' Garcia interjected. 'He told you that he was going to disappear forever, which was practically a confession that the whole suicide-vest thing was a scam. Unless he was also counting on you dying in there. No witnesses, no confession, case closed.'

'Possibly,' Hunter agreed. 'But Lucien knew that even if I escaped that warehouse, it didn't matter if he had confessed to me or not, Carlos. With no concrete proof, it would all be hearsay, because what we would have would be a site blown up by a suicide vest, a detective who very luckily escaped the explosion, and bone fragments that had been severely destroyed by the blast and the blaze. With DNA testing failing to produce a positive ID from the bone fragments, we would be left with one thing only.'

'Assumption,' Kennedy confirmed, knowing full well what Hunter was getting at. 'We would have to assume that the bone fragments found in the warehouse belonged to Lucien because as far as everyone knew, at the time of the blast, there were only two people inside that location. Whether Robert, or any of us, believed or not that Lucien was still alive would make no difference whatsoever to the US Attorney General. To him, Robert would be nothing more than a detective suffering from post-traumatic stress disorder. Since bone fragments were found at the scene and the DNA test results proved totally inconclusive, the Attorney General would see no argument to approve a new budget for a new manhunt. On the contrary, he would've been more than happy to finally put Lucien and this entire case to rest forever.'

'And with that,' West jumped in, 'Lucien would've been ... born again. He would've been completely free to start a whole new life somewhere else, with the knowledge that he wouldn't have to be looking over his shoulder because no one would be looking for him anymore.'

'Lucien knew what he needed to do,' Hunter said. 'When you have the US Marshals Office, the FBI, the NSA, the ATF, Homeland Security, and pretty much every law enforcement agency in the country looking for you, you know that they will never give up.'

'Unless they all believe that you're already dead,' Holbrook said, concluding Hunter's line of thought.

'I'll admit,' Kennedy took over again, 'it was a great plan, executed to almost perfection.' He addressed Hunter. 'If you hadn't realized that Lucien was up to something when you got to Echo Park and put the tracker in your mouth, his plan would've worked, you would probably be dead, and we would've had nothing to stop us from believing that Lucien was dead too.'

'What happened with that, anyway?' Garcia asked. 'The tracker thing.'

'Probably exactly what Peter suggested yesterday,' West replied. 'Some sort of signal failure. Maybe some of Robert's saliva got into the tracker once he placed it in his mouth and interrupted the signal, but not enough for it to completely stop transmitting.'

'Maybe,' Hunter accepted it. 'I'm just happy it worked.'

'Good move,' Captain Blake congratulated Hunter. 'Very good move.'

One Hundred and Ten

'Director Kennedy,' Captain Blake called, as they all left Hunter to rest, 'could I have a moment of your time, please?'

'Of course,' Kennedy replied.

Garcia, Holbrook and West all moved to the end of the corridor to use the coffee machine.

'I wanted to get your opinion on something,' the captain said.

'Sure, how can I help?'

'I know that you know Robert well,' Captain Blake began. 'And by tomorrow he'll be out of here, doctor's consent or not, you know that, right?'

Kennedy chuckled. 'Yeah.'

'You also probably know that as soon as he's out, he'll go straight back to the UVC Unit and his desk. He'll go straight back to work.'

'And that worries you.' Kennedy didn't phrase it as a question.

'It doesn't worry you?' the captain replied. 'You know what happened, right?

'You're referring to the woman he was seeing?'

'Yes.'

Kennedy leaned shoulder first against the wall.

'I understand your concern,' he began. 'But one thing that I can tell you with absolute certainty is that mentally and psychologically, Robert is the strongest person I've ever met. Sure, he's also human like all of us. He also gets hurt like all of us. His mind goes through turmoil every now and then, just like all of us, but if there's something that Robert knows how to deal with better than all of us, that something is psychological pain and stress.'

'I was just wondering if it wouldn't be best if I gave Robert maybe two weeks on his own . . . no work, nothing, just so he can heal . . . psychologically and physically.'

Kennedy gave Captain Blake a sympathetic smile.

'The brain is the most complex organ we know, Captain,' he explained. 'It occupies itself with something at all times – thoughts, dreams, wonders, whatever – but it's always working . . . *always*. If we don't give it something to occupy itself with, it finds something on its own. In extreme psychologically traumatic situations, people like Robert, myself, and I'm pretty sure you too, we all try to rationally occupy our brains with something so it doesn't keep on going back to those traumatic memories. Usually, we try to do it with something that makes us feel good, something that gives us worth. To Robert, that something is work because that's what he's good at, that's what he loves – solving crimes and putting bad people behind bars. If you take that away from him at a time when he needs it the most, what do you think his brain will occupy itself with?'

'The traumatic memories,' Captain Blake accepted.

'Bingo.' Another smile from Kennedy. 'Let Robert do what he does best, Captain. He'll be OK.'

'But Robert pressed that "send" button on that phone,' Captain Blake said. 'He didn't know that the suicide vest wouldn't go off. Some might see that as attempted suicide, and if a law enforcement agent feels suicidal . . .' Her eyebrows lifted at Kennedy. 'You know protocol.'

'Robert isn't suicidal,' Kennedy said with overwhelming conviction. 'He didn't press that button to kill himself, Captain. He pressed it to stop a psychopath from killing again, and we're not talking about just any psychopath here, we're talking about the most dangerous psychopath any of us have ever known, including the FBI. What he was doing was giving his life so no one else would *ever* have to die again because of Lucien. He doesn't deserve to be suspended, Captain. He deserves a medal.'

The captain nodded before smiling at Kennedy. 'Thank you.'

Right then, Garcia, Holbrook and West got back to where Captain Blake and Kennedy were.

'Well,' West said, taking a long sip of his coffee and addressing Director Kennedy. 'The good news here is that, if you'll pardon my French, Lucien is fucked. This time he was arrested in California, where the death penalty is alive and well. If it were up to me, he'd get the chair tomorrow, end of.'

Those words took Garcia back to the moment they finally arrested Lucien back at the burned-down warehouse.

As Lucien was being ushered into the back of the police car, he paused and looked at Garcia.

'You'd better hope that they give me the chair, Detective,' Lucien said, his eyes flashing red. 'Because if they don't, I can promise you that one day I'll get out again and when I do . . .' – he winked at Garcia in a way that put a knot in the detective's throat – '. . . I'll be coming for you and everyone you love. You can bet on that.'

'If you do . . .' – Garcia winked back at Lucien – '. . . rest assured that I'll be waiting. *You* can bet on that.'

FIND OUT MORE ABOUT
CHRIS CARTER

Chris Carter writes highly addictive thrillers
featuring Detective Robert Hunter

To find out more about Chris and his writing,
visit his website at

www.chriscarterbooks.com

or follow Chris on

 @ChrisCarterBooksOfficial

All of Chris Carter's novels are available
in print and eBook, and are available to
download in eAudio